THE TRAHE CHRONICLES: BOOK ONE

THE CHOSEN ONES

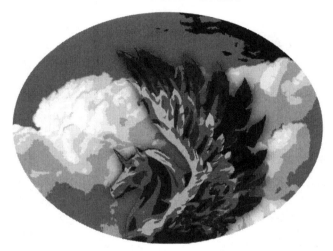

BY
D.L. PRICE

COVER DESIGN & ARTWORK BY JERECO PRICE

The Trahe Chronicles—The Chosen Ones is a work of fiction. Names, characters, places and incidents are the product of the author's imagination. The events described in this story never occurred. Any resemblance to actual events, locales, or persons—living or dead— is entirely coincidental. This story has no purpose other than to entertain the reader.

A Story Tyme Realm LLC Trade Paperback Original

Copyright © 2012 by D.L. Price

All rights reserved. No part of this book may be reproduced or transmitted in any form or by any means, electronic or mechanical, including photocopying, recording, or by any information storage and retrieval system, without permission in writing from D.L. Price and/or Story Tyme Realm LLC.

Published in the United States of America.

Registered with Library of Congress
ISBN:-10:1478220406
ISBN-13:978-1478220404

First Edition

ACKNOWLEDGMENTS

Michael — Thank you for reading my manuscript and being supportive. You persuaded me to pick up the pen and start writing again. My books were finally developed because of your support, patience and love.

Diana — Thank you mom for reading and proofing my manuscript. I appreciate all the time that you put into assisting with my work. You taught me to reach for the stars and accomplish many things. So I did!

Jereco — Thank you for doing a fabulous job on the illustrations and artwork design of my book. You stepped up to the plate when this tough client was in need. You are a hard working, patient person. I am proud of you

Maria — Thank you for reading my work. This book and its sequels were put into motion because of you! Over ten years ago you discovered my secret hobby. Your inspiration gave me confidence to complete my first manuscript, and to continue my dream.

Cynthea Liu — Thank you for doing a fantastic job of copyediting my manuscript. I appreciate the additional feedback and advice.

Charlie Courtland — Thank you for sharing wonderful tips and information that contributed bringing my manuscript full circle to publication.

God — Thank you Creator!

DEDICATIONS

I dedicate my first book to my first child, Nicolas. You are truly a gift from God and a blessing in my life. Some day you will be old enough to read and enjoy this book.

CONTENTS

PROLOGUE: The Trahe Chronicles...........................1

PART ONE: Cleo...3

1. I Am..4

2. Blizzards and Crashes.................................5

3. Diana and the Talking Cat............................12

4. A Brief History Lesson...............................26

5. Space plane to Bermuda...............................36

PART TWO: Trahe, the Sister Planet.....................42

6. Crash Landing..43

7. Green Eyes...52

8. Snake Charmer..56

9. Sir Bolivar..61

10. We Are Not Alone....................................68

11. Saved by Grandpa....................................74

12. The Creatures' Council..............................79

13. Untold Stories Unfold...............................86

PART THREE: Pegasus and Willow.........................91

14. Midnight..92

15. The Secret Stronghold...............................99

16. Whispers in the Wind...............................108

17. The Green Mark.....................................116

18. A Storm Is Brewing.................................129

19. Nature's Fury and Friends..........................136

20. Leaving Willow.....................................143

PART FOUR: Mermaids and Unicorns.......................151

21. Riding Horseback in the Air.............................152

22. The Island of the Pegasi.................................159

23. Brandon's New Friend..................................175

24. Abijam... 181

PART FIVE: Bears, Caves and Dragons....................190

25. Friends and Foes of Great Rock Canyon.................191

26. Thou Shall Not Kill a Talking Beast.....................204

27. Talking Sheep in Bethemek.............................219

28. Ancient Methuselah....................................231

29. The Living Rock 244

30. Diana's Dragon.......................................259

PART SIX: The Lost Evadeam Tribe.......................274

31. Evadeam City...276

32. The River People......................................292

33. A Day of Peace.......................................302

34. The Gray Protector....................................311

35. The Beginning..321

Book Two Preview....................................324

Glossary..330

PROLOGUE: The Trahe Chronicles

In the beginning, all was created, including many galaxies of stars and planets. The Creator of the universe formed the planet Trahe. On this planet, he created numerous living species, including seven tribes of two-legged creatures. The seven tribes were named the Evadeam, the Edamave, the Evemada, the Madeave, the Madevea, the Suhman, and the Muhans.

Evadeam was the first of the seven tribes, and its members were given the responsibility of recording the history of their planet Trahe. Their writings were known as the Trahe Chronicles.

As recorded, peace and harmony reigned for the first one thousand years of the new planet. But as history patterns of Trahe's sister planets revealed, evil transpired. The Creator wept as Trahe was embraced by sin. The Creator's tears caused nature's fury, and the planet was gripped by natural disasters. Howling winds, thundering rains, screaming squalls, blizzards, and thrashing waters ravaged Trahe. But small voices broke through the pounding storms. They begged for the Creator to stop, to help, and to forgive. The Creator remembered forgiveness and listened.

The voices belonged to the Evadeam tribe. High atop Evadeam Mountain, their voices praised the Creator and prayed for hope. The Creator answered.

Hope was given in the birth of a child—a baby girl to the Evadeam chief.

"You shall call her Skylar," said the Creator, "and she shall grow and become Princess Skylar of your nation. She will give birth to the Chosen Ones who shall save your world."

Chief Evadeam and his wife were grateful, but they worried of their new daughter's safety. So the Creator blessed them with the Protector. The Protector came in the form of a white tiger cub.

"You shall call her Bright Eyes," said the Creator, "and she shall grow and protect Princess Skylar. Bright Eyes' cubs of many generations shall save your world."

With the birth of Princess Skylar and Bright Eyes, the Creator let nature rest into peace on the planet Trahe. Many had witnessed and believed the Creator. Peace reigned once more. On Princess Skylar's eighteenth birthday, many men of the seven tribes of Trahe came forth to seek her hand in marriage. All were refused by Princess Skylar's heart.

The Creator spoke to Chief Evadeam and Princess Skylar. "I will send a man named Ibhar. He is my choice to be father of all fathers of the Chosen Ones."

Ibhar was a humble man. He did not feel worthy to marry a princess of the Evadeam tribe, for he was merely a laborer of the Madeave tribe. The Creator spoke to him and he listened. With the blessing of the Evadeam Chief, Princess Skylar and Ibhar were married.

They were told by the Creator to journey from Evadeam Mountain to the ancient lands of the Madeave. In the jungle lands of the Madeave, belief in the Creator would be reborn. Princess Skylar and Ibhar led many years of peace, praise, and teachings.

Harmony ended on Princess Skylar's fortieth birthday. Many men of another Madeave tribe attacked her village. Peace had reigned for so long that the attack was a surprise. New evil creatures encouraged the bloody battle between the different Madeave tribes. The creatures slithered through the jungle and became known as the Large Snakes.

The Large Snakes clashed with jungle tigers. Among the fighting tigers was Bright Eyes. She roared as she saw her tiger mate fall to the ground. The howl summoned the Creator, and the rains began to fall.

Bright Eyes listened as the Creator spoke.

"Take your children and the children of Princess Skylar north. I will send a guide who will take you to a large tree that will protect the children until they can return to Evadeam Mountain."

Bright Eyes and Princess Skylar gathered the children as they watched the destruction of the village unfold. Dead and injured creatures lay upon the earth. She saw her husband Ibhar as he was struck down by a snake. Princess Skylar picked up a fallen spear and ran screaming toward him. She threw the spear into the attacking snake's eye as a lightning bolt, generated by the Creator, struck the other snake's eye. The Large Snake fell. Princess Skylar thanked the Creator, and then she fell to her knees next to Ibhar.

Ibhar lay on the jungle floor and forced a smile. "My love," he murmured. He kissed her and prayed to the Creator to watch over his wife and bless his children. The Creator answered with another lightning strike in the sky, and Ibhar died in Skylar's arms.

Bright Eyes kept her promise to the Creator. Her cubs, Princess Skylar, and her children found refuge in a huge fortress north of the jungles. They continued to stay safe through their journey back to Evadeam Mountain.

The Trahe Chronicles continued in Evadeam City, where some stories were lost and new legends were written.

PART ONE

Cleo

In the darkness, I seek.
In the darkness, I come.
The calling, I shall answer.
The answer, I shall protect.
Protect all those who shall protect us all.
- Cleopatra, Messenger of the Creator and Guide of the Chosen Ones

Book One: The Chosen Ones

I Am

On one starry evening, a white, pure snow fell from the sky and developed into one of those perfect snowstorms. It dropped fluffy snow down like it was raining in April. In the midst of the storm, a small creature of black and white was born.

Before the creature opened her eyes, she heard a voice. "You will be one of my messengers. You shall travel between many of my worlds. You shall be taught to guide many to my path. Now open your eyes, little one, and see beyond your internal sight."

The creature opened her eyes. She was scared for she saw the great evil in all the worlds.

"Do not fear," said the Creator. "For as long as you see me, you will be protected, and I will grant you my power."

The creature believed the Creator and started a long journey towards her destiny.

Blizzards and Crashes

These are stories that take place during our time, your time, another time, and a time when believing is needed most. These are the times and adventures of the Evadeam family.

The Evadeam family lived on a planet called Earth in a small town of Nashville in the state of Michigan. As the stars beckon in the sky overhead, a light shined in a farmhouse bedroom.

In the bedroom, a little girl named Diana heard a loud boom. She sat up in bed. The crash was heard all through the farmhouse. It shook the entire home.

Diana ran to the steps that led downstairs. She was met by her two older brothers, who had already taken positions on the stairs. A closed door was between them and the living room where their parents were on the phone, reporting the crash.

"It sounds like they are talking to Grandpa Evadeam," Jereco whispered.

"Shouldn't they be calling 911?" Brandon questioned as he pushed his glasses farther up his nose.

Before Jereco had a chance to answer, the door flew open. Their dad did not look at all surprised that his three children were sitting on the staircase, listening to the conversation.

Dad put on a heavy, winter coat. "Grandpa and Uncle Larry are on their way over to help investigate the crash. Diana, your mom needs help in the kitchen. Boys, come with me." He turned and walked towards his bedroom.

Jereco and Brandon looked at each other and followed their father.

"What is going on, Dad?" Jereco asked. "Was it a plane crash?"

Jereco had been watching the weather outside. It wasn't good. The weatherman on the television had said one of the worst snowstorms in years was coming to Nashville. Jereco was bummed because that would mean the schools would be closed. He didn't like missing school. Living on a farm meant more chores if they had to stay home.

The boys followed their dad into his bedroom that was adjacent to the living room. Dad opened a hidden door in the bedroom wall. "The airports have been closed due to the weather. Any airplanes that may have been flying are doing it under the radar."

Chills ran up Jereco's back as they stepped into the secret closet. He knew what Dad stored in there.

Brandon, who was the younger of the two boys, had a look of surprise when his dad handed them shotguns. His dad didn't like guns. He didn't even like to hunt. Brandon looked at Jereco and waved one hand at the closet. "Did you know about this?"

Jereco didn't get a chance to answer. Their cousin, Brooke and her father, Larry, had just arrived. Brandon was surprised to see both Brooke and his uncle armed with guns. *Brooke knew how to handle a gun?* When Brandon went

Book One: The Chosen Ones

hunting with his grandpa and uncles, Brooke never went along. In fact, she always made a funny face if she was invited to come and would take off for the mall with her friends instead.

"We could see flames and smoke on the way here," Larry said. "It looks like it landed on the back forty acres."

"Then we better hurry." Dad closed the hidden panel closet door. He led them into the kitchen.Diana was sitting at the kitchen table with her mom when she saw everyone walking in with shotguns. "Why does Brandon have a gun?" The pitch of her voice got higher. "Why does Daddy have a gun?"

Her father kneeled next to her. "A small aircraft had crashed due to the storm outside. We have to get to the crash site quickly in case there are any survivors. The guns are just a precaution. It is dark and stormy out, and we don't know what we might run into."

That answer didn't ease her mind. Her wild thoughts were interrupted by the arrival of Grandpa Ovid Evadeam.

Grandpa stepped into the kitchen from the adjacent back breezeway. "Are we ready yet?" He clapped his hands. "How exciting!" He looked around and pointed at the gun. "There will be no need for those. Now come on." He waved to everyone to follow him.

After the back screen door shut, Dad looked at his wife. "Agnes, why don't you take Diana upstairs to her bedroom? Everything will be fine."

Agnes took Diana upstairs. Larry turned to Brooke and Brandon. "Brooke, you cover the window in the upstairs foyer near Diana's bedroom door. Brandon, you cover your bedroom window."

Brandon nodded and followed Brooke. He was still confused about what was going on, but he knew better than to disobey his uncle. Everyone respected him. He was once a high ranking officer in the military. He joined right after high school and made a career of it until he was forced into retirement by a war injury. He now worked in the recruitment office in the nearby town of Grand Rapids.

"Brooke, what is really going on?" Brandon asked as they climbed the enclosed staircase leading up to the second floor where the kids' bedrooms and bathroom were located.

Brandon was four years younger than Brooke, but he was very street smart. Brooke knew better than to try to hide anything from him. She paused for a moment and looked back down at Brandon. "Commercial flights are not flying, so our dad thinks that something else crashed into the field."

"Like a war plane?" Brandon asked.

Brooke shook her head. "We are not at war, Brandon. He didn't say, but he thinks it is a drug dealer's plane." Brooke continued up the stairs.

"But wouldn't they have called 911?" Brandon was aware of drug dealers planting drug plants in the middle of farmers' fields. The local authorities were always scanning the fields by helicopters. "Maybe one of their helicopters crashed," he continued.

The Trahe Chronicles

Brooke paused again and looked over her shoulder. "No one called 911?"

"I don't think so, and every time I ask, the subject gets changed," Brandon responded. Brooke's right eyebrow shot up, and then she got the look on her face that she always got when she started thinking about something serious. As if testing Brandon's theory, she peeked into Diana's bedroom. "Did anyone call 911?" she asked Aunt Agnes.

Her aunt just looked at her from Diana's bed. She was lying next to Diana. Aunt Agnes put a finger to her lips and waved her away.

Before Brooke walked away, she noticed the gun on the floor underneath the bed. Brooke glanced at Brandon.

"See?" Brandon whispered.

Brooke bit her lip and motioned to him to go to his bedroom. She also reminded him to keep his door open, so she could see into it from her post. Brooke peered out the window that overlooked the back breezeway's roof and the farmland. It was a very dark night only lit up by the blowing, white snow. It was a bad night to drive back to the last forty acres of the farm. At least all of her family members had four-wheel drive vehicles. Speaking of which, she saw more trucks pull into the farm.

She squinted to see if she recognized them, which she did. Her other three uncles had shown up with Aunt Rhonda. She decided that Brandon was right. Something was odd about all of this. Why would all her family members arrive before the authorities?

Brooke reached into her pocket and pulled out her cell phone. Her father was out there with Jereco, so chances are one of them would see something that would make sense. It was about time she did some investigating.

Jereco felt overwhelmed and uncomfortable. He didn't like to hold a gun. Brandon was the hunter of the family. Jereco was more like his father. Jereco and his dad would rather sit in front of the computer than in a deer blind in the woods. Jereco never understood why his dad still had the farm.

His dad had an office job with a government agency and hired out the farm work that his family couldn't do. Jereco wondered if his dad would ever sell the farm. Probably not, since most of the Evadeam family owned farms or large properties, except for Aunt Rhonda, who lived in Grand Rapids. He loved that city! There was so much to do there. They had three big malls, multiple movie theatres, and lots of restaurants. And now that Brooke had her driving license, he often would catch rides with her into town.

Jereco felt the vibration of his cell phone as he rode in his dad's truck between his dad and Grandpa. He pulled it out and read a text message from Brooke.

So what's up?

Jereco knew what she was asking.

He texted a message back.

Don't know yet. Weird.

Book One: The Chosen Ones

"There it is! I told you, son! I told you," yelled his Grandpa as he clasped his hands together.

Jereco's dad slowed down the truck. The trucks drove to the middle of a field.

Jereco looked up from his phone. His mouth dropped as he stared at the scenery in front of him. The headlights shined upon a small aircraft that was enflamed by fire. Smoke was billowing into the air.

His dad got out. "Jereco, stay in the truck."

Jereco didn't have to be told twice.

"And get behind the driving wheel," his father continued. Then as an afterthought, his dad looked back and yelled, "Put the gun in arms reach!"

Jereco didn't have a driver's license yet, but he had been operating farm equipment since middle school. He naturally got behind the truck's steering wheel, but he had to take deep breaths to calm his nerves.

He was not sure what was going on or what he was seeing. He was so nervous that he felt sick to his stomach. As Jereco rubbed his stomach, he leaned over the steering wheel to get a better look at the scene in front of him. The aircraft was dark in color and looked larger than a small jet but not as big as a jumbo jet liner. And it did not look commercial. *Military or perhaps foreign.* Then he saw a slight shimmer around the aircraft. *Definitely foreign!*

He felt the phone which was still in his hand. Technology. That was his comfort zone.

He quickly texted another message back to Brooke.

You won't believe what I am seeing. You won't believe it. I will send you a picture.

He looked over at his gun and finished his message.

Keep your gun handy.

Jereco took a picture of the scene with his cell phone and sent it to Brooke.

Brooke watched the rest of the Evadeam men drive out to the fields as the women made their way into the farmhouse. Everything else was quiet as she read Jereco's texts. She waited patiently for the picture that he promised. It finally appeared in her phone. Her mouth dropped. She blinked, and then she zoomed in on her phone.

Are you kidding me?

Jereco had watched the scene in front of him changed. He rubbed his eyes as the jet's shimmering body revealed an aircraft unknown to him. He snapped another picture and sent it to Brooke's cell. A few minutes later, he felt his phone vibrate. No doubt it was Brooke questioning his picture. He didn't blame her. He wouldn't have believed it himself if he wasn't staring at it right now.

Through the blowing snow and the billowing smoke, he saw before him

The Trahe Chronicles

what looked like a UFO, an Unidentified Flying Object—a type of aircraft he had never seen before. His dad and relatives were approaching the aircraft. It suddenly dawned on him that this was dangerous. What was he doing here? Why was his family here? *Shouldn't there be a government agency out here?* he thought. *Some police officers? Emergency units or something?*

Maybe Jereco really didn't know what his dad did at his government agency office. None of this made sense. Why would his dad drag *him*—a teenager—out here and not call the government or better yet, the U.S. military?

Then Jereco finally noticed that his dad seemed to be talking to someone low to the ground. Jereco rubbed his eyes and looked again. Whatever Jereco saw was now gone, and his dad was walking quickly toward the truck. As his dad got closer, Jereco noticed he had something in his arms. Jereco squinted to make out what it was. It looked like an animal that might have gotten hurt in the crash. Chances are the aircraft landed on one of their farm animals, but it looked too small to be a calf, goat, or sheep. Plus, none of them were out in the middle of this storm. Before Jereco could get a chance to identify the animal, his dad wrapped the animal in a blanket and handed it over to Jereco's grandpa.

Jereco looked down at his phone. Brooke was insisting on being filled in on the scene, but Jereco was hesitating on answering. He followed his gut feeling and text one word.

Alien.

Hours went by, and soon a new dawn approached. With the doors locked and his hand on the gun, Jereco had fallen asleep. He woke up with a start when someone knocked on the truck window. It took Jereco a minute to focus. He had forgotten where he was and why he was sleeping in his dad's truck. His dad's voice grabbed his attention. Jereco used his jacket sleeve to wipe the frost from the interior of the truck window. His dad instructed him to unlock the truck.

Jereco unlocked the truck, and the first thing Jereco noticed was how tired his dad looked. "Everything all right?" Jereco asked.

"Yeah, we can start heading back now," he replied.

"Is it safe?"

His dad nodded.

Jereco got out and took in the scene around him. The new morning sunlight was streaming across the field. Smoke was still smoldering where the UFO had landed, but the UFO wasn't there. Jereco heard a loud sound come from one of their large diesel trucks. He turned and saw the truck begin to haul away what now looked like a small, private jet liner. Jereco rubbed his eyes with his hands and looked again. "What? I don't understand."

His dad did not respond and proceeded to start the truck's engine. Next Jereco saw his grandpa walk away from the diesel truck and toward them. Grandpa also looked tired, but there was a sparkle in his eyes—a sparkle that

Book One: The Chosen Ones

Jereco has not seen in a long time. With determination, Jereco walked up to his grandpa. He pointed toward the small aircraft that was being towed away. "What is that?" Jereco asked.

Grandpa looked over his shoulder. "Well, it looks like a small jet that crashed neatly into our wheat field."

Jereco gave him a stern look, knowing that his grandpa wasn't good at lying to him.

His grandpa shifted uncomfortably and looked over Jereco's head toward his son, Ronald. Then Grandpa turned, looked directly into Jereco's eyes, and whispered, "Your dad would be mad at me if I say anything. It is an old argument," He paused. "Jereco, you are a smart and logical boy. Let's just say that your eyes do not deceive you." He patted Jereco on the shoulder. "Come on. Your dad is very tired. A nap and a big breakfast will help clear our minds."

As his grandpa walked him back to the truck, Jereco knew in his mind that he did not dream what he saw last night. Something strange had landed in their winter wheat field, and he was certain it was not a small jet liner.

As they rode back to their farmhouse, Jereco looked out the window. He was sitting in the backseat this time. He glanced at the rising sun in the east. He looked at the sky and watched some birds rise with the sunlight. Some of the northern birds were heading in the direction of the farmhouse where there are bird feeders.

The morning cries of the birds echoed through his ears as his thoughts wandered. He wondered where that small aircraft had come from. *Alien? Military plane? An experiment of some sort?*

Jereco's eyes looked up higher at the sky. When he was a little boy, he was interested in the stars. He got a telescope for Christmas one year, and he used it to watch the nighttime sky every night. But as he got older, he stopped believing in and dreaming about outer space. His grandfather always tried to encourage him to continue any dream that would lead him to the sky above. Jereco looked at the back of his grandpa's head and remembered how disappointed his grandfather had been when he had found Jereco's telescope collecting dust in their attic. Determined, his grandfather had cleaned up the telescope, and to Jereco's surprise, he handed it to Diana.

Jereco smiled as he remembered how excited his little sister was to use Jereco's telescope. She still reports her sky findings to Jereco. Jereco's eyebrows came together as a thought occurred to him. Not only did Grandpa get another grandchild involved with astrology, but Jereco also was pulled back into his old hobby by his sister's new interest.

As the truck pulled into the farmyard, Jereco saw their diesel truck begin to haul the small jet into his dad's private barn. As the sunlight danced across the plane, Jereco thought he saw funny-looking waves on it. Was there a cloaking device that was able to change the appearance of the aircraft? For it seemed to transform right before his very eyes. Then the moment passed as

10

The Trahe Chronicles

the small jet disappeared into the barn.

Jereco stepped out of the truck. He watched the barn doors close as a flock of singing birds flew above. As he listened, he wondered if his grandfather's belief was right. What if there were other planets beyond theirs? What if he was now witnessing the collision of two different worlds? Jereco was determined to find out the truth.

Book One: The Chosen Ones

Diana and the Talking Cat

The truth never came, at least not in the next few days after the mysterious crash. The Evadeam household became chaotic. Strangers dressed in black suits had shown up at the farmhouse the night of the aircraft crash.

Jereco had peered outside his bedroom window and saw several black vehicles pull into their driveway. People piled out of the vehicles. Jereco assumed that these people were with a government agency or maybe with an aeronautic agency. Some of the people were dressed in outfits that looked similar to astronaut suits. They walk around the farm property and used tools and machinery that he had never seen before. Perhaps they were checking the place for aliens, alien debris, or something dangerous like radioactive material.

As Jereco walked out of his bedroom and headed down the stairs, he heard voices. He picked out his mother's voice. She was upset about something. Jereco sighed and paused at the door that opened into the living room.

Yes, he was eavesdropping. But how could he not? Something weird was happening to his family and their farm.

From what Jereco could gather from the conversation, the government people wanted some Evadeam family members to go to Washington DC. He overheard the words, *in the best interest of the universal affairs*. Jereco wondered why his cousins in the Washington DC area could not handle it. Apparently, his mom had been thinking the same thing. Jereco leaned in farther when he thought he heard a strange voice say some family members had disappeared.

The stairway door flew open, and Jereco almost fell to the floor.

Uncle Larry caught Jereco's arm. "Eavesdropping?" he said.

Before Jereco could answer, Uncle Larry continued, "Come on. Now you are old enough to find out the truth about the family. Besides, you, Brooke, and Grandpa will be in charge while we are gone."

"Gone? Where are you going?"

"To put out some fires," Uncle Larry said, nonchalantly.

Jereco followed his uncle into the dining room area. No wonder his mom was freaking out. Her dining room was a mess. It looked like a computer lab. The small room was packed with technical equipment and more people dressed in black suits. As Jereco scanned the room, he saw Brooke. She looked up at Jereco. Brooke had that look she got when she was holding back a secret. Then it dawned on him. *She knew.*

It was now two weeks later. Jereco's parents and Uncle Larry were sent out of town. The people dressed in black suits and the astronaut uniforms were gone. Their dining room was back to normal. Well, almost normal. A few people dressed in military attire were left behind. "Guard duty," Grandpa had explained.

The Trahe Chronicles

Grandpa Evadeam and Brooke were now staying with them until Jereco's parents came back. This was all fine with Jereco. He was a little nervous after what he saw the night of the aircraft crash on their farm.

Jereco was up in his bedroom, sitting on his bed, with his laptop balancing on his legs. He looked over at Brandon's empty bed. Brandon was downstairs, watching a movie with Grandpa and Brooke. No one had told Brandon or Diana the truth about their family. That was really hard for Jereco. He did not like keeping secrets, especially from Brandon, who was really good at figuring things out. Jereco was sure he would slip up and say something to Brandon.

Jereco sighed and looked at the computer screen. He was looking at aircraft designs. He was trying to find something that looked like the picture he had taken on his cell phone. Aircraft pictures flashed across his screen. Then he heard a familiar sound from Diana's bedroom. He quickly placed his laptop on the bed and ran to Diana's bedroom.

Diana heard a funny sound, like someone was banging against the wall. Was it herself? Was she shaking? Was she having an attack? Yes. She was having one of her attacks. *Please, God. Let it be over.* Then she heard a voice. Was it her brother?

"Jereco?" she tried to say, but as always, nothing came out.

"Diana, Diana!" said the voice. "It is okay. It is almost over. You are okay."

It is Jereco, she thought.

In less than a few minutes, it was over. She slowly came out of her trance. She was very weak and sweaty. She felt like she had just run a marathon. She tried to speak, but again, nothing came out.

"Rest," Jereco ordered. "Save your energy."

She heard her other brother Brandon in the background. "Grandpa is coming," he said.

Grandpa. She was confused. She slowly looked around and started to recognize her bedroom. Diana reached out and grabbed Jereco's arm. "I had a dream. Before my attack, I had a dream. Our parents are in danger."

At that moment, her grandpa and cousin Brooke walked in. Brooke ordered the guys to leave the room, so she could change Diana's clothes, which were soaking with sweat.

Before Jereco left the room, Brooke asked him to get a drink of water and one of Diana's pills. When Jereco came back, Diana was changed and refreshed. Even though she was still weak, she was sitting up and leaning against her bed's headboard. Jereco handed the glass of water and a prescription pill to Diana. Diana swallowed the medicine and proclaimed she was feeling better.

As Grandpa headed towards the door, he said he would call the doctor in the morning. He then motioned the boys to also leave. Diana grabbed

Book One: The Chosen Ones

Jereco's arm and asked him to stay. Grandpa let him, knowing that Jereco's presence would comfort Diana after a seizure.

As soon as Diana was left alone with Jereco, she announced again that their parents were in danger.

Jereco sighed. "Did you have another dream?"

Diana gave him a disgusted look. "Jereco, you know it wasn't a dream. It was a *vision*."

Jereco put his hand gently on hers. "We have yet to determine that."

Many people have told Jereco he was a very patient brother for listening to Diana's stories. But Jereco had discovered over the years that his sister had a gift. She had many dreams. All of which she remembered in detail, and sometimes, on rare occasions, the dreams came true. She called them *visions*. Few people took Diana's dreams seriously though. Jereco, on the other hand, found it was much easier to help Diana work through her visions. Yet, he still had to convince Diana it was in her best interest that she didn't share the visions with too many people.

Diana was very frustrated that no one, but Jereco, believed her. Other people blamed her dreams on her age or her epilepsy medication.

Diana knew epilepsy was a disorder of the nervous system that caused her to have convulsions. Those convulsions, sometimes called grand mal seizures, became less frequent if she took her medication every day. Sometimes, the medication made her see things. At least, that was what the doctors had said.

Jereco believed that she really could see things others could not see. He watched as his sister closed her green-blue eyes. Jereco thought about how frail his sister looked as her small body lay in bed. Her pale face surrounded by straight, light brown hair.

Jereco grabbed an extra blanket to spread over Diana. She was four years younger than him. She was still in grade school while he was in high school.

Jereco was tall and lean. He had curly, sandy brown hair and hazel brown eyes. The girls at school thought he is cute, but he didn't have much interest in girls. His interest was in electronics, or more specifically, his laptop computer and video games. However, he did love to swim. He was one of the fastest swimmers on their swim team at school. He wished it was summer time. He missed swimming in the Michigan lakes.

Jereco shivered as the chill in the house reminded him that it was not summer. He tucked the extra blanket around Diana. Their second-floor bedrooms often got cold during the winter, and there was only one heating vent that came up through the middle of the hallway floor. The heat did not travel very well to the children's bedrooms. His dad was going to update their home, which was over one hundred years old.

Their very old farmhouse was located on over forty acres of farmland and swamp. The first floor of their home had a back mudroom that led into the kitchen. Off the kitchen is a bathroom that is combined with the laundry

14

The Trahe Chronicles

room. To the left of the kitchen was the back porch entrance. The farmhouse was built like a box. One had to walk through the kitchen to get to the dining room. Off the dining room was an enclosed front sun porch. To the right of the dining room was the living room. Stairs leading up to the second floor were off the back of the living room.

Two bedrooms were upstairs. The smallest was Diana's, and it faced the backyard and the farm. Jereco and Brandon shared the largest bedroom, which was located at the front of the house. Their parents' bedroom was downstairs, off the kitchen. There was a small hallway that led from the parent's room to the basement door. The basement was considered an old Michigan basement. It was large enough to hold the furnace and hot water heater and had some room for storing their canned vegetables. Jereco thought the basement could also be used as a tornado shelter or, perhaps, a war shelter.

Diana slowly opened her eyes and watched Jereco get lost in his thoughts. She got along the best with Jereco because he acted like an older, protective brother. Maybe Brandon was too close to her age.

Brandon was shorter than Jereco, but Brandon had a stocky body frame. His hair coloring was similar to Jereco's, but Brandon had different colored eyes. One eye was blue, and the other was green. Diana would tell him, "You have special eyes."

She used to love to play trucks with Brandon, but now she always wanted to play with dolls and unicorns and read fantasy books. Jereco was always sitting in front of the computer or wanting to hang out with his older friends. So Brandon got stuck trying to find rides to his friend's house or spending time with his dad, which usually led to working on the farm.

Their farm had dairy cows, beef cattle, chickens, and vegetable fields. All the kids had chores on the farm, but their mom wanted them to do well in school and have fun while they were still kids. Most of the farm work was a combined effort of their dad, uncles, and other hired help.

Diana's chores consisted of helping their mom around the house and feeding the chickens. Because of her epilepsy, Diana was not as athletic as her brothers. However, she did like to dance, ride their horses, and write stories about imaginative places, people and things. In fact, she constantly had stories in her head. Sometimes she felt like she couldn't write them down fast enough. Then there were times the thoughts were lost for a while. And maybe if she was lucky, they might come back to her in the dreams.

Diana's thoughts were interrupted by her brother. "Now tell me about the vision," Jereco asked.

Diana gathered her thoughts. She suddenly felt very sad and weak. She settled deeper into her pillow and bed. She looked up at Jereco with tears in her eyes. "There was a great wind. Then a crash. And weird-looking people." Diana leaned forward and whispered, "And dad turned toward me. Like he

Book One: The Chosen Ones

was talking directly to me."

"What did he say?"

He said, "Tell Grandpa. Tell Grandpa that we made it, but we need help from the messenger." Diana slumped back against her bed pillows. "Then he was gone. The dream was gone, and I awoke to one of my seizures. Jereco, our parents are in trouble. I just know it. I can feel it and there isn't anything I can do about it."

"Yes, you can," replied Jereco. "Remember what mom told you to do when you feel like you can't help someone?"

Diana nodded.

Jereco took her hand. "Come on. We will do it together."

Jereco and Diana held hands as Jereco led them into a prayer. "Dear God, please help our parents. Protect them and guide them. And please help Diana get some rest tonight with no more visions. Amen."

Diana mumbled an "amen".

Jereco got off the bed. "Okay. It's time to go back to sleep. Are you okay, or do you want me to sleep here on the floor tonight?"

"No, I am okay," Diana replied. "You can go back to your bedroom, but first, will you tell grandpa what Daddy said?"

"Yeah. I will go tell him right now. Are you sure you are okay?" Jereco imagined how scary it had to be for his sister to have a bad dream followed by a seizure. She insisted that she was okay, so he said his goodnight and headed toward the staircase.

As Jereco walked by the hallway window, he looked outside. It was a cold and starry evening. He wondered if it was cold where his parents were. He turned and hurried downstairs. He was convinced Diana's dream had a meaning. He just had to convince his grandpa.

Diana did not go to sleep after Jereco left. She started to think about her dream that seemed so real. She glanced outside her bedroom window. Her bed was against the north window overlooking the back of the house. It was a cold, clear, and brisk night. This was the month of November, and school winter break was just around the corner. It had been snowing for over a month. The yard and fields were covered with blankets of the white stuff.

Diana thought that it looked beautiful outside. The snow was white and pure. It had developed into one of those perfect snowstorms. One that dropped fluffy snow down like it was raining in April. The snow covered all the rooftops, the driveway, the tree branches, and even the farm trucks. As luck would have it, the snowstorm rolled in before the school winter break. Many children in the town were excited because this would mean sledding, skating, and an easier path for Santa (but that was another story).

Diana continued to look out of her bedroom window. She loved to watch snow fall in the evening when the stars were out. Diana thought there was something magical about the snow. She also enjoyed watching the animals

The Trahe Chronicles

make tracks in the snow. From her window, she could watch their farm animals eating in the fields, squirrels climbing trees, birds flying in the sky, and bunny rabbits hopping in the yard. Tonight, however, they were all tucked away in their own homes, keeping safe and warm while the snow continued to fall. Except for one animal.

Diana could barely make out the creature under the large farm light that shined across the backyard. The creature appeared to be a very large cat. Diana had now seen this cat for the past two weeks. It always appeared just outside Dad's private work barn. Every time Diana saw the cat, the cat would follow the same routine. The cat would come out of the barn, sit under the glow of the farm light, and then looks up at Diana's window.

Diana thought the cat was waiting for her. Diana would wave to the cat. Then the cat would nod and go after unexpected prey. The cat usually disappeared into the woods or the barn. When Diana first saw the cat, she had asked her dad about it. They had many barn cats, but that one didn't look like any of those cats because it was so large. Diana guessed it was as big as a medium size dog. The cat was black with white markings on its stomach, neck, and paws. Her dad never acknowledged the cat existed, so Diana dropped the subject. And now her dad was gone.

Diana's eyebrows came together as she thought about her parents. She was worried about them. Diana continued to watch the cat. *Odd*, she thought. *The cat did not run off this evening.* Instead, it ran across the yard and climbed up an old willow tree that was planted next to their garage. The cat picked a branch, lay down, and swung its tail back and forth. The motion of the tail had a hypnotic effect on Diana. Diana yawned and settled back into her bed. For some reason, the cat seemed to calm Diana. She suddenly felt very tired and calm. She slowly drifted to sleep and did not have any more nightmares that evening.

The next morning was a Friday, and Diana was happy to awake to cancellation of school. The snow that had fallen during the night had turned into a major snowstorm. The whole family was sitting at the breakfast table as Grandpa listened to the weather on the radio. They did own a TV, but their mom wouldn't allow the television to be turned on during meals. Diana noticed that Grandpa was sticking to their parents' rules while they were gone.

They heard the repeated message on the radio that the area schools were cancelled due to the winter storm taking place. "At this rate," Brandon said, "we will hardly have any school before it is time for Christmas break."

"Yes," replied Jereco, "but don't get too excited because if we run out of winter snow days, then they will have to extend our school year into our summer break."

Brandon shook his head. "That is dumb. Why don't they just have us stay later during the day? We are already there, so they should make us stay an

Book One: The Chosen Ones

hour later to make up the time.”

“I can’t imagine you staying any longer at school, Brandon,” Grandpa said. “Besides, your dad needs you home before it gets dark to help with the farm chores.”

“Hey, the weather forecast is coming on,” Brook said. “And please pass me the orange juice.”

The weather forecast was not looking good for the weekend. They were getting a break during the day, but the evenings were blowing in storms all the way through Sunday.

During the rest of breakfast, they planned what needed to be done with the farm and animals during this storm. Brandon and some other cousins were going to help with the cattle. Jereco was going to cut and stock up more firewood; their farmhouse was equipped with old-fashioned fireplaces just in case the power went out. Grandpa was going to make sure there was enough gas for the backup generators, and Diana was going to feed the chickens and help Brooke with the house.

After breakfast, Diana bundled into her winter gear—snow pants, boots, coat, gloves and hat. As she headed into the chicken coop, she noticed tracks. She went into the coop cautiously, knowing that there could be a fox, barn cat, or even a coyote that might have gotten into the chicken coop. She peered into the coop. Everything seemed calm and fine. She shrugged, did her daily routine of feeding, and made sure the coop was nice and secured when she left.

Out of curiosity, she followed the tracks to see where they would lead. They led straight to Dad’s private barn, which the kids called “Dad’s cave.” The children were not allowed to go in this barn. So Diana faced a dilemma. The tracks seemed to lead right into Dad’s cave. She wasn’t allowed into the cave, so she couldn’t check to see if an animal was in there. Besides, what if it was a coyote or something large? She really should just tell someone. Just when she turned around, she heard a meow.

She glanced back, and sitting right at the door was the black and white cat!

“Well, hello,” Diana said. “So you are not part of my imagination. Or are you?”

The cat meowed as if answering her question.

Diana smiled and bent down to pet the cat. The cat came right up to Diana and started purring.

“Oh, what a nice kitty,” Diana said. “You don’t even look like a barn cat. You are too clean and plump. Have you been eating well?”

The cat meowed again.

“I wonder if you belong to the neighbors. Maybe I should take you back to the house and call around.” As Diana said this, the cat turned to run away. “Oh no. Don’t go.”

The cat actually stopped and turned to look at Diana.

Diana looked at the cat, curiously. “I do believe you understand every

The Trahe Chronicles

word I say. Or is it coincidence? Hmm … would you like some cream?"

The cat meowed again and walked back to Diana.

"Well, Mom doesn't like me to bring animals into the house, and Dad would be mad if I brought you into the dairy barn, so I have to find a spot to bring you some cream. But then again, neither of my parents is here right now."

As if on cue, the cat turned and walked toward Dad's cave.

"Oh no," Diana said. "I can't go in there. That is Dad's barn. It is the cave, and we aren't allowed in there."

The cat looked at Diana and said, "Its okay. Follow me." It proceeded to walk toward the back of the barn.

Diana just stood there. She shook her head, looked around, and called out, "Okay, Brandon. Are you playing a practical joke?" Diana swore she just heard the cat talk and say, "It's okay. Follow me." But that was impossible.

Diana looked around again, but there was no one in sight. She shrugged. *It must be my overactive imagination.* She proceeded to follow the cat's tracks. The paw prints were pretty clear in the fresh fallen snow. They took her around to the back of the barn, but there was no door. The tracks seemed to just disappear right into the barn. *That makes no sense*, thought Diana. *There is no door here, yet the cat prints seem to walk right into the barn wall.* She pushed on the wall and sure enough, a board slipped to the side and a small opening appeared.

Diana bit her lip and looked around. She knew she wasn't allowed to go in this barn. But curiosity was getting the best of her. Maybe she would step in for just a minute. As she was thinking about it, a high wind blew against her, knocking her right into the barn. Diana looked behind her to see snow furiously blowing hard. She could hardly see outside. *Where did this wind come from?* she thought. The wind and snow got colder and colder and kept blowing her into the barn. Her mind reasoned that taking cover from the unexpected snow gale was a good enough reason to crawl into the barn.

Diana stepped through the hole in the wall. At first, she couldn't see anything. Her eyes had to adjust to the darkness. It was so bright outside from the white of the snow, but the barn was dark and gloomy. All of a sudden, Diana felt something rub against her leg. She let out a small scream, and then covered her mouth, remembering she wasn't supposed to be in the barn.

Meow.

The sound came from a fur ball rubbing against her leg.

Diana sighed with relief. It was just the cat. She bent down and started petting her. "Is this your home? I wonder why Dad doesn't see you in here. No matter. Want to show me where to bring the cream? But I'll only stay a moment because I am not really supposed to be in here."

Once again, the cat took off as if it understood Diana.

Diana followed the cat farther into the barn. The barn had high ceilings

Book One: The Chosen Ones

with lofts. They walked into a back room. The cat took Diana to a corner that had a cat bed made out of old blankets. Some food dishes lay next to the bed.

"Now, that is curious. Who would get you these blankets and dishes if no one is supposed to be in here? It must be Grandpa because Dad doesn't know anything about you."

The cat opened its mouth to say something when Diana heard Grandpa's voice calling for her.

"Oh no," Diana said. "I have to go, so he doesn't see me in here. But I will be back to bring you cream as soon as I can." Diana noticed the look on the cat's face. It almost had a look of disgust and irritation, like the cat was upset by the interruption.

As Diana had promised, she came back to the barn with cream for the cat the following day and every day after that. They had formed a special pet and owner bond. Diana looked forward to seeing the cat. She started talking to the cat like it was a special friend, and she shared her special thoughts and dreams with her.

One afternoon, Diana felt lonely and depressed. Diana sat on the barn floor, petting the cat as the cat drank her cream. Diana told the cat about her sorrows. Diana really missed her parents. They had not heard from their parents since the night of her dream. Jereco had told Grandpa about Diana's vision, and Grandpa had seemed worried, which made the kids worry even more. To make matters worse, they were still stranded on the farm due to the winter snowstorms, and aside from the cat, Diana only had one other very good friend, Annette, whom she had not seen for a while.

"I wish I was normal," Diana said to the cat. "Normal like all the other kids at school. I do well in school, but I miss so many days of school because of my epilepsy. I am always behind in my homework, and I have a hard time making new friends. I wish I was more like Annette. Everyone likes her."

"You don't want to be like someone else," the cat replied, "because then you wouldn't be you. And you are very special. No, you definitely want to be who you are."

Diana shrieked and jumped up. *Did you just talk?* No, of course, you didn't. You are a cat. It must be my medication," she mumbled, shaking her head.

"No, it's not the medication," the cat replied. "I can speak very clearly, thank you very much."

Tears welled up in Diana's eyes. This was exactly why she wished she didn't have this disorder. Her medicine was making her hear things now. She knew she could sometimes see funny things, but she had never heard anything imaginary before.

"Why are you crying?" asked the cat.

"Because you can't talk, and I am imagining it," Diana replied. "Oh, I

The Trahe Chronicles

really wish you could talk." She wiped the tears from her eyes.

The cat jumped up to a nearby countertop so she could look straight into Diana's eyes. "Now, Diana, listen to me. I can speak your language, so you can hear me just fine. I am not like the rest of your barn cats, who are Earth cats. I am a cat from another world. My name is Cleopatra. But you may call me Cleo."

Diana just stared at the cat, still not believing her. "I know! This is a trick, not my medication. One of my brother's pranks. Probably Brandon."

Diana started yelling, "Brandon! Brandon!" She looked around the small room for him.

She didn't find him. She looked at a door that led into the rest of the barn—a door she had never opened before.

She looked back at Cleo.

The cat nodded, pointed her paw at the door, and said, "Go ahead."

Diana hesitated. "No. This is a trick by you, Brandon. You are trying to get me into trouble and have me get caught by Grandpa. But it isn't going to work!" And with that she turned around and said to Cleo, "You were supposed to be my friend, and you let Brandon train you into playing a trick on me. It isn't funny or very nice." With tears in her eyes, Diana ran out through the hole in the back wall.

She stumbled on her way back to the house, and just before she opened the door, a snowball hit her on the back. Looking for the culprit, she turned around with hot tears running down her face. It was Brandon. He wore a devious smile as he packed another snowball.

"That isn't funny, and you are so mean," Diana said. "I am telling Grandpa. No, I am telling *Brooke!*"

That caught Brandon's attention. Brooke was in charge while their parents were gone. Brandon only listened to Brooke because she was older, bigger, and knew how to throw a mean punch.

"Why would you do that?" Brandon said. "It is just a snowball. It's not like it hurt you or anything." He slowly walked toward her as he packed another snowball in his hand. He paused. "Hey, have you been crying? Why are you crying? I didn't hit you that hard." Brandon looked at her more closely and realized she had been crying longer than the few minutes it would have taken to feel his snowball on her back.

"Hey, have kids been picking on you again?" he said. "You just tell me who they are. I will take care of them!" He was quite aware that some kids teased Diana behind her back about her disease. He was protective of his little sister.

"No, it isn't the kids," Diana replied. "And don't pretend that you don't know why I am upset, Brandon!" Her tears of hurt were quickly replaced with anger. "Teasing me like that. It isn't funny. She was my cat. I found her first. Stay away from her, and stop training her to do mean things."

Brandon just looked at her, confused. "What are you talking about? Did

21

Book One: The Chosen Ones

you skip your medication today?"

All the hurt and anger was enough to set Diana off. She took her fist and punched Brandon in the face.

Brandon fell back, more from surprise than from the force of the hit. "Hey, what did you do that for?" *Brooke must have taught her*, he thought. He wanted to hit her back. But the one and only time that he hit a girl, he got in big trouble with his dad.

Diana looked at him with satisfaction. "That is for playing the trick on me with Cleo, and don't do it again!"

Brandon rubbed his cheek. "Who in the heck is Cleo?"

"Stop pretending!" yelled Diana.

"You know what?" Brandon turned and started to walk away. "I have better things to do than argue with you about an imaginary friend."

"Imaginary? Oh, is she so imaginary that you trained her to move her lips and talk to me?"

This caught Brandon's attention. Now he was starting to worry about his sister. Since when had Diana ever hit anyone? And now she was talking about some trick and someone named Cleo? Maybe she did forget her medicine, or maybe she was about to have a seizure. "Diana, why don't we go in the house and get warmed up. I think you need to lie down." He grabbed her arm to steer her into the house. He needed to get Grandpa before she had an attack.

Diana would have nothing to do with it. She pulled her arm away. "Stop pretending, Brandon. Just admit that you played a bad trick on me with my cat. And maybe, just maybe I won't tell Brooke."

Brandon was tempted to agree that he had played a trick on her just to get her in the house, but he hesitated because their parents had taught them not to lie. As he weighed his options about what to say to Diana, he suddenly heard a sound.

Meow.

Brandon looked down, and a stray cat rubbed against his legs. He had never seen this cat before in the barns. It was quite large, almost as large as a small dog. It was black with a white strip that ran down its forehead and covered most of its face. The white ran underneath its belly and down all four legs. "Now where did you come from?" asked Brandon.

Diana picked Cleo up. "Like you don't know. I am warning you. Stay away from my cat."

"*Your* cat? Where did you get this cat?" Brandon knew very well that there was no way their parents would allow them to have any more animals.

Ignoring Brandon's suspicious gaze, Diana just looked down at Cleo. "I didn't get her. She got me. She came to me."

"Where has she been staying?" Brandon asked. "I haven't seen her in the barns."

With accusing eyes, Diana looked at Brandon. "You know very well where she has been staying—in Daddy's barn."

The Trahe Chronicles

"Dad's barn!" yelled Brandon. "Are you nuts? You want to be grounded forever?" Diana was confused. Why was Brandon acting so surprised by all of this? She started to wonder if he was not behind it. Maybe it was Jereco, but he wasn't the type to waste time on pranks, especially on his little sister.

Diana was still deep in thought when Brandon grabbed her arm. "Show me. Show me where you have been hiding her." Brandon dragged her toward Dad's barn. "I can't believe you," he said, shaking his head. "You know how much trouble you can get into?"

Diana yanked her arm away and looked around. "Where is Grandpa?' All of a sudden, she was afraid that Grandpa might see them sneak in Dad's barn.

"He went back to his house to get some things. Lucky for you!" Brandon walked them up to the barn's front door. He pointed at the lock. "Now how did you get in?"

"Not through here. Come on, around the back." She headed toward the back of the barn. Once they arrived, Cleo looked up at the kids, meowed, moved the loose board, and walked into the barn. Brandon just stared after her. He looked more closely at the loose board. "Did you do this, Diana?"

"No, it was already like that. In fact, Cleo showed me into the barn. Come on." She followed Cleo.

Brandon looked behind him to make sure no one was watching and reluctantly walked into the barn. At first, it was very dark, and it took a moment for his eyes to adjust. He followed her into a small room. The room had shelves, a desk, and a cabinet that was loaded with old, dusty books and stuff.

Diana waved Brandon over. "Over here." She walked around a cabinet and some shelves piled full of random things. In a corner were a cat bed, blanket, water bowl, and a food dish.

"Where did you get this stuff?" asked Brandon.

"I didn't." Diana gestured toward Cleo's corner. "It was already here."

Brandon's eyes were drawn to a map above Cleo's bed. The map was brown and seemed ancient-looking. It looked like a world map, but he didn't recognize any of the countries.

"I've never noticed that before," Diana said. "Is that Earth in ancient times?"

"I don't know. I don't recognize any of the countries, yet they seem kind of the same so it must be a map of Earth, like hundreds or maybe thousands of years ago." Brandon loved maps. Studying maps was one of his favorite hobbies. He liked to collect, memorize, and pretend to explore the places on the maps. Brandon reached for one of the pins that kept the map on the board.

"What are you doing?" asked Diana.

"What do you think I am doing? I am going to take the map. It obviously hasn't been looked at in many years. It is all old and dusty. No one is going to

Book One: The Chosen Ones

miss it."

"But it isn't yours to take," argued Diana.

Brandon rolled his eyes. "Who says—"

"It is not yours to take," a women's voice interrupted. "Besides, don't you think your dad would be a little mad for breaking into his barn and stealing his map?"

Brandon and Diana both jumped, and then they turned, half-expecting to see Brooke standing there. But the only person standing there was the cat.

Diana blinked. "Oh no. Here we go again."

Brandon looked at her. "What?"

Diana just looked at him, doubting that he was the one who had made Cleo talk earlier.

"Just follow my lead," Brandon whispered. "I will cover us. Who goes there? Brooke? Grandpa? We are sorry, but we followed this cat into the barn." Brandon looked accusingly at the cat.

There was no answer.

"This is the trick I was talking about," Diana said. "If it is not you, then do you think it is Jereco?"

"There's one way to find out," Brandon replied as he started to search the little room. It didn't take long since the room was very small. It was only big enough to hold a desk, a chair, a file cabinet some shelving units, and the cat's area. "No one is in here, but I bet it is wired with some voice activation system. I need a flashlight or a light." Brandon started to search the shelves. A small light bulb clicked on. Brandon and Diana were startled and looked over at the desk. Cleo was sitting on the desk and had pushed a switch that was hidden under the map.

"That's where the light switch is!" exclaimed Diana.

Brandon looked at the cat. "Did the cat just do that?"

"Yes, the cat did do that," said the cat. "In fact, I can talk too."

Both kids froze.

"This isn't funny anymore, Brandon," Diana whispered. "If you or Jereco is up to this, you need to tell me now."

"I'm not doing this," Brandon whispered back. "It must be Jereco." This was a pretty good joke for Jereco. Jereco was a computer whiz kid, and he obviously was testing something out on this cat. "Hey, I bet this cat isn't even real. It is probably a computerized stuffed animal that Jereco created." Brandon picked up the cat and looked it over. "Feels real. Wow, this is good. I wonder where the batteries are on this thing." He started poking the cat.

"Do you mind?!" hissed the cat. She took a swing at Brandon and scratched his cheek. "Ouch! Hey, that hurts." Brandon dropped the cat and touched his cheek. "Great, now I am bleeding. A scratch on top of the black and blue bruise."

Diana gave him a guilty look, but she didn't apologize. She still wasn't fully convinced that he didn't have anything to do with this.

24

The Trahe Chronicles

"Brandon! Diana!" boomed a voice from outside the barn. Jereco was calling for them.

"Good, let's get to the bottom of this now," said Brandon. He walked through the hole to the outside.

Diana could hear them talking, which quickly became arguing. The voices got louder as they came closer to the barn.

"I really can talk, Diana," Cleo said. "And we are really wasting valuable time."

Diana's mouth was still open when Brandon, followed by Jereco, came through the hole.

"What is so important that you dragged me into Dad's barn?" Jereco's voice boomed. "Do you know how much trouble you are in?"

Jereco had a look of surprise on his face when he saw Diana. She never got into trouble.

"Okay, Brandon, what kind of trouble are you trying to get Diana into?"

"Why does everyone blame me? I have nothing to do with it." Brandon pointed toward the cat. "If anything, this is your fault."

Jereco looked at the cat. "Where did the cat come from?"

"I am Cleopatra," said the cat in a very musical and loud female voice. "The guide of the Creator. I have been sent here to find and bring back the Chosen Ones to Trahe."

Jereco's mouth dropped, but then he stepped toward the cat to examine it closely. He obviously was more curious than afraid. "Wow, this cat looks real. Who made it? Where did you order it from, Brandon?"

"*I am real,*" said the cat.

"Wow, this is good. Seriously, where did you get it? I have to get one of these." Jereco reached for the cat.

"I wouldn't do that if I were you." Brandon rubbed his cheek again.

"This fake cat did that to you?"

"Uh-huh."

"Wow. Just amazing. Looks so real." As Jereco touched the cat, it hissed. Then the most amazing thing happened, the cat glowed a bright yellow-white color!

"I am Cleopatra," the cat repeated. "The guide of the Creator for the Chosen Ones. Time is here for the Chosen Ones to go to your sister planet—Trahe." All three kids stared at the cat, mesmerized.

"Who are the Chosen Ones?" Diana asked.

"Children of the Evadeam tribe," replied Cleo.

Book One: The Chosen Ones

A Brief History Lesson

"The Evadeam tribe?" asked Brandon.

Jereco looked over at Brandon. "That is our last name."

"I know that. I am not a dummy. But why *tribe*? And why is she glowing? Except for the talking, she sure looks real and acts real."

Cleopatra shook her head sadly and mumbled, "This is what the modern world and technology has done for me. It is time to call in some reinforcements." She glowed brighter, closed her eyes, and just sat there.

Diana looked back at her older brothers. "What is she doing?"

"I don't know." Jereco studied Cleopatra closely without touching her. "Maybe she is recharging herself."

"Well, she said she was calling in for help, so maybe she has, like, telepathy," guessed Brandon. "Maybe she is mediating."

Jereco still believed she was some sort of robot. "Who do you think invented her?""Well, isn't it obvious?" Brandon said. "She has been in Dad's barn, so Dad must have made her. It must be a top secret government project. Cool! Dad is a secret agent disguised as a farmer." Brandon pointed at the map. "And this must be a secret planet or something. How cool is that?! Our dad is a *spy*."

"Don't get your hopes up, Brandon," scolded Grandpa. "He is not a spy or a secret agent. But he would be very upset, knowing his three kids are in his restrictive barn."

All three kids jumped at the sound of Grandpa's voice. They had not heard Grandpa walk in behind them.

"Now we are in trouble," Brandon whispered into Diana's ear. "And it is your fault."Diana just gave her brothers a panicked look. She knew they were all in trouble. Grandpa loomed over them. He was easily over six feet tall with huge muscles. He was like an older replica of Jereco. His gray hair had once been a dark sandy brown color. He had light brown skin that made them look tan all year round. His big brown eyes looked accusingly at them. "Well, I am waiting for an explanation."

Cleo walked toward Grandpa. "There is no one to blame but myself and the Creator."

Grandpa looked surprised, but he quickly regained his thoughts. His anger now seemed to be directed at the cat. "What is the meaning of this?" he whispered angrily.

"It is time," Cleopatra replied. "The Evadeam tribe has been called upon and the Chosen Ones have been found." Cleo pointed a paw at the children. "They are the Chosen Ones."

"No, no. They are having no part of it," Grandpa said. "You leave the children out of it.""You know that we have no choice in the matter, Ovid Evadeam."

"Grandpa?" Jereco was now beyond the point of worrying about getting

26

The Trahe Chronicles

in trouble. He was more worried about what the cat was saying and what the heck was going on.

Grandpa looked at his grandson. At that moment, Jereco looked so grown up even though he was only a teenager.

"Grandpa, what is going on?" Jereco waved at everything in the room. "Does Dad work for the government? Or is he some sort of secret mad scientist?"

Grandpa looked around the room. It was filled with evidence of something he had hoped he would never have to share with his grandkids. That was his son's responsibility. But his son just wanted them to have a normal American life. Grandpa sadly shook his head. His eyebrows came together as though he were deep in thought.

"Ovid, you might as well forget it," said Cleo. "I know that look. Unfortunately, this is not something we can get out of."

Grandpa just sighed. "Your dad is not going to like this. Where do we begin?" He clapped his hands together. "I guess we start here." as he waved his arm around the room as Jereco did earlier.

Grandpa turned toward Jereco. "Remember after the airplane crashed in the farm field? We told you and Brooke our family secret?"

Jereco nodded.

"Well, we did not tell you everything."

"What family secret?" asked Brandon.

Jereco crossed his arms and stared at his grandfather. "You mean the secret where Dad, Uncle Larry, and several other family members work for a government agency that investigates UFOs?"

"What?!" Brandon said.

Grandpa rubbed his chin. "Yeah, that one." He walked behind the desk and moved the map. "There is a little bit more to it."

Diana gasped.

"Whoa," Brandon said.

In front of Jereco was an oversized safe, like something he might see in a bank. It had been hidden behind the large map.

Grandpa clasped his hands together. "Now, let's see if I can remember the combination." He thought carefully, his tongue sticking out just a little as he turned the large combination dial."There. That should do it." He pulled on the handle. It did not open.

"Hmmm …" Grandpa rubbed his jaw and then snapped his fingers. "I know." He dialed another combination. But again, the safe did not open.

Cleo jumped on the desk. "You know how I hate wasting time, Ovid Evadeam. Let me try."

'Oh, never you mind, you mangy cat."

'Why do you always have to argue with me, old man?" said Cleo.

"That's it!" exclaimed Grandpa. "My sweet, dear Adeline used to call me *old man*. The combination is her birth date. Bless her soul." Grandma Adeline

Book One: The Chosen Ones

had died ten years ago. Now Jereco wondered if what was in this safe had anything to do with the cat. Jereco studied Cleo. Was Cleo the animal Grandpa had carried away from the crash site?

"That did it," Grandpa said. "See, I told you I knew the combination. Cleo, you were distracting me."

Cleo just shook her head. The two of them walked into the safe. Grandpa peeked out "Well, come on in, kids. I know you are curious." He flicked on a switch and the room lit up.

The kids walked inside what looked like a small storage room. Grandpa waved Jereco over. "Help me move this shelf."

Jereco helped him move what seemed to be an empty, metal storage shelf. The walls of the room were lined with more shelves filled with miscellaneous supplies. The supplies looked like things one would need in case of an emergency.

"Grandpa, is this a tornado shelter?" asked Diana. They did get some tornadoes on occasion, but they usually went into the house basement when a warning siren sounded.

Grandpa paused to look at Diana. "Well, yes, I guess this could be a tornado shelter. And if anyone asks, this is exactly what it is—a tornado shelter." He nodded, and then he spoke to Jereco. "Now push."

Diana gave Brandon a questioning look. *Why would anyone think this room was a tornado shelter, especially if it needed a combination to get in?*

Brandon just shrugged.

After the shelving unit was moved, another steel door was revealed. But this one did not have a combination lock—just one door handle with some sort of screen next to it. Grandpa put his hand over the screen, and it blinked yellow. Then Grandpa looked into the screen, and it scanned his eyes.

"Cool." Brandon pointed at the screen. "It's a retina scanner."

"Yes, it is." Grandpa pulled on the handle. "And that should do the trick." The door opened, and Grandpa clasped his hands again. "Here we go."

The kids followed Grandpa down a flight of cement stairs. At the bottom, Grandpa pressed a button on the wall that lit up a huge room.

"Wow." Brandon could not believe his eyes. From the outside, the building looked like an ordinary barn. But from the inside, a secret passageway had led to this large room. It had a small kitchen and a work area. A wall was lined with books. There were tables, chairs, and a few sleeping cots. There was even a separate wash room. However, the main attraction was right in the middle of the room.

Brandon pointed to the focal point.

"What is that?"

At first glance, it appeared to be a dark multi colored small jet with rounded and sleek curves. But it looked too modernized for an ordinary jet. Brandon wondered if it was military.

28

The Trabe Chronicles

"That? Well, that is the road to my dream," replied Grandpa.

"Hey," Jereco said, "isn't that the aircraft that crashed in our field?"

"Yes, it is. It's revolutionary and sleek design makes it look like a jet. However, it is technically classified as a winged space plane."

"Space plane?" questioned Brandon.

"Yes, as in a type of spacecraft which is defined in the encyclopedia as a vessel designed for spaceflight. Is that correct Grandpa?" asked a voice from behind them.

They looked over their shoulders to see Brooke who had just walked into the room.

"Brooke!" squealed Diana.

"Hi, Squirt." Brooke gave her a big hug. Then she turned toward Grandpa. "Aunt Rhonda is back, along with some guys in dark suits and the sheriff."

Grandpa looked anxious. He picked up the cat and ordered the kids to follow him to the house. Brandon was surprised that the cat let Grandpa handle her so roughly.

As they walked back through the small office, Grandpa asked Diana to gather Cleo's things as it looked like Cleo would be living in the house now. "Brandon," Grandpa said, "can you bring that map? Be careful as you carry it. It's very old and fragile."

They left the barn, and Grandpa filled Brooke in about their new house cat. Jereco also informed Brooke that the crashed aircraft was in Dad's barn. Jereco noticed that Brooke didn't seem too surprised by this new information.

Once they were in the house, Grandpa sent the kids upstairs to the bedrooms. But the Evadeam children found themselves eavesdropping again while sitting on the second floor stairs. Conversations between their relatives and the uniformed strangers were taking place in the kitchen. The children had a hard time hearing all of it. It sounded like bad news. Worried about their parents, Brooke finally left the sanctuary of the staircase and marched into the kitchen. The rest of the children followed.

They did not like the scene they walked into. Aunt Rhonda was crying while Grandpa was arguing with some guy wearing a black suit. Other men in suits and the sheriff were also there, wordlessly watching the argument.

Jereco noticed that Cleo was lying on the kitchen table casually licking her paws as her tail flipped back and forth.

"I don't care what your company may think," Grandpa said, jabbing a pointed finger into the man's chest. "I know, you know, we all know that they are not dead. We know exactly where they are at, and we need to go get them."

"Who is dead?" Diana whispered.

All the adults in the kitchen turned toward Diana. One of the men in the dark suits cleared his throat. "We are done here. We are truly sorry for your

Book One: The Chosen Ones

loss."

Jereco noticed that the man did not look at anyone as he said those words. Instead, the man just packed up his briefcase. The other suited men followed him out the door, leaving the sheriff standing there, holding his hat.

The sheriff muttered an apology to the kids and turned to leave. Before he left, he mumbled in a low voice "Ovid, don't do anything foolish. But if you do, be safe."

Grandpa just stood there with a grim face, arms folded. He looked like he was restraining himself from kicking someone's butt.

The sheriff let himself out. After the door shut, there was silence for a while.

Brooke finally said, "Well?"

Aunt Rhonda stood up. "Kids, I don't know how to tell you this, but—"

"Rhonda!" Grandpa interrupted. "Let *me* tell them the truth."

Aunt Rhonda looked like she was going to argue, but then Cleo stood up on all four paws and meowed. Aunt Rhonda just sighed and sat back down.

Obviously, the cat was in charge thought Jereco.

Grandpa walked over to Diana, picked her up, and set her on his knee. Then he looked up at his other grandchildren. "We have some sad news. Your parents were in a plane crash." He held up his hand before the kids got a chance to speak. "No, they are *not* dead. But we do believe they crashed in an area that our authorities cannot reach."

"What does that mean?" asked Jereco.

It was Brooke who replied this time. "It means that you are about to get a crash course on our heritage."

At that moment, Aunt Rhonda's cell phone rang. After Aunt Rhonda walked away with the phone, Brooke turned to Grandpa. "Dad has been trying to teach, or should I say, *convince* me for years, but I didn't want to believe him."

Grandpa put one arm around Brooke's shoulders. He then waved Diana over and held her in his other arm. "I know. At least you were a little bit more prepared than your cousins."

"Prepared for what?" Brandon asked. "Is this the part where you tell us the rest of our family secret?" Jereco grumbled.

Grandpa looked at him. "There is no easy way to say this, so I am just going to say it." He took a deep breath. "We, our family—the Evadeam family—were not created on Earth. We come from another planet."

As the children slowly went into shock over what their grandfather had just told them, Cleo started to glow. "I am what crashed landed onto your farm," she said. "I was brought here to gather the Chosen Ones. I brought word that a war of the worlds is foreseen; only the Chosen Ones can prevent it. Unfortunately, your parents chose not to believe me. They wanted to change the path."

Grandfather set Diana down. "They left in one of our family's small

30

The Trahe Chronicles

aircrafts to meet with the President. Unfortunately, their plane went down and they've disappeared."

"Where did it go down?" asked Brooke.

Grandpa hesitated, and then he looked Brooke straight in the eye. "The Bermuda Triangle."

Jereco's head snapped up. "Where?"

Brandon walked over to Grandpa. "What president?"

"I am guessing the President of the United States," Brooke replied. "But Grandpa, isn't the Bermuda Triangle southeast of Washington DC?"

Grandpa looked at Brooke like something had just occurred to him.

Cleo jumped off the table. "I think we need to go back into headquarters—the barn."

Aunt Rhonda walked back into the room. "That was Gregory. He and the rest of the family are on their way over." She walked over to the kitchen counter and mumbled something about making coffee.

"Make that coffee strong," suggested Grandpa. "I think it is going to be a long night."

Brooke, Jereco, Brandon and Diana sat back in their dad's barn room where the infamous space plane displayed as a centerpiece. Aunt Rhonda shoved cups of hot liquid into their hands. She insisted they drink what she had made; assuring them that it would help with the shock. As the children sat, they watched other family members arrive—four uncles and two aunts— all of Dad's siblings. Dad was the seventh child of Grandpa Ovid.

Brandon elbowed Jereco and nodded toward Cleo. The children switched their attention to the cat.

Cleo welcomed the relatives, one by one. "Welcome, Gregory Evadeam. Welcome, Brandon Scott Evadeam. Welcome, Coby Evadeam. Welcome, Tricia Evadeam, and thank you, Rhonda Evadeam."

Once everyone was settled, Grandpa pointed at the map that he had unrolled on the table.

"Isn't this an old map of Earth?" said Brandon.

"It does sort of look like it, doesn't it?" Grandpa replied. "That is the magical wonder of it. It looks like Earth a little bit, but it isn't. This is a map of Trahe."

"What is Trahe?" asked Jereco. "Does anyone want to explain what all of this is?"

"Yes, and we do need to start moving," Grandpa said. "Take a seat, and I will give a little history lesson. Gregory, can you dig out the family book?"

Jereco waved his hand over the table. "I am assuming you are going to explain how all this ties into our missing parents?"

"Yes," said Cleo. "Patience, Jereco."

"Wait a minute," said Brooke. "Can we start with the talking cat?"

"I am Cleopatra," the cat said. "The guide of the Creator for the Chosen

31

Book One: The Chosen Ones

Ones. I came from your sister planet—the world of Trahe. It is very important that I bring the Chosen Ones back to Trahe." The cat began to glow again as if to make her speech more appealing.

Brooke looked warily at the cat, and then she looked at Grandpa. Grandpa walked over to Brooke and gave her a hug. "It is okay. We can explain this." The other relatives nodded in agreement, as Uncle Gregory dropped a pile of old, large, dusty books in the middle of the table. "Here they are," he said. "Dad, do you want to do the honors?"

Grandpa gingerly picked up one of the books. "It's been a long time. Gregory, why don't you just give the kids the short version, and we can give them more details during our Trahe lessons."

"Lessons?" the kids chimed.

"We already go to school," said Brandon, who particularly didn't like school. "What kind of lessons are these?"

"Ah, there are a variety of lessons regarding Trahe," Grandpa replied. "But I will start out with a brief history lesson." He rubbed his chin. "Where do I start?"

Cleo hopped on the table and walked over to the smaller of the two books. "How about if I start with these?"

Grandpa simply nodded, knowing it was more of a statement than a question.

Cleo turned toward the children and sat on the table, with her tail flicking behind her. She glowed as she talked. "Do you know how Earth was created?"

Jereco and Brooke nodded. Brandon just shrugged. "I know some of it," Dana replied.

"God, the Creator of all things," Cleo continued, "created Earth and other worlds including the world of Trahe."

"I knew it!" Jereco replied. "I knew our planet couldn't be the only planet with life in the universe."

"Oh no, far from it," Cleo said. "In fact, there are many worlds, but we are only going to concentrate on Trahe. Now, after Earth was created, God decided to create another world. He went far away from here and created the planet called Trahe. Trahe was created to be similar to Earth, but with some differences. Trahe has the same type of air, water, and land."

Cleo walked across the table. "You humans were created before those on Trahe. Hence, the Trahe two-legged creatures were created in your likeness. Seven tribes were created on Trahe. The first was the Evadeam, who were placed in a mountainous region that had an abundance of lakes, trees, and wildlife to eat. The second tribe was the Edamave, who were put on the other side of the Great River. The third tribe was the Evemada, who were put on the south side of the mountain. The fourth tribe was the Madeave, who were placed much farther south into the jungle region. The fifth tribe was the Madevea, who were put on the edge of the jungle in the great swamps. The

32

The Trahe Chronicles

sixth tribe was the Suhman, who were put on the other side of Trahe in the flat desert lands. The seventh tribe was the Muhans, who were placed in the grand desert caverns."

Cleo paused to take a drink out of a water dish provided by Aunt Rhonda. "Once the Creator had assigned each tribe their area, he also assigned a chief to each tribe. Each chief was given a wife. Then the Creator called for a meeting of the tribes at the tallest and biggest mountain in the Evadeam territory. He went over his rules and what was expected of each tribe. He gave the first tribe, the Evadeam tribe, the authority to keep order. But don't think the Evadeam tribe is the leader of all tribes. No, the Creator made it very clear that all tribes were to be equal and run themselves in their own land. The Evadeam was to do such things as write down the history of Trahe. They were to also keep the peace and enforce the Creator's laws with all of the seven tribes. These laws are very similar to your ten commandments. We will go over these laws in more detail later, but I'll start with the four that significantly changed the history of Trahe."

"Keep in mind the rules in Trahe are all equally important though. They are not to be put in any special order. One rule states that the two-legged creatures and other animals will have the capability to speak the Trahe language. This is how they will be able to communicate with each other."

"Another rule states that a Trahe-speaking creature shall not kill another Trahe-speaking creature."

"I thought the Trahe language was universal? Why do some animals not speak it?" interrupted Jereco.

Cleo paused in her history lesson to explain this better. "For example, I am a Trahe-speaking cat. As you recall, I said earlier that the Creator had provided an abundance of wildlife to eat. But most species of wildlife are not universal Trahe speaking beasts, so you can eat them. However, you must never kill or eat a Trahe-speaking creature."

Brandon raised his arm to ask a question.

"Yes, Brandon?" said Cleo.

"So how can you distinguish a talking creature from a non-talking creature?"

Uncle Gregory dropped another large, old-looking book on the table. Brandon leaned over and read the title. *All Creatures of Trahe.* "You are kidding," he said. "Do we have to memorize that book?"

"Well, the simpler way is to ask the beast before you kill it," explained Cleo. If the talking beast answers in the ancient Trahe language, then you cannot kill it."

"Still not buying it, are you, Brandon?" asked Grandpa.

"No, but it is a great story, so go ahead, Cleo."

Cleo looked at Brandon and shook her head. "Okay, where was I? Oh yes, you cannot eat a Trahe-talking beast. The other rules are that all the tribes and creatures of Trahe will have their own separate language, and you must

Book One: The Chosen Ones

love, respect, and be at peace with each other and the Creator." She paused. "There are many more rules, but these are the important ones for this history lesson." Cleo looked over at Grandpa. "Ovid, would you like to take it from here?"

"Yes," Grandpa Ovid replied. He stood and clasped his hands again as he often does. He looked deep in thought. "Well, since the beginning of Trahe's time, the world lived in peace and harmony. There was a natural order of things. It was not perfect since we know that nothing is perfect, except for the Creator. The planet Trahe was magnificent. Picture a world much like ours but fresh, clean, and peaceful. It was almost what I might imagine heaven on Earth to be like. But, alas, as always, all good things come to an end." Grandpa sadly shook his head.

"See, Trahe is not modernized as our world," he continued. "People on Trahe live much like our people did many years ago. They live in harmony with Trahe and each other. So what was happening is that the tribes grew in population and started to overgrow their areas. The Creator saw this, and to avoid any conflicts between the tribes, he took matters into his own hands. He created natural disasters on Trahe to slim down the population. This worked, except that this was the first time in Trahe's history that natural disasters had occurred. We are used to them on Earth, but imagine seeing a tornado, an avalanche, a hurricane, or a sandstorm for the first time. The people of Trahe became frightened. Some stopped believing in the Creator. Peace around the world dissolved, and the inevitable happened. Wars broke out. Evil had emerged."

Grandpa paused for a moment and took a drink. While he did, he noticed Brandon was yawning, Jereco was texting someone, and Brooke looked like she was ready to leave.

"Okay. Let's speed this up a little." Grandpa pointed toward the ancient-looking books. "You can read these history books at your own leisure for more details."

Cleo walked over to one of the large books. "It is this book that tells about one of the most important events ever recorded." She looked at Grandpa. "May I?" He nodded even though he looked like he wanted to continue the storytelling himself.

"The Creator had sent a message that the world of Trahe would follow the path of destruction if the seven tribes did not live in harmony. The Creator's heart was very heavy after he had seen another world destroy many of the beautiful things that he had created. So he decided to try something different with Trahe. During one of the meetings of the Seven Tribes of Trahe, he advised that each tribe pick a family that would be sent to another place. And in time, descendants of these tribes would be sent back to help save the world of Trahe. The tribal leaders were hesitant until one of their prophets stepped forward, proclaiming that what the Creator wanted was foretold in the ancient writings, and therefore, it must be fulfilled. So each tribe picked people to be sent away to this place of peace, harmony, and safety."

Cleo stopped and hopped off the table. Everyone patiently waited for her to finish the tale, but she seemed to be taking a long time. Finally, Brandon looked at Grandpa. "What happened?"

Grandpa waved a hand around the room. "*We* are what happened next."

The kids looked confused.

Grandpa continued. "We are the descendants of some of those tribal members sent from Trahe long ago."

"Yeah, right," said Brandon as he sat back in his chair.

Grandpa shrugged.

"I know it seems hard to believe, Brandon," Uncle Gregory added. "I was just as skeptical as you were at your age. But the proof is in these books. The proof is in the talking cat." He pointed toward Cleo, who was returning with a piece of paper in her mouth.

Cleo dropped the paper into Uncle Gregory's hand. He read it and then walked towards the crashed aircraft. He pointed. "And the proof is in that. I have heard this story before, so now I am going to get some work done."

As Uncle Gregory disappeared behind the aircraft, Jereco asked the next obvious question. "So if the planet of Trahe was not modernized at the time that story was written, how did our ancestors get from that planet to this one in a spaceship?"

Grandpa looked at Cleo, who took her cue and hopped back on the table.

Cleo flicked her tail. "The Creator has many resources, and at that time, he decided to intervene by sending assistance from another world." She paused as if she needed to be careful about what she said next. "There is another world much more advanced than Trahe and Earth. We are fortunate that those inhabitants are very wise and very receptive to the Creator. They willingly offered to supply transportation from one world to the next."

Jereco was excited about the possibility of aliens from other worlds. "Where is that world? What is it called? Is it on the charts?"

"It is a world far away from here, and it is known to your family as the planet Heart. That is all I can say."

Before more questions could be asked, Cleo stated very clearly that there would be no more discussion about Heart. To do so would be a breach of an inter-world treaty.

Jereco and Brandon started to argue with Cleo over that, but the sudden glow that formed around Cleo's body freaked them out. They decided to save the questions for Grandpa when Cleo was not around.

Brooke gently rubbed her eyes and temples. All this information was overwhelming. She wished her dad was here. Being a military man, he was extremely knowledgeable. *Dad.* She had to find her dad. She decided she heard enough history lessons. Action was in order.

Book One: The Chosen Ones

Space plane to Bermuda

Brooke had grown impatient as her cousins had listened intently to the history lessons of this planet called Trahe. She pushed back her chair and walked over to the small refrigerator that stood in her uncle's barn. As she popped open a can of soda, she glanced around. She was impressed by her uncle's secret complex. The barn is similar in size to a small airplane hangar. It had multi levels to help hide the large scale of the interior unit.

What was most notable was the large space plane that was parked in the middle of this floor's work area. Jereco had told her that this was the same aircraft that he saw weeks ago in the field. Brooke noticed that someone had been fixing it up. Brooke walked to the other side of the barn and saw a door that opened to a small room. As she walked in, she saw a closed, steel door with buttons on it. *Another hidden room*, she thought.

The steel door slid open and standing there was Uncle Gregory. He waved her in. Brooke walked into a computer room. Actually, it looked like it could have been a small airport control tower.

"Pretty impressive, huh?" Uncle Gregory asked.

"Yeah."

"Getting bored of the history lessons?"

Brooke nodded. "I can't stand sitting here, listening to these stories. Shouldn't we be trying to find my dad, aunt, and uncle?"

"These are not just stories, Brooke. They are our family's history."

"Whatever."

Uncle Gregory put his hands on Brooke's shoulders and looked into her eyes. "We are going to find your dad. They are my brothers too. But these lessons are important. It is like taking a crash course on flying a spaceship. I know your dad told you a little bit about this stuff. I guess he felt like you needed to know the truth after your mom and brother died."

Brooke turned away.

"Think about it, Brooke. How do you think we were going to try to find your dad?"

Brooke looked back up at Uncle Gregory, bit her bottom lip, and shrugged.

Uncle Gregory waved her over to a monitor. "Here. Here is where they were reported missing. Do you know where that is?"

"Grandpa said something about the Bermuda Triangle."

"Exactly. The best way to find them is to follow their air pattern. We'll need to fly straight into the Bermuda Triangle. Unfortunately, the people who have the best experience and knowledge about flying are your dad, Ronald, and Agnes."

"Aunt Agnes? I didn't think she even liked to fly."

"She doesn't, but she is a semi-retired ambassador to Trahe."

Brooke's right eyebrow shot up. "Trahe?"

36

The Trahe Chronicles

"Yeah, that is where they were headed. Apparently, there is some war going on there. It was important for an Evadeam family member from Earth to go there."

"And this type of request does not happen often," Grandpa said from the doorway. Cleo was with him, purring between his legs.

Cleo walked toward Brooke. "But the request was not for them, and therefore, they were lost."

Brooke, who was getting used to the talking cat, asked, "What is that supposed to mean?"

Uncle Gregory just looked at Grandpa. Neither of them said anything.

Cleo jumped up on a cabinet and looked Brooke in the eye. "The request was to be fulfilled by those of the prophecy. Your dad, Ronald, and Agnes were not the ones to fulfill the prophecy even though they insisted on going to Trahe."

"*Cleo*," Grandfather warned.

The cat just flicked her tail and hissed.

Grandfather backed down, and it was obvious to Brooke that the cat was in charge.

Cleo continued. "The prophecy says that five people on Earth from the ancient Evadeam family shall return to Trahe. At the right time, the five family members shall help the Trahe creatures return to peace. It also says that the five family members shall stop evil from spreading beyond Trahe into their own world."

"But the prophecy in the Book does not say which five Evadeam members," argued Grandpa.

Cleo nodded. "That is true. However, the prophecy does say that a messenger shall reveal the five Evadeam members through the voice of the Creator." Cleo looked away from Grandpa and back at Brooke. "I am the messenger. The Creator has revealed the answer, and I know which five Evadeam family members are supposed to travel to Trahe."

Cleo moved closer to Brooke. Now Cleo's head was so close to Brooke that the cat's whiskers touched Brooke's nose. "You, Brooke. You are one of those five."

Brooke just stood there with her arms crossed. She was not surprised by Cleo's words. She saw it coming. She took a deep breath and sighed. "So how do we go find my dad?"

Uncle Gregory walked over to Brooke and handed her a piece of paper—the same paper that Cleo had given to Gregory earlier. Brooke stared at the coordinates on the paper. Her father had taught her well. She knew exactly what they meant. She put her hand over her stomach. She was not sure if it was nerves or hunger that had made her stomach turn. "I think I need to go eat before I start packing."

An hour later, the older family members decided it was time to take a

Book One: The Chosen Ones

dinner break and history lessons were adjourned. Brooke, Jereco, Brandon and Diana were all sitting in a corner, eating pizza. Aunt Rhonda and Aunt Tricia were arguing with Grandpa and Cleo. They could not agree on who was going to go on the search for their missing family members. They did not seem to care about the prophecy or the mission to the planet Trahe.

Cleo revealed that Brooke, Jereco, Brandon, Diana and Grandpa were the ones to fulfill the prophecy. That's when the yelling started. After all, Cleo was talking about sending a bunch of kids and an old man to a foreign planet. None of them had any knowledge or training about how to conduct a rescue mission to another world.

Cleo calmly shook her head, licked her paws, and groomed her tail. She continued to insist that she did not control the prophecy or the Creator's plan. She was just a messenger. She also reminded everyone that if they did not follow the Creator's plan, then they too would meet the same fate as Larry, Ronald and Agnes. Lost. Vanished.

The discussion would have continued all night long if it wasn't for Aunt Rhonda, who demanded that the children get some sleep. It had been a very shocking and emotional day for everyone, so everyone agreed to get a good night's sleep and start fresh the following morning.

It was nearly midnight before Brooke, Jereco and Brandon found themselves in the boys' bedroom. Even though they were very tired, none of them could sleep. It was a very stressful day with incredible discoveries about their family. Plus, they were still worried about their parents. They talked quietly among themselves under the low lights of flashlights. They did not want to let the adults know they were awake or wake up Diana, who was in the bedroom next door.

"I have been doing a lot of thinking," Brooke said. "What if we really are supposed to go to Trahe? What if our parents will never be found if we do not go?"

"I think we need to go," agreed Brandon.

"I keep waiting to wake up from a bad dream. This is unreal." whispered Jereco.

The other two nodded in agreement. They both had been thinking that since the aircraft landed on the farm.

Crash!

A loud sound came from Diana's bedroom.

Brandon jumped up. "I will go check on her. She probably just fell out of bed again."

Brandon slowly opened Diana's bedroom door to find that she was awake and moving around, using a flashlight for light.

"What are you doing?" he whispered.

"Don't you know how to knock?" Diana said.

Brandon walked in and noticed clothes and other items spread across her

38

The Trahe Chronicles

bed. "Why are you packing a backpack?"

Diana hesitated, then turned to Brandon. "Because we need to go. I had a dream. Mom and Dad are alive. They are waiting to be rescued."

Brandon put his hands in his pockets. "Diana, I think you are partially right. We need to go find them, but I think you need to stay here. You are too young. Plus, you have epilepsy."

Diana shook her head and turned away. She continued packing. "It was in my dream, and I am supposed to go. Besides Cleo told me I am one of the Chosen Ones."

Just then, Cleo came from behind and jumped on the bed. "We do not have much time. Grandpa is loading up the aircraft now and plans on going without you kids. If he does, he will fail and be lost with your parents. Brandon, you must take this list. Go pack and bring a sleeping bag. I've already talked to Brooke and Jereco. They're both packing now."

Brandon looked at Cleo and was amazed that he was taking orders from a talking cat. He remembered Cleo teaching them that anyone who could hear her talk was a believer. A sign from the Creator she had explained.

Cleo looked at Brandon, straight in the eyes. "We must hurry. We must take off before the morning sun rises."

The children quickly gathered their sleeping bags and backpacks loaded with supplies. They quietly walked down the stairs and dashed to the back door. Brooke noticed a note had been left on the kitchen table for the other family members. It was from Grandpa, and it explained that he was off on a rescue mission. Brooke grabbed the pen beside the note and signed below Grandpa's signature.

After she set down the pen, Jereco took it. "I feel like I am signing my life away."

"Or maybe," Brooke whispered, "we will just wake up from a dream in the morning."

Brandon took the pen next. "Or maybe, this is the beginning of a great adventure. Stories will be told about us, and this piece of signed paper will be worth millions one day."

Jereco stifled a laugh. "Always thinking about money."

Diana signed last.

Diana Lorraine Evadeam, a Chosen One, who is going to find her parents.

The kids snuck out to the yard and quietly walked into the big barn that hid their family secrets, including the spaceship. They could not see well at first, but when their eyes adjusted to the darkness, they finally noticed it. A new space plane was parked in the middle of the barn room. It was identical to the crashed one.

"Wow!" Brandon said. "Where did this come from?"

Grandpa came walking around the aircraft, wiping his hands. He paused, shocked to see his grandchildren standing there. He noticed their luggage and

Book One: The Chosen Ones

then gave Cleo a dirty look. The cat meowed something to him, and the kids watched as their grandfather seemed to give in with a slump of his shoulders.

"Well, just don't stand there." Grandpa motioned for them to follow him into the space plane. "Start piling your stuff in."

Brandon raced to the front. "Where did this come from? Is this what we are flying?"

Grandpa waved a hand in the direction of the crashed aircraft. "You didn't think we were going to be able to fly that piece of junk, did you?" The *junk* was on a hoist that was going down into a lower level of the barn.

Jereco noticed Grandpa still hadn't answered Brandon's question. "So where did you get this space plane?" Jereco asked.

"Yeah," Brooke added. "It seems that our family has many hidden secrets. More hidden rooms or barns, perhaps?"

Grandpa turned to Brooke. He noticed that her tone of voice was not the best. "This secret aircraft is going to help us find your father."

Brooke adjusted the backpack on her shoulder. "Then let's get on with it." She walked past Grandpa and then turned back around "Oh, and just a few more questions. Who is going to fly this ship? And how are we going to get past the local authorities? The *federal* authorities?"

Grandpa walked by Brooke and touched her shoulder. "What? Do you think this is my first rescue mission into space?" And with that question left unanswered, Grandpa walked into the space plane, expecting his grandchildren to follow.

Brandon trailed Grandpa. "Cool!"

Jereco paused, took out his phone, and took pictures.

Brooke looked back at him. "Just in case this isn't a dream?"

Jereco nodded. "Just in case. I need proof."

"Whoa!" Brandon said as he examined the inside of the most modern aircraft he had ever seen.

"Whoa is right," said Jereco from behind. He could not believe the technology. He was seeing stuff that he couldn't even dream about.

Brooke was beginning to realize what they were about to do. "Is this safe for us to take to another planet?"

"About the safest out there," Grandpa said as he showed them where to store their stuff.

"Isn't she a beauty?"

The kids answered in *ohs* and *ahs* as Grandpa took them on a brief tour.

They had boarded the space plane right behind the cockpit area which was to their left side. The cockpit had three seats in front of the windshield. There was another seat to the side overlooking a huge computer panel. And three more seats at the back of the cockpit. Cleo explained that capsules will enclose the chairs before they leave the Earth's atmosphere. Before leaving the cockpit, she also mentioned that the chairs turned into health incubators.

Grandpa followed Cleo and continued the space plane tour. There was a

40

The Trahe Chronicles

small kitchen, medical room, bathroom and some storage areas.

As they walked through the ship, Cleo described how the technology would keep them safe while traveling from Earth to Trahe.

"Who came up with this technology?" asked Jereco. "Our government?"

Cleo shook her head. "There are many other worlds beyond your world. Like your leaders, their leaders want to keep all of the worlds safe from destruction, so they contribute when it is necessary."

"But how do they keep our government from stealing their technology?" Jereco said. "We could be so much more advanced."

"Your government has learned to take only what is given. They are not the strongest of all the worlds. They take only what they can control; they have learned to do the will of the Creator."

"We have permission to take this aircraft?" asked Brooke.

"Permission granted," Grandpa replied. "But only for a small amount of time. And we are running out of that time."

"Yes, it is time," agreed Cleo. She started to glow. A soft light surrounded her. Then she looked into Brooke's eyes and gently spoke. "Brooke Ashley of the Evadeam family, you must look within you for strength and belief. Now please sit in that chair next to mine. We need an additional driver. I will give you instructions and explain as we take off."

Cleo proceeded to give more orders. Grandpa was the main pilot while Cleo and Brooke were copilots.

Brandon's job was to make sure everything was secured and to follow the checklist Grandpa handed him.

Jereco was to sit at the computer panel and follow orders as necessary. "Watch for red lights and you might want to read this manual." instructed Grandpa as he tossed a heavy book onto the control panel desk.

Diana was to sit next to Brandon. Her job—hang on and keep calm.

They all buckled their seat belts, ready for launch.

Cleo walked up to each Evadeam kid. First, Jereco. "You will need to help Brooke. Use your wisdom, and do not forget your inner strength."

"Brandon, you must stop and listen to the elders. They are wise. Be patient, stay close to your family, and use your physical strength only when necessary."

"Diana, do not fear. Use your instincts-your inner guide. Believe and all will be fine."

Finally, she walked up to Brooke and pawed at the cell phone that Brooke held in her hand. "Phones will not always work. Sometimes you have to go back to the basics. Dig deep within yourself for strength. You are a strong girl who is becoming a woman."

Then Cleo jumped on Grandpa's lap. "Ready to fly this plane?"

Grandpa rubbed his hands and grinned. "Ready as I will ever be. One space plane to the Bermuda Triangle."

41

Book One: The Chosen Ones

PART TWO

Trahe, the Sister Planet

In the beginning, the Creator created the heavens.
In the beginning, the Creator created the planets.
In the beginning, the Creator created the stars.
In the beginning, the Creator created all beings.
In the beginning, the Creator decided to have no single One.
In the beginning, the Creator decided to have no End.
- Author unknown

The Trahe Chronicles

Crash Landing

Diana could hear only silence. She slowly opened her eyes and saw blinking red and green lights. *It must be Christmas lights*, she thought. She closed her eyes again and dreamed of a Christmas tree, presents, candy canes, and angels.

Yes, angels. They were Christmas angels that were white and soft. Then slowly one of the angels turned colors. It was gray and white with green eyes. The angel was not an angel at all. It was Cleo.

Cleo spoke. "Wake up, child. This is only a Christmas dream. It is not Christmas yet. Wake up, and when you do, you must remember that what you see may not always be true. Believe in me, and believe that I will be there to guide you. Do not lose faith. When you wake up, don't forget the love in your heart and the power of prayer to heal. Wake, my child."

Then the voice changed to Brandon's voice. "Wake up Diana. We have made it. I think we are at Trahe."

Diana woke up to find Brandon hovering over her.

"Are you all right?" asked Brandon. "Are you hurt?"

Diana checked herself over. "No, I don't think so." Just some bumps and bruises, but nothing was broken. She sat up and noticed blinking green and red lights in the ceiling. "So those are the lights that I saw in my dream." Then she remembered Cleo in her dream. "Where is Cleo?"

"I don't know," replied Brandon. "I just woke up myself."

Diana closed her eyes again. She gently rubbed them as she tried to remember what had happened. It slowly came back to her.

They had decided to take off in the middle of the night and head toward the Bermuda Triangle. She remembered Jereco being amazed that they flew through the night with no interruption from any authorities. Grandpa and Cleo had assured him that they had clearance.

After what seemed like a very long flight, they had finally arrived at their destination. Diana remembered looking outside the front window to see only blue skies and white clouds. It wasn't as scary as she thought it would be. Then all of a sudden, there it was.

Cleo called out orders for everyone to tighten their seat belts. Diana suddenly felt scared. She put her hand in her pocket and clung to a worn piece of her baby blanket. This was her security blanket when she was away from home. *Home*. She wished she was home. She remembered changing her mind and crying out that she wanted to go home.

In front of them, a strange storm cloud appeared out of nowhere. Jereco yelled something about it being a horizontal tornado, and then he yelled at Grandpa to turn them around. But it was too late.

Unknown to the children, the aircraft was being sucked into a wormhole—a third dimension phenomenon that was used for space travel between different worlds. Cleo told everyone to stay in their seats and hang

Book One: The Chosen Ones

on tight. Then she hit a button that caused large, plastic cylinders to enclose around everyone. Cleo pushed another button and a shield began to close over the front windshield.

Diana watched in horror as the storm enveloped them. Then the shield blocked the sight from her eyes. She felt the space plane move about roughly, jostled by the wormhole. Diana felt light-headed and wondered if an epilepsy attack was coming. She looked over at Brandon, who also looked frightened. She felt tears running down her face. The last thing she remembered was Brandon mouthing the words, *it will be okay.*

How long ago had that been? Diana thought as she opened her eyes. She was still buckled into the seat, but the cylinder that had enclosed her was gone.

"Are you okay?" asked a voice.

Diana turned and saw Brandon. Relief swept over her and she nodded.

"Do you want to try to get up?"

She nodded again, and Brandon unbuckled her seat belt. They stood and looked around.

Brandon noticed Grandpa, Brooke, and Jereco were all slumped over in their seats.

"Oh, God no!"

He rushed to their sides and tried to wake them up. None of them responded. "Where is Cleo?"

Diana looked around and let out a horrible cry. She rushed to a pile of rubble. A black and white paw stuck out of it. "Brandon, help me," Diana said.

Brandon rushed to her side. He wasted no time moving off the debris. He needed help from Cleo.

"Be careful," cried Diana.

Once they unburied Cleo, they found she was bruised and bleeding.

"Is she dead?" asked Diana with a shaky voice. "Is she dead?"

"I don't know, but she doesn't look good." Brandon gently moved his hands over her. "I don't feel her breathing," he said, panicked.

"We have to do something, Brandon."

"I know, but I don't know what to do! I haven't taken CPR at school yet."

There was no one else to help them. *It's just Diana and me,* Brandon thought. *Okay. Think. Think. Breathe. Breathe.* Brandon could feel an asthma attack coming on. *No, not now. Football. Football.* He thought about football and what he did when he started to run out of breath.

He went into his wind-down breathing exercise to calm his thoughts. *This is like football. A game with a team that needs me. I need to think. Calm down.* Green flashing lights on the dashboard caught his attention. The green lights reminded him of Cleo.

What would Cleo do?

She would think logically.

Brandon glanced over at Jereco and Brooke. He slowly walked over to

44

The Trahe Chronicles

them, afraid to touch them now. What if they were dead? He took a deep, raspy breath and placed his fingers on Brooke's neck. He felt for a pulse. *There! Yes, there.* He found a pulse. He was sure of it. Then he rushed to Jereco. Yes, he found a pulse again. They were alive!

He just needed to wake them up. He thought of football again and what would happen if he got knocked out during a football game. The couch would give him smelling salts. That was it!

He rushed to the back of the plane where there was a medical room. As he rushed in, he could hear Diana call out, "What are you doing?"

"Not now, Diana!" He rummaged through a medicine cabinet, found smelling salts, and rushed back to the cockpit.

Brooke felt nauseated. She grabbed her stomach and thought she must have eaten something bad. She would need to run to her bathroom. She opened her eyes and tried to get up, but Brandon pushed her back down. *Brandon?!*

What the heck is Brandon doing in my bedroom? she thought. She yelled at Brandon to get out of her room, and then she thought she heard Brandon say that she wasn't in her bedroom. Then where was she? And why was Brandon bleeding?

Brandon's voice suddenly became clearer. "Brooke, you are disoriented," he said. "Just sit there for a minute. Boy, am I glad you are all right. I have to go check on Jereco."

Jereco, Brooke thought. *Why does Brandon have to check on Jereco?* Then the pieces started to come together. Brandon's bloody face. Her own aches and pains. They had been in an accident. *A car accident! Oh no! Dad is going to kill me. I have been in a car accident.* The very thought of crashing her car and getting in trouble snapped her awake. But when she sat up and looked around, she realized she wasn't in a car. She looked over and saw Brandon hovering over a slumped Jereco.

A little voice kept talking to Jereco. Jereco kept thinking, *I need to wake up. It is important that I need to wake up, but I am not sure why.* Green eyes. He kept seeing green eyes. Cleo's eyes. "No," the voice told him. The voice kept telling him that he needed to wake up. It was important for him to wake up. He was important.

Jereco slowly opened his eyes. He saw green. Then … not green. Green … not green. The green was blinking. Those weren't eyes. They were lights on the dashboard. Dashboard. Computer board. Cockpit. Spaceship! Jereco sat bolt upright. He frantically looked around.

Jereco saw Brandon looking at him with a happy grin, bloody face, and teary eyes. Then Jereco saw Brooke looking over with disbelief.

"Boy, I am sure glad you are awake!" cried Brandon. Then he rushed over to Grandpa.

Book One: The Chosen Ones

"Where are we?" asked Jereco.

Cough. Cough. Grandpa slowly woke up.

"Well, I am guessing that we made it to Trahe," sputtered Grandpa as he brushed away the smelling salts in Brandon's hand.

"Doesn't Cleo know where we are?" asked Jereco.

"Cleo!" Brandon said. "Oh my gosh. I totally forgot. I was so busy saving your lives that I forgot about Cleo."

"Saving our lives?!" asked a disbelieving Brooke.

"Come on. Cleo is hurt." He pointed toward the pile of rubble where Cleo was.

Jereco and Brooke looked at each other and the realization of the situation hit them. They both jumped up to help Cleo, but then they quickly had to grab their seats.

"I don't feel so good," said Jereco.

"Me either," replied Brooke. "We better check ourselves for broken bones and bruises. Jereco, you have a bruise on your head."

"And so do you," Jereco replied as he rubbed his forehead. "We probably have concussions. And from what I remember, if that's true, we have to lie down but not fall asleep."

"Well," Brook said. "I am not lying anywhere until I know where we are, so come on." She grabbed Jereco's arm, and they supported each other as they made their way over to Cleo.

Grandpa, Diana and Brandon were kneeling over Cleo.

"Are you guys okay?" asked Diana.

"We will live," said Jereco. He nodded toward Cleo. "But what about her?"

"We can't tell if she is dead or alive," Brandon said. "I think she is in a coma."

"Let me have a look at her," said Brooke.

Brandon stepped away, knowing that Brooke was the most qualified. She had her CPR certification and was a licensed lifeguard.

Brooke felt Cleo all over. "She isn't breathing." She whispered to Grandpa. "I think she is gone."

Grandpa looked very sad and nodded in agreement.

Everyone looked at Cleo, helplessly.

Diana gently pet her. "She can't be gone. She just can't be. She is our guide, our angel. She can't die!"

"But she isn't breathing, Diana," said Brooke. "I am sorry."

"Well, do something!" Diana said angrily. "You know CPR. Bring her back!"

Brooke put her hand to her own throbbing head. She couldn't take it anymore. She had just experienced something unbelievable today, her head hurt, and she felt like she was going to throw up. And now she was supposed to give CPR to a dead talking cat?

The Trahe Chronicles

Tears slid down Brooke's face. "Diana, I can't do anything for her. It's too late. I am sorry." She put her hand to her mouth. "I think I am going to throw up." She ran to the spaceship bathroom.

Diana had never felt such grief. Her cat—her best friend—lay in her arms, lifeless. She started to cry uncontrollably. Brandon and Jereco looked on, with their own tears developing in their eyes. Jereco got up and sat next to Diana. He put his arm around her, squeezed her, and put his other hand on Cleo.

Odd, he thought. *Cleo's body felt warm.*

He gave Brandon a look and nodded toward Cleo's chair. "Diana, I think it is time we put Cleo in her chair. Just a temporary spot while we figure out what to do with her. She wanted us to come here for a reason. We do not know what do to without her, so we need to figure out how to get back home. She wouldn't want us to sit here, crying and wasting time while our ship sits in an unknown land."

Diana knew deep down he was right. She slowly pet Cleo. Then she looked up at Brandon and Jereco and noticed the blinking green and red lights. "My dream," she murmured.

She eagerly looked at the boys. "I had a dream before Brandon woke me up. In my dream Cleo spoke to me." Diana recited her dream. "Do you think Cleo will come back as an angel to help us?"

Brandon started to speak, but Jereco interrupted him. "Maybe. I also had a dream with green eyes in it. I was told that it was important for me to wake up too. So maybe you are right, Diana."

"Oh, give me a break!" exclaimed Brandon. "They are just dreams. And yes, it was important for you to wake up, Jereco. *Hello,* we are stranded in a spaceship in a foreign world with God-knows-what out there!"

Diana got up, with Cleo in her arms. "That is it. God! We need to pray to God to help Cleo."

Brandon just rolled his eyes.

Jereco scornfully looked at Brandon. "It wouldn't hurt," Jereco whispered. "Plus, the sooner we put Cleo to rest in her bed, the sooner we can get out of here."

"Okay," Brandon reluctantly agreed. He shuffled his way to Cleo's chair.

Diana placed Cleo in her chair and asked that they all hold hands. The people at the end had to place their hands on Cleo. "Wait," said Diana. "What about Brooke?"

Jereco went to check on Brooke. He came back and announced that she was sitting on the bathroom floor and wasn't about to get up. Jereco decided to leave out the part where Brooke told him she wouldn't pray for a dead talking cat and suggested that they pray for their own lives instead.

So they proceeded without Brooke. Diana put her right hand over Cleo's heart and held hands with Jereco, who held hands with Grandpa, who held hands with Brandon. Brandon reluctantly put his left hand on Cleo's body.

Book One: The Chosen Ones

Diana said a small prayer. "Dear God, or Creator of our world and this world that we've landed on, Cleo was not only a good cat, but she was also my best friend. She brought us here to help, but we can't do it without her. We don't even know where we are. So please God, bring Cleo back or bring someone who can help us."

"Preferably the U.S. military elite," murmured Brandon.

Grandpa elbowed Brandon, and Diana ignored him. "I know that you can help," Diana continued. "Cleo told me you create miracles. The fact that Cleo can talk to us, operate a spaceship, and bring us to this world is all the proof that we need."

At that moment, she opened her eyes and stared at Brandon, who quickly closed his eyes. "Thank you for bringing Cleo into our lives," Diana said, "and I hope she is happy now with you or wherever she is. She was a good, brave, and loving cat. And please God, don't forget about us and our parents. I pray that all of our bodies heal, especially Brooke, who is still sick in the bathroom. Thank you. Amen."

"Amen," mumbled everyone else.

After a moment of silence, Jereco said to Diana, "Why don't you see how Brooke is doing?" After Diana left, he turned to Brandon. "Did you notice that Cleo's body is still warm?" "Yeah," Brandon replied, "I thought that when you're dead your body gets cold, clammy, and hard."

"Maybe it takes time to do that," Jereco said, "or maybe she doesn't turn that way because she's an alien cat. But I was thinking about our chairs that turn into health incubators if we pushed a red medical button. Maybe her chair will heal her." "Why didn't you say anything to Brooke or Diana?" asked Brandon. "It could have saved us from that lame prayer."

Grandpa scowled at Brandon.

"If you haven't noticed," Jereco said, "Brooke isn't in the best state of mind, and I didn't want to get Diana's hopes up. So let's try to find this button before the girls come back."

Jereco and Grandpa searched the chair capsule. Finally, Jereco found a little latch underneath. When he pulled it, a side panel in the chair opened.

"Cool," exclaimed Brandon. There were several buttons, including the red medical one. "Boy, whoever designed this ship sure did like green and red."

"Here goes!" Grandpa said as he pushed the medical button. Suddenly, all the other lights went out, except for some yellow emergency lights in the ship. A see-through plastic cylinder rose from the bottom of the floor. It surrounded the chair and enclosed it. The red medical button flashed.

The girls came running out of the bathroom and into the lounge. "What happened?" asked Brooke in a panic.

Grandpa quickly turned to Brandon. "You need to take care of that cut on your head. Take Diana to the medical room, and she can help you clean and bandage it."

Brandon understood Grandpa was trying to distract Diana. Brandon

48

The Trahe Chronicles

pulled Diana along, assuring her that everything was fine.

Jereco quickly explained to Brooke what they were doing.

"Are you nuts?!" Brooke said.

"Keep your voice down," ordered Grandpa. "I don't want Diana to hear this."

"But you are obviously using up our power on a dead cat! Who knows how long these emergency lights will stay on?" Brooke turned toward the front windshield. "And what if the protective shield is off now?"

"Well, it is not like I knew that would happen," said Jereco. "Besides, if there is any chance that this will work and bring Cleo back, we have to take the chance. Remember, she is a *talking cat* and we need her!"

Brooke crossed her arms and shut her eyes. He was right. "Okay, but we have to figure out what to do until something happens. How long before we know if this will work?"

Jereco looked to Grandpa for an answer.

Grandpa was staring at Cleo in the capsule. Without looking up, he replied, "I am thinking that light will stop when it is done, and then we will know. Until then, we have to think of this as an emergency crash landing. Kind of like when you have an emergency at the lake. Brooke, what are you trained to do if a boat crashed on a deserted island?"

Brooke took a deep breath to regain her patience and gather her thoughts. "Well, first, we would have to examine everyone for injuries. Treat them and ourselves. Then we would go through our supply checklist to determine how many days we would last. Oh, and we should inspect the boat for damages and determine if we can get it moving again."

Grandpa stood up. "Very good. I'm not hurt at all, so no need to examine me. I will check the aircraft for damages now. Brooke and Jereco, you check each other and Brandon and Diana for injuries."

Jereco nodded and headed toward the medical room. As Brooke followed, she glanced at Cleo, and she swore she saw a slight uplift of Cleo's mouth, like the cat was smiling. Brooke just shook her head, and thought, *no way.*

Brooke summarized everyone's injuries in her head. She was pretty sure she had a slight concussion, which was manageable. Brandon had a gash on his head that was cleaned and bandaged, but luckily, there were no other signs of head injury. Jereco seemed to have only bruising on his forehead, and by some miracle, Diana had just a few bumps and bruises. Brooke hated to admit it, but she wondered if that darn cat had something to do with Diana's fortunate state.

Grandpa ordered all of them to eat, drink and rest. While the children slept, Grandpa thought about Cleo and their predicament. He didn't want to tell the children that he was worried Cleo would not come out of her coma. He also had an idea where they had landed, but he also knew that they were stuck. He looked at his grandchildren and was upset with himself for putting

Book One: The Chosen Ones

them in this bad situation. He bent his head back and looked up at the roof. "Adeline, I fear I have failed. Have I used poor judgment and put our grandchildren in danger?"

An answer did not come. He sighed and rubbed his eyes. He knew he needed to sleep, but he thought sleep would not come.

He was wrong. He did sleep. It must have been pure exhaustion or, perhaps, it was the change in atmosphere. Grandpa woke with a start when he heard something. His eyes blinked open and he listened intently. He silently scolded himself for falling asleep even though he knew he needed it.

Grandpa was still tired. He calculated that he had gotten only a couple hours of sleep. Something had woke him up. He decided it was time to see what it was. The protective shield was still down, so he couldn't see the outside. As he looked at his grandchildren, who were sleeping in their chairs, he hesitated before opening the shield. It might wake them up. He decided to take the more dangerous route. He walked back to a different part of the aircraft and pushed some fancy-looking buttons. A panel door slid open and revealed some very old-looking equipment. Grandpa loaded up and left a note in the kitchen for the kids.

He paused at an exterior door. He pushed some buttons and put his hand on a small white panel. The door opened. Grandpa stood there for a moment before stepping onto the planet Trahe.

The sound of the doors sliding open was enough to wake up Brandon. The other children slowly woke up too. Brandon noticed Grandpa wasn't in his chair. Maybe he was in the bathroom.

Brandon volunteered to take a flashlight and inspect the interior of the ship again for any signs of damage. Plus, he wanted to look for some food. His stomach was growling. Diana went with him and brought a battery-operated handheld communication system. Brooke insisted they take it even though the ship wasn't that big.

Brandon and Diana found some stuff tipped over. Nothing major seemed to be wrong. The exterior door seemed to be intact, and there were no openings that would let outside creatures into the ship. They also found some food in the small kitchen for dinner.

The kids decided to take a break to get some food in their stomachs. As they started to eat, Diana wondered where Grandpa was.

"Isn't he in the bathroom?" asked Brandon.

Brooke shook her head. "I was just in there." Panic rose within her. "Brandon, stay here with Diana. Jereco, come with me. We will check the ship."

Jereco and Brooke went through the entire ship and did not find Grandpa.

"What did you think happened to him?" Brooke whispered.

Jereco's eyebrows closed in as he thought about it. "Well, we didn't hear any screaming, so I do not think he was abducted by aliens. Based on what

50

we know about Grandpa, he probably went outside the ship to explore our surroundings."

"Don't you think he should have told one of us?"

"He probably thought he would be back before we woke up."

"He should have left a note or something."

Brandon approached them. "Um. This note." Brandon found it buried under the food they put out on the counter.

Brooke grabbed the note. "He went outside to investigate our location."

Jereco was right. He went to explore our surroundings. Hopefully he was right about Grandpa not being abducted by aliens. But what if something bad does happen? What if something or someone finds their ship before they leave, and what if they were not friendly? What if Grandpa doesn't come back? Brooke suddenly felt anxious.

They agreed to take turns standing guard during the night. Jereco and Brooke took the first round of night watch.

Brandon had searched all over the ship for weapons. He had found nothing. He couldn't believe that Cleo and Grandpa hadn't packed any type of protection. Diana kindly reminded him that Cleo was supposed to be their protection.

"Like she is doing us a lot of good now," Brandon had said.

Diana hadn't been happy with Brandon's response.

Brooke and Jereco agreed to guard the door by sitting down, back to back. They had flashlights, handheld communication pieces, and what looked like two walking sticks that they had found in a storage room. The walking sticks were the best weapons that they could find.

As they sat, they talked about stuff that they missed at home. Their favorite television shows were probably playing now. A big box office movie was coming out this weekend. And they both started to crave sodas and candy.

Soon, they stopped talking and quietly missed their parents. They wondered if they would ever find them. They wondered if they would ever return to Earth. Eventually, they got sleepy and nodded off.

Book One: The Chosen Ones

Green Eyes

Brooke was dreaming this time. She was dreaming about white Christmas lights—lovely white lights that shimmer on white snow. She was home. Tons of snow was everywhere, glistening in the darkness. She saw herself in her house, looking outside the window. A pile of snow fell off the roof. Then a bigger pile of snow fell off. Then a loud bang made her jump. She thought the snow had made the roof cave in.

But it wasn't the roof. Brooke woke up with a start. She heard another bang from above. Jereco jumped up, making her fall backwards; they had been sleeping with their backs against each other.

"What was that? Jereco said.

"I don't know," Brooke whispered. She was too scared to move.

All of a sudden, they heard someone come running from behind them, making them both jump and point their walking sticks in defense.

It was Brandon. "What was that noise?" he asked.

"That wasn't you?" Brooke said in a worried voice.

Diana came up behind Brandon. "No, that wasn't us."

Suddenly, the spaceship door slid open, and Diana screamed when Grandpa came tumbling in.

He shut the door and fell to the floor. "Turn on the shield and get this thing moving!" He passed out.

Brooke immediately started looking him over while Brandon ran to get some smelling salts.

It was quiet for a few minutes. Then they heard the loud banging noise again.

They all looked at Grandpa. If the noise they heard wasn't Grandpa banging on the door, then who or *what* was it?

"I think we have company," yelled Brandon as he came back.

They all looked at Brooke. Since Grandpa was unconscious, Brooke, being the eldest, was in charge.

Luckily for them, Brooke had a leadership personality that included strong determination. This thing banging above them was making Brooke mad. She looked at Jereco. "How are you feeling?"

"Okay. Why?" he asked nervously.

"I have a plan."

"I am not going out there."

"Don't be silly," said Brooke. "Of course, you are not going out there. None of us are!" We need to do as Grandpa ordered. So take your brain over to that cockpit, along with your handy-dandy computer, and get the shield up!"

"Sounds like a plan." Jereco dashed to the cockpit just as Grandpa came to.

"Is the ship moving yet?" asked Grandpa with a strained voice.

52

The Trabe Chronicles

Brooke let out a sigh of relief. "You all right?"

He nodded. "Just sore and a few bruises."

"You've got a little bit more than bruises," Brooke said. "You're bleeding too. Can you walk to the medical room?"

Grandpa nodded again.

Brooke and Brandon helped him up. "Lean on me," Brooke ordered. Then she turned to Brandon. "You and Diana go back to the cockpit, and stay with Jereco." Jereco worked on the spaceship's computer as fast as he could. Diana and Brandon just sat there in the chairs, constantly looking upward as if they were expecting something to come crashing through the ceiling at any minute.

Bang!

They all jumped.

"Hurry, Jereco," yelled Brandon.

"Don't rush me. I need quiet. Genius at work." But deep down, Jereco knew he often did his best work when he was under pressure. He hoped that would be true this time. He also repeated to himself, *I am important. I am important. Boy, Cleo, I could sure use you now.* At that moment, a computer formula popped in his head as if someone had put it there. He typed it into the system as fast as he could even though it didn't seem familiar to him. The lights came on and the shield surrounded the ship.

"Yeah!" Brandon exclaimed. "That is my bro. My bro. The computer genius."

"Okay, everyone," yelled Brooke as she came in to the cockpit, "get in your chairs just in case Jereco can get this baby to launch." She slid into the driver's seat.

"How is Grandpa?" Jereco asked.

"He will live."

"I am more than living," Grandpa said in a gruff voice from behind. "Diana and Brandon, take your seats."

Diana looked over at Cleo's seat. Tears of grief and fear started forming in her eyes. What would become of them without Cleo?

All of a sudden, the front shield opened. It was dark outside.

Brooke looked to the right, at Jereco. "What did you do?!"

"I don't know, I don't know, I don't know." He frantically typed on the computer. "This can't be right."

"Guys, guys, *guys!*" yelled Brandon.

They all looked at Brandon. He had a look of horror on his face. He was pale and his lips trembled as he croaked a whisper. "Please tell me that you see what I see?"

They all turned to the front window.

Brooke jumped and screamed.

Jereco tightly held his laptop, with shaking hands.

"What is that?" Diana said. "What is that?"

53

Book One: The Chosen Ones

Large, bright green eyes peered in at them.

As Brooke's eyes adjusted to the nighttime darkness, she could make out a head of a large snake. A red tongue flicked out at her and came in contact with the window.

"Jereco, close the shield!" ordered Brooke. "Close the shield!"

Jereco paled at the sight of the snake, but he snapped out of his frozen trance when Brooke hit his arm. He looked at her with a scared look on his face.

Brooke grabbed him by the shoulders and shook him. "Jereco, snap out of it. The shield needs to be closed before he breaks through the window."

"How do you know it's a he?" Jereco said.

Brooke looked at him with disbelief.

"Yeah," Brandon said. "Maybe it is a she. And she has a nest with eggs that we landed on."

"You are not helping, Brandon!" Brooke said angrily.

"Sorry, but I am just being realistic," Brandon replied. "She looks like a she, and she is really mad right now!" He turned to Grandpa. "Did this thing attack you outside?"

Grandpa nodded. "This thing is just a taste of what we might run into in this world. I should have never brought you here." He shook his head. "I should have known better."

Bang! The snake attempted to break through the window. They all jumped.

Brooke grabbed Jereco again. "Jereco, you can do this. You are the smartest kid I know. You are a computer genius. All those bad jokes about being a computer smarty-pants—well, I was actually jealous because you are smarter than me."

"You made jokes about me?" said Jereco in despair.

"Oh, forget about that for now! I am trying to tell you that you are a smart kid, and you can close that shield!"

Jereco looked at the snake. It seemed to be studying them. Digesting the situation. *Digesting,* Jereco thought. "There's no way I am going to be your dinner." With newfound determination, he started typing on his computer again. The shield started to close.

"Yeah, yeah! You are doing it!" exclaimed Brandon.

The snake frantically tried to stop the shield from going down by throwing itself against the window. Luckily, the snake didn't succeed, and the shield closed successfully.

Everyone fell back and took in a breath.

"Now what?" asked Diana. "The snake is still out there."

Cleo's voice came from behind them. "Don't worry about the snake. I will take care of her. Meanwhile, good job everyone! Good teamwork!"

They all looked at each other and then looked behind them. Cleo was standing there!

"Cleo!" they all yelled at once.

54

The Trabe Chronicles

She jumped on Diana and rubbed her whiskers against Diana's face. "Thank you for believing in me!" Cleo said.

"You are alive. How?"

"It's simple. Your prayer, your faith, and a little modern technology saved me." Cleo looked at Jereco and winked. "Plus, do you think that a cat having nine lives is just a myth? I am a guide of the Creator, after all."

Diana hugged her with tears in her eyes. Cleo was alive and sitting on her lap! They had been so busy with the snake that they had not noticed Cleo's chair capsule had opened.

Cleo turned to Jereco. "Thank you for your ingenious wisdom. You knew to use the health chamber that I mentioned. Excellent job. I told you that you would be important."

Then Cleo jumped onto Brooke's lap. "As for you, you still lack faith, but your leadership skills that I had been counting on took over. Good job!"

Brooke smiled. "Thank you," she said shyly. She couldn't believe that Cleo was on her lap, alive and well.

Cleo then turned her attention to Brandon.

Before she could say anything, he said, "I know, I know. I lack faith. Blah, blah, blah. But I am a realist. And reality is, that yes, the talking cat is by some miracle sitting here, no longer *dead*. And reality is that a large snake bigger than you, and maybe longer than this spaceship is still out there. How are you going to take care of that?"

"Brandon, your faith will come, but for now, your realistic outlook in life is an asset to our assignment. It is true. We have an enemy outside our doors." Cleo jumped into her seat and looked toward the shielded window. "Now what do we do with this enemy?"

Book One: The Chosen Ones

Snake Charmer

In a spaceship stranded somewhere on the planet Trahe, the Evadeam family chattered nervously about their situation.

It was Cleo who decided it was time to call upon some long-term friendships. Now the trick was to reach these friends without the snake noticing. After much discussion, the group came up with a plan.

They would distract the snake at the windshield while Cleo got help. Cleo explained that there was a second door on the spaceship—an escape hatch. The small hatch was hidden under a rug beneath the medical table, and the hatch was only to be used for extreme emergencies. If the hatch was opened from the outside, an emergency alarm would turn on to notify the ship that someone was entering through the hatch.

To exit the ship, the invisible shield had to be shut down. That was the tricky part. The shield was protecting the ship from the gigantic snake. So how were they supposed to distract the snake and prevent it from trying to break open the front windshield?

It was Brandon who came up with the best idea. Brandon always had a fondness for snakes back home. He once read that some snakes could be hypnotized by a flute instrument. A snake would sway in time with the musician's tune. Brandon had learned that snakes cannot actually hear the tune being played, though they can, perhaps, feel the vibrations from the music and any tapping done by a snake charmer.

Brandon explained that most snakes are timid in nature; they prefer to scare off possible predators rather than fight them. He continued to say that snakes back home weren't that dangerous, and cobras were incapable of attacking things above them. Brandon had nicknamed the snake outside Green Eyes, and Green Eyes looked like an oversized cobra to Brandon. If Green Eyes was in the cobra family, then it might be possible to put some type of pressure on a particular nerve behind the snake's head that would cause the snake to stiffen up.

Diana, Brooke and Jereco looked at Brandon like he was nuts. They didn't believe in the snake-charming theory, and none of them wanted to try to pinch some nerve on the back of the snake's head!

Cleo spoke. "I know someone who would be more than happy to pinch a nerve, even take a bite of that snake's head."

They all looked at Cleo in astonishment.

"You have to be kidding! Who would try to attack that snake?" asked Brooke.

"His name is Sir Bolivar. Not only would he be of great help with the snake right now, he would also be a good guide for us. By Grandpa's description of the terrain outside, I have a good idea of where we landed on Trahe. Sir Bolivar should be nearby and he knows this jungle like the back of his hand."

The Trahe Chronicles

"Great!" Brandon said. "A snake charmer and a jungle guide. He sounds like my kind of guy. How do we get a hold of him?"

"First, he isn't really a snake charmer," explained Cleo. "He likes to eat snakes on occasion. Second, I will use the bird signals to call him. Oh, and third, he isn't a guy, as in *man*." She then walked toward the back of the ship and uncovered the hidden hatch.

Cleo went on to explain that Brandon's idea could work. Jereco would need to come up with some charming music. There was a button on the front console that would run the sound to an outside speaker. If Jereco gave the music some loud bass, then that would amplify the vibration and hypnotize the snake. While the music played, Brooke and Diana could open the hatch and Cleo could slip outside. Brooke and Diana would need to stand by the locked hatch and wait for Cleo's return.

Cleo revealed that she would be able to communicate with Diana through her thoughts—similar to telepathy. At this point, she had only communicated during dreams. Cleo was confident that with great concentration, Diana would be able to hear Cleo's thoughts announcing her return.

The plan was in progress, and so far, everything had gone well, except Cleo had yet to return. Hours had slipped by. Diana was getting worried. She wasn't sure how much longer Green Eyes was going to sway with the music. The snake appeared to be in a sleeping state, but Diana feared the night's noises could wake the snake from the trance.

Diana decided to pray and concentrate really hard on Cleo. Diana rubbed her head. Over and over, she kept calling out to Cleo in her thoughts. She really tried hard. The morning light was approaching, but she refused to give up on Cleo.

Meanwhile, the boys quietly watched the snake for any signs of awakening. Jereco and Brandon were getting tired and hungry, but neither dared to move. Then Brandon noticed a break in the snake's rhythm. It seemed to be stirring a little—perhaps, *awakening*. Brandon looked over at Jereco.

Jereco's eyes told Brandon he had noticed the same thing.

Grandpa, who was standing behind the boys, gently squeezed their shoulders. He motioned to Brandon to sneak out and warn the girls.

Brandon slipped out of the cockpit and went to the medical room. He kneeled next to Brooke and Diana. They whispered to each other, afraid of awakening the snake.

"We think the snake is waking up from the trance," Brandon said.

Diana opened her eyes for a moment, then, desperately closed them. She concentrated on calling Cleo again. "I can't get a hold of Cleo, Brandon. She must still be too far away."

Brooke decided to give telepathy a try too. Maybe it is like praying. "Give

57

Book One: The Chosen Ones

me your hand, Diana, and yours too, Brandon. Perhaps if we all call to her through our minds, she can hear us."

"A group effort can't hurt," Brandon commented.

They huddled together and sent their thoughts to Cleo.

Suddenly, Diana yelled out.

Brandon covered her mouth. "What is it?" he asked.

"I felt a horrible knock in my head," explained Diana.

"Well, maybe Cleo got hurt," said Brooke. "Concentrate on her. Come on, hold hands, try again, and whatever you do, don't yell out."

They tried it again, and, sure enough, Diana felt another hard knock to her head. She could barely stand the pain. She sent a screaming thought out. *Is that you, Cleo?*

A thought came rushing back to her. *Yes, it is me. How did you reach me?*

Diana sent thoughts explaining to Cleo what they were doing.

Wow. I am impressed, Cleo responded.

Diana quickly explained that the snake was coming out of the trance.

Cleo reassured her that she and Sir Bolivar were almost to the ship. They would knock three times and use a code word to get back in. The code word would be their secret name for the ship. She was going to break off now, so they could keep moving.As soon as Cleo left her thoughts, Diana fell to the ground, holding onto her head. When she opened her eyes, she saw that Brooke and Brandon were also doing the same. She got Brandon's attention and whispered what Cleo had said. He nodded in acknowledgement. He started toward the cockpit but stopped to rummage through some drawers. He found a pencil and paper and wrote a note explaining the latest update from Cleo. Then he ran up to the cockpit.

Jereco was getting worried about what was happening in back of the spaceship. He was tired of watching the snake. Brandon finally arrived and shoved a piece of paper into his hands. Jereco read the note then passed it to Grandpa.

Jereco felt a jab into his rib cage. Brandon pointed towards the windshield. Jereco glanced up to see the snake no longer swaying back in forth. The snake was looking around as if it had just awoken from a nap.

Jereco looked up at the snake, and then down at the console. He turned up the music volume. Jereco and Brandon held very still, holding their breaths. They both hoped that the snake wouldn't try to break the windshield. Suddenly, the snake noticed them. It started to slither toward the windshield.

Meanwhile, at the hatch, the girls heard the music grow louder. "Oh no! The snake must have awakened," Brooke said. "Diana, we have to turn put the shield up."

"No, not yet," insisted Diana. "Cleo said she was almost here."

58

The Trahe Chronicles

Grandpa walked up quietly behind them. "Diana, I am sorry, but we can't risk our lives or jeopardize the ship."

Diana looked up at Grandpa and then at Brooke. She saw tears forming in Brooke's eyes. Brooke seemed to know how hard of a decision this was for her. Grandpa was right. Diana replied by simply nodding her head.

Diana stayed at her spot at the hatch while Brooke went back to the cockpit. As Brooke snuck up behind Jereco, she saw the snake peering into the windshield. Brooke tapped Jereco's shoulder and whispered, "Cleo isn't back yet, but as soon as that snake starts breaking in, bring up the shield."

Jereco nodded, never taking his eyes off the snake.

Brooke started to head back, but the movement must have been enough to catch the snake's attention. It noticed the kids, raised its head high, and lashed its tongue toward the windshield.

Brooke ran towards the hatch. "Grandpa — the snake is awake!"

Crash.

The Snake had butted its head against the windshield. It hadn't done any damage — yet.

Grandpa yelled, "The shield, Jereco!"

Diana called from the back of the plane. "No, Cleo is here!"

"Diana, you'd better not be playing games," Brooke said. "That snake is about to break through."

"I'm not," Diana replied. "I just heard three knocks."

"Are you sure it wasn't the snake?"

"Yes, I am sure, now be quiet, Brooke." Diana dropped to the floor, put her ears to the door, and listened. Brooke also dropped to the floor, desperately wanting to hear the knocks.

Knock, knock, knock.

That was all Brooke needed to hear. She ran to the front to stop Jereco from bringing up the shield.

Diana yelled, "Password?"

"The Ark!" Cleo responded.

Grandpa yanked on the hatch handle, but he couldn't get the hatch open. He didn't have enough strength.

"Brooke, I need help," he yelled.

Brooke skidded to a halt and yelled to Jereco, "Don't turn on the alarm!" She turned back around.

"What did she say?" as Jereco reached for the button.

"I think she said, don't turn on the alarm," Brandon replied just as the snake struck the windshield again. This time, the blow left a crack in the glass.

"Brooke!" yelled Jereco. "I need to get the shield up!"

As soon as the hatch was opened, Cleo flew into Diana's arms.

Brooke looked down to the outside. "Where is that Bolivar you promised? We have to get the alarm system back up!"

Cleo turned to Brooke. "Not to worry. Close the hatch. Put the alarm on

59

Book One: The Chosen Ones

and watch from the cockpit."

Brook saw Jereco's hand freeze over the shield button as he saw something jump on the snake's back. "*What the?*"

"Well, look at that," Grandpa said, stepping into the cockpit.

The snake coiled back with surprise and tried to see what had landed on its back.

Jereco squinted and moved closer to the windshield. "What is that?"

"That is Sir Bolivar," answered Cleo.

The Trahe Chronicles

Sir Bolivar

The big serpent twisted and turned, fighting vigorously as Sir Bolivar attacked the snake. The four kids stood frozen by the windshield, watching in amazement. They could not believe their eyes.

Diana looked back at Cleo. "Is that a big ferret? It looks like a ferret, but it's as big as a dog."

"Sir Bolivar is a mongoose," Cleo replied. "He comes from a very strong tribe. The tribe's agility, cunning, and thick coats make them the best fighters in this region. Sir Bolivar is one of the bravest and most intelligent of his tribe."

As Diana studied the creature on the snake's back, she thought he did look like an overgrown mongoose.

"While Sir Bolivar is taking care of the snake," said Cleo, "we should pack up our supplies in preparation to depart this ship."

The kids, however, had no intention of moving as they watched the fight between the overgrown snake and the large mongoose. The mongoose was riding the snake like he was a cowboy on a bull. As hard as Cleo tried, she could not get the kids to break away from watching the scene in front of them. Finally, the snake moved away from the ship, trying to buck off the mongoose that had hopped on its back.

As the snake slithered away, Brandon caught another glimpse of the mongoose biting into the snake's neck. "Is that thing really going to kill the snake?"

"That *thing* has a name—Sir Bolivar," Cleo said. "It would be best that you remember that when you speak to him. And yes, he probably will kill the snake." She turned toward the doorway.

"Come on, kids," ordered Grandpa. "Cleo is right. We need to start packing."

As Grandpa turned, Brandon noticed a sheath attached to Grandpa's waist. Brandon pointed at it. "What is that?"

Grandpa looked down and pulled out a sword from the sheath. "This is a piece of fine craftsmanship."

"Sword? I thought we had no weapons on the ship."

"Follow me," Grandpa instructed as he walked towards the back of the ship. "This was stocked in the secret storage compartment. We'll get you kids something to defend yourselves with too."

Cleo agreed "You may need the weaponry once we are on the outside."

"We are not going out there in that jungle with overgrown snakes, are we?" asked Diana.

"Can't we just take the ship and fly wherever we have to go?"

The others looked at Diana because it was not like her to challenge Cleo. Apparently the snake attack had been enough to scare her and question her beloved friend.

Book One: The Chosen Ones

"This is where the ship must stay," said Cleo. "There may be swords on Trahe, but I can guarantee there are no spaceships. It must stay hidden until we are ready to return. From here, we continue on foot."

"On foot?!" Brooke crossed her arms. "No way! There is no way we are walking in a jungle with large snakes." She turned to Grandpa. "We need to go home."

Grandpa looked very sad. "We should go home, but we have to remember why we came here in the first place. Do we want to leave without trying to find your parents?"

Brooke was torn. She badly wanted to turn this ship around and go home, but Grandpa was right. They all had agreed to go on this mission to find their parents. Now that they had finally made it to Trahe, how could they leave without searching for them?

"My dear Brooke," Cleo said, "I am glad you are taking the initiative to step up and voice your opinion. However, I assure you that all of you will be safe with Sir Bolivar and me."

Brooke found it hard to believe Cleo. "The overgrown mongoose is going to protect us?"

"Yes, come on. We have no time to waste." Cleo turned and ran into the other room. Grandpa followed.

The four kids just looked at each other, waiting for someone else to make the next move.

Finally, Brandon spoke up. "Well, if that overgrown rat can kill a large snake, then I think we will be safe. I am going to see where Grandpa found his sword."

Brooke uncrossed her arms. "Good idea. You gather anything that looks like a good weapon. Jereco, you pack your laptop and any other type of electronic thing you think we might be able to use. Diana, you pack up the supply of food and water, and I will ransack the medical cabinet. I don't particularly want to go outside, but I don't want to be left behind without Cleo either, so I guess we are stuck doing as we are told."

The others nodded in agreement and went off to pack their things and gather the items Brooke had assigned to them.

"Well, this is the last of it." Jereco added a bag of stuff to the accumulated pile sitting in the middle of floor. "Cleo, if we are walking, how in the world are we going to carry all this stuff? We have our camping backpacks to use, but all of that won't fit in them."

Cleo nosed through the pile. "I believe there are some items in here that we do not need."

"We need all of it," insisted Brooke. "I am not backing down on this one, Cleo."

Cleo stood at the top of the pile, flicking her tail. "Well then, you can figure out how all of you will carry this."

62

The Trabe Chronicles

Brooke placed her hands on her hips. "Cleo, we are humans, not cats. We have to wear clothes, we have to eat food, and we need certain things that you don't need.

"I think I know a way to haul all of this stuff," said Jereco before Cleo and Brooke could have one of their stare-downs. "It is quite simple, actually. We need to make a sled or wagon. Like the sleds that the Eskimos might have used for their dogs to pull."

"Who is going to pull the sled?" Brandon said. He looked at Cleo.

"Don't be ridiculous," Cleo said. "I am not pulling any sled. Besides, I am your guide and that might require jumping up a tree now and then."

"This time I will have to agree with Cleo," said Brooke. "Besides, she is way too *small*." She emphasized the word *small* as if it were an insult.

Cleo hissed at Brooke and then thumped her tail for emphasis.

"Well, I think Jereco's idea is a smashing idea," Grandpa said. "Why don't we all think of ways to put a sled together while we wait for the mongoose—I mean, Sir Bolivar—to come back."

Diana had an idea to use the top of their sleeping capsules as a sled. Jereco came up with the idea of using shelves from the storage room for the bottom of the sled, and Brooke suggested the shower curtain to help keep all of their things covered and together. Cleo rejected all of the ideas because they involved taking items from the ship that were not supposed to be brought onto Trahe.

Brandon finally came up with the idea of using vines and wood from the jungle. This seemed to be the best route, but they agreed that they could not venture outside until Sir Bolivar returned with a clearance of safety. So the making of the sled would have to wait for his return.

"*If* he returns," mumbled Brandon.

"Oh, he will return," Cleo said. "Mark my words. However, I admit that he has been gone longer than I expected."

"Cleo, while we are waiting," asked Diana, "can you tell us more about Sir Bolivar?"

"Yeah," Brandon said, "especially since it sounds like the rat is going to be with us for a while."

Cleo growled at Brandon for the *rat* remark.

Grandpa excused himself claiming he heard this story before. He wanted to secure the ship and check the supplies one more time. Meanwhile, the children stayed in their seats and listened to the tale of the mongoose.

"On this world of Trahe," Cleo began, "there is a place called Mangus Village. We were lucky to arrive just south of the village. Of course, I didn't realize this until I ventured outside. Sir Bolivar is from this community. He was raised at a very young age to be a hunter. He is very good at it, and he is one of the bravest mongooses I have ever encountered. I have been lucky enough to witness him battle an evil serpent. He won and had enough food to feed his tribe for many moons."

Book One: The Chosen Ones

"Evil serpent?" asked Diana.

"Yes, similar to the one attacking our ship. So it is fate that Sir Bolivar was hunting in this area of the jungle. He will guide us to his village. He is smart, proud, and a very good tracker. He will be a perfect addition to our search party. Now, when he comes back, please refer to him as Sir Bolivar, not the mongoose or rat." She looked at Brandon.

As if on cue, Cleo heard a knock on the hatch. She jumped on top of the hatch and meowed some words. Then Brandon heard what sounded like squirrel or ferret chatter.

"It is Sir Bolivar," Cleo said. "Quickly, Brandon, open up the hatch."

Brandon shook his head. "I didn't hear the password."

"Well, of course, he said the password. Otherwise, I wouldn't tell you to open up the hatch." Cleo looked at the kids, who just stared back, waiting for better reassurance. "Oh, for goodness sake," Cleo said. "He said it in mongoose language."

Brooke's and Jereco's eyebrows shot up.

"Oh, very well." Cleo turned back to the door and said something in her cat language. "Ark!" boomed a husky voice.

"Now quickly," ordered Cleo.

Jereco and Brandon opened up the hatch while Brooke and Diana stood back.

An overgrown mongoose crawled through the hatch.

The mongoose stood inside the spaceship. He slightly shook his body and then bowed to Cleo. "It is an honor and pleasure to serve you, Cleopatra of the Creator."

Sir Bolivar then turned to Brooke. He dramatically bowed again. "Sir Bolivar, at your service, Madam."

Brooke smiled in return. She decided that Sir Bolivar's character was probably a combination of cowboy and pirate, all wrapped into one, with some English manners thrown in. She just had to get past the fur, rat-like nose with whiskers, squinty mouse eyes, and the fact that he was covered in dirt and dried snake blood.

"Please, I beg your pardon," Sir Bolivar continued, "I am not presented at my best for such two young and beautiful ladies."

Brooke clasped her hands and slightly curtsied. "Not at all, for you have saved our lives, and we are forever grateful."

Jereco and Brandon rolled their eyes at Brooke putting on an old English act.

Diana giggled, joined in with Brooke, and curtsied too. She thanked Sir Bolivar for coming to their rescue.

At that moment, Cleo coughed up a fur ball. "Oh, excuse me for my interruption. Now may I introduce everyone? Sir Bolivar, you have just met Brooke, the eldest child of the human tribe that I have brought to Trahe for an important mission. The youngest here is Diana, my beloved friend."

The Trahe Chronicles

Sir Bolivar squinted at Diana and walked around her. "Remarkable."

"Yes, she is," replied Cleo. "Isn't she?"

"What is remarkable about Diana?" asked Brandon.

Cleo ignored the question. "And this is Brandon, who is as brave as you."

"Is that so?" Sir Bolivar replied. "Well, then, it is an honor to meet you, Brandon. I will be happy to fight by your side."

Brandon seemed to grow a little taller from this comment and completely forgot his question about what was remarkable about his sister.

"And finally, the brains of this mission," Cleo continued, "This is Jereco, the eldest son of the clan."

"Ah," Sir Bolivar said. "Tall, lean, and wisdom in your eyes. Wisdom is lacking in this world right now." He turned toward Brandon. "Brandon, we must protect Jereco at all costs, along with the damsels!"

Jereco looked embarrassed. "I don't need protecting. I am not a girl."

"No, but Sir Bolivar is right, Jereco," said Brooke. "You, Grandpa, and Cleo are the ones who know how to run the laptop, this ship, and who-knows-what-else we will need." "Actually, we are all important," Brandon said, trying to make Jereco feel better. "So we just need to watch each other's backs."

Sir Bolivar looked at Cleo. "You have a great small army here. I like them. So when should we be off on our mission?"

"Excuse me, Sir Bolivar," Diana said. "But you have not met our grandpa yet."

Sir Bolivar turned to see an older man had entered the room.

Cleo piped up. "Oh yes, Sir Bolivar, let me introduce the children's guardian. He has been taking care of them since their parents have gone missing."

"Yes," Sir Bolivar said, "the stars have told us about the fate of the parents." He shook his head.

Grandpa cleared his throat and took the moment of silence.

"But do not worry," Sir Bolivar continued. "Sir Bolivar is here to assist you in your journey!" He turned to Cleo. "So let us begin."

Brooke stepped forward. "I was thinking since it is now nightfall that we should bed down for the night in the comforts of the ship and pursue our mission early tomorrow morning. Plus, you probably haven't had dinner yet, and I could make you something to eat."

The other three kids looked at her in shock. Brooke never volunteered to cook, and her idea of cooking was microwaving pizza.

"Unless you already ate the snake?" asked Brandon.

"No, I am afraid the devil snake got away," Sir Bolivar replied. "But don't worry. Her time will come, and I am sure she is hiding and licking her wounds. Yes, food sounds wonderful. I normally like to travel at night, like my friend Cleo here. However, I am aware that you humans are day travelers due to a lack of night vision. So let's have dinner and talk. You all can fill me

65

Book One: The Chosen Ones

in on this mission." He looked down at himself. "Perhaps, I should be excused to clean up first."

"Of course." Brooke pointed out where the bathroom was and asked Jereco to help Sir Bolivar figure out how to use the modern facilities.

As Jereco walked Sir Bolivar back to the bathroom, he noticed how Sir Bolivar and Grandpa had avoided each other. Jereco was really good at reading facial expressions. During the introductions they looked like two old friends sharing a secret. Jereco had a sneaking suspicion that Grandpa wasn't being totally honest with them about all of his knowledge regarding this planet. Grandpa's exploration outside the ship had tipped Jereco off. He felt uncomfortable thinking that his Grandpa held secrets about this planet and its inhabitants.

After Sir Bolivar cleaned up, they all sat down for dinner. It would be their last civilized meal before they ventured out to the jungle. The kids could not imagine that any future meals on this planet would be any better. They sat around talking and getting to know each other. They told Sir Bolivar about their home planet and how they had come to Trahe. Sir Bolivar did not seem too surprised by the kids' stories. Apparently, Cleo had informed Sir Bolivar about many things when she had found him the day before.

Soon they decided to get some sleep. Even though the kids were anxious about venturing out to the jungle the next day, Sir Bolivar's presence eased their minds. They slept soundly until the sun rose.

Cleo was kind enough to let the kids sleep in a little bit while she and Sir Bolivar discussed some things in private. Finally, Jereco was woken by the touch of Cleo's paw on his face. She was acting as an alarm clock, and one by one, she woke the other children.

Sir Bolivar's booming voice came from the cockpit. "The sun has risen, and too soon, it will be at its peak! We must eat and be on our way before it is too hot to walk in the midst of the jungle."

Everyone sat up when they heard Sir Bolivar's voice. Remembering he was there brought confidence to their souls. They ate a hearty breakfast and cleaned themselves up, knowing this might be their last hot showers for a while. The boys were ready first and decided to put the sleds together while the girls finished getting ready.

"What is a sled," asked Sir Bolivar. "And what is its purpose?"

The boys explained to him that they needed to make something to haul all of their supplies. Sir Bolivar paced back and forth as he listened to the explanation and their ideas about how to make the sled. "The jungle gets very dense," Sir Bolivar said. "It will not be easy for you to pull a sled over the jungle floor. I shall help!"

Sir Bolivar went right to work with the boys to make the sleds out of fallen old wood and vines. They made two sleds—one for Sir Bolivar to pull and another for Jereco and Brandon. Brandon insisted that Brooke and Diana could pull a third sled, but Sir Bolivar refused. He said the backpacks

66

The Trahe Chronicles

on their backs would be heavy enough. So to Brandon's dismay, the boys would have to haul more than Brandon had hoped.

It was mid-morning before they were packed and ready. When they started off, the kids looked back at the spaceship, a little sad to leave the security of the aircraft.

"Wait a minute," said Brooke. "If no one is supposed to know about this spaceship, shouldn't we hide it? We shouldn't leave it in the open like this."

"Very good, Brooke," Cleo said. "I am glad you are thinking like a true leader. Our friends from above will hide the space plane."

Above in the sky were many tropical birds. They were pulling vines into their beaks. "They will cover the ship with the jungle plants," continued Cleo. "Are you sure you have everything you need out of the spaceship?"

They all nodded their heads.

"No, wait a minute." Diana ran back to the cockpit. She went to her chair and grabbed a picture beside it. It was from their last Christmas family dinner. She smiled as she looked at her parents, aunt, and uncle. "We are going to find you all." She gave the picture frame a kiss and stashed it in her backpack. She took one last look at the space plane and left the cockpit.

Book One: The Chosen Ones

We Are Not Alone

The Evadeam family was very nervous now that they were outside the spaceship and deep in the wilds of Trahe. Jereco was certain that they would die from exposure to strange things on this planet. He was convinced that they should be wearing a spacesuit to protect themselves.

Cleo and Grandpa assured the kids that Earth was not the only habitable world in the universe. In fact, there were many Earth-like planets. Trahe was one of the planets that the Creator made almost exactly like Earth.

However, Jereco still was not convinced. So he said a silent prayer to the Creator and then waited for his body to explode into a million pieces. That didn't happen.

Jereco felt a hand on his shoulder.

Grandpa grinned from ear to ear. "Relax, Jereco." He took a deep breath. "Isn't it beautiful?"

Jereco looked around and saw jungle. Rainforest, actually. The jungle was overgrown. It was thicker and darker than anything he had ever seen before. He swatted at a bug. "Did you, by chance, bring any bug spray?"

As Grandpa reached into his bag, Cleo ran up to him and meowed. Grandpa responded as he handed Jereco a bottle. "Cleo, I know this bug spray is modern technology, but I am not having my grandchildren die because of some disease carried by a Trahe bug."

Cleo hissed. "All of you have been vaccinated for any possible Trahe diseases."

"Yeah, but even you mentioned that you have not been here in a while," Brooke pointed out. "So maybe there are new diseases." She also reached for the bug spray.

Sir Bolivar had just come back from sniffing the area. He started sneezing. "What is that odor?"

Grandpa apologized, and Cleo explained what the scent was.

"I highly recommend that we make haste," Sir Bolivar said, sniffing the air. "If the spaceship doesn't attract attention, then this bug-killing poison certainly will."

"Sir Bolivar is right," agreed Brandon. "I learned through hunting back home that any new sight, sound, or smell in the area can attract predators."

"Like a snake?" asked Diana, nervously.

"Yes," Sir Bolivar said as he started walking, "that is why we must move quickly before she comes back with reinforcements." Then he explained to the small group that the jungle was very thick and walking would be slow-going for the humans. They would have to go single file. Sir Bolivar would take the lead and break down a path as needed. Cleo would take up the rear.

Another new journey began as they walked through the thick jungle. The kids trudged along, nervous and jumpy, but thankful for being between their two guides. The morning quickly turned into the afternoon. They felt like

The Trahe Chronicles

they had been walking forever, not just hours. As their weary bodies continued to trek through the jungle, their thoughts wandered.

Diana felt safe walking behind Sir Bolivar, but she wished Cleo was next to her. She started to think of home. It seemed so far away now. She missed her parents and worried about them.

Behind Diana, Brooke was batting at a bug. *Of course, this planet would have bugs,* she thought. They couldn't pick a planet that was bug-less. At least they were small bugs and not big human-eating bugs. Brooke was also realizing how out of shape she had become. She had been skipping her workouts back home. She usually had a daily routine to keep her body in shape for her lifeguard job. But the indoor winter blues and dating kept her from her daily exercises.

As Brooke trudged on, Brandon was busy looking around. He was the only one truly enjoying the walk in the jungle. He always dreamed of going to a jungle someday. Michigan was far from any tropical paradise; the only jungles he'd seen were on TV and in magazines, and he loved looking at all the greenery.

Then there was Jereco. Out of the group, he was the one worrying the most. He was concerned about where they were headed. He was worried about his parents; were they all right? Then his thoughts wandered to his home and school. Were they going to be gone too long? Would he miss too much homework? He really didn't want to fail his classes just because he was absent. He was a straight-A student working hard to receive a scholarship to college. He couldn't afford to be gone much longer.

Then he thought about all the technology he had with him. If there were no modern facilities here, then that would mean they would run out of battery life for the cell phones and his laptop. Maybe Cleo was right. What was the point of bringing the laptop if he couldn't charge it? What good was his technical knowledge if he had no technology to use? What had they gotten themselves into?

They walked on through the thick green jungle. Despite being so engrossed in his thoughts, Jereco was the first to notice the beautiful tropical birds above in the trees. Somehow, the birds seemed to calm his nerves. One with a bright yellow head caught his attention. It seemed to be moving closer and closer to him. Jereco thought it was a parrot, at least it looked a lot like one—a yellow-headed parrot to be exact. Those kinds of parrots were almost extinct back home. The bird landed on a branch right in front of Jereco. Its body was green with some red, yellow, and black markings on its wings. Its tail was yellow at the tip.

"You look like a friendly bird," Jereco said.

"Friendly, friendly," squawked the bird.

"Whoa!" Brandon stopped dead in his tracks, and Jereco ran into him from behind. "Did that bird just talk?" asked Brandon.

"Friendly, friendly," repeated the bird.

Book One: The Chosen Ones

"I think it just knows how to copycat words," explained Jereco. "It just said *friendly*."

"I don't know, Jereco," Grandpa said as he came up behind the boys. "A lot of creatures can speak the language." He looked up at the bird. "What is your name?"

"Koa, Koa," replied the bird. "Koa is my name."

Jereco and Brandon gasped. Before they had a chance to say anything, Cleo approached them. The moment Koa saw Cleo, he flapped his wings nervously and flew up a little higher.

Cleo started meowing to Koa, and soon the bird settled down. Koa cocked his head and seemed to be listening to Cleo's musical voice. He responded to Cleo by squawking. They were having a conversation.

Sir Bolivar also joined the conversation. He sniffed the air and barked. Once again, the bird seemed flustered, but he settled down quickly. After the conversation ended, Cleo translated.

"Things are even worse than I expected," Cleo said. "A great war is going on between the Madeave and the rest of the Creator's followers. There is a new evil that is unknown to this part of the world, and it's stirring up the Madeave and fueling the war. Koa lives very south of here, but he has left his native home to become part of a Trahe bird chain. This bird chain is a way to facilitate the exchange of communication quickly among our allies."

"Danger, danger," squawked Koa. He flew to another branch and pointed a wing in the direction of their spaceship. "Danger, danger."

"Koa is right." Sir Bolivar lifted his nose and sniffed again. "I can smell it in the air. Danger is close behind us. Forgive me, but my new two-legged friends are moving too slowly. We must go faster. We must run."

"Run!" exclaimed Brooke. "I am dead tired. I can't run."

Koa turned around, cocked his head toward Brooke, and then looked at Diana. "No run. Water. Go water." Koa flew over to another branch just east of them. "Water, water."

Sir Bolivar walked under the tree branch where Koa was perched. He sniffed the air once more and then looked up at Cleo. "Koa has a good idea. We can get to my village quicker if we go across the sea."

Cleo jumped into a tree and walked quickly across some branches. "We will need boats. The bay of sea is too large to swim across, and we need to keep our supplies."

Koa flapped his wings. "Yes, yes, two-legged village. Friends, friends." He flew off between the trees.

"Come on," yelled Cleo to the others.

Everyone quickly grabbed their things, including the sleds of supplies. They ran as fast as they could, following Koa and Cleo. This time Sir Bolivar followed last, keeping his nose to the air to smell for any upcoming danger.

Sweat was pouring down Brooke's face and back. *So much for not running,* she thought. She was really concerned about Diana, who was running in front

The Trahe Chronicles

of her. Diana had not had any epileptic seizures since they left Earth. Brooke was wondering if it was a coincidence, or maybe the vaccines provided by Cleo had special healing powers. Brooke lightly touched a belt that she had hidden under her clothes. It was filled with emergency items, including Diana's medications. She hoped they had enough medicine until they got back home because she doubted that they would come across a pharmacy on Trahe. Brooke quickly glanced around as she followed Diana. No, there definitely would not be a pharmacy in this forest.

Brooke heard the parrot squawk up ahead. Everyone slowed down to a stop at the edge of a clearing. A village stood in front of her, followed by more rainforest and a large body of water just beyond the trees. The village was made up of many wooden huts. Small fire pits were lit up throughout the village. The fires burned bright against the sky, making Brooke realize that dusk was fast approaching.

Brooke studied the village's inhabitants—Sir Bolivar had called them two-legged creatures. There were men, women and children, who looked a lot like humans. They had dark skin, jet black hair, and dark eyes. Several of them, holding handmade spears, walked toward the Evadeam family.

Koa flew between the men and Brooke's party. He squawked away, and the men seemed to be listening to Koa, but their gaze never left Brooke and her family. Cleo and Sir Bolivar greeted the villagers. They talked to them in another language. The men nodded and motioned for everyone to follow them."It is safe," Grandpa said to the kids. "They want us to meet their chief."

One by one, the children followed. They walked through the village as the inhabitants stared at them.

"This is so cool!" exclaimed Brandon.

"I don't know," replied Jereco. "I don't like the looks of those spears."

Brooke nodded in agreement, but she didn't say anything. She kept her eyes open, with one hand on Diana and the other on her knife.

They were brought into a hut where several villagers were sitting. They were directed to sit across from a gray-haired man who was introduced as the chief. Formal greetings were made and then a conversation started with the chief, Cleo, and Sir Bolivar.

There was a point during the conversation where there was a disagreement. Grandpa leaned over to the kids and whispered, "The chief isn't willing to give us any of his boats. He says he needs them in case the Madeave decide to attack his village."

Brooke, who had been watching the discussion intently, said, "How about we borrow the boats and offer them something for letting us do that? He can send some of his men with us, and they can bring the boats back after we get to our destination."

"Good idea," Brandon said, "but what do we have to offer them?"

Brooke smiled. "What seems to always make the world go round?" She

Book One: The Chosen Ones

reached around her neck and removed a gold chain. She handed it to Grandpa. "I think the offering needs to come from *our* gray-haired man."

Grandpa huffed and took the chain. He stepped forward and spoke to the Chief in his language. The chief looked surprised. He took the chain and dangled it in the air as he inspected it. Afterward, he shook his head.

Grandpa's shoulders slumped, and he turned toward Brooke. "He is not interested in the offering."

"I have something!" Diana volunteered. She grabbed her backpack and walked up to the chief. He watched her as she dug out an item—a gold picture frame. She removed the picture and handed the frame to the chief. The chief took the frame, but he also pointed to the picture. Diana reluctantly handed the picture of her family to him.

The chief was quiet for a moment while he looked at the picture. Jereco studied the chief. He thought that it was odd that the chief hadn't act surprised to see the modern objects that had been handed to him. As if reading his mind, the chief looked up at Jereco. He spoke clearly in the Trahe language, which the Evadeam family understood.

"Travel close," he said. "To the swamplands. To the land of the Tree God. There you will find the first of many answers." He looked into Jereco's eyes. "A mark. Travel to many places. Travel afar." He held up the picture and pointed to their parents. "Writings on the walls lead to those you seek."

Brooke jumped up. "You know where our parents are?"

The chief shook his head.

Brandon also stood. "What? You just pointed to them." He looked at Grandpa. "He must know."

The chief pointed to his head. "Only dreams."

"Liar!" yelled Brandon as he drew out his small sword.

Younger men of the tribe quickly guarded the chief by pointing their spears at Brandon. The chief just sat calmly as Grandpa got between Brandon and the tribesmen.

"Whoa, Brandon," Grandpa said.

"Brandon, back down," ordered Jereco. "I don't think the Chief really knows. He probably has visions like Diana."

"But he talks in riddles," Brandon protested.

"Sometimes visions are not always clear," replied Jereco.

Diana put her hand on Brandon's arm. "I believe the chief too, Brandon."

Brandon lowered his sword, but he still wasn't convinced.

"Sit," ordered Grandpa in a rough voice. "I said *sit*, Brandon!"

Brandon hesitated, but he eventually listened.

The moment Brandon sat down, a light started to glow around Cleo. She spoke to the chief in his native tongue. There were a few minutes of conversation between the cat, Sir Bolivar and the chief. Finally, the chief nodded and spoke to his tribesmen. He motioned one of the men over and whispered something. Afterward, the man led the other tribesmen out of the

The Trabe Chronicles

hut.

The chief held up the gold chain and frame. "We will take. I send four short boats and four men. Men bring back boats. You go now."

Sir Bolivar thanked him and led the way outside of the hut. Jereco and Cleo were the last ones to leave. Jereco held out his hand and thanked the chief. The chief took his hand and held it. "Do not forget. You will know the way."

Jereco hadn't forgotten and thought he'd always remember meeting the chief—this man of another world.

Book One: The Chosen Ones

Saved by Grandpa

When they stepped out of the hut, Grandpa pointed toward the bay. "Good. We will have calm waters for traveling."

Brooke looked across the waters to the darkening sky. "We can't travel now. It will be too dark."

Grandpa disagreed, "We can travel across these waters in the dark."

"How are we going to see? Are there headlights on the boats?" asked Diana.

"I don't think so," replied Brandon as he watched the tribesman load the canoes with supplies.

"You've got to be kidding me," Brooke retorted.

"That is enough," Grandpa snapped. "I will not have any more ungrateful comments. Don't you understand that our being here puts these villagers in danger?"

Brooke looked around and noticed the women and children seemed to be protected by only men with spears. She shuddered as she thought of the huge snake that attacked the spaceship. The snake alone could probably destroy the entire village.

One of the natives came up to Grandpa and asked for an article of clothing. They wanted to use it to make a new scent trail that would lead away from the village.

Grandpa took a recently-worn shirt from his backpack and ripped a sleeve off.

Before the man left, Brooke stopped him. She dug in her pack and grabbed a small bottle of her perfume. "I think this will help."

Grateful, he smiled and ran off.

Brooke watched him go to the edge of the forest. He handed the items to another man. Brooke thought she also saw a large white creature standing beside him. Before Brooke turned away, she watched the large creature walk back into the jungle.

Brooke couldn't figure out what kind of large white creature would live in a green jungle. She thought animals usually blended in with their surroundings. But then again they were in a different world. She mentioned the creature to Sir Bolivar. He sniffed the air and assured Brooke she had nothing to fear of the mysterious white creature.

The canoe glided quickly off the jungle coast. The chief had loaned out their fastest canoes and best tribesmen. *Fast for a canoe maybe. But not as fast as a motorized speed boat*, thought Brandon. He looked back toward the jungle. For some reason, he was getting more nervous as they paddled farther away from the forest. The tribesmen had suggested that the Evadeam family eat and sleep while they traveled during the night. Brandon ate dinner and wondered what type of large white creature hung out with jungle villagers.

74

The Trahe Chronicles

Brandon didn't like the idea of sleeping in the canoe with strange men around him. But his eyes got droopy, and soon he was sleeping to the soft sound of the waves lapping against the boat.

Moonlight shimmered over the ocean. Jereco had been keeping an eye on the other canoes as they made their way across the water. He had watched his brother fall asleep, and he felt like he needed to sleep too. They all needed to sleep, but unlike his brother, Jereco didn't completely trust the strange men around him. However, sleep could not escape Jereco. He slowly drifted off, sitting up.

Bump! Something had nudged the canoe and awakened Jereco. Startled, he grabbed a knife that Grandpa had given him. He looked around — nothing stirred — not even the tribesman who was paddling Jereco's canoe. The canoes were still gliding over calm waters, and everyone seemed to be asleep — including the tribesmen. *Who's manning the canoes?* Jereco thought.

Bump. Something gently nudged the canoe again. He looked over the edge of the water and an animal fin surfaced. His thoughts formed images of a dolphin or perhaps a manatee. As he tried harder to make out the shape in the water, he realized that there were many of them swimming with their canoes. These sea creatures were moving the canoes along the water! *What are they?*

Jereco leaned over and dropped his head closer to the water, hoping to see the animals better. Suddenly, water splashed against his face. As Jereco wiped the water away, a slight tingly feeling and a great sense of calm washed over him. He was safe and comfortable. His desire to sleep again grew strong.

Jereco's mind kept screaming, *don't fall asleep!* The situation was not normal and he should wake up everyone. But something deep inside him felt differently. It was all right to sleep. He needed his rest. Jereco's mind eventually lost the battle, and he fell asleep to the gentle rocking of the ocean waves.

Bump. Jereco jumped and opened his eyes. In front of him was land. The sun was rising, shining upon the jungle stretched in front of him. This jungle was different from the one they had left. The greenery wasn't as tall or dense. In fact, Jereco felt like he was staring at a Florida coastline back on Earth.

The canoes had landed on a stretch of beach. Jereco looked back at the ocean. He didn't see any signs of the animals he saw the night before. He rubbed his eyes and wondered if he had just imagined them.

"Jereco!" yelled Diana. She stepped out of her canoe and ran toward him while everyone else unloaded supplies from the canoes. "Look!" She pointed toward the trees. "Doggies!"

Jereco glanced in the direction Diana was pointing. Dogs were galloping out of the jungles. They were all different species, but they had something in common. They were all as large as small ponies.

Sir Bolivar and Cleo greeted the dogs. Cleo jumped on one of the dog's backs as they walked toward the canoes.

75

Book One: The Chosen Ones

"Welcome, Chosen Ones," a dog barked in the Trahe language. "I am Cheyenne. Our pack will guide you to Mangus Village." After introductions, they took a break to eat breakfast and freshen up before their short journey to Mangus Village. Then the tribesmen said their goodbyes and departed with their canoes.

Cheyenne reassured everyone that the village wasn't very far. They could make the journey in a day. As they started to leave, a huge flock of various birds came out of the jungle. Two of them landed on the beach in front of the group. One was Koa, the yellow-headed parrot, whom they had met in the other jungle. The other was a large osprey.

The osprey was at least two feet tall and had a huge wingspan. His backside was brown, his head and underside were white, and his wings were black. He wore a black eye patch and talked to Koa and Cleo by making screeching sounds. After their discussion, the osprey flew up into a tree and watched the newcomers.

Cleo explained that the osprey had claimed this area as his territory. He was very guarded about other birds, like Koa, coming into his area. Luckily for Koa, the Osprey knew Cleo and Sir Bolivar. The Osprey approved of Koa's mission and would let Koa fly into his territory. He even volunteered to watch and guide them from the skies. He felt honored to be among the Evadeam family.

"What is his name?" asked Diana.

"His name is too hard to say in any language you know," explained Cleo. So they just called him Osprey.

Osprey, Koa, Cheyenne, Sir Bolivar and Cleo led the way into the small jungle. The rest of Cheyenne's pack surrounded the group on all sides. The Evadeam family felt well-protected as they went into the tropical forest.

Indeed, the jungle was different from the rainforest from before. The jungle looked more like a swamp. They saw many creatures, including otters, alligators, crocodiles, tortoises and hawks. Sir Bolivar advised everyone to watch out for king snakes. "These snakes were a little smaller, but faster than the ones we have encountered," explained Sir Bolivar. This made everyone a little uneasy and encouraged them to move quickly.

They made great time, and Sir Bolivar said they would make it to his village by dusk.

They didn't make it by dusk though.

They first heard the warning barks from the dogs, and then the birds' squawks. Brandon even thought he heard a roar. Then, out of the corner of his eye, he saw a king snake, slithering across the jungle floor toward them.

It reminded him of the snake that attacked their ship. Except now, they had no spaceship shield to protect them. All they had was themselves, a bunch of large dogs, some birds, Sir Bolivar, and Grandpa.

Grandpa? Brandon could not believe his eyes. His old, gray-haired grandpa

The Trahe Chronicles

had pulled out his sword and was yelling at the approaching snake. Brandon watched as Grandpa told Brooke and Diana to stay and then he turned and charged the snake.

'Huh?' Brandon shook his head in disbelief at Grandpa's boldness, and then Brandon pulled out his own sword and rushed after Grandpa. He got to the snake in time to see Grandpa fight like he had never seen him fight before. Apparently, Grandpa was an excellent swordsman.

Unlike Grandpa, Brandon was not very good with the sword. Brandon slashed away, but he was no match for the snake. Grandpa ordered Brandon to stay away. Brandon looked around for help, but snakes were attacking from all sides. Everyone was in danger. Brandon had no choice but to fight. He turned toward Grandpa to tell him so, but a snake took him by surprise. It coiled around Brandon, and its fanged mouth came toward Brandon's head. Brandon thought he was going to get eaten when suddenly; a roar came from behind them.

The roar caught the snake's attention. The snake's head turned just in time to meet his fate with a black panther. Several panthers, actually. One by one, the black panthers jumped on the snake and attacked. Grandpa grabbed Brandon and dragged him away.

"What were you thinking?" demanded Grandpa.

"I was thinking I was going to save your life."

"And how did that work out?"

"Not too well," Brandon mumbled.

Another snake suddenly crossed in front of them and was intercepted by one of the dogs. Grandpa and Brandon watched as the snake grabbed the dog with its fangs and snapped the dog in half.

"We have to get out of here," exclaimed Grandpa.

Brandon silently agreed. He had just lost his motivation to fight after seeing the dog die in front of him.

But it was too late. The king snake had spotted them and was slithering toward them.

"Run!" yelled Grandpa.

They ran, but Brandon thought there was no way they could outrun the snake. He silently said a prayer. "God, Creator, whoever you are. Can you help us? We really, really need some more help. Like now! Please!"

Whip! The sound emanated from the jungle, followed by more of the same. *Whip, whip, whip!*

Grandpa stopped and looked back.

'Grandpa!' yelled Brandon. "Keep moving!" Then Brandon saw what Grandpa was staring at. The whipping sounds were jungle vines whipping through the air. A vine had just whipped around the snake that was pursuing them.

"Thank the Creator that the vines are on our side," Grandpa said.

"Who is on our side?" asked Brandon.

Book One: The Chosen Ones

"The trees."

"The what?"

"The trees! Come on. Let's go before they accidentally snatch one of us."

"Grandpa!" Diana ran into his arms, crying.

Brooke also raced into Grandpa's arm. "I lost sight of you. The dogs saved our lives." She peeked over at Brandon "You okay?"

Brandon simply nodded feeling a little choked up after seeing tears in the girls' eyes.

Cleo jumped out of a tree and landed at Grandpa's feet. "We need to get out of here. Who knows how long the jungle can keep the snakes away?"

As if to demonstrate Cleo's point, a snake broke free from a vine and slithered their way. Cheyenne started barking orders. "Grandpa, put Diana on my back."

Grandpa didn't hesitate.

"The rest of you," Cheyenne barked, "get on the others."

Everybody climbed onto neighboring dogs. There were dogs even large enough for Grandpa.

Cleo, Sir Bolivar, and Cheyenne led the pack, with Koa and the Osprey flying overhead. The pack moved fast. The Evadeam family had never ridden dogs before. Brandon was very uncomfortable. It was like riding a small horse, bareback, at full speed, with no mane to grab onto. Brandon found it best to reach around the dog's neck and grab onto some fur to hold on. He hoped he wasn't hurting the dog.

Brandon tried to see where they were going, but it was too hard to see much of anything. Branches and foliage were whipping against his face and body. So he just closed his eyes and prayed.

He never prayed much before. He didn't really believe in it. But he thought it wasn't coincidental that the trees came alive and rescued them right after he asked the Creator for help. Brandon could hear the continued sounds of fighting between the tree vines and snakes. Soon the sounds faded and suddenly — the branches stopped whipping his face. Brandon opened his eyes and looked ahead. It seemed like the forest was slowly opening for the pack. A very small path was being made for them as they ran into the darkness.

The Trahe Chronicles

The Creatures' Council

The early morning light streamed in through the cracks in the walls. Brooke slowly opened her eyes. As her eyes adjusted, it took a moment for her to remember where she was—Sir Bolivar's village. She was sharing a bed with Diana, who was still asleep. Brooke smiled slightly and snuggled deeper under the covers. They were safe, rested, well-fed, and warm. She felt good.

A curtain dividing the small bedroom separated the girls from the boys and Grandpa. Sir Bolivar's wife Bathsheba had offered separate rooms, but Brooke did not want her family to be separated. They were in a foreign land on a foreign planet, and she was not going to let her cousins and Grandpa be far from her reach. Thankfully, Grandpa agreed, and Bathsheba came up with the curtain divider.

Bathsheba often had guests. She had said her home was a safe haven for many. Brooke had smiled when Bathsheba used the word *home*. The home was actually a sprawling compound. It had many different types of rooms to accommodate a variety of creatures.

Brooke's thoughts were interrupted by the sound of Grandpa suddenly snoring. It had been a long couple of days and nights. Bathsheba insisted that her guests get plenty of food and sleep. Brooke constantly heard her shooing visitors out. Apparently, Bathsheba Bethharan was a very important person in this community.

Brooke had to smirk when the daring Sir Bolivar was scolded for the condition he was in when arrived at his home. He was forced to bath, eat and rest as well. Sir Bolivar tried to insist that they bring the council together for important business. However, Bathsheba, in her busy huff, informed that not all of the council members had shown up yet.

Brooke was wondering how many hours they had slept when she heard yelling outside. The voices grew louder as they entered into the house and came closer to the bedroom. She could hear Bathsheba tell the new visitors not to disturb the children. Their voices were brought down to a whisper. Brooke then recognized Sir Bolivar's voice. The other voices faded off. Then she heard their bedroom door open and Sir Bolivar gently waking up Grandpa. They moved out of the bedroom.

Brooke closed her eyes for a moment. Peace and tranquility seemed to be gone. She needed to know what was going on. She pushed the covers off and pulled back the curtain. Jereco and Brandon were both getting up.

"What is happening?" whispered Brooke. "Any idea?"

"Apparently, an infamous Hachmoni has just arrived at the village," whispered back Jereco.

The bedroom door opened. Bathsheba peered in. "Oh goodness. They did wake you. Well, you might as well get up, wash, and dress. Hachmoni has arrived and there will be council this afternoon. I will have breakfast fixed for you."

Book One: The Chosen Ones

In addition to housing a variety of guests, Bathsheba also had a live-in staff, including cooks who could prepare a human meal.

Brooke and the boys nodded and thanked her. As Bathsheba closed the door, Brandon stopped her with a question. "What is he like? This Hachmoni? Is he a mongoose too?"

"Oh goodness, no. He is a human. He is very old and very wise. They say he speaks directly to the great Creator himself. He is the one who told our council to prepare for your arrival so the prophecy could be fulfilled. He is respected by many and feared by our enemies. But don't worry. He has waited a long time to meet all of you, and he will be very pleased, indeed. Now come. While you were resting, we went to the market and bought you some fresh clothing and items for your personal needs."

She proudly held her head up. "Ever since I knew you were coming, I have been reading about your type of people and your planet." She looked down, shyly. "And with Cleo's help, I think I have gathered what you need."

Brooke stepped forward and touched Bathsheba's shoulder. "Thank you. Thank you for all that you have done for us. We have never felt more at home since we left our planet."

The boys nodded in agreement.

Bathsheba's eyes got a little teary. "Well, then, you're welcome. Now we must not delay anymore. Boys, you use the washroom first. Brooke, you wake up Diana, and I will come for you girls next."

Brooke went back to her side of the room where Diana was still sleeping. Brooke smiled. She didn't want to wake her. In fact, she would love to climb back into bed again. But then again, meeting Hachmoni and the council members might bring them closer to finding their parents.

At that moment, Cleo ran into the room and jumped on top of Diana.

"Where have you been?" asked Brooke.

"I have been hunting for two things: food and information," said Cleo. With her paws, she started kneading Diana awake.

Diana moaned and turned over.

"Come on, sleepyhead," said Cleo. "It is time to get up." She licked Diana's face.

Diana opened her eyes and looked up at Brooke and Cleo. "We are on winter break. We don't have to get up for school." She rubbed her eyes.

"Come on, Diana," Brooke said. "We are not at home, remember? We are at Bathsheba and Sir Bolivar's house."

Diana quickly sat up. "How long have I've been sleeping?"

"I don't know," said Brooke.

"You all have been sleeping for about twenty-four hours," reported Cleo. She cleaned herself with her tongue as cats do.

"Twenty-four hours!" the girls exclaimed.

"Wow — we must have been tired." Brooke said as she gathered her stuff.

The Trahe Chronicles

"Well, you had one major flight, and with jet lag ..." Cleo's voice trailed off.

"And the snakes ..." pointed out Diana.

"And the jungle trek," added Brooke. "And now Hachmoni is in town."

"Yes, I know," Cleo said. "I have already met with him. He will be meeting with the council this afternoon. I will take all of you there after you have dressed and had breakfast."As if on cue, Bathsheba walked into the bedroom, carrying a basket. She set it on the floor. "Well, good morning, Diana."

"Good morning," replied Diana, shyly.

"Do you remember me?" asked Bathsheba.

Diana nodded.

"Well, I have a surprise for you and Brooke." She gestured for them to go over to the basket. Inside was some new clothing and containers. The containers had beautifully scented liquids and soaps.

"I didn't think I would be so happy to get clean clothes and soap," Brooke commented excitedly. Brooke picked through the items, "So by chance did you get these from a mall?"

"A mall?" asked Bathsheba. "What is a mall?"

"Brooke, not now," Cleo said. "It's time for you girls to bathe and get ready."

The girls and Bathsheba walked away. Carrying the basket, Brooke turned towards Bathsheba, "Now let me explain what a mall is."

Cleo hissed and flicked her tail, but Brooke just smiled and kept on walking.

During breakfast, despite Cleo's disapproval, Brooke filled Bathsheba in on such things as malls, stores, and other amenities from Earth.

As they filled up with a wonderful breakfast, Jereco and Brandon shared thoughts on how this food was similar to the cuisine back on their own planet. Bathsheba found that to be most interesting.

Afterward, Brooke insisted that they brush their teeth. Brandon, of course, could care less about brushing his teeth, especially since his mom wasn't around to tell him to do so. But Brooke insisted that they keep their civilized habits intact. Once Bathsheba understood why humans needed to brush their teeth, she agreed with Brooke, and to Brandon's dismay, she ordered him to do it, just like his mother would have.

After Brooke and Bathsheba felt everyone was finally ready to meet with Hachmoni, they headed for the council building. During the walk, they talked about the village and the surroundings.They arrived at the large hut, which was being guarded by two mongooses and two men. The men were armed with swords.

"Cool," said Brandon.

Cleo complained about the swords. "Yes, it appears that metal has been

Book One: The Chosen Ones

discovered since my last visit."

"Just how long has it been since you have been here?" asked Jereco.

"A long time," said Cleo.

"Not that long," said Bathsheba. "You were here when I first met my mate, my Sir Bolivar. Remember?"

"And when was that?" asked Brandon.

"Oh, it will be one hundred years ago this coming spring."

"One hundred years!" Brandon said. "Just how old are you anyway?"

"It's not polite to ask a lady how old she is," scolded Brooke.

"But Brooke—" Brandon started.

"Well, just in time," Sir Bolivar interrupted as he walked out of the hut. "I was telling Hachmoni about our little adventure in the jungle. He was asking about you. It is time for you to meet him. Follow me." Sir Bolivar led them into the hut.

The hut was one large room that had torches in each corner. As Jereco's eyes adjusted to the darkness, he wondered how the torches had not set the grass hut on fire already. Then he noticed that the hut was not made of grass at all. The walls, ceiling, and floor were made from brick or hardened mud. In the middle of the room was a large rectangular table surrounded by chairs and large pillows. At the end of the table, sitting on one of the pillows was a very old mongoose who was introduced as a leader of the community. He gestured toward the kids to sit down.

They sat in four empty seats next to Grandpa, who was already in the room.

"I have waited a long time to meet you," said a deep voice.

The kids turned their heads towards the other end of the table. In the shadows sat a human. "Hachmoni," presented Sir Bolivar.

Hachmoni was dark skinned with black freckles on his face. He had short, curly black hair that peeped out of a small hat. He stood and walked towards them. Even though he paced with a wood walking stick, he was still taller than Grandpa. He stopped in front of them and smiled. The kids relaxed and already felt comfortable.

"You must be Brooke," Hachmoni said, bowing his head slightly.

"Yes, I am," Brooke whispered.

Hachmoni nodded. "I see the resemblance. You have the features of the Evadeam tribal women. You are tall, slender, and quite beautiful."

Brooke blushed. She could barely manage a thank you.

"You are the oldest and will be a great leader of your people," he continued.

That remark surprised Brooke.

Hachmoni turned toward Jereco.

"Jereco, the oldest son. We and the water people have been waiting a long time for you."

As Hachmoni turned toward Brandon, Jereco mouthed, *water people?* at

82

The Trahe Chronicles

Brooke. She shrugged.

"Brandon." Hachmoni placed his hands on both of Brandon's shoulders as he looked down at him. "You are very brave. You come from a line of great hunters. I see that you will be very needed, but not necessarily for hunting."

Brandon, who was not as shy as Brooke and Jereco, asked, "Sir Hachmoni, what is that supposed to mean?"

A hearty laugh rippled through Hachmoni. "You may call me Hachmoni. It means many things. One is related to the laws of our world. Would you know which law that might be? The one about hunting?"

Brandon thought for a minute. "Find out if the animal speaks the Trahe language before shooting it. It is against the law to shoot a Trahe-talking beast."

"Very good, Brandon. You learn quickly."

Brandon beamed and looked at Jereco. "See? I am wise too."

Hachmoni laughed again, looking over at Grandpa. "You are much like your grandfather."

Hachmoni kneeled next to Diana, who was standing in front of Jereco. "Hello, little one." Diana backed up a little into Jereco.

Jereco placed his protective hands on her shoulders.

Hachmoni nodded with approval as he looked at the three older kids. "It is very important that you watch over Diana and keep her safe."

"Safe from what?" asked Jereco.

"The unknown," responded Hachmoni.

Brooke quickly found her voice. "You are scaring her."

Hachmoni looked at Diana. "I do apologize. I do not mean to scare you, Diana." He smiled. "You look so much like her."

Curiosity got the best of Diana. "Like who?"

"Have you heard of Skylar?" he asked.

"Yes, I read about her in the family history books. She was an Evadeam princess, who had a white tiger as a pet."

"Not a pet," said a growling voice. "But a dear, dear friend who protected her."

The kids jumped, and out of a dark corner came a great shadow. The kids backed up as the shadow came closer. "Bright Eyes!" exclaimed Brandon.

Hachmoni shook his head. "No, I am afraid not. Bright Eyes died many years ago." Brandon turned to the white tiger. "Are you a descendant of Bright Eyes?"

"I am the cub," said the white tiger. "I am Skylar named after your Princess Skylar."

"Wow," asked Brandon. "So how old would that make you?"

"What is it about age with this kid?" asked Bathsheba.

Brandon looked at her. "Humans don't live this long. We're lucky if we live to be one hundred."

83

Book One: The Chosen Ones

"Really, Cleo?" Bathsheba said.

Cleo nodded.

One of the guards walked in and whispered into Sir Bolivar's ear.

Sir Bolivar cleared his throat. "Ladies and gentleman, may I announce the leader of the Evadeam tribe, Archelaus?"

Chairs scraped against the floor as everyone rose. The door opened.

"Wow, another human?" whispered Brandon.

Brooke let out a small gasp. Not only was he human, but he was also a very good-looking human. He was not as tall as Hachmoni, but taller than her. He had medium-toned skin similar and dark hair that fell to his shoulders in messy waves. She thought he looked like a knight in shining armor. Brooke felt a tug on her sleeve.

She looked down at Diana, who whispered behind her hand, "He's cute." So it wasn't just Brooke's imagination.

Brandon, who had overhead Diana, just rolled his eyes.

Suddenly, Skylar roared and leaped into the air. She jumped on Archelaus. The man and the tiger rolled onto the floor.

Brandon, who was standing there in shock with the rest of them, snapped out of it first and drew his knife.

Brandon headed toward the pair on the floor, but was tackled by a man.

Meanwhile, Jereco's instincts took over. He grabbed both Diana and Brooke and pushed them underneath the table.

"What is happening?" asked Diana.

"I don't know. All I see is feet." Brooke held onto Diana, sheltering her from whatever came their way. They heard a lot of scuffling and yelling. Then they heard some laughing and someone saying, "Bravo."

Brooke and Diana looked at each other, confused.

"Sorry," said a man's voice, "you can come out now." Archelaus kneeled and looked under the table. He held out his hand. Diana looked at Brooke, who nodded and slightly pushed Diana forward. Diana took Archelaus hand, and he helped her up.

Brooke was just about get out herself when Archelaus was back, peeking under the table and offering his hand to her. Brooke smiled slightly and took the hand, hoping her palms were not too sweaty. Once they were up from under the table, Brooke looked up at Archelaus. "Thank you, your highness."

"Please, no formalities. I am just Archelaus to my friends. And a big cat toy to Skylar." He laughed.

They looked over at Skylar, who was sitting and licking her paws.

Bathsheba scolded the tiger. "That prank and rowdy behavior scared the wits out of these children, and you almost got yourself killed by Brandon."

"Yeah, sorry about that," said Brandon.

The big cat got up and walked over to Brandon. "Brandon, you did a brave thing. You were protecting your kind, and that was the right thing to do."

The Trahe Chronicles

Brooke looked around. "So who stopped Brandon?"

Hachmoni spoke. "I think some introductions are needed to prevent any more misunderstandings. You know who Archelaus is now, with that grand entrance." Hachmoni chuckled. "Archelaus, may I introduce to you the Evadeam family?"

After Archelaus introduction, Hachmoni turned, "And this is the man who leaped across the table and stopped Brandon. May I introduce Silver Kat?"

Everyone turned to look at another tall man. *This keeps getting better and better*, thought Brooke. A very good-looking man with long, straight black hair stepped forward. However, he was not as sociable as Hachmoni and Archelaus. He just politely nodded and quietly stepped back.

He looks like a Native American thought Brandon.

Hachmoni quickly went around the table finishing the introductions of others who had entered into the hut. "Please sit."

As the talks began, Brooke's mind kept wandering to Archelaus, who was now quietly sitting next to her. She watched as Archelaus attention was focused on Sir Bolivar and Cleo.

They were reporting on the children's adventures thus far. Then there was much talk about large snakes, some tribe that was on the move, and questions about how the children tied into everything. During the talks, Diana leaned over to Brooke. "I'm hungry."

Then Archelaus leaned over from Brook's other side. "I'm hungry too." He announced a lunch break and suggested the meeting resume after they had feasted.

Book One: The Chosen Ones

Untold Stories Unfold

Indeed, the lunch was a feast that extended past the dining time. There was much visiting, laughing and storytelling. When someone tried to regroup the council and start the meeting again, someone else would start a story, reminiscing about the past. Soon dusk fell upon the land. It was at that time that a final decision was made to move the council meeting to the following morning.

With that decided, Archelaus had a good bonfire built. The fire became bigger and bigger as many other villagers joined the festivities. Soon there was more eating, drinking, and dancing. As the party carried on into the night, many became tired, but some still sat along the fire to relax and talk to old friends. Eventually, children who had fallen asleep were taken back to their huts by their mothers, and the only children left at the fire were Brooke, Jereco, Brandon, and Diana.

They sat with Grandpa, Archelaus, Hachmoni, Silver Kat, Bathsheba, and Sir Bolivar. Everyone was quiet, except for the crackling of the fire.

Diana slowly fell asleep in Brooke's lap. Brooke continued to watch the flickering flames of the bonfire. A movement caught her eye as she saw Cleo wander off into the night shadows. Her thoughts were interrupted by Bathsheba.

"The poor little girl is exhausted. I can bring her into the house," offered Bathsheba. "No, that is okay," replied Brooke. She wasn't quite ready to go in herself, and she still refused to be separated from Diana. "She is fine. I will bring her in shortly." "You are close to your sister?" asked Archelaus.

Brooke smiled. "Actually, she is my cousin. Jereco and Brandon are her brothers."

Archelaus was surprised. "You are close for cousins."

"Aren't you close to your cousins or other relatives?" Brooke asked.

Archelaus shook his head. "Not really. I lost most of my closest relatives in a raid eight years ago."

Brooke studied him, and she could see the pain of his memories. "Oh, I am sorry. I know how you feel. I lost my brother and mom in a car accident." She paused. It occurred to her the accident was also eight years ago.

Archelaus eyebrows gathered together. "How old was your brother?"

"He was twelve." Brooke then looked away as tears started to form in her eyes.

"Twelve?" said Archelaus. "I was twelve when the raid happened. When my sister and brother were captured, they were ten."

"Captured?" asked Brooke.

Archelaus nodded and looked back at the fire. "Witnesses saw the twins taken away, but could not identify their abductors. We never found their bodies, so I assumed they were kidnapped by the Madeave. I have been searching for them since that day."

86

Brandon, who was sitting on the other side of Brooke, was listening to the conversation. "Is it just me or is that a weird coincidence?"

Heads turned toward him, but no one replied. "Brooke's brother died eight years ago—the same year that Archelaus siblings were taken away."

"It is just coincidence," said Jereco.

Archelaus nodded his head. "It would be a twist of fate if Adamah—"

Brandon interrupted. "Adamah?"

"Adamah is my brother."

Brandon jumped, Jereco's mouth dropped open, and Brooke's face paled.

"What?" asked Archelaus, softly.

"My brother's name was Adam," Brooke said in a shaky voice. Tears slid down both cheeks. She looked at the fire and tried to blink the tears away. She was just about to excuse herself when Archelaus laid a hand on hers and squeezed it.

No, Brooke thought. *Now I really will start crying.*

Diana woke up with a start and bumped her head on the bottom of Brooke's jaw. "Ow! Diana?" Brooke went from wiping her tears to grabbing the bottom of her jaw. Brooke looked down at Diana whose eyes were wet with tears. "What's wrong, Diana? Are you crying? Did you have a bad dream?"

She nodded.

"It's okay; it was just a bad dream. It is time we get you to bed anyway."

"No. I don't want to go to bed," whimpered Diana. "I might dream again about the bad men painted in black and yellow stripes."

"You dreamed about men in black and yellow stripes?" asked Archelaus.

Diana nodded.

Archelaus looked over at Hachmoni and Silver Kat. He then said something to them in a language that the kids have never heard before.

Archelaus reached over to Diana and stroked her head. "I know this may be a hard thing for you to do, but can you please tell me about your dream?"

Brooke and Jereco gave Archelaus a questioning look.

"Why?" asked Brandon.

Jereco answered instead, "It might be a vision." He looked at Archelaus and then back to Diana. "Is it okay if I tell them about the kind of dreams you have?"

Diana hesitated.

"I think Archelaus already knows about this type of dream," Jereco continued, "and that is probably why he is asking."

Diana sat up more and looked at Archelaus. "Do you have visions?"

"I don't know. Why don't you tell me about them, and we can figure that out together."

Diana went to wipe her tears, and Archelaus handed her a blue cloth that he pulled from his pocket.

Diana smiled. "This is a pretty handkerchief." She wiped her tears and

Book One: The Chosen Ones

blew her nose.

Archelaus pulled out another one and handed it to Brooke.

Brooke blushed and thanked him.

Diana took a deep breath. "See, I sometimes have these dreams. They're not always bad, but sometimes, they seem so real. Sometimes, they come true." Diana proceeded to talk about how she had a dream of her aunt and cousin, Adam, being in a car accident. In the dream, they came to her and told her something that she had to tell Brooke. The car accident end up being real and they died.

Hachmoni, who had been very quiet, asked her what the message to Brooke was.

Diana looked at Brooke.

Brooke spoke up. "It was a long time ago; we don't remember." The fact of the matter was that Brooke did remember, but she thought it was too personal to tell strangers.

Hachmoni just nodded.

Archelaus took Diana's hands in his own. "Can you tell me about the dream you just had?"

Diana nodded and squeezed Archelaus hands as she told the story; it was still kind of scary to remember.

"Well, there were some men painted in black and orange stripes. They were using some sticks and stones to hit some nice people. The nice people kind of looked like you. And then there were some big snakes in the woods. Like the ones we saw in the jungle. And then some big black and orange tigers jumped onto the snakes and fought with them. And then a big black bear took a boy away. The boy was kicking and screaming. And then a tall shadow took a little girl away, who was crying for her mom."

Diana pulled up her knees. "And I miss my mom."

Everyone was quiet for a moment.

Brandon was the first to speak. "So, is it a vision?"

Archelaus brushed Diana's hair away from her face. "Thank you for sharing your dream." He then looked at Hachmoni to answer Brandon's question.

Hachmoni replied in his deep, gravelly voice. "Yes, it is a vision. But Diana, not all of your dream was bad. True, there were some bad men, but the tigers and the bears were good warriors."

"Hachmoni," Jereco asked, "why don't you tell us your whole story? I have a feeling we need to know."

Hachmoni looked into Jereco's eyes and nodded. "Diana's dream was about Archelaus village raid eight years ago. The men painted themselves with black and orange stripes to try to disguise themselves as tigers. The tigers were friends of the Evadeam tribe, but these men were from the Madeave tribe."

"Hey, Grandpa told us about the Madeave tribe," said Brandon. "Their

88

The Trahe Chronicles

chief married Skylar, who was an Evadeam."

"Very good, Brandon," replied Grandpa.

Brandon turned his head. "I thought you were sleeping."

"Just resting my eyes and listening," said Grandpa.

Hachmoni continued. "These men raided Archelaus village. I came upon the village too late. Many of the Evadeam men were killed. The women and children had scattered into the mountains. I knew I couldn't be much help but I saved what I could. I, like you, Diana, have visions. I had a vision about the raid and brought help. That is why the tigers and bears came. Sadly, Archelaus parents were killed."

Hachmoni bowed his head in a moment of silence. "It was then that I knew I had to save the rest of the family—Archelaus, his brother, and his sister. The black bear you saw in your dream was a friend who took Archelaus brother, Adamah, to safety. I am that tall shadow who took Archelaus sister, Areli, to safety."

"What?!" yelled Archelaus as he jumped up. "You took my brother and sister and never told me? I thought they were kidnapped. Why? Why didn't you tell me that you took them?"

Hachmoni looked up at Archelaus and quietly said, "They would be safer if you didn't know."

Archelaus walked toward Hachmoni and drew out his sword. The rest also jumped to their feet. Silver Kat and Skylar ran between the two men.

"You took the only immediate family I had left and never told me. For eight years, I have been searching for them. Praying for their safe return. For eight years, I have avenged the Madeave tribe." Archelaus voice changed to a low growling whisper. "I thought you were my friend. After my father died, I looked up to you. Up to you as a father."

Hachmoni finally stood. He put his hand on Archelaus shoulder. "I did not think I could keep all three of you safe, together. I did what I was told to do. I had to separate you to fulfill the prophecy."

Archelaus shook Hachmoni's hand off his shoulder. "Prophecy! What prophecy? A prophecy that peace would come back to Trahe? All I have seen in my life are bad things, evil, war—there is no such thing as peace! There is no such thing as this prophecy!"

Hachmoni narrowed his eyes. "You once believed, Archelaus."

"I once believed in you too," growled Archelaus. "Now where are my brother and sister? You tell me, old man."

Hachmoni jaw clenched, and then out of the uncomfortable silence came a small voice.

"The boy is living in a mountain," said Diana, "and the girl was sent somewhere warm, tropical, with pretty colorful birds. But I don't think she is there anymore."

Heads turned toward her.

She shrugged. "At least that is what I saw in my other dreams."

89

Book One: The Chosen Ones

"Other dreams?" asked Archelaus.

"I told you." Jereco stood. "She has these sign dreams."

"How many and how often do you have these sign dreams?" asked Hachmoni.

Diana shrugged again. "A lot, I guess."

"Yeah," Brandon added. "She has always had these dreams since she was little."

"I think I've had more since Cleo came to visit me," said Diana.

Cleo. They had all forgotten about Cleo, who, at that very moment, decided to join them.

"Midnight snack," she said, licking her chops.

"Speaking about Midnight." She paused from licking herself and looked up.

Everyone else did too.

Whoosh!

The sound was made by large flapping wings. Everybody stared at a large black shadow flying above.

"Can it be?" said Archelaus in disbelief. "No, they are just legends."

Silver Kat who had held his tongue for quite some time finally said, "Is seeing believing for you, Archelaus? You once believed in prophecies until your mentor followed a prophet you didn't like. You must open your eyes. Prophecies are being fulfilled all around you." He gestured toward Brooke, Jereco, Brandon, Diana, Grandpa, Cleo and then, the skies above.

The dark creature slowly flew down and landed in front of Archelaus. It then bowed and said in a deep velvety voice, "Leader of the Evadeam tribe, son of the Creator, brother of Adamah and Areli; I now join you to fulfill the prophecy and bring peace to Trahe."

The Trahe Chronicles

PART THREE

Pegasus and Willow

*Stories are told.
Legends are believed.
Myths are stories.
Faith makes legends.
- Silver Kat*

Book One: The Chosen Ones

Midnight

Brandon could not believe his eyes. *This world keeps getting better and better*, he thought. He could tell that Jereco, Brooke and Diana were thinking the same thing.

"I knew it!" Diana exclaimed. "I knew pegasi were real! It all makes sense. They were in the book about Trahe that I read. I bet these creatures were on Earth too! That is why there are legends of them."

Brandon thought Diana could be right. It made sense. Legends and things that seem to be make-believe back home were real on this planet. Maybe these creatures had existed on Earth many years ago. Maybe the legends were from true stories told by the earlier settlers of Earth.

He looked over at the creature Cleo called Midnight. Midnight was a perfect name for a magnificent horse that was black and shiny. Or maybe Midnight was better described as a pegasus, for this large horse had wings just like pegasus in the stories back home.

Midnight stomped his right front hoof. He then shook out his mane and wings and stood tall. *Taller than any horse he has ever seen*, thought Brandon. Even their farm work horses were small in comparison.

Diana kept thinking Midnight was the most beautiful horse she has ever encountered. If it wasn't for the brightness of the fire, she thought she would barely see him because he was so black. *Midnight black*, she thought. "I wonder if we can pet him," whispered Diana.

"He isn't a pet, like we think of our horses," Jereco whispered back, "That might be disrespectful. Remember, some of the animals here are creatures equal to man." He looked at Midnight with awe and respect. "I am pretty sure he is someone great."

The others nodded in agreement, and as if on cue, Midnight turned to them.

"These are the great legendary Evadeams." Midnight slightly bowed down on his forelegs, and his wings spread magnificently. "I bow in honor and am humbled by your presence." His wingspan was twice the size of the width of his body. The wings shimmered with tints of dark blue that matched his mane, tail, and eyes.

The children were dumbfounded. They did not know what to say, for in their minds, the creature in front of them was magnificent and almost unbelievable.

Sir Bolivar stepped forward. "It seems that they are at a loss for words, Midnight. I believe it is because they have never met a pegasus before. In fact, I am learning that there are many creatures of our world that do not exist in theirs, like myself."

Understanding, Midnight nodded and spoke in his deep, rich voice. "Ah. So the stars, our forefathers, and the legends speak the truth. The Creator will bring Evadeam family members from another world, much like ours, but this

The Trahe Chronicles

other world will have lost the great creatures of Trahe. Only written legends will be left of their ancestry. And someday, the legends will also be lost forever."

Midnight walked up to Diana. "And you look so much like the ancient one."

"I am Diana." Diana kept her hands behind her back to resist the urge to pet his nose. "Such a small creature with so much weight of two worlds upon her," said Midnight. "It never ceases to amaze me what our Creator thinks and does. But if he has faith in you, so do I." He bowed again.

Before Midnight stood, Diana's urge to pet him overcame her. Her hand went to touch his nose. She paused. "May I?" To her surprise, Midnight nodded. She stroked his nose, then his head, and ran her hand down his neck toward his wings. She hesitated, looked at Midnight, and he nodded with approval again. Her fingers gently touched his wings. "You are so lovely," she said, smiling at Midnight.

Sir Bolivar stepped forward and introduced Midnight to the rest of the family. After that, Bathsheba insisted that the children go off to bed. It was now very late, and the morning sun would be rising very soon. Sir Bolivar showed Midnight where he could bed down for the night while the rest of the party said their goodnights and were off to bed.

Bathsheba was right. *The morning sun came much too early*, thought Brandon. He had dreamed of flying horses, snakes, and tigers. He was thankful that Bathsheba had let them sleep late. Soon the sounds of the household woke the rest of the Evadeam family, just in time for a lunch.

Following lunch, the council met again. The kids and Grandpa pretty much sat there and listened. There was a lot of talk about people and creatures of Trahe that the children did not know.

Brandon, who did not like to sit still for too long, got bored with all the talking. The discussions didn't mean anything to him as far as he was concerned. When he rose from the chair, Jereco looked at him. Brandon mouthed that he was going outside, and he quietly slid out, unnoticed by anyone else. He decided to do some exploring in the village.

Brandon, who was a very sociable person, stopped and talked to the villagers as much as possible. He got to know many of them. He walked past a home with a large front porch. A human elder and his grandson waved Brandon over. They offered him to sit in one of their rocking chairs.

The village elder was talking about how he once was part of the council but had since retired. Now he enjoyed time with his grandson. His son has taken his place on the council, sitting in on the boring meetings. "In my day, the council meetings were often about who should marry whom— uninteresting stuff like that. But there were times when the meetings were about war and keeping peace. Yes, those would have been the exciting times."

Book One: The Chosen Ones

Brandon looked up at him. "Isn't that what the meetings are about now?"

"Oh, are they? Well, if they are, then those are the meetings I surely would have wanted to attend." Then he rocked some more and looked off in the distance.

Brandon was just thinking that maybe he should return to the council meeting. He was about to say goodbye when he noticed a concerned look came over the elder's face. The elder leaned forward, squinting to see something.

Brandon looked up and pushed his glasses farther up his nose. There was something out in the horizon. He stood up and used his hand to shield the sun from his eyes. "What is it?" "Not what—*who*?" said the elder. "That is one of our scouts from the western side. Something is wrong."

As the scout came closer, Brandon could see he was staggering as though he were hurt. He needed help.

The elder looked at his grandson. "Quickly, go sound the alarm." The elder turned back to say something to Brandon, but Brandon was already off and running toward the scout.

Brandon heard an alarm bell ringing in the background. Brandon's eyes searched the horizon, looking for any other danger. Once Brandon reached the scout, the scout fell into Brandon's arms. He was bloody and barely could talk. He grabbed Brandon's shoulders and looked into his eyes. "They know. They know you are here." Then he collapsed.

Brandon felt his pulse. Nothing. No breath either. *No way*, he kept thinking. *No way. This can't be happening. There's so much blood. Who knows we are here? What is going on?* Brandon heard others running up behind him. Brooke dropped down beside him. She asked Brandon to assist with CPR by doing the breathing while she and Jereco pushed on the ribs. Brandon heard a cracking of the ribs and cringed, but he knew that would happen so the compressions could reach the scout's heart.

The scout sputtered and coughed. He was breathing again.

"Oh, great Creator, it is a miracle," someone said from behind.

The scout opened his eyes, looked at Brandon and whispered something. Brandon lowered his head closer to the scout. "What?"

The scout raised his head — repeated his message — dropped back to the ground.

Brandon heard Hachmoni ask one of the man villagers to carry the scout to the healing building. Hachmoni patted Brandon on the back. "Well done!" He helped Brooke up from the ground.

As Brandon started to get up, he noticed that everyone was leaving and following the carried scout. "Wait!" he yelled. "Wait, he said something."

That caught everyone's attention. Brandon was trying to catch his own breath. He looked into the horizon and did a quick scan. He saw no sign of intruders — yet. He turned back to the group. "He said, 'They know. They know you are here.'"

94

The Trahe Chronicles

Brandon could tell by the looks on their faces that this small message was important, indeed. Skylar, who was already sniffing the ground where the scout fell, turned toward them. "He is right. I can smell Madeave."

"But how can the Madeave possibly know that they are here?" asked Archelaus.

"As we have legends and prophecies, so do the Madeave. It is wise to think they also are aware of the stars' stories," replied Midnight.

"It was only a matter of time," said Bathsheba.

Silver Kat nodded, "It is time to move the children and prepare for an attack. Skylar and I will go out and see how close they are. This scout was assigned to the western side of the marshes. We will start there."

"If the great snakes are ready to strike, then they are coming from the south," said Midnight. "I will fly overhead to those marshes."

"I will ride on Midnight and warn the other scouts," said Hachmoni. He turned toward Midnight, "With your permission, of course."

"Are you up to it?" asked Midnight. "It has been a long time."

"Of course, I am up to it." Hachmoni grinned as he patted Midnight's shoulder. "I may be old, but I still can out-fly any of these young villagers."

"Can I go?" asked Brandon.

They all turned to him.

"I want to go. I want to do something."

Hachmoni grasped Brandon's shoulders "You have done something. Because of you, we now know this village and your family are in danger. You did a brave thing, and with the help of your cousin, you may have saved a life. However, Silver Kat is right. You must be moved. Not only are you in danger here, but the longer you stay here, the more danger this village faces." Hachmoni turned to Bathsheba. "We need to prepare to leave. Can you help the children prepare and pack?"

"Of course," Bathsheba said with slight tears in her eyes. She was sad the Evadeam family was leaving and worried about the danger that lay ahead for them. "Come." She waved the children to follow.

Brandon stood firmly. "But where are we going?"

"A safe place," replied Hachmoni. "We will discuss that later. Now we must not waste another minute."

With hesitation, Brandon and the rest of the Evadeam family followed Bathsheba while the others went off their separate ways. As they walked back to Bathsheba's home, Brandon noticed that there was much bustle throughout the village. The community was preparing for an attack.

Bathsheba shooed the Evadeam family into the house. They started packing. All of the kids felt scared, but there wasn't much time to discuss their feelings about it. Now and then, Bathsheba or Grandpa would tell them that it would be all right, and there was no reason to be frightened; they had the great ones and the good Creator on their side.

The kids had their doubts but kept quiet. In between the packing,

Book One: The Chosen Ones

Brandon would step outside to look up into the sky to check the distance for a sign of Midnight, Silver Kat, Skylar or the Madeave. Nothing. He wasn't sure if that was a good sign or not. Every time he stepped out, he noticed the village looked more and more prepared. Homes were shut up and barricaded. The men were now heavily armed and stationed around the great fence that surrounded the village. Brandon's heart started pumping as it did when he had run toward the scout. He shook his head. "I can't just run away."

Archelaus returned and stepped onto the porch. "You are not running away. You are running toward your parents, and you are fulfilling the prophecy. You will be of no good to any of us if you stay here and get killed."

"But I don't know where our parents are and what the prophecy really is." Brandon said impatiently.

"Did anyone tell you that the scout is still alive? The Healer said that he will heal and live."

Brandon shook his head.

"Maybe that small act is part of what you are meant to do. You were the one who heard his message, saved him, and warned the village."

Brandon was happy to hear the scout would live. "And maybe I am supposed to stay here and fight."

"Nay, I believe you are to live by leaving," said Archelaus. "Why else would the Creator let the scout survive and warn you?"

"But how can I leave and let my new friends be under attack? I can't abandon them."

Archelaus put his hand on Brandon's shoulder. "They know you are not abandoning them. But they will be very upset with themselves if something happened to you on their watch. They will stay here, fight, and be happy, knowing you got away safely to fulfill the prophecy."

"Which is?" asked Brandon.

"What the Creator desires of you."

"Riddles," said Brandon in frustration. "You all talk in riddles and nonsense."

Archelaus pointed to the sky. "Look."

The sun was setting, and through the rays of light, Brandon saw a dark blob in the sky.

"Midnight?" asked Brandon.

"Yes." Archelaus stepped off the porch to meet Midnight and Hachmoni.

Brandon was amazed by how fast the horse flew. Midnight was just a dark speck in the sky, and in a matter of minutes, he was landing in front of the council house.

Clouds of dust stirred as he hit solid ground. Hachmoni slid off Midnight's back.

Brandon noticed that there was a new large saddle with all kinds of pockets on Midnight's back.

Hachmoni said, "There are definitely snakes and Madeave coming from

96

The Trahe Chronicles

the south and western marshes."

"Not very creative, are they?" replied Archelaus.

"No, they are not much for surprises," Hachmoni replied. "There are not too many of them, and we can easily fight them off."

As if reading Brandon's mind, Archelaus said, "But we still need to get these children to safety."

Midnight and Hachmoni nodded in agreement, and Brandon's shoulders dropped.

The council quickly met in the council building. Silver Kat and Skylar had not yet returned. "We counted only about ten great snakes and less than fifty Madeave," reported Hachmoni. "They will be easy enough to fend off. They will probably arrive late tonight. Their pattern seems to be to attack at dark when they think we are asleep. The Madeave probably will attack the homes while the snakes slither underground, looking for the Evadeam children."

"Why would they slither underground?" asked Brooke.

"Many years ago, we built caverns below the earth to hide our females and children. But because this is a swampy area, that didn't work well; the caverns kept flooding. However, we still pretend to hide our females and children there. Now and then, we get lucky and drown a snake or two."

"So now where does everyone hide?" asked Brandon.

"In our stronghold," said Sir Bolivar, proudly.

Brandon's eyebrows came together. He was puzzled because he had explored the village already and hadn't seen any stronghold. He looked up. "Where is that?"

"Funny that you asked because that is where you will be heading with the elders, females and children." replied Sir Bolivar.

Brandon just scowled at him.

"So what is the plan?" asked Grandpa.

Hachmoni said, "Midnight is going to fly you to the stronghold until we can meet up with you."

"Who is *we?*" asked Brandon. "Are you staying behind to fight Hachmoni?" He still didn't like the idea of leaving.

"Yes, so there will be plenty of help."

"But sir," piped up Diana, "how can we all fit on Midnight's back?"

"Small, but wise," said Midnight. "While Hachmoni and I were scouting, we put word out to our friendly cranes of the marshes. They are going to fly and get us recruitments." He turned to Archelaus. "It should not take long for them to get here, but the Evadeam family should start out for the stronghold."

They were all in agreement and decided to move Grandpa and the children now in case they were incorrect about the timing of the expected raid. Bathsheba and Sir Bolivar led them toward the house to gather their things, and the rest of the council stayed to discuss counterattack strategies.

Book One: The Chosen Ones

As Grandpa and the children walked to Bathsheba's home, Brandon couldn't help but notice the armed men in the village. He wished he could stay and fight with them.

"Didn't you learn your lesson in the jungle, Brandon?" asked Grandpa.

"What? You read minds now?" Brandon grumbled.

"I just know my grandson." Grandpa tousled Brandon's hair.

Brandon shrugged off Grandpa and jogged ahead of everyone. He was upset and frustrated. He wished he was old enough to stay and fight. "Maybe I will anyway," he said aloud.

Just then, the wind picked up, and a tree branch slapped the back of his head. He turned toward the tree, and the wind got stronger.

"Come. Come to me," a woman's voice said. "I am waiting for thee. Come where it is safe."

A chill went up his back. The voice sounded like his mother's. "Mom?" he whispered.

Brandon looked around, but he saw no one. He turned and rushed to Bathsheba's home to go pack.

The Trabe Chronicles

The Secret Stronghold

Brooke and Diana were very quiet as they gathered their stuff. They both didn't dare speak, knowing they might start crying. It was very overwhelming for them at this point. They had been comfortable living in Sir Bolivar and Bathsheba's home, and Bathsheba was like a mother figure to them.

Bathsheba walked into the bedroom and saw their glum faces. "Now don't worry girls." She gave them a big smile. "Everything will be all right. Besides, I am coming with you to the stronghold."

"You are?" said Diana.

"Well, of course. Now do you have all your stuff?"

The girls nodded.

"Then off we go."

Jereco, Brandon, Brooke, Diana and Grandpa stepped outside. Many of the other villagers were saying goodbye to their loved ones.

Diana pointed. "Look!" About fifty large dogs were getting packs put on their backs.

Brandon recognized some of the dogs as the ones that had helped rescue them in the jungle with Sir Bolivar. Brandon waved, and Cheyenne came trotting over.

"Howdy, Brandon," said Cheyenne.

"Where have you been?" asked Brandon.

"At the stronghold. Are you ready to go see it?"

Brandon nodded, now a little more eager to go. It helped to know that he was going to a new place with family and friends including Cheyenne.

Cheyenne began to introduce the rest of the pack to the Evadeam family; there were a lot more dogs here than there had been in the jungle.

As he was doing so, Diana suddenly began to feel sick. Her brain was telling her that she was going to pass out, but she couldn't mouth the words for help. Her brain was filled with thoughts, but her body wasn't reacting to her thoughts. It felt like she was falling in slow motion. She heard voices and barking. She saw white and black stripes. Felt something large and soft underneath her. She heard foreign words like a chant of some sort. Was it Silver Kat? Then everything went blank. She had another one of her dreams.

In Diana's dream, something was rubbing against her face. It kept trying to grab her head. It was a long tree vine. Diana slowly turned her head. She saw a village under attack. It was the Madeave. They were human, just like herself, except their skin was a little darker, and they had long, darker hair. They almost reminded her of Silver Kat, except they were dressed in tiger skins, and they were dirty and muddy. They were burning the homes and trying to hurt everyone in sight.

"No!" shouted Diana, and the vision froze.

The vine that had been trying to grab her spoke. The vine whispered in a

99

Book One: The Chosen Ones

soft, female voice. "This will happen as it is foretold, Diana. You can stop it. You must tell them that everyone must go to the stronghold—all females, males, cubs, including the members of your party who plan to fight — except for Silver Kat and Skylar. They will know what to do and will go to the stronghold when the time is right.

"Now wake, small child, and tell them to all leave by tomorrow's setting sun."

The vine released Diana and it disappeared. Diana then heard another voice. "Now wake, my child."

Diana's eyes fluttered open, and staring right into her eyes was Cleo. Diana was lying on her bed in Bathsheba's home. She smiled and petted Cleo. Cleo licked Diana's face and purred.Jereco and Brandon were sitting on the end of the bed. They had been worried about her. She hadn't had a seizure since they'd been in Trahe.

"Diana's medicine must not be working," thought Jereco.

Diana saw their worried looks. "I am fine," she assured them. "I had an important sign dream."

"It is true," said Cleo. "We must retrieve Hachmoni, Archelaus, Sir Bolivar, Silver Kat and Skylar. And hurry, for we do not have much time." She jumped off Diana's bed. "Bathsheba, get Diana some of your herbal soup from the kitchen to help her recover. Brooke, help the boys find everyone, including Cheyenne."

Diana was sitting up, finishing the herbal soup when everyone piled into the bedroom. A few of them asked Diana how she felt. She assured them she was fine.

Cleo began to speak. "Diana is a little weak, but she will be fine. She had an important sign dream, and you must all listen very carefully. Go ahead, Diana."

Diana hesitated because she really didn't like being the center of attention, but as the dream started to come back to her, she remembered how important the message was. She slowly recited the dream back to everyone.

Afterward, everyone was quiet for a moment.

"My home," Bathsheba said as she looked up at Sir Bolivar. "We can't permanently leave our home, our stuff. How can we possibly pack up everything and move it to the stronghold by tomorrow night?"

"We are not!" replied Sir Bolivar. "No, my love, we will stay here and fight. I am not letting any Madeave run me out of my home."

"That is right, Sir Bolivar," said Archelaus. "I will stay and help you defend your village."

They started to make plans on how to defend the town.

Diana's eyes started to tear up. She pleaded for help. "Cleo, Jereco, Brooke, they have to leave. They have to do what the dream said."

Jereco nodded in agreement and tried to get everyone's attention, but at

The Trahe Chronicles

that moment, no one seemed to want to hear him.

"This is ridiculous," whispered Brooke. "We were brought to this planet for a reason, and I believe this is one of them. They will listen!" She turned to the crowd, stood on top of the bed, and yelled at the top of her lungs, "SHUT UP!"

Heads snapped up. Brooke's gaze shifted from one party to another make sure she had everyone's full attention. "Are you insane?!" she exploded in her best military voice that she had learned from her father. "We all agreed the other night that Diana's sign dreams are real and important. You can't just go pick and choose the ones you want to listen to. The Creator thought this one was so important that she caused Diana to fall into a dead faint. We have been told that *all* must go to the stronghold, and that is exactly what *all* of us are going to do. Silver Kat and Skylar, you may stand behind, but make sure you get to the stronghold when it's time. Since you also have visions, I assume you will know when."

Silver Kat and Skylar both nodded in agreement.

"Good. Now for the rest of you, we have some serious packing to do. Sir Bolivar and Bathsheba, you also have some serious convincing to do. All of the villagers have to leave. This village needs to be totally emptied before the Madeave arrive. Now let's get cracking!" Brooke remained on the bed with her hands on her hips.

Hachmoni stood up and moved to Brooke's side. "You heard her," he said in a low, demanding tone. Now let's get cracking."

They nodded and went off to plan and organize the evacuation of the village. Hachmoni looked up at Brooke. "Very well done, my child." He hesitated. "But may I ask, what does "get cracking" mean?"

With Hachmoni's help, Brooke stepped down from the bed. She explained what she meant.

Archelaus and Sir Bolivar approached them. "We are a little concerned about the Madeave following us into the stronghold. We are, after all, moving an entire village there."

Silver Kat and Skylar stepped forward. "We are taking care of that."

"Just the two of you?" asked Sir Bolivar.

Silver Kat's eyebrow shot up.

"Oh, forgive me." Sir Bolivar bowed. "I forgot to whom I was talking."

Silver Kat turned to Hachmoni. "We will meet you at the stronghold."

Silver Kat shook hands with everyone and then bowed to Diana. "You are a brave little girl. You did a good thing today. Follow your dreams, and they will lead you to much happiness. We will see you soon, little one."

Diana smiled at him, gave him a big hug, and whispered, "Please be careful." Then she gave Skylar a big hug. He licked her cheek.

Once outside, Silver Kat and Skylar had a few words with Midnight before they walked south of the village.

Jereco and Brandon approached Sir Bolivar. "So how can Silver Kat and

101

Book One: The Chosen Ones

Skylar keep the Madeave from following us?"

"It is a long story that is best saved for another time," replied Sir Bolivar. "Let's just say that Silver Kat's tribe is called the Ghost Tribe. Now come along, we have some packing to do."

It did not take long to convince the rest of the villagers to pack up and go to the stronghold. Hearing the words of Hachmoni was all the convincing they needed. It was a long night of packing and not much sleeping or eating as everyone prepared to go. By the time the sun rose again, much had been accomplished, and everyone was a little more optimistic about going to the stronghold.

That morning, the Evadeam family had breakfast with their hosts and was now packing the remaining provisions. Jereco and Brandon were assigned to the supply room.

"How are we going to get everyone and their stuff to this stronghold?" asked Brandon. "It is not like they have cars and trailers here."

"I guess they will just use packs and carts," replied Jereco.

Brandon nodded. "Then we better get a move on because the Madeave will be right on our heels."

"Well, maybe Silver Kat and Skylar are going to delay them?" replied Jereco.Brandon's mind kept thinking. "What about weapons? Shouldn't we have more weapons just in case the Madeave catches up with us?"

"I am sure Archelaus will make sure we have enough weapons, Brandon."

"Shouldn't we have better weapons? We need some guns."

"We don't have any guns here on Trahe. Our knives and swords will be fine." But Jereco had to admit he was starting to miss the shotgun that his dad had handed him those many weeks ago when the spaceship first landed on their farmland.

"How about a bow and arrow?" suggested Brandon. "I have seen those here, and I know how to use them. I use to hunt deer with Dad and Grandpa on the farm."

Diana came running into the room. "Hey, come see this!" she shouted.

Curious and wanting a break from packing, they followed her outside. They looked at the sky and saw many large and different-colored objects flying overhead.

"What are they?" asked Brandon. "Big birds?"

The objects were coming from the north, and as they got closer, cheers erupted from the villagers.

Brooke came running out of the house. "Oh my gosh."

Jereco turned to Brandon, smiling. "I think prayers have been answered. Here is our transportation."

"Cool," said Brandon as he continued to look up. He now saw the forms of many flying horses. They were each unique in size, color or markings. Most of them were as large as Midnight. Midnight was already at the north

102

The Trahe Chronicles

end of town greeting them.

Bathsheba walked up behind the children. "Now that is a pretty sight." Some of the pegasi bowed down to Midnight. "Midnight is their leader," she explained.

"I see," said Diana. "He is like the leader of their herd."

After all of the pegasi landed, Midnight and two very large brown horses walked over. Diana thought the two horses looked like Clydesdale horses with wings.

"I would like you to meet Clyde and Dale," introduced Midnight.

Diana and Jereco looked at each other. They were both thinking what a weird coincidence it was that the horses' names sounded just like the breed of horse on Earth.

After Midnight made all the introductions, he said, "Brooke and Diana will ride on my back to the stronghold. Jereco, Brandon, and your supplies will ride on Clyde and Dale."

"What about Grandpa?" asked Diana.

"He has already chosen his ride." Midnight nodded to his right. They looked over and saw that Grandpa was talking to a big black horse that looked a lot like Midnight. Grandpa and the horse walked over to the group. "Kids, I would like you to meet Luke Thunder. This is Midnight's father."

"I see you came out of retirement, Dad," said Midnight.

"When I heard that the legendary Evadeams from Earth were here, I couldn't resist." Luke Thunder said. "Besides, I wanted to see an old friend." He nodded to Grandpa.

The kids looked at Grandpa, confused. Jereco's suspicions about Grandpa having been to Trahe before seemed to be true.

Grandpa just cleared his throat, and Midnight changed the subject.

Midnight looked down at Bathsheba. "We will make arrangements with Cheyenne's pack to carry your supplies."

"Thank you very much," said Bathsheba. "Perhaps you can also take some of the smaller cubs with you. The rest of us can travel fast on ground."

Midnight agreed and walked over to Cheyenne. Grandpa and Luke Thunder wandered over to the rest of the pegasi herd that was eating grass on the north side of the village.

"Aren't they beautiful?" asked Diana.

"I wish we had pegasi back home," Jereco replied.

"Maybe we did at one time," Brandon said. "So what's with Grandpa and Luke Thunder?"

"I think Grandpa has been here before," Brooke said. "Do you know anything about that, Bathsheba?"

"It is not a story for me to tell," said Bathsheba. "Besides, we have lots of work to do. Come." She sent the kids back into the house.

Soon after the arrival of the Pegasi herd, things moved quickly. Perhaps,

103

Book One: The Chosen Ones

the arrival of the herd had brought hope. By late afternoon, everyone was ready to leave. It was agreed that the pegasi would start getting the children and cubs out first. After the pegasi made their drops at the stronghold, they would turn back to pick up more.

Sir Bolivar, Archelaus, and Hachmoni insisted on being the last ones to leave. They wanted to make sure everyone got out, safe and sound. Bathsheba also wanted to stay behind, but she was convinced she was needed most at the stronghold to get everyone settled in their new homes.

When it came time to load up, the Evadeam children said their goodbyes.

"Goodbye? That is nonsense," Archelaus said as he tied their supplies onto Clyde and Dale. "We will see all of you soon."

Archelaus walked over to Brooke and Diana. Blankets and saddles had been provided for the pegasi's backs. He explained that the pegasi never used to allow anyone or anything to ride on their backs, but during these times of war, they made exceptions to help their fellow friends.

Midnight insisted that he would be the one to care for the two Evadeam daughters of the Creator. Archelaus lifted up Diana first onto Midnight. Brooke was to ride behind Diana and make sure Diana didn't fall off. Luckily, all of the children had horse riding experience.

Archelaus turned to Brooke before lifting her onto the pegasus. "Hang on tightly to Diana and to Midnight. Midnight will get you there safely."

Brooke nodded. She felt a little uncomfortable. She and Archelaus hadn't talked much since the night they had discussed the loss of her brother. Archelaus started to lift Brooke onto Midnight. Brooke then quickly turned toward Archelaus. "Don't become foolish by staying here to fight. I trust Diana's dream. You must make sure that Sir Bolivar and everyone else safely arrives at the stronghold."

"I will," said Archelaus.

"Promise?" Brooke asked.

Archelaus smiled. "I promise. Besides, being stuck in the stronghold will give me time to get to know this Brooke that stood up to a roomful of men earlier."

Brooke smiled. "I will see you soon, Archelaus." She turned back to Midnight as Archelaus lifted her up onto the grand horse.

After Midnight flew into the air, Archelaus turned to Jereco and Brandon. "I didn't want to say this in front of the ladies, but we are in a time of war. There will be a time for training, but until then, take these." He handed Jereco a large knife in a sheath.

Jereco hesitated for this knife was larger than the one Grandpa gave him.

"I have a feeling you will need this," explained Archelaus. "Even if only to use for gutting fish."

Jereco nodded and thanked him. He tied the sheath onto his belt.

Archelaus turned toward Brandon. "I hear that you are good with a bow."

The Trahe Chronicles

He held out a bow and some arrows.

Brandon broke out into a big smile and took them.

Archelaus hesitated for a moment and very seriously spoke to both of them. "Use these wisely, and remember to never, *never* use them on a talking creature. Except, maybe a Madeave."

Brandon's eyebrows came together. "Well, how are we supposed to know if the creature talks? What are we supposed to say? Pardon me, but are you a talking creature?"

Archelaus said, nonchalantly, "Well, of course." He showed Jereco how to mount onto Clyde.

Brandon wanted to argue that it sounded strange to ask an animal if it talks before you shoot it, but he wasn't given time to argue as it was his turn to climb onto Dale.

Grandpa hoisted himself upon Luke Thunder like an old pro, which raised even more suspicions with Jereco about Grandpa's history with Trahe.

Other villagers bid their goodbyes as they were lifted onto pegasi. One by one, pegasi lifted into the air.

The older and healthier mongooses walked on their own, following Cheyenne and his pack.

Brooke watched from above. She felt the wind whisk her hair back as Midnight galloped into the air. Flying was more breathtaking than she had imagined. At first, it was scary to leave the ground with only the support of a large horse underneath her. The flapping sound of the large wings drowned out the voices of those left behind on the ground.

The kids peered down below. They saw the mongooses and dogs taking off toward the north.

"Boy, they sure can run fast," said Brandon.

"Yes, but we will fly faster," responded Dale.

And sure enough, they flew fast and low over the grounds. They wanted to keep out of sight as much as possible in case the Madeave were close enough to see them above.

The swampy everglades quickly turned into taller green foliage. The pegasi had to fly higher to avoid the larger trees. As Diana looked down, she saw more and more willow trees, and the farther they flew, the larger the willows became. Pegasi began to fly upward to clear a huge forest of willow trees. The forest was thick. It was hard to tell where one tree ended and another one began. After what seemed like only a short time, the pegasi carefully started to fly downward. Diana held on tighter to the saddle horn. "Brooke, I think we are going to crash right into the trees."

Brooke, Jereco, and Brandon were thinking the same thing. But right at the moment they thought they would hit branches, the branches pulled back. Diana blinked and looked again. With the wind blowing in her face, her vision wasn't clear. She kept blinking tears away, so she could see what was in

Book One: The Chosen Ones

front of her. Midnight slowed down, and Diana began to make out the branches in front of her. They were just like the ones in her dream. The branches were bending away, making a path for the pegasi.

It was incredible. As the branches bent away, she could see the wooded ground covered with old willow tree debris. She recalled how one of her chores back home was to pick up the broken old branches that fell from their farm's willow trees. Here, they were left on the ground as a natural covering.

Midnight was flying very close to the ground and was approaching the biggest willow tree Diana had ever seen. In fact, it was so large that she could not see all of it.

As they approached the tree, branches opened in the middle, and Midnight flew up into the opening. Willow branches softly brushed against Diana's face, and they reminded her of the feeling in her dream.

They seemed to fly forever in the darkness of the willow tree branches. Finally, a soft light came from above and guided them to the middle of the tree. The branches became thinner, and Diana's mouth dropped as she saw what was in front of her.

It was a wooded city made out of the willow tree's branches and roots. It reminded her of a very large tree-house city. It was incredible. One by one, pegasi landed on the forest floor in the middle of the stronghold.

There, awaiting them, were many different creatures including a variety of dogs, birds, and reptiles. Diana turned her head. She thought she even saw some oversized ferrets.

Midnight landed softly and trotted to a halt in front of a white dog that Diana thought looked a lot like a golden retriever. In fact, the dog looked a lot like Cheyenne, except Cheyenne was red in color.

Midnight and the dog bowed to each other, and then the dog said, "Welcome. We heard of the grave news; our home is now your home." She walked over to Midnight's side and looked up at the girls. "Ah, we are blessed, indeed." She peered at Diana. "Remarkable. She looks so much like her."

Midnight turned his head back toward the dog. "Yes, Diana does look much like her."

Meanwhile, some very large Great Dane dogs had come up to the pegasi and were letting themselves be used as stepping stools for everyone to get off.

When Diana and Brooke were safely on the ground, they were introduced to Sheba, who was the white dog. Once they got closer, they noticed some gray and red hairs mixed with the white. They were told that Sheba was the mother of Cheyenne, and she was considered to be the wisest of the pack.

Once everyone's things were unloaded, the pegasi left to fly back to the village for more passengers.

The kids quickly learned that this stronghold was shared by many different creatures—

The Trahe Chronicles

herds, packs, and tribes of all kinds. The willow tree that housed the city was ancient and alive; it was simply called "Willow." She was greatly respected. Willow hid the city and kept all those inside safe. Nothing evil was ever allowed to enter Willow Woods, the forest surrounding Willow, and to date, no enemy knew specifically where Willow was.

"Why can't everyone just live here all the time?" Brandon asked.

Bathsheba explained that Willow only offered sanctuary to those in need and when requested by the Creator. Besides, the whole world of Trahe could not fit under the branches of Willow.

I guess that makes sense, thought Brandon. Then he wondered if he could live there safely forever. Before Brandon could ask that question, they were quickly introduced to their new surroundings and friends.

It was decided that the Evadeams were to stay with Hachmoni, Archelaus, Bathsheba and Sir Bolivar in their new home, which was up in a tree house close to the middle of the tree city.

As they walked toward their new tree home, Brandon looked around anxiously for any signs of his mother. He had been sure it was her voice he had heard back at the village, but now he wasn't so sure. He sighed. He missed his mom very much.

Book One: The Chosen Ones

Whispers in the Wind

Willow was larger than anyone could possibly imagine. The tree city was magnificent with many overgrown tree houses to accommodate the humans. Homes were built into living trunks and branches. Even a running stream of fresh water ran through the city. There was a pasture for the Pegasi. Grandpa and the kids thought the tree city was simply incredible.

The kids especially enjoyed their new home. Once everyone was settled into a new daily routine, they started exploring the tree city. They actually felt a little more freedom in this new place. The children were allowed to wander around to explore. Bathsheba told them that Willow would protect after them.

One afternoon, Brandon and Jereco decided to explore higher into the tree while the girls stayed back and spent some "girl time" with Bathsheba and other female friends. Brandon and Jereco started to climb a large branch that reached high above the city. The higher they climbed, the darker it got and the denser the branches became.

"I wonder if we can reach the top and see out to the rest of the world," commented Brandon.

"I don't know," said Jereco, "but it sure would be worth a try. It has been days since we left the village and we haven't heard any word from the outside. I am curious to know if Diana's dream has come true. I wonder if the Madeave burned down Sir Bolivar's village. Maybe if we climb high enough, we can look out and see it."

Brandon's breathing became heavier as he climbed upward. "I don't know. We seemed to have travelled a long way to get to Willow. It might be too far away." He stopped to catch his breath. "I wonder if they have towers built up high for inhabitants to see outside of Willow? To watch for enemies or something?"

"Yeah, you would think so," asked Jereco. "Hey, are you okay? Is your asthma kicking in? Did you bring your inhaler?"

"I will be okay. Let's keep climbing."

They moved on, but it wasn't too long before Jereco heard raspy breaths coming from his brother again. Knowing that Brandon was very stubborn and wouldn't admit that his asthma was getting the best of him, Jereco decided to claim he needed to stop for a break.

"You should have brought your inhaler," said Jereco as they leaned against a branch.

"I didn't think I would need it," explained Brandon. "I haven't even unpacked it since we left the spaceship. Besides, why would I need an inhaler here? It is clean and fresh air."

"I think it has to do with the altitude," said Jereco. "We might be higher up, so the air is getting thinner. I think we should head back. What if your asthma kicks in? We don't have your inhaler."

The Trahe Chronicles

"Yeah, I suppose you are right. I should always have an inhaler in my pocket. We could always come back up here another day." Right after Brandon said those words, the wind kicked up, bringing in some fresh air. Willow branches brushed against the boys. The wind got stronger, and the boys were afraid they would fall off the big branch. As the branches moved about, Jereco noticed a flat surface just a little higher up among the branches. He pointed it out to Brandon, and they agreed to climb to that spot to rest. If Brandon could sit down, he might be able to breathe better.

They climbed up slowly. Jereco followed Brandon to make sure he was all right. They finally reached the flat surface. It was like a floor was right in the middle of the branches. They both sat down, leaning against the thick branches of the tree. They just sat, closed their eyes and rested.

As the wind died down, Jereco heard something. It sounded like a flutter. Wings, perhaps. He slowly got to his feet and squatted, trying to peer through the branches.

Brandon started to say, "What?" when Jereco put his fingers to his lips.

Brandon, who was still breathing pretty hard and raspy, decided just to sit there and cover his mouth with his hand to quiet the sound of his breathing.

Jereco slowly drew out his knife and stood in front of Brandon. His eyes squinted in the direction that he had heard the noise. He saw a shape flying in the air, coming toward them. The willow branches seemed to move apart for the creature. As it got closer, Jereco noticed it was a large bird. He saw colors. Tropical yellow colors. "Koa?" whispered Jereco.

The large tropical bird was flying above them now.

Brandon jumped up. "Koa, is that you?"

Koa squawked. "Me — me —arrive at Willow. Put to work. Something for Brandon."

The boys noticed that Koa was gripping something in his claw. "Catch!" He dropped an inhaler into Brandon's hands.

Both boys just stared at the inhaler, dumbfounded.

"Don't stare at it — do" Koa was annoyed. He felt there was more important work than acting as a delivery bird. The boys sat back down, and as Brandon got his breathing under control, Koa decided to fill them in on what had been happening outside of Willow.

Jereco listened to the broken language of Koa and concluded what had happened. After Koa had arrived back home in the jungle, Koa noticed much activity. There were rumors that the snakes were on the move. After much investigation, Koa and many of his friends found the rumors to be true, and even worse, they found out that the snakes had teamed up with the Madeave. Many types of birds joined together to spy on the new enemies. Word was sent to Koa that both — Madeave and snakes — were heading to Mangus Village. The Madeave believed that the Chosen Ones were hiding there.

When Koa and his flock arrived at Mangus Village, they were shocked to

109

Book One: The Chosen Ones

find the village in ruins. The buildings had been burned and were still smoldering.

Koa panicked, as birds sometimes do, flying from house to house, building to building trying to find any signs of life from the town. He was completely shocked to find nothing, except a bunch of snake tracks and Madeave tracks.

The local swamp cranes flew in and told Koa what had happened. The Madeave and the snakes had attacked the village, trying to find the Chosen Ones, and when they found no creatures, they set everything on fire. They were very angry and on a warpath. Worst of all, the large snakes slithered around, trying to find clues as to where the villagers went. Being close to the ground, they found some clues and discerned the direction in which the villagers went, leading toward the hidden stronghold. The swamp wildlife, including the cranes and alligators, fought the snakes and Madeave, trying to throw them off, yet they still travelled in the correct direction, trying to find the villagers.

So Koa and his bird friends decided to pull a trick on them. One early morning, while the Madeave and snakes were resting, the birds got within earshot of their enemies and made up a story about going to the stronghold to the East to warn their allies of the enemies' presence. It worked, and as soon as the flock of birds took off in the air, the Madeave and snakes followed them from below.

"Once the goose chase was on," said Koa, "I snuck to the stronghold."

"And you are sure you were not followed?" asked Brandon.

Koa looked at Brandon, disapprovingly. "Followed! No! Fly undercover."

The willow branches started to move around.

Koa fluttered his wings, not looking very happy. "Okay. Help from the trees."

The wind and branches stopped moving again.

"Had help from the trees?" asked Brandon.

"Yeah," said Jereco, "and you said that Willow told you Brandon needed his inhaler. How did you know that? How did Willow tell you?"

Koa looked at the boys like they just asked the most ridiculous questions. "What do you mean? Willow talks. " He started to take off.

Jereco stopped him. "Wait a minute, Koa. You didn't answer my question. How did Willow talk to you?"

Koa stopped and looked at the boys, confused.

Brandon stood up. "Willow is a tree. How can trees talk? All we hear is a bunch of branches blowing around." He waved his arms around to demonstrate.

Koa shook his head and whistled, "Apology. Forgot not from this world. Trees don't talk on Earth?"

The boys shook their heads.

"Interesting." said Koa with a thoughtful look on his face.

110

The Trahe Chronicles

A willow branch reached down and hit Koa, sending him backward. He dropped into the branches below. The boys ran to the branch where Koa had been perched and looked down. Yellow feathers were flying everywhere, and they heard a lot of screeching. Then all was silent for a moment.

"Koa?" yelled Jereco.

Koa flew up behind them. He looked a little upset. As he was flying in midair, he yelled, "Didn't mean anything. Tree take personal." Then he dropped his voice to a whisper. "It would be nice to not have talking trees. Sometimes, they get bossy."

"Lookout!" yelled Brandon as a willow branch came up from behind Koa.

Koa flew out of the way, dodging the hit. "Okay, okay, sorry."

The willow branches were now making all kinds of noise.

"Seriously!" exclaimed Koa. The wind picked up, and the branches were now slashing around even harder. Jereco and Brandon had to get out of the way before they got hit themselves.

"All right!" yelled Koa. "All right, I said!"

The branches calmed down, slightly swaying.

"Willow has given great task of teaching tree talk." Koa did not look happy about his new assignment.

Brandon walked up to Koa and petted his feathers. "Look at it this way. You will be teaching the great Evadeams an important language."

Koa just gave him an unhappy look.

Brandon shrugged. "Well, thanks for my inhaler."

"You're welcome," mumbled Koa.

Koa looked above them. "It is getting late. Your first lesson will be on the walk back."

Jereco looked at Brandon. "Do you feel good enough to start walking again?"

Brandon nodded. "It is a lot easier to climb downhill."

Jereco agreed that this was true.

As they started walking down, Koa started their lessons on tree talk. "First lesson. Willow can hear and understand at all times."

"Obviously," said Brandon. The boys laughed, remembering the tree branch that hit Koa.

Koa ignored them and continued. "Second lesson. Willow hears all within her city." He spread his wings. "And can hear beyond into the Willow Woods. She is connected to all living willow trees."

Jereco eyebrows came together in thought. "So that is why there aren't any towers to look out beyond the tree city. She is aware of our surroundings, so she would know if the enemy has found us."

"Precisely," replied Koa.

"But how does she talk to us?" asked Brandon. "How do you hear her?"

Koa landed on a branch and looked at Brandon. "You are impatient boy. No wonder you forgot inhaler." He let out a low whistle. "Third lesson.

111

Book One: The Chosen Ones

Willow, speaks the Trahe language. You speak universal language, you speak to the trees."

Jereco and Brandon looked at each other.

"But Cleo gave us the gift to speak Trahe," said Brandon, "and we can't hear Willow talk."

Jereco nodded in agreement.

"Then you are not listening carefully," said Koa. "Tree talk is a language derived from the Trahe language, but it's not that hard to decipher. Brandon, ask Willow a question."

Brandon looked at Jereco, who shrugged.

"Try something easy," Jereco said.

"I feel dumb," replied Brandon. "Talking to a tree, I mean."

A tree branch swatted at Brandon and hit him lightly on the head.

"Hey!" Brandon exclaimed.

Koa shook his head. "She hears everything!"

"Yeah," said Jereco, "and she doesn't like to be insulted."

"Then you ask her something." said Brandon.

"Okay. Willow, can you hear me?" asked Jereco.

Brandon rolled his eyes.

The branches fluttered in the breeze.

Both boys listened intently.

"Nothing," said Brandon. "I hear nothing but branches."

Koa sighed. "Try again and listen with your soul. Listen with your insides."

"My insides tell me I am hungry," mumbled Brandon.

Koa just shook his head. "Come then. Go back."

As they descended downward, Jereco was deep in thought. He wondered if talking to Willow was like listening to nature back home on Earth. You have to listen to all the sounds around you and interpret what they mean. If the tree branches start blowing hard, you know the wind is picking up and a storm is coming. Maybe Diana can hear Willow. She seems to have a gift. Or what does Brooke call it? A female instinct. Why does a girl have good instincts? Boys should have that too. *Maybe we are just too impatient*, he thought as he looked at Brandon walking ahead of him.

Jereco stopped. Maybe he could concentrate harder without Brandon distracting him. Jereco closed his eyes and started speaking. "Willow, can you hear me? Help me hear and understand you, just like Koa can." He just stood there and repeated the question. The tree was silent. No wind. No branches blowing. Just silent and calm.

Brandon's head was down, concentrating on the limbs below him. Now and then he would look up to make sure Koa was not too far ahead of him.

"Brandon!"

Brandon's head popped up as he heard Jereco calling his name.

"Brandon!"

112

The Trahe Chronicles

Brandon yelled back to Jereco as he kept on walking. "What?"

There was no answer.

"Brandon!" the voice echoed again. Growing impatient, Brandon stopped and looked back. "WHAT?"

But as he turned around, he saw that there was no Jereco in sight. "Jereco!"

Brandon heard Jereco again. "Brandon!"

A bad feeling came over Brandon. Something must have happened to Jereco. He must have fallen.

"Koa! Koa! Something happened to Jereco." Brandon started to run in the direction from where they had come. He stopped at a point where the branches broke off in multiple directions. "Jereco!" he yelled. He didn't see him. Which way should he go?

He looked back over his shoulder "Koa!" *That darn bird*, Brandon thought. *Where did he go?*" He started to panic. He looked around and all he saw were willow branches, branches, and more branches. No sign of Jereco or Koa. His breathing started to get raspy as his panic worsened. He put his hand in his pocket and clutched the inhaler.

"Brandon!"

Brandon whipped his head around. One of the big tree limbs moved. The increased wind pushed back more willow branches. "Willow?" he whispered, following the path that the tree was opening for him.

Brandon finally found Jereco, who was standing on a large tree limb, with his eyes closed. Brandon looked around to see if there was anyone or anything keeping Jereco there. Nothing. Brandon reached into his pockets. He had no knife. No weapon to defend himself. The wind picked up a little. Brandon stepped forward, cautiously. "Jereco?" he whispered.

Jereco jumped slightly and opened his eyes "Oh, it is just you."

Brandon came closer. "What do you mean, just me? Didn't you call for me?"

Jereco shook his head. He sheepishly looked down. "I was trying to talk to Willow, but I heard nothing." He shrugged and then started moving forward.

"What?" asked Brandon. "Didn't you call my name? Several times?"

Jereco shook his head.

Brandon stood there for a second.

"Where is Koa?" asked Jereco.

"Shhhhh!" said Brandon. Jereco was about to say something when Brandon put his finger to his lips. Brandon looked above them. "Willow? Willow, did you call for me?"

The wind picked up again. Branches swayed slightly, and a quiet, but strong female voice said, "Brandon."

Brandon looked at Jereco. "Did you hear that?"

Jereco nodded his head.

113

Book One: The Chosen Ones

"That is what I heard," said Brandon, "and the voice brought me here."

Jereco got excited. "That means it did work. I was talking to Willow, trying to get her to communicate. She did, but to you. Ask her another question, Brandon."

Brandon looked up. He wasn't sure why he felt a need to look up when Willow was really all around them; but nevertheless he looked up when he spoke "Willow, can you hear me?"

"Yes," said the hushed, but strong voice again.

"She has a pretty, musical voice." whispered Jereco.

Brandon looked up again. "Can you hear Jereco?"

"Yes," said the voice.

Jereco looked pleased but then wondered why she didn't talk to him earlier. He had Brandon ask her that question.

The wind stirred and branches blew. She said, "Brandon is the Forest Friend."

The boys looked at each other, confused. In fact, Jereco was a little offended. "But I can be your friend too," said Jereco.

"Yes, not your time. Brandon's time. Brandon is the *Forest Friend*." This time, the voice was loud enough to shake the large overgrown branch they stood on.

Both boys had to grasp other tree limbs to keep their balance.

Jereco shook his head. "I don't get it. You hunt animals with Dad back home. How can you be a Forest Friend? More like an enemy."

"Hey, don't blame me," Brandon said. "She called me the Forest Friend. Whatever that means. I don't know."

"What that means is — you Forest Friend," cracked a voice behind them. Koa was flapping in mid-air. "You talked to Willow. Quick learners. Good teacher."

"But why is he a friend, and I am not?" asked Jereco.

Koa landed on a branch. "You are Willow's friend, Jereco. Brandon is the Forest Friend. Old legend."

Both boys just looked confused.

Koa blew out a loud whistle. "Hachmoni not told you about your Trahe names?"

The boys shook their heads.

Koa started to whistle a happy tune and bounced back and forth as birds sometimes do. "I am the teacher. I am the teacher."

The boys waited for Koa to settle down.

He ruffled his feathers. "Now where were we?"

Jereco rolled his eyes. "You were about to explain to me why Brandon is a friend to the forest, and I am not."

Koa bobbed his head back and forth. "No, no, you have it wrong." He let out a low whistle. The branches shook, and the wind blew again.

Jereco and Brandon lifted their heads but heard nothing.

The Trahe Chronicles

Koa took on a calmer, stronger voice as if Willow was speaking through him. "It is foretold by old Trahe legends that the prophets and saviors of our world will come from another world. Throughout the spoken legends and written languages, they would be of the long lost Evadeam tribe. They have special powers that would help defeat the Madeave and their enemies. Each of them had been given a Trahe name. Forest Friend was one of them. Do you know what this means?" asked Koa.

The boys shrugged their shoulders.

Koa got excited, ruffling his feathers. "You are the Evadeam prophets as legends foretold. I knew it. I saw big shiny bird fly out of the air and land in the jungle. Cleo said so. But others doubted. Did not believe that Evadeam children could bring peace. Yes, much doubt. Much doubt. But now — Willow has confirmed."

Koa looked at Brandon and continued. "No doubt. Legends are true. Faith. Believe. For you have been named the Forest Friend."

Book One: The Chosen Ones

The Green Mark

"Do not worry, Jereco," purred a voice behind Koa. "You will be named when the time comes." Cleo had snuck up behind Koa, scaring him. Feathers flew everywhere as Koa flew into the tree limbs above.

Koa came back down, wings flapping. "You scared me! Please do not sneak."

"I did not sneak up on you," said Cleo. "You were just so busy teaching that you did not hear me."

Koa landed on a tree limb, looking a little bit upset. He ruffled his feathers and said something in his native bird language to Cleo. Cleo just shrugged it off and meowed.

"So you are the Forest Friend," said Cleo to Brandon.

Brandon shrugged. "I guess." He was a little embarrassed about the whole thing and felt bad for Jereco.

Cleo narrowed her eyes and turned to Jereco. "Each of you has been given a name by our Creator. In time, your name will be revealed to you. No name is greater than another, and the roles that go with the names are also equally important. You are all friends of the forest. If you were not, you would not be able to hear Willow at all."

Jereco said nothing as he shuffled his feet back and forth. He decided to add mind reader to Cleo's imaginary list of powers. A willow branch softly brushed against Jereco's face. "Another mind reader." He scowled.

The wind picked up, more branches stirred, and Willow spoke. "The Forest Friend and the Vision Keeper have been revealed. The others will be revealed in time. The enemy stirs. Lessons have begun with Willow. Lessons must continue with Hachmoni."

The wind died down, and the branches went still once again.

Brandon and Jereco looked at Cleo.

Knowing what was on their minds, she said, "I believe it is time to start school."

"School!" both boys said in unison.

Cleo smiled, purred, and swished her tail. "Yes, school. But enough lessons for today." She began to walk away. "Come. It is late. Time to get back for dinner."

Food. Jereco had forgotten how hungry he was. He grabbed his stomach, which had been growling fiercely. As they walked back down to the center of the tree city, Jereco started putting his thoughts together. He was remembering the things he read in the old Trahe books back home and on their spaceship. He couldn't remember any certain Trahe names of the prophets in the book. *Besides,* Jeremy thought, *does it really matter? They're just names. And who is the Vision Keeper?*

Jereco stopped in his tracks. *Diana! Of course! Diana, who has sign dreams, is the Vision Keeper.* So maybe the names did mean something after all. That

The Trahe Chronicles

made sense. Even though Brandon hunted deer and turkey back home, he was kind of a woodsman taking after Grandpa and his uncles. So maybe that was why he was the Forest Friend.

So what am I good at? thought Jereco. He kept this thought in the back of his mind as the night wore on.

Word got around that Brandon and Jereco had talked to Willow. It was a good excuse to turn the dinner into a feast. There was much storytelling, eating, and laughing. Cleo also relayed the message from Willow about the lessons from Hachmoni. Hachmoni nodded his head in agreement. The kids soon discovered that they would be starting school the following day. It would be a different kind of school than what they were used to. While confined inside the stronghold of Willow, the boys would be taught a variety of lessons recommended by Willow.

Hachmoni would teach them a more in-depth history of the legends of Trahe. This excited Jereco because he hoped his new name would be revealed. Archelaus and Sir Bolivar were going to train them on fighting and protecting themselves. Midnight was going to teach them how to read the stars and ride flying horses a little better. Cheyenne and some of his pack were going to teach them how to hunt for food for themselves in the wild. Bathsheba and some of the women were going to teach them how to prepare and cook food, along with other housekeeping survival skills. Then there was Silver Kat and Skylar — who had arrived safely at the stronghold — they would help in all the categories, in addition to teaching a spiritual class.

And so their lessons began.

"Why do we need to leave Willow?" asked Brandon, during one of the lessons. "I like it here. It is safe."

"Yeah, why do we need to leave?" asked the other Evadeam children.

"It is written in the stars," answered Midnight. "The stars forecast the return of the Evadeam tribe. Back to where it all began. Back to the home of the ancestors."

"Yes, it was foretold in my dreams," Silver Kat agreed. "The Evadeam prophets are to journey to the old civilization and bring peace. Then, you will be able to return to your homeland."

Grandpa had walked up behind them. "Besides, we can't find your parents in the confinements of Willow."

The kids looked at each other. Their parents. Home. They suddenly felt guilty about not wanting to leave Willow. They need to search for their missing parents.

"How could we have forgotten about searching for our parents?" Brooke shook her head. "From now on, we must never forget why we came here. Each and every day, we must talk about them, so we don't forget."

"We could tell stories about them at bedtime," suggested Diana.

They thought this was a good idea. And from that night forward, they told stories and shared memories about their parents. It became easier when

Book One: The Chosen Ones

Diana offered her family picture as a focal point. Their families, their friends, and their home had seemed so far away. Their memories seemed almost like a distant dream, but soon their memories became more vivid. And they became more determined to learn their lessons.

"Where actually is this place that we are supposed to go?" asked Brooke, during one of their lessons that was taken place in a small tree house.

Like the others, Brooke was now anxious to start searching for their parents, even though she was not fond of the idea of moving again. They had just gotten comfortable in their new home. She was tired of traveling, packing, and unpacking in another strange place.

"I see in my dreams that we should go to a place in the mountains," replied Silver Kat. "Is that it?" asked Brooke.

When Silver Kat did not understand what Brooke meant by that question, she explained. "Don't you, like, have an address or something?"

"Address?" asked Silver Kat.

"She means something more specific," said Jereco. "Do you know how to get to this place?"

Silver Kat shook his head. "I know of only two who are still alive and have been to the ancient grounds of the Evadeam."

"And who are they?" asked Jereco.

A low voice said, "I would be one." Skylar had just walked into the classroom. "But I am not the only one who has been there and is still alive. There are more than you realize," she said to Silver Kat.

"Who else has been there?" asked Brandon, now curious about this ancient place that had only been seen by Skylar, the white tiger.

"A very wise ancient man," she said in her low tiger voice.

"Ancient? Speak for yourself," said Hachmoni as he walked into the classroom.

Jereco looked at Hachmoni closely. "Are you the one who has been to this ancient mountain?"

"Yes, I have," said Hachmoni, "but that was not so long ago. I think ancient is not the right word."

"I do agree with you, Hachmoni," said Silver Kat. "Ancient is thousands of years old, not hundreds of years."

"A hundred years!" shouted Brandon. "Just how old are you anyway, Hachmoni?"

"Didn't your mom tell you that it is not polite to ask someone his age?" said Hachmoni.

"Only women, but not men," replied Brandon.

Brooke smiled. "It applies to anyone who is really, really old, Brandon."

Hachmoni gave Brooke a disapproving smile, and she burst out laughing. Silver Kat also could no longer contain his laughter, but the younger kids just looked at Hachmoni with disbelief.

Diana stood up and put a hand on Hachmoni's arm. "It is okay. Besides,

118

The Trahe Chronicles

you look really good for your age."

Hachmoni saw the seriousness on the young child's face. "Well, thank you, Diana." He smiled down at her.

"So how old are you anyway?" persisted Brandon.

Hachmoni looked at Brandon. "Old enough."

"Well, how old is that?" he insisted. "Are you talking one hundred years old, two hundred, five hundred?!"

Brooke shook her head. "Brandon, give it up. He isn't telling."

Brandon gave Skylar a questioning look. Skylar, who was now lying down licking her paws and enjoying the teasing of the ancient man, lifted her paw and replied, "Age is just a moment of time. A number. It is the experience that you will appreciate."

Brandon's eyebrows came together. He didn't like this answer.

Skylar looked over at Hachmoni and said, "Let's just say that he was very old when I was just a young cub myself."

Hachmoni harrumphed. "Enough of this talk. We have lessons to continue." And so the next class session began.

It was decided to start out their mornings by having spiritual classes after breakfast. Hachmoni and Skylar's Trahe history lessons would follow Silver Kat's lessons. After that, they would go down to a clearing where they were taught self-defense. Silver Kat and Hachmoni taught techniques similar to what the kids would consider martial arts back on Earth. Even Archelaus found these lessons helpful and decided to become a student. Afterward, they would break for lunch before moving onto sword fighting, knife throwing, and archery taught by Archelaus, Silver Kat, and some other men from the village.

They also practiced hunting. However, this was done on fake animals because all those living in Willow were talking animals. Because of the Trahe nature law, they could not be hunted.

"So what is the point of hunting again?" grumbled Brandon.

Patiently, Sir Bolivar explained again. "Once we leave Willow and go beyond our home boundaries, we may need to hunt for food."

"But how are we supposed to know which animals we can hunt?" complained Brandon. Sir Bolivar sighed. This same discussion had come up several times during their lessons.

"You know how, Brandon," said the frustrated Sir Bolivar.

"Oh yeah. We are supposed to say, 'Hey, Mr. Deer, can you speak the universal language because if you can't, I am going to shoot you now and eat you!' That is dumb!" exclaimed Brandon.

In all honesty, the rest of the kids thought it was dumb too. But they didn't bring it up because the rest of the Trahe creatures seemed to think this was a natural thing. They just went on with their lessons thinking they would never use this skill. If anything, it was good archery practice.

And so the lessons continued. They would pick and find food to cook for

119

Book One: The Chosen Ones

dinner while the women would teach them how to prepare it. Most of the food was similar to those on Earth like berries, vegetables, and bread. However, there was nothing close to a pizza or a juicy hamburger, which the kids craved one day.

While they sat around eating dinner, Brandon explained fast food to everyone. Silver Kat thought this type of food sounded unnatural and not at all pleasing. However, Archelaus thought it was interesting. So the conversation slowly turned to the differences and similarities of the two worlds.

The conversion did cause the children to start thinking about their home planet and of their home. They became more sad and quiet — lost in their own thoughts.

Jereco remembered the dinners they had back home. They all ate at the dinner table. Mom and Dad were always interested in learning about how their day at school had gone. Then, as if Grandpa was reading Jereco's mind, Grandpa asked how the kids' classes had gone that day.

Usually, Grandpa did not join the kids in the daily lessons. At first, he claimed he did not need them and said he had other important things to do. However, one day Jereco had forgotten his knife and sheath for his lessons and had to go back to their tree house; he saw Grandpa taking lessons with Hachmoni and Skylar in the classroom. He quietly concluded that for whatever reason Grandpa wanted to take his classes separately. Maybe he was far more advanced than they were with the history and spiritual lessons and not as far advanced in the physical classes. After all, he was Grandpa. Jereco had mentioned this to the rest of the kids, and from then on, they never questioned where Grandpa was when they were having their lessons.

One morning, while in their spiritual class with Silver Kat, Diana confessed she felt bad about not praying to God or going to church, so that became their discussion for the day. After speaking with Silver Kat, they realized that the Creator of Trahe was very similar to their own god. They wondered if the Creator and God were the same being as Cleo had indicated before they took this journey to Trahe.

They also discovered that Silver Kat's tribe has similar worship services to that of the Earth church. Silver Kat clarified that when he was away from his tribe, he worshiped by himself. There was no need for a church. In fact, Silver Kat goes down to the small lake every day after lessons and does his own prayer ritual. He thanked their Creator for many things and asked for his guidance. The Creator's guidance often came into his dreams, just like Diana's dreams. Silver Kat offered to have the kids come with him to the lake that day, and he said he would talk to Bathsheba about them skipping their cooking class.

As it turned out, the cooking class was making a dish that they had already prepared, so she agreed that the children could go with Silver Kat. Bathsheba

The Trahe Chronicles

and Silver Kat thought it would be good for the children to become closer to the Creator on a more regular basis. So the children went down to the lake with Silver Kat every other day for some individual prayer, meditating, or whatever kind of worship they desired.

Of course, the children did not feel as comfortable or as disciplined as Silver Kat to do their own silent prayers, so Hachmoni joined them and started group worship. Brandon and Diana's attention span were not last as long as the others, so they were allowed to do a little swimming afterward. It was time for the children to have some fun back in their lives. As the kids swam, Silver Kat and Hachmoni sat cross-legged on the bank and continued their silent prayers to the Creator.

Brandon noticed that Silver Kat always kept his eyes closed, but Hachmoni always seem to have at least one eye open. Hachmoni said he was keeping an eye on him.

Eventually, as the days went by, Skylar and Archelaus also joined the early evening worship and swim event. Jereco teased Brooke that Archelaus only came down to see her swim. After all, women on Trahe did not swim in cut-off pants.

Brooke just shook her head.

Hachmoni suggested that Brooke put something more appropriate on.

Brooke placed her hands on her hips. "If you think for one moment that I am going to put on more clothes while I swim, you are crazy." She gestured at her hacked tee shirt and shorts. "This isn't revealing where I come from."

Hachmoni continued to argue and Brooke just shook her head, calling him an old-fashioned ancient man. Silver Kat laughed and assured Archelaus and Hachmoni that even women of his tribe swam in clothing no more revealing than what Brooke had on; it was perfectly acceptable. Brooke smiled at Silver Kat, thanked him, and dove in the water.

Jereco laughed and said to Silver Kat, "I think you just enjoy seeing Archelaus flustered over my cousin."

Silver Kat laughed and shook his head, but Jereco could tell by the expression on Silver Kat's face that Jereco was right.

Jereco was still laughing when he went in the water himself. All the children were great swimmers and often swam at a lake on Earth. Swimming in this small lagoon was just as enjoyable.

Brooke was on the swim team at high school and tried to talk Jereco into joining, but Jereco preferred to use his time on academic classes. Brooke couldn't understand why he didn't want to take a fun, easy class like swimming. Jereco had to remind her that he wanted to go to college and needed to keep his grades up. Back home on Earth, Brooke was always trying to get Jereco away from the computer and the books to have some more fun.

If my parents could see me now, he thought. There was no laptop, computer, or books here. Even their classes were all verbal teachings as Willow did not have any books in her city. Jereco thought that was sad. When the villagers

121

Book One: The Chosen Ones

packed up their stuff, no one packed any books. Their history lessons had all been done by Hachmoni and Skylar from memory. When Jereco mentioned this to Hachmoni, Jereco said that he intended to collect more books and one day bring them back to Willow. The children of Mangus should have them.

As Jereco was thinking all these thoughts, he swam farther away from the group. When he looked over to the banks and realized how far he had swum toward the other end of the lake, he decided he should head back. He was stopped by a sound.

It was an odd noise. He paused and listened. It sounded musical. Like a musical instrument. "Hey, who is there?" he called. No one answered. The noise had stopped. He looked back toward the bank to see if the others had noticed anything. No, they were all carrying on. They hadn't even noticed how far out Jereco had swum.

Jereco shook his head and decided he had better head back when he heard the sound again. "Koa? Is that you?" Again, no response. He listened intently, but he didn't hear the musical sound anymore. He decided whoever it was had left or was playing games with him. He started to swim back to the bank.

As he swam under the water, he noticed all of the fish. Then he heard the sound again, but it was much clearer. It definitely was a musical tone of some kind. In fact, he swore he had heard something like that before. He came up for a breath of air and dove back down into the water. This time he turned away from the bank, toward the noise. Not only did he hear it, but something very large was swimming in the shadows. He couldn't make it out. A large fish? Not an alligator. It had fins. He came up, took another breath, and went back down. This time there seemed to be more of the large creatures. They were dark shadows below and upstream from the lake. Must be large fish. The sound now came to him again. It was very similar to those of whales that he had heard about on their family trip to the Hawaiian Islands on Earth.

He came back up, took a breath, and waved over to Brooke and Brandon. "Hey, there are really large fish over here. They sound like whales."

"What?" Brooke said. "I can't hear you?"

Jereco waved her over. "Whales!"

"Agggh!" Jereco screamed as something tugged on his leg. It took all his strength to break free. He took gasps of air and started to swim toward Brooke, but something grabbed his leg again and pulled him down. This time, he went under the water.

Brooke saw Jereco being pulled underwater. She yelled back to Brandon, "Get Diana out of the water."

Brooke dove into the water after Jereco. Archelaus, who was nearby, also yelled to Silver Kat and Hachmoni. "Get Brandon and Diana out of the water." Archelaus then dove into the water after Brooke.

Meanwhile, Jereco decided to face his attacker and gulped in water while doing so. He was surprised when he found himself staring into a face of a

122

The Trahe Chronicles

woman. She had flowing hair, yet she didn't look like a woman he had seen before.

The attacker released Jereco and pushed him up toward the surface. Jereco gasped for breath and coughed up the water. Brooke and Archelaus hadn't reached him yet. The waters were turning rough, making it difficult to swim toward him.

Jereco looked back in the direction of the attacker. *What was that?* he thought. Now angry and curious, he dove back in and searched for the woman. But all he saw were large figures swimming away. He looked hard and saw long wavy hair, arms maybe, and a fin.

Mermaids? he wondered. The musical sound started again. He stayed underwater, just looking and listening. Just when the last figure was about to swim away into the depths of the water, it looked back. Jereco saw her green, bright eyes. *Snake!* The eyes looked like the snake eyes from the jungle. Panic overcame him, and he swam up. He bumped right into Brooke.

He gasped for air and coughed up water, trying to talk at the same time. "Snake, woman," sputtered Jereco.

"Jereco, be quiet," said Brooke. "You have to catch your breath. I got you."

Archelaus had now caught up to them.

"Can you see what is down there?" Brooke asked Archelaus.

Archelaus dove into the water.

Meanwhile, Brooke held Jereco from behind in a rescue hold. She tried to calm him down.

Archelaus popped back up. "Nothing," he said.

"Down deeper into the dark, upstream," coughed Jereco.

Archelaus dove back down and came up a few minutes later. "Nothing. Whatever it was is gone."

"Then let's get out of here before it decides to return," ordered Brooke.

Archelaus nodded.

"Can you swim, Jereco?" Brooke asked.

Jereco nodded and headed toward the bank, with Brooke and Archelaus following.

As they climbed up the bank, Brandon came running toward them. "Did you see that?" he shouted. "Did you see that?"

"You saw them too?" asked Jereco.

"Them? What them? I am talking about the waves. The stream turned into stormy waters just like that." Brandon snapped his fingers to make his point.

Brooke was now sitting down on the bank, catching her breath. "Yeah, that is what took us so long to get to Jereco."

Diana handed them towels. "Are you okay, Jereco?" She was concerned about her big brother. She was so scared when she saw him get pulled underwater.

123

Book One: The Chosen Ones

Silver Kat and Hachmoni were kneeling beside him. They were looking him over and asked if he was okay. Jereco kept nodding and didn't say anything; he was catching his breath and trying to figure out what had just happened to him.

It was Hachmoni who snapped him out of his thoughts. "Jereco, Jereco, who grabbed you under the water?"

The question of *who* caught Jereco's attention. "Did you see her, Hachmoni?" he asked.

"*Her?*" asked Silver Kat.

Jereco looked from Silver Kat to Hachmoni, not sure how he should answer. He thought it was a she, but then the eyes told him it was a snake.

"Jereco, where were you grabbed?" asked Hachmoni.

Jereco pointed to his ankle. "Wait, what the —"

Wrapped around his ankle was a green mark. It almost looked like seaweed, yet it seemed to be embedded in his skin. He rubbed his skin and couldn't get it off. "Get it off. What is it? Get it off, Hachmoni!"

"Hold still, Jereco," ordered Hachmoni. "I want to take a look at it." Hachmoni studied it closely. Silver Kat bent down and also looked at it. Soon the entire group had crowded around Jereco to look at this green ring of seaweed wrapped around his ankle.

Jereco couldn't even see the ankle anymore with all everybody in the way. "Are you getting it off, Hachmoni?"

Diana's head popped up. "Are you feeling okay, Jereco?"

"Yes, why?" he asked in a panicked voice. "Don't I look okay? What is wrong with my leg?"

Brandon popped up. "Nothing if you like having seaweed for an ankle bracelet."

That did it. "Everyone, get off of me!" He pulled himself up. He looked down at the green ring, or bracelet, as Brandon had called it.

Jereco pointed at his ankle. "Why didn't you get this off?" he asked Hachmoni.

Hachmoni shrugged, stood up, and leaned against his cane. "It is not for me to remove."

Jereco looked at him, bewildered. "What?! Stop talking in riddles. What is this thing? Get it off me!"

"Is it hurting you?" Hachmoni asked.

Jereco shook his head. "That is beside the point. I don't want a piece of seaweed stuck to my skin." He tried to tug it off himself, but it was like it had become embedded into his skin. "I have to cut it off."

"*No!*" Hachmoni and Silver Kat said.

Archelaus finally stepped in. "As leader of the Evadeam tribe, I demand to know what this thing is wrapped around Jereco and how we can remove it."

Hachmoni's eyebrow popped up. Ever since Archelaus found out that

124

The Trahe Chronicles

Hachmoni knew his siblings were alive, he had not been friendly to Hachmoni. "Well," explained Hachmoni, "I believe that this is the sign of the water people."

Everyone looked at him in silence.

Brandon, who spoke his mind often, asked, "Water people?"

"Water people are legends," said Archelaus. "It is said that they live in the waters of Trahe. However, no one whom I know has ever seen them, so they are just legends." Archelaus turned toward Hachmoni. "Or am I mistaken?"

"Mermaids!" yelled Diana. She ran toward the water, turned back toward them, and clasped her hands. "Mermaids! Make them come back, Jereco. I always wanted to see a mermaid."

"But they are not real," said Brooke.

Jereco thought for a minute and finally spoke. "I could be wrong. For a moment, I thought I saw green eyes. Green eyes like the jungle snake."

"Snake!" Diana ran away from the water and crouched behind Skylar.

Silver Kat spoke up and pointed at Jereco's ankle. "No, this is no marking of a snake. If it was a great snake of the jungle, Jereco would not be with us now."

Hachmoni nodded in agreement, and relief washed over the group.

"Silver Kat is right," said Hachmoni. He turned toward Archelaus. "And so are you, partly. Water people are legends, and true legends they are. And they are not seen often, except on rare occasions. In fact …" He rubbed his chin, thoughtfully. "… they usually do not come in from the great seas. Never this far inland. Especially in freshwater."

"Yes, that concerns me too," said Silver Kat. "So how and *why* did they come in this far?"

Silver Kat and Hachmoni lowered their voices and turned to look at the stream and lake. They discussed how the water people could have come to Willow in freshwater so far away from the sea.

Jereco, who was looking back and forth between the two, finally said, "Excuse me, excuse me. *Excuse me!*" All faces turned toward him. He pointed at his ankle. "Hello, people! What do I do about this green thing on me?"

Hachmoni waved Jereco's words away. "Oh, that won't hurt you. It is of no concern."

Jereco's mouth dropped, and he was about to speak again when Brooke stepped in. "Excuse me!" Brooke said. "But my cousin has a foreign object on his ankle. So either do something about it, or at the very least, tell us what it is. Will it go away? Can we fix it? Are you sure it won't harm him?" She lowered her voice with the last question.

The great white tiger Skylar, who had been lying in the grass observing and listening, finally got up and walked over to Jereco. "Forgive the ancient one, Jereco. He sometimes forgets that you are neither of this world, nor as old as he; thus you do not have as much knowledge of our world or of our legends and stories. He often forgets to take other's feelings into

Book One: The Chosen Ones

consideration."

"Feelings?" said Hachmoni, "Feelings from an overgrown cat who spends most of her time, lying around, eating, and bathing?"

"Enough already," ordered a different voice among the crowd.

All heads turned to see Cleo standing there. "Jereco sit."

Jereco did as Cleo asked.

She went over to Jereco's ankle. She pawed it, sniffed it, and licked it. Then she jumped on Skylar's back. Standing on all her four paws, she had everyone's attention.

"It has begun," she said.

No one said a word. The kids didn't know what to make of it. Hachmoni and Silver Kat looked in deep thought. It was Archelaus who asked the question, "What has begun?"

Cleo nodded. "First, the Vision Keeper." She pointed a paw at Diana. "Then the Forest Friend." She pointed at Brandon. "And now, the Water Guardian." She nodded at Jereco.

The Water Guardian. It slowly sank into Jereco's thoughts. It was the name that he was seeking. But a green mark wrapped around his ankle was not what he desired. He pointed to his ankle. "What about this?"

Cleo jumped down and sat next to Jereco. "It is the mark—the mark of the water people. It will not harm you. It will help protect you. It is a great honor to have a mark from such worthy people, who are not seen by many in their lifetime."

So Jereco was right. He did see a woman fish. "A mermaid," he whispered.

Diana squealed with delight. "Mermaids! Oh, Jereco, how exciting. You saw mermaids. Can you call them? Can they come back? I want to see them."

Silver Kat shook his head. "No, little one. It does not work that way. They will come to him when needed, like they did here."

"Which brings us to the question," said Hachmoni, "why did they come here, and how did they get this far? I thought they could only swim in salt water?"

"We do know one thing for sure," growled Skylar. "They came here, sought Jereco out, and marked him; Cleo is right. It has begun."

"What?" asked Jereco. "What has begun?"

"The prophecy is coming true," replied Hachmoni. "We are that much closer to bringing peace to our world."

"Can we discuss bringing peace to your world tomorrow?" asked a tired Jereco.

It was agreed they should head back to their houses to clean up, put on some dry clothes, and eat supper. After a good night's rest, they would discuss what this all meant.

As they started to head back, Jereco hung back and looked at the waters one more time. *Why me?* he thought. *The Water Guardian.* Brooke was a much

126

The Trahe Chronicles

better swimmer than he was. It didn't make sense to him. He wasn't as overjoyed as he thought he would be. He sighed and turned to walk away. Then he heard the musical sound again.

This time, he was standing on land and not in the water. He listened intently. Yes, he could still hear it. He closed his eyes. It sounded so much like the sound of whales. Musical. Relaxing. Then very faintly, he swore he could hear "*Jereco.*"

He opened his eyes and looked around. There was Brandon still standing at the bank while the rest had walked on. "Did you call my name?" Jereco asked.

Brandon shook his head.

"Did you hear that music?" Jereco asked.

Brandon shook his head again and walked down to Jereco. Given the experience Brandon had with Willow—a talking tree—he didn't argue with Jereco about the existence of the sound. In fact, Brandon persuaded him to listen again.

Jereco nodded, closed his eyes, and heard the music again. Once again, he heard his name as if they were calling him.

He opened his eyes. "There, there! Did you hear that?"

"No, but I think Willow did." Brandon pointed up at the tree's branches. Sure enough, with no wind in the air, the branches were swaying, making a rustling noise as they moved.

"What is she saying?" asked Jereco.

"I don't know," replied Brandon. "She is speaking a language I don't recognize."

"Maybe she is talking to the water people," suggested Jereco. Both boys continued to listen. Jereco listened to the water people's musical voices while Brandon tried to make out Willow's conversation.

"I hear them, Jereco," said Brandon. "I hear the sound. It sounds familiar."

"Yeah," said Jereco, "it sounds like the whales we heard on our Hawaiian trip." Brandon got excited. "You are right. It does. Wow. Do you think we do have or did have mermaids back home on Earth? These water people sound so much like our own whales."

"I don't know. Maybe," replied Jereco. They both stood there, listening to the conversation between the land trees and the water people. Eventually, the music of the water people faded away, and the tree branches stopped.

The boys looked at each other and started up the bank. They walked in deep silence until Brandon suddenly stopped. "Hey, what was I thinking?" He looked at Jereco. "I wasn't." Brandon looked up as he always did when speaking to Willow. "Willow, can you tell us what you said to the Water People, or if there is anything we need to know?"

A soft voice came down from the tree branches. "The Water Guardian of the water people has been found. He has been chosen. His time will come.

Book One: The Chosen Ones

Now you must prepare to leave. The enemy approaches, and it is time to fulfill part of the prophecy."

Jereco and Brandon looked at each other. They did not like that news. *Leave?* They didn't want to leave. They both sank down to the ground and leaned against Willow's trunk. It was all too much to bear right now. But they knew not to question Willow, so they just sat there, overwhelmed.

The Trahe Chronicles

A Storm Is Brewing

During dinner that evening, the boys revealed what they heard between the water people and Willow. Brandon repeated what Willow had said, "The Water Guardian of the water people has been found. He has been chosen. His time will come. Now you must prepare to leave. The enemy approaches, and it is time to fulfill part of the prophecy."

"Leave? Leave again?" Diana shook her head. "But we just got here."

Brandon turned to the elders. "I don't want to leave. I like it here." But he could tell by the look on their faces that they were going to listen to Willow. Brandon shook his head. "I don't want to leave Willow."

"Our parents are not here. We must continue the search for them." reminded Jereco.

Brooke agreed, "Jereco is right. I love being here. It feels secure under Willow's branches, but we have to find our parents."

"I think this is enough talking for tonight," said Bathsheba. "We are all tired and hungry. Besides, Willow did not say when you had to leave. It could be next month. Now everyone eat their supper."

Bathsheba had become like a mom to the kids, and they listened to her. They picked at their food as they slowly ate in silence. Brandon had lost his appetite, but he knew from his lessons that he must eat to keep up his strength. After he finished eating, he excused himself and wandered to his favorite resting place.

It was a spot way up in the tree where he could talk to Willow alone. He sat there in silence for a long time until a willow branch came up and brushed his cheek.

"What is wrong, Forest Friend?" asked Willow's hushed voice.

Brandon just shrugged and picked up an old piece of bark.

"I think my Forest Friend will miss me when he is gone," continued Willow. "You are a good friend, and your heart is where it needs to be for your journey to continue."

"Continue?" huffed Brandon. "I don't want to continue. Why can't Hachmoni and Archelaus search for our parents? I am tired of moving around. I like it here."

"And you will miss me," stated Willow.

Brandon noticed it was not a question. He leaned his head against the tree trunk and sighed. "Yes, I will miss you." A tear flowed down his cheek. One of Willow's branches wiped the tear away. Then other branches cradled Brandon like she was holding a child. More tears came, and Brandon just sat there in silence, crying. He was going to miss Willow, and he was tired of missing people. He missed his mom and dad. He missed his friends back on Earth. He even missed the farm animals. He missed home.

Willow was feeling more like home, and now he had to leave. He was tired. He was tired of missing people and places. He was tired of moving

129

Book One: The Chosen Ones

around. He thought he would like this adventure — rescuing his parents. He thought it would be simpler. Who would pass up the opportunity to journey to a different planet, a different world. Traveling and seeing places, things, and creatures he only imagined or read about back home. This was a chance of a lifetime. Wasn't it?

He felt Willow's branches brush against him. He sighed and leaned into her. "I do not want to leave," he whispered. He felt many branches envelope him, and then he was slowly being rocked to sleep. At least he thought he was asleep, but he could hear Willow speaking to him in a low, hushed voice. It reminded Brandon of the sound of rustling leaves back home—when leaves start dropping in autumn. The sound when there is a slight summer breeze blowing through the trees. Or the sound when a rainy storm blows the tree branches into the air.

"Forest Friend, we are friends, and you are a Chosen One. You have learned to respect and love me as I respect and love you. I shall not forget you, and you shall not forget me. Most importantly, I will always be there. I will always be in your heart and your spirit. The wind and the Trahe energy will take my spirit to you, for I will always be with you. We are one under this universe. Under your universe. There will be no need to miss me because I will always be there. Listen. Listen, Forest Friend, for me. Listen, Forest Friend, to me. And I will guide you to your destiny. Now listen and sleep."

Brandon did sleep. He slept well. When the morning came, his eyes popped open, and he knew what had to be done. It was time to get up and prepare.

Brandon felt fresh, but he didn't smell fresh. So he decided to take a bath before breakfast. Afterward, he took his time, walking back to the tree house he called home. He was deep in thought when he noticed a slight movement. He caught it out of the corner of his eye. His senses became more alert. He heard the slight rustle of Willow's branches. He slightly smiled, knowing she was with him.

A chilly sensation ran up the back of his neck. It was a warning. Instinct took over. He quickly jumped toward a tree vine, pushing away with all his might. He swung around to face his assailant with his knife in hand.

His aggressor was also quick. He was only inches away from Brandon.

Brandon thought, *Willow, up! Please! Now!*

The branch he was hanging onto pulled him up, out of the attacker's reach. Brandon flung himself onto a higher branch.

"*Grrrrrrrr!*" growled the white tiger. "I believe that is cheating!"

"No, I call it improvising," said Brandon. "And enough already. I just bathed."

"Oh, is that what I smell?" exclaimed Skylar as she walked next to Brandon. Her big paws rested on Willow's branches.

"Funny, at least I don't smell like a wet cat or a dead animal," said Brandon as he kept walking away from Skylar.

The Trahe Chronicles

"Mmmm … dead animal," said Skylar. "Fresh kill. You are making me hungry, Forest Friend."

Brandon rolled his eyes and kept walking.

Skylar paused to smell the air. "We both will smell like wet creatures if we don't hurry to cover soon."

Brandon stopped and looked back at Skylar. Brandon noticed how dark it had become. *It shouldn't be this dark in the morning,* he thought. His eyebrows came together, and he looked at Skylar.

As if reading his thoughts, Skylar said, "A storm is coming." She jumped over Brandon and starting running down the branches.

"Willow?" whispered Brandon.

"Go. Warn the others," the huge tree replied. "I need all my strength to protect the stronghold."

Willow worried Brandon. He followed the same path that Skylar had just traveled. He caught up with Skylar, who had stopped again. She let out the loudest roar Brandon had ever heard, and then she turned to Brandon. "Hop on. It will be faster."

Brandon shook his head. "I am too heavy."

Skylar gave him an *are-you-serious?* look.

Brandon did a mental evaluation. Skylar was very similar to an Amur tiger on Earth. Amur tigers were very large. On Trahe, they were even larger. He guessed she weighed over six pounds and was over eleven feet long.

"Get on," Skylar said.

Skylar lowered herself down, and Brandon had to pull himself up by gripping her fur. "Sorry," he mumbled as he pulled himself up onto her back.

Skylar didn't answer and plunged forward. Brandon was holding on for dear life. *Boy, Skylar is fast,* he thought. It was a fast and rough ride down Willow's thick branches. Soon, they were at the center of the stronghold.

By the looks of it, they were not the only ones who had noticed the storm. The crowd was large and included the elders, Archelaus, Hachmoni, Sir Bolivar, Brooke, and Jereco. Silver Kat was running from the front of the stronghold.

When Skylar, Brandon, and Silver Kat arrived at the center of the tree city, the crowd became quiet. "A storm is coming," said Skylar.

"We should speak to Willow and see how bad it is." said Archelaus.

Brandon slid off Skylar. "I already have. She said that she can't talk to us now because she needs all her strength to protect the stronghold."

"That is not a good sign," replied Sir Bolivar.

"I don't get it," said Brooke. "What is the big deal? Don't you get storms here? Rain?"

"Yes, we do," answered Hachmoni. "In fact, we've had some rain and thunderstorms since we have been here. You just did not notice because Willow has protected us. She is capable of letting in water only to the stream and lake." He looked up. "But this is different."

131

Book One: The Chosen Ones

"And we will have company," said Silver Kat. "Some of the forest creatures are coming in to seek shelter." He pointed toward the front of the stronghold. Breaking in through the branches were animals of all kinds. There were alligators, crocodiles, deer, panthers, birds, and even some otters.

Sir Bolivar turned to Brooke. "Let Bathsheba know that we may have company." Then he turned to Silver Kat and Archelaus. "Get some groups together and tie down anything that the winds might pick up. Hachmoni, let's meet our friends and see where we are going to put everyone."

"Hachmoni, can I come with you?" Brandon asked.

Hachmoni put his hand on Brandon's shoulder. "Yes, you are the Forest Friend. Come." So Brandon went off to help welcome the new friends to the stronghold while Jereco helped Archelaus and Silver Kat.

Everyone was busy doing something to prepare for the storm. All the women were securing things in their homes. Diana and Brooke were helping Bathsheba tie down items in their tree house.

"How bad can this storm be?" Brooke asked Bathsheba.

"Well, if Willow's roof is looking that dark, and she needs all her strength to protect us, us, then it's pretty bad." She turned back to work.

Brooke looked at Diana, wishing there was a better answer.

Diana shrugged her shoulders. "It is a Category Five hurricane."

"What?!" said Brooke. "How do you know?"

"I had a dream about it," replied Diana, "and Cleo told me so."

At that moment, Cleo jumped on the kitchen table.

"Is this true?" Brooke asked.

"Yes, the child is right," replied Cleo. "The storm is similar to what you call a hurricane back on Earth."

"A five?" Brooke insisted.

"Yes, I believe that is the number the U.S. weather system uses to classify the strongest hurricane."

Brooke's jaw dropped. She looked back and forth between Cleo and Diana. "But, you need an ocean to make a hurricane."

"We are closer to the sea than you realize, child," said Cleo. "Plus, the strength of this one will carry for many miles."

"Can Willow hold it off?" Brooke asked.

Cleo looked up as if she could see through the roof of the house. "I don't know."

That answer worried Brooke.

"Bathsheba," said Brooke, "this is bad. This is very bad. Back home, whole towns, cities, and homes are destroyed by a hurricane this big. This could cause flooding of the stream, the lake! Everyone needs to get to higher ground and be secured. I need to go warn the others." She started to rush out.

"Wait, Brooke," said Diana. "I want to come with you."

"No, you stay here," ordered Brooke. "Cleo and Bathsheba, keep Diana

132

The Trahe Chronicles

safe.""Brooke is right, Diana," agreed Cleo. "You need to stay here and help Bathsheba. Brooke will be back. They all will be back."

Diana reluctantly nodded okay and sadly watched Brooke as she left the house.

The winds had picked up, and Brooke's hair kept blowing in her face. The first person she found was Archelaus. "What are you doing outside, Brooke? You need to get back inside." He ordered.

The hurricane winds were getting stronger, so it was hard to hear and speak over the airstream. "We need to get everyone to higher ground and away from the streams," she yelled back.

"What?" said Archelaus as he tied down supplies. "I can't hear you."

Brooke moved closer to Archelaus, so they were cheek to cheek. "A hurricane is coming. A really, really bad storm that will cause high winds and flooding." She brushed her hair out of her eyes.

Archelaus was listening and looked up into Brooke's eyes. He was about to ask her what a hurricane was when a high wind blew against him. He knocked into Brooke and grabbed her by the waist to keep her from falling. When their eyes met, time stood still for a moment.

The moment passed with the sound of a low growl.

Archelaus and Brooke broke apart and found Skylar standing there. Archelaus, who knew Skylar well enough, thought he saw a smug look on Skylar's face.

Silver Kat ran up to them, yelling, "The bad storm is coming. We need to go to high ground." The wind grew stronger.

"That is what I have been trying to tell you, Archelaus," Brooke said. "We need to make sure everyone is up in the tree houses." She pointed upward. "Have the horses fly to higher ground."

Silver Kat nodded. "Skylar and I can run quickly and warn them. You find Jereco and Brandon. Get them to the tree house."

Archelaus nodded. "Jereco went down to the stream to tie down the fishing supplies." Brooke started to turn away. "I will get him, and you find Brandon."

Archelaus shook his head. "Brooke, Brandon is with Hachmoni; he will be fine. Let's stick together and get Jereco first."

Brooke agreed and followed Archelaus as he raced off toward the watering hole in the stream. The rain was pouring in now. Brooke was a pretty good athlete, but she was not used to running over slippery ground with tree roots sticking up everywhere. She kept slipping and then fell down really hard. Her right knee hit a tree root.

"Oh dag it!" she screamed.

Archelaus looked back. "Are you okay?"

Brooke rubbed her knee. "Yeah, it's just a bruise."

"Why don't you go back to the house, and I will find Jereco."

"No, I will help." She looked around at the pouring rain. "And I don't

Book One: The Chosen Ones

think we should separate."

Archelaus looked toward the center of Willow and couldn't see it. Sheets of rain blinded his vision. He could only see a few feet in front of them. "Then take my hand." He reached out for her. When she hesitated, he said, "We can move faster, and I won't lose you."

Brooked nodded and they were off again.

When they got to the stream, they didn't find Jereco or the fishing equipment.

"There!" Archelaus pointed to muddy tracks. "He is walking to the lake."

They ran forward, slipping and sliding. When they got to the lake, they still did not see Jereco. It was difficult to see anything in the storm. They yelled for Jereco at the top of their lungs.

Whoosh. Something yellow came swooping down on them.

It was Koa. "Storm coming. Storm coming. Take cover."

"Koa, where is Jereco?" yelled Archelaus.

"Up hill," squawked Koa. "Up the trees. Tying. Tying."

Brooke yelled above the winds. "He needs to come down and take cover. Go tell him, and we will wait here."

"Storm is coming. Storm is coming." Koa flew back up the way he had come.

Archelaus and Brooke stood there, waiting. They were soaking wet, and Brooke started to shiver. She wrapped her arms around herself.

"You are cold," said Archelaus. "Here, take my cloak."

"No, I will be okay," said Brooke.

"Take my cloak," Archelaus insisted. He started to put it around her. "You will catch a chill."

"What about you?"

"I will be fine."

As Archelaus wrapped the cloak around Brooke, they had a moment of eye contact. Brooke shivered. Archelaus wrapped his arms around her and slightly bent down.

Brooke peered up at Archelaus, she began to realize how close they were. A thought occurred to her. *Is he going to kiss me? Yes, I think he is going to kiss me. Should I let him? Why not? He is a good man.*

"Archelaus." she said softly. She was sure he was going to kiss her, when suddenly a huge splash came from the lake and got them even wetter.

Nothing like a big splash of cold lake water to disrupt them.

"What was that?" asked Archelaus.

They looked at the lake and saw a tail fin splash again and then dive into the depths of the lake.

"It was a mermaid, I believe," Brooke replied.

"A mermaid?"

"A water person," she explained.

"Storm is here," interrupted Koa. "Storm is here."

134

The Trahe Chronicles

Archelaus and Brooke jumped apart.

Koa seemed to ignore them and flew by.

"Koa?" said Brooke.

"Hey, is that you Brooke?" a voice boomed from uphill.

"Jereco, where have you been?" scolded Brooke.

"I was tying up the equipment to some higher ground," he responded. "This isn't just a bad thunderstorm. We have a hurricane coming."

Brooke looked confused. "How did you know that?"

"The water people told me," he said matter-of-factly. "Come on. We have to get back to the house." He started heading toward the tree houses.

Brooke could barely look at Archelaus as she thought about what had almost happened before Jereco showed up.

Archelaus motioned her to go in front of him. They followed Jereco.

As they walked back to the center of Willow, Archelaus thought about the kiss that he almost had with Brooke. What was he thinking? He cannot deny that there was something between them. He was definitely attracted to her, but she was a prophet, a legend, a woman not of this world. Nothing could happen between them. He had to be more careful.

Book One: The Chosen Ones

Nature's Fury and Friends

"Storm is here," cracked Koa's voice. "Storm is here."

A torrent of water and sand hit the mainland with 160-mile-per-hour winds. The gusty winds were deafening to the ears. The howling winds roared across the lands. Outside of Willow, there was the sound of the land breaking apart as the storm blew in from the waters. Then there was the booming and lightening that also came with the storm.Inside of Willow, creatures who had taken cover on high ground came back down due to the strength of the winds. Many took shelter in Willow's massive tree roots and caves away from the waterways.

Those who took cover in the above tree houses prayed that Willow and the homes would hold up to the winds. The Evadeam family and friends had made it safely to Bolivar and Bathsheba's tree house. As the vibration of the storm shook the ground, Jereco wondered if an earthquake felt like this. He prayed that the water people were safe. He prayed and hoped that Willow could hold her ground and protect all of them.

The Evadeam family was with Archelaus, Hachmoni, Silver Kat and Skylar. Bathsheba insisted that they eat some supper. The day had gone by quickly when everyone was preparing for the storm, and most of them had forgotten to eat their breakfast and lunch.

They ate in silence, listening to the winds. Bathsheba and Diana surprised them by bringing out a dessert. That cheered them up a little bit, and they started to talk. Most of it was about their day and the storm.

Brooke and Jereco explained what a Category Five hurricane was. No one had ever seen or been in a storm similar to a hurricane, except for Hachmoni. He went on to tell a story about how he was on an island when a hurricane hit. Most of the island was underwater, and at one point, he thought he would drown. Then remarkably, he was saved by an underwater creature, which he later learned was one of the water people. It was his first contact with one of them. He had heard many stories about the water people.

"Hey, that reminds me," said Jereco at the end of Hachmoni's story. "The water people who came to tell me about the hurricane said that the Madeave were getting close to the woods surrounding Willow. The water people hoped that the storm would delay and confuse the Madeave. As soon as there was a break in the storm, the water people would send word for us to leave."

Archelaus, who seemed to be a little moody, said, "Don't you think you should have mentioned this earlier?"

Brooke was quick to defend her cousin. "I don't know if you noticed, but everyone, including Jereco, has been a little bit busy today."

Archelaus looked a little stunned by Brooke's remark.

Hachmoni lifted an eyebrow, wondering why Archelaus and Brooke were acting upset with each other. He decided that was not a question to ask at the moment, so instead he said, "What is important is that Jereco remembered to

136

The Trahe Chronicles

tell us, and yes, we all have been a little busy. Did they say anything else, Jereco?"

Jereco's eyebrows came together as he thought about it. "They said something about needing to go to the ancient grounds of Evadeam, but they would first stop where the great winged creatures run. Midnight would lead the way."

Hachmoni nodded. "This is one of the signs we have been waiting for. I will speak to Midnight when the winds die down. Meanwhile, everyone should ride out the storm by getting rest and eating well." He pointed to his dessert. "Thank you, Bathsheba and Diana, for the meal. Do you think you and the other womenfolk could prepare some food for our journey?"

Bathsheba looked at Brooke and Diana. "Of course, and you girls can help, but not until tomorrow. I think we need to relax the rest of the night. We may need our energy if this storm doesn't let up and does too much damage."

Everyone agreed and broke off into smaller groups to play some games or talk about their next journey.

Jereco took a moment to approach Hachmoni. "Can I speak to you alone?"

"Of course." Hachmoni led Jereco to an enclosed porch area.

Jereco looked up. "I think the storm is over. The winds have died down, and it seems quieter."

Hachmoni shook his head. "No, I believe the eye of the storm is now overhead."

Jereco lowered his voice. "The water people told me something else too, but I did not want to bring it up in front of Bathsheba."

Hachmoni nodded for him to continue.

"They said that the Mangus village — everything south of it — to the sea would be destroyed during this storm."

Hachmoni looked very sad and put his hand on Jereco's shoulders. "This is sad news, indeed. You were wise not to tell everyone at dinner. I will tell Sir Bolivar and Bathsheba myself."

"Hachmoni, I have been thinking," said Jereco. "Do you think that the attack on the village was meant to be? I mean, with the storm destroying the village, we could have all been destroyed by the storm if we did not leave the village and come here to the stronghold."

"Yet another very wise perception, Jereco. I have always believed that the Creator has worked in miraculous ways. I think we all should thank him for putting us out of harm's way. Yes?"

Jereco nodded, and they prayed to the Creator in silence. Later that evening, Hachmoni broke the news about the destruction of Mangus Village, and everyone prayed, giving thanks to the Creator for their survival. It was a solemn evening, and everyone gave goodnight hugs and promised to check on each other throughout the storm. Archelaus and Brooke were the only

Book One: The Chosen Ones

two who did not give each other a hug. They just looked at each other and nodded a goodnight before retreating to their own beds.

The worst of the storm lasted two and a half hours, but thunderstorms continued for another full day. It wasn't until the third day that there was a break in the winds and rain. Everyone pitched in to survey the damages and fix anything that needed to be repaired. Overall, Willow did a great job protecting the fortress. There was minimal damage and injury. However, the damages outside of Willow were extensive. The creatures that could risk being seen left the safety of Willow and went to help anyone in need outside of the stronghold.

Everyone was busy working—cleaning or healing. Hachmoni, Sir Bolivar, Silver Kat, Skylar, Archelaus, and the elders met to discuss the news relayed by Jereco from the water people. It was inevitable that they depart Willow as soon as possible. This made everyone sad, especially Brandon.

After the storm had passed, Brandon noticed all of the willow branches scattered about the fortress. His heart broke for Willow's loss. He tried speaking to her, but she didn't answer. Koa had told Brandon that she was still protecting the fortress and probably was exhausted. She would speak when she was able. This news did little to lift Brandon's spirits.

On the fifth day after the storm, Brandon began to pick up Willow's broken branches. He wasn't sure what to do with them, except put them in piles.

Silver Kat walked up to him. "Brandon, you are doing a good job cleaning up after Willow."

Brandon just nodded.

"I am sure Willow would be pleased that you are caring for and respecting her. Did you know that her dead branches help build this fortress?" Silver Kat picked up some twigs. "These can be planted to bring birth to Willow's children. This forest that surrounds us grew from Willow's branches. I think Willow would be pleased if you collected them and gave them to Bathsheba, so she can replant them back at their village."

Brandon looked up at Silver Kat. "But the village was destroyed by the storm."

"What better way to start rebuilding the village? By planting the birth of Willow's children."

Brandon gave that some thought and decided it was a good idea.

"Maybe Diana would like to help you," suggested Silver Kat. "You may be able to collect enough to take with you on our journey."

Not only did Brandon agree, but he started to think about all the things he could make out of Willow's branches. If he could take her with him, he might not feel so far away from her. Diana agreed to help, and they started their project right away. It was a good thing because on the sixth day after the storm, it was announced that they would be leaving soon.

138

The Trahe Chronicles

A great dinner feast was planned in honor of those leaving to continue the fulfillment of the prophecy. Grandpa and the kids expressed concern about leaving when Willow was not completely cleaned up from the storm. But the villagers and creatures assured them that they could handle it. Hachmoni also knew staying longer would only stall the inevitable.

While eating at the feast, Jereco asked Grandpa why he was so eager to start out on this next leg of the journey.

"Well," Grandpa said eagerly, "every passage of this trip — I hope — leads us closer to finding your parents. And Midnight reminded me what the water people said to you. That Midnight will lead us to his home of the great winged creatures. We will be able to see the rest of his herd, including Prisca. I can't wait to see Prisca."

"Who is Prisca?" asked Brooke.

Grandpa glanced up and looked over at Midnight, who was on the other side of the feasting table, eating a pile of greens on the ground. Midnight nodded his approval for Grandpa to continue. "Prisca is Midnight's partner."

The kids didn't reply and didn't seem impressed.

"And ..." Grandpa continued with an exaggerated pause, "... she is a unicorn."

Diana squealed with delight. "A unicorn!"

Grandpa just nodded as he stuffed his mouth with some berries.

"A unicorn?" asked Brandon.

Grandpa nodded again.

"A unicorn married, partnered—or whatever you want to call it—to a pegasus?" Brandon continued. "How is that possible?"

"Duh, they are both horses," Diana said, defending the couple. "One just has wings and one has a horn. What is the big deal?"

Brandon reached for some more food. "It just seems odd."

"I think it is cool," commented Brooke. "What a powerful couple. A mighty horse with wings and a horse with a horn. How cool is that?"

Brandon just shrugged and stuffed his face.

"Well, I can't wait to go now," said Diana. "Just imagine. Meeting a unicorn. Doesn't she have powers or something? Isn't her horn magical?"

"Oh, she is a powerful unicorn, indeed," answered Grandpa, "but her secrets have never been revealed to a human. Maybe you will be the lucky one."

And so the conservation continued about Prisca and what her magical powers might be, lightening up the mood of the feast. Jereco, however, noticed that Grandpa had said, "I can't wait to see Prisca." He didn't say, "I can't wait to meet Prisca." Grandpa almost acted like he would be visiting a long lost friend. Jereco just decided to keep this observation to himself for the moment.

The feast went late into the night as all special feasts do. The morning

Book One: The Chosen Ones

came fast, and the day was spent packing for the journey. "I thought we were leaving today," asked Brandon.

"I guess we are leaving tomorrow morning before the sun rises," Jereco said. "One of the bird messengers said that many of the Madeave were either killed or scattered about during the storm. Hachmoni wants to make sure that one of them doesn't accidently come across us as we are leaving Willow. Silver Kat and Skylar are going to head east, hoping to lead any of the Madeave away from us. Then we will fly north on the horses into the darkness. Hachmoni does not think we will be spotted in the northern mountain ranges. We will then fly southwest toward Midnight's home. Are you done packing?"

"Yeah, I thought I would walk up and try to speak to Willow before we leave."

"I will come with you." Jereco packed his last item. "I want to walk down to the lake and see if I can say goodbye to any of the water people."

Jereco went for a late night swim and was able to catch glimpses of some water people in the deep darkness of the water. He tried to say his goodbyes, but every time he got close, they swam deeper and farther away. He wondered if they came from a deep underwater cavern. Afraid that he would run out of breath, he didn't want to swim too far. He finally gave up trying to personally say goodbye to them. Instead, he sent the thought out to them and swam back to the surface. As he broke through the water, he looked toward the shoreline to get his bearings. He was just about to do a free-form swim stroke toward the shore when he felt a slight tug on his leg. He ducked underwater to see a female water person holding his ankle that had the green mark on it.

In Jereco's opinion, she was a beautiful mermaid. She had big green eyes that seemed to change with the color of the water. Her dark and colorful face was surrounded by massive sea grass hair. Yes, she had a fishy look to her, with the scales and the huge fin, yet there was something magical and alluring about her. Jereco was so memorized by her that he forgot how long he was under. All of a sudden, the mermaid grabbed Jereco and brought him up for air. He gasped, coughed, and thanked her in a strangled voice.

She just smiled at him.

He pointed at himself. "I am Jereco."

She looked confused.

"Jereco," he said again.

She shook her head and went underwater. She tugged his ankle again, so Jereco popped underwater.

She looked at Jereco, pointed at him, and said, "Water Guardian."

At first, Jereco didn't understand what she had said. She sounded like a combination of a whale, dolphin, and a human who might be trying to talk underwater. Her words had a musical, bubbly sound to them. After she

140

The Trahe Chronicles

repeated it a few times, he finally understood.

Jereco nodded and said, "Water Guardian." He pointed at himself. Then he pointed at her. She immediately understood. She pointed at herself and said a name in a language that Jereco did not understand. Jereco tried to repeat it, and she just laughed. Once again, she brought him back up to the surface for some air.

"Chislon," said a deep voice from the shore.

They looked back and saw Hachmoni standing there. He seemed to be bowing down to the mermaid. Jereco looked back at the mermaid, and she said something to Hachmoni in her native language. Surprisingly, Hachmoni answered back. She then dove back underwater and tugged on Jereco's ankle again. Jereco looked back at Hachmoni, who nodded for him to go ahead.

When Jereco looked at the mermaid underwater, she spoke to him in the universal Trahe language that he understood. "We will look after you as you will look after us. After all of us," she said. "I bid you safe travels, Water Guardian." She came forward and kissed him on each cheek. Before Jereco had a chance to reply, she quickly swam away.

Jereco thought about swimming after her, but then he heard his name being called. He looked behind him, and there was no one else underwater but other fish. He heard his name again, but now it seemed like it was coming from above. He swam to the surface and saw that it was Hachmoni calling him. Hachmoni waved Jereco over to the shoreline. Jereco hesitated and looked back toward the water. He reluctantly turned and swam toward shore.

It had become dark outside, so Hachmoni was holding a lighted torch. He handed Jereco a towel with his other hand. Jereco quietly dried off, deep in thought.

Hachmoni broke the silence. "Her name in our language is Chislon. It means hope. She is the daughter of King Abijam and the hope of their people."

"Chislon," repeated Jereco. "Hope of her people? Are her people in danger?"Hachmoni nodded. "There is a prophecy that their people will be in great danger one day. Unlike the Evadeam people, their time has not yet come. But there is no need for you to worry about this now. We must go to bed and get some sleep." With that said, Hachmoni turned and started to walk back to the village.

Jereco looked back one last time at Willow's lake. "Good bye, Chislon," he whispered. Jereco had a deep feeling that he would see Chislon again and that he had just made a new friend. Water dripped down his face. As he brushed the droplets away, he felt something. In the darkness, he couldn't see what his fingers had removed from his cheek. He smelled it and then tasted it with his tongue. Salt. It was salt. *That is odd*, he thought. The lake and the streams in Willow were freshwater, yet Chislon left salt on his cheeks.

"Hey, Hachmoni, is Chislon a salt water mermaid?" Jereco asked. He turned and realized Hachmoni was too far to hear him.

Book One: The Chosen Ones

Jereco just shrugged and tried to catch up to the lighted torch leading the way back home. Home. Willow was another home that they were about to leave. Jereco sighed, and willow branches lightly touched his shoulders as he walked on.

The Trahe Chronicles

Leaving Willow

Grandpa was sound asleep, snoring, when he was woken by Hachmoni.

"It is time," Hachmoni told Grandpa.

Grandpa wanted to roll over and go back to sleep, but the urgency in Hachmoni's voice told him he had to get up. Grandpa slowly sat up. He squinted at the window.

As if reading his mind, Hachmoni said, "The birds have reported that the Madeave have moved farther east. This would be a good time for us to leave without being spotted. I want to be in the air before the sun rises." He paused. "The Madeave might have left some scouts behind."

"Yes, the Madeave seem to have grown wiser over the years," replied Grandpa as he got out of bed.

During their time at Willow, Grandpa had been informed of the major events that had transpired on Trahe. The Madeave had broken up into many different tribes. Each tribe had claimed different territories, trying to conquer as much land as possible. By doing so, they almost eliminated the Evadeam tribe. That was one of the reasons his Evadeam family had to return.

The prophecy stated that the return of the original Evadeam tribe would save the Evadeam from perishing altogether on Trahe.

Archelaus was determined to find any Evadeam tribe members that might have been scattered during the tribal wars. Grandpa was not sure what his family's role was, but he knew to follow Hachmoni's lead. He just hoped and prayed that he wouldn't have to sacrifice his own grandchildren while doing so. He also prayed that they would find the children's parents even though he had doubts that they would.

The children were not as easy to wake up as Grandpa had been. They complained to Grandpa that is was too early; it was still dark outside. They did not want to leave. The children did not move until Hachmoni walked into the bedroom, "We must go *now!*"

Their departure happened very quickly. There was barely time to wash up, eat breakfast, and gather their things. The horses had flown to the center of the village to pick up them up. Sir Bolivar decided to stay behind to make sure that Bathsheba and the rest of the villagers would be safe. Besides, he was not fond of flying horseback.

The children wanted Sir Bolivar to travel with them, but it was Willow who finally convinced the children that he must stay. "There will be a time when you will see him again," whispered Willow's branches.

Reluctantly, the children mounted the flying horses. It was decided that they would use flocks of birds as decoys just in case there were any Madeave in the area. Koa, however, was flying out with the horses.

"You are going with us?" asked Brandon.

"Oh yes," he said. "Koa go home."

"Home?" Diana asked. She looked a little scared. "Why are we going back

143

Book One: The Chosen Ones

to that snake jungle?"

"Jungle with snakes?" replied Koa. "No. My home is Midnight's home."

"Where is that anyway?" asked Brooke.

"You will see. You will see," Koa replied as he flew away.

"Why doesn't anyone want to tell us where we are going?" demanded Brooke.

"It is like a military strategy," Brandon replied. "Midnight's home is probably a secret place. If one of us falls off a horse, and the Madeave captures us, then we can't tell them where the rest of us are going."

"Don't worry," Archelaus told Brooke and Diana. "No one is falling off a horse."

"But it makes sense to me," whispered Jereco.

Brandon nodded.

Then they were whisked into the air. Even though it was hard to get used to flying on an oversized horse with large wings, they enjoyed the flight. This was the closest they would probably come to really feeling like they were flying.

As they left the center of Willow, friends below waved goodbye. The horses went single file, following Midnight. Midnight circled around within Willow, so the Evadeam family was able to get a final look of the place they had called home for the past weeks.

Jereco thought he saw Chislon in the lake. He waved goodbye just in case it was her, and as they headed out of Willow, the branches pulled back to let them out.

Brandon was the last one to leave, and as he did, the willow branches caressed his cheek. A raindrop or perhaps a tear fell down from a willow branch and blended in with the tears that had already slipped down Brandon's face.

Brandon knew that they had left the heart of Willow, but the others couldn't tell. There seemed to be an endless sea of willow branches around them. Eventually, they could see the difference between Willow's branches and the branches of the smaller willow trees. The woods surrounding Willow were larger and taller than they remembered. Originally, they had entered Willow from the south. Perhaps the woods were taller on the north side.

Finally, the woods started to thin, and a large mountain range lay ahead to the north and west. They squinted adjusting to the light. The sun was not up yet, but it had been much darker within Willow.

As they continued northward, there were signs of the devastation left behind by the hurricane. They could only imagine how bad it must have been on the southern side where the storm had originated. Brooke and Diana wanted to go south and help anyone struck by the storm, but they were told they must continue to their destination. Koa assured them that there were many volunteers from the north and west regions, helping their fellow creatures.

144

The Trahe Chronicles

As the sun started to rise from the east, they noticed bands of volunteers heading south, which made everyone feel better about the decision to continue. As the rising sun's rays reached across the sky and land, Jereco thought how similar this sun was to their own back on Earth. Through squinted eyes, he watched the sun shine magnificent colors over the land. He could barely see the tops of the willow trees as they headed up into the mountains.

The rest of the party was also watching the sun rise. *It's beautiful*, thought Brooke. She couldn't remember the last time she had watched a morning sunrise. She would have to do that more often. As she turned her head, she caught Archelaus watching her. They had not said too much to each other since the moment they almost kissed. He smiled at her, and she smiled back.

Archelaus was riding on a pegasus named Stal Lion, who suddenly took a sharp turn. It took Archelaus by surprise, and he had to hang on tightly to prevent himself from falling off.

Brooke laughed at him.

He laughed back. "Do you think that is funny? Falling off into those rugged mountains down there?"

Brooke shook her head and shouted back over the sounds of the large winged horses "You wouldn't fall off. You are an excellent rider, but you should have seen your face." She continued to laugh.

Archelaus did not think it was that funny that he almost fell off his pegasus, but he enjoyed hearing Brooke laugh. It was hard to hear each other over the noise of the great winged horses, so they just laughed and smiled at each other as they flew up into the mountains.

After hours of riding, the horses descended into a small valley surrounded by sharp cliffs. The horses had great eyesight and had spotted a secluded spot that offered a mountain stream for water and grass for food. The friends on their backs were grateful for the opportunity to stretch their legs.

"Is this your home, Midnight?" asked Diana.

"No, we are many miles from my home," he replied. "We will fly in between these mountains and go south until we see the great sea."

They all walked to the stream for some water.

"How long will it take to get there?" Brooke asked.

Midnight who realized he may have said too much about their next destination went to eat some grass.

Hachmoni offered the answer. "It will take a few days. Come drink, and fill your water containers."

Brandon, who was watching the horses eat, asked, "What are we supposed to eat?"

Archelaus jumped up and rolled back his sleeves. "I believe I see fish in this stream." "Fish? I don't think I can eat fish now," said Jereco. "I am the Water Guardian.""Jereco," asked Hachmoni, "what do you think the water

145

Book One: The Chosen Ones

people eat?"

Jereco just shrugged.

"They eat many things that come from the sea, including fish," replied Hachmoni as he waved his hand toward the stream.

Diana piped up. "But isn't there talking fish?"

"Yeah," said Brandon, "and how are we supposed to catch fish? Are we to ask them if they are talking fish before we try to catch them or after we catch them?"

"I assure you Brandon that there are no talking fish in this stream," said Hachmoni. "All freshwater fish are non-talking and very edible."

"But the water people were in a freshwater stream and lake," pointed out Jereco.

Hachmoni scratched his chin. "Yes, that did surprise me."

"So they are from the sea?" asked Jereco. "I tasted salt. Was that from salt water?"

"What are you talking about, Jereco?" asked Brooke.

The others looked at him.

"Never mind," he mumbled and decided to ask Hachmoni his questions later.

Midnight's head popped up from the grass. "We cannot stay here all morning. You better catch some fish, so we can move on."

As Archelaus started to head toward the water, Brandon asked him how he was going to catch fish.

"With my hands," he replied.

"Hands?" Brandon asked. "I have to see this."

Archelaus stopped. "How else would you catch them?"

"With a fishing pole and hook," said Brandon.

"What is a fishing pole?" asked Archelaus.

Cleo jumped between them. "Midnight is right. We do not have time to catch fish now. Bathsheba has packed some food. Come." She gave Brandon a warning look to remind him about not sharing modernized ideas with Archelaus. But Brandon decided that there was nothing modern about fishing techniques and decided he would show Archelaus how to fish his way when Cleo was not around.

Brooke started to unpack their food. "Besides, we would have to build a fire to cook fish."

"Cook fish?" asked Archelaus.

"Well, how else would you eat it?" she asked.

Archelaus shrugged. "Just eat it."

"Raw?" said Brandon.

Archelaus smiled slightly and nodded his head.

"Yuck," exclaimed Brandon. "That is like eating sushi."

"It is not that bad," said Brooke.

"Oh yes, it is," said Brandon. "And since when do you like sushi?"

146

The Trahe Chronicles

Brooke just shrugged and continued handing out the food.

They sat down near the stream. As they ate, Brandon proceeded to explain to Archelaus how and why one should cook fish. It was not until after lunch was eaten that Brandon caught on that he was being fooled. Indeed, Archelaus did cook most fish to prevent sickness. Archelaus and everyone else were just teasing Brandon. Brandon didn't appreciate being the center of a joke, and Archelaus apologized. "Tonight I will catch and cook the fish. You, Brandon, will get first taste."

Brandon grumbled something and wandered off to the stream to wash up. Jereco decided to join him and was silently grateful that they didn't eat fish. He wasn't sure he could ever eat fish again now that he had been appointed the Water Guardian.

Soon they were flying north, deeper into the mountains. It was colder here than it had been in Willow. They often made stops, so everyone could take a break. They were not used to riding on large horses for hours at a time. Brandon even heard one of the horses complain about the extra load on his back. Brandon had forgotten that the pegasi of Trahe usually did not have creatures riding on their backs. Hachmoni assured everyone that their new travel arrangements would become habit over time.

The sun was setting, and it was decided it was time to find a spot to settle in for the night. They found another secluded spot near a mountain stream. Archelaus and Brandon volunteered to go fishing while Brooke and Diana made camp. Jereco and Hachmoni would gather broken tree branches from the mountain floor.

Before Jereco and Hachmoni could gather wood though, they needed permission from the trees. Brandon tried to talk to the trees, but he didn't get a response like he had earlier with Willow. He got frustrated, but Hachmoni said it would take time. All trees were different, and their language varied. Brandon wanted to know how Hachmoni could understand the trees.

"Because he is ancient," Archelaus replied.

Everyone laughed, except for Hachmoni, of course.

"Come on, Brandon." Archelaus pointed at the stream. "Let's go catch some fish."

While Archelaus and Brandon fished, Hachmoni taught Jereco how to start a fire without matches. Brooke approached Hachmoni once a small fire was roaring. "It seems Archelaus has forgiven you for not telling him about his brother and sister," she said.

"Forgiven?" Hachmoni replied. "I am not so sure. Maybe he has forgotten for a little while. But I am sure he will understand my motivations in time."

"I was a little worried," admitted Brooke, "that you two wouldn't get along after your fight in Mangus Village."

"Ah, we have known each other for a very long time," said Hachmoni. "I

Book One: The Chosen Ones

have known Archelaus since he was born. I promised to watch over him like my own son. So I suppose we have disagreements like a father and a son. What about you? Have you and Archelaus worked out your differences, Brooke?"

"Differences?" she pretended. "I don't know what you mean."

"Differences?" asked Grandpa, walking into the middle of the conversation. "You and Archelaus are fighting?"

"No, not at all, Grandpa." Brooke excused herself.

Grandpa looked at Hachmoni with a suspicious eye. "Am I missing something here?" Grandpa asked.

Hachmoni just shrugged.

Grandpa looked at Brooke. Then he glanced at the stream where Archelaus stood and back at Brooke. His head turned sharply to Hachmoni. "Now look here, Hachmoni," Grandpa said strongly. "My idea of helping the Evadeam tribe does not include leaving my granddaughter on Trahe. I promised the family that I would bring all the children back, safe and sound to Earth, and I have every intention of doing that. Are we understood?"

Cleo and several pegasi heads perked up. Not too many people raised their voices to Hachmoni.

"It is understood," replied Hachmoni.

Everyone went back to what they were doing. However, Grandpa walked away with nagging, worrying thoughts in his head.

That night, they ate cooked fish for dinner. The fish smelled good, but Jereco still could not get himself to eat it. He ate Bathsheba's packaged meal instead. Midnight was concerned that the smell of the cooked fish would bring unwanted visitors, so they set up watches throughout the night. Koa, who had ridden in one of the horse's bags and slept through most of the day, volunteered to take the night shift.

As it turned out, the night was uneventful, and everyone got a good night's sleep. Well, as much as they could have gotten. Sleeping on the ground under the cool night stars was not as comfortable as sleeping in the tree houses in Willow. The night had brought back some memories of sleeping on the ground in the jungle. Now and then, the kids would wake up, hearing things in the woods. However, having so many friends to protect them helped.

The next day, they headed south. After many days of traveling, moods clashed from weariness. Then one day, they saw a great view from the sky. Ahead to the south was a large mass of blue.

Brandon pointed. "What is that?"

Jereco smiled. "I think that is an ocean."

Brandon squinted. "Is it?" He asked Dale, the flying horse he sat upon. "Is it an ocean?"

"That is our great blue sea," acknowledged Dale.

Spirits lifted. This was a sign—a sign that they soon would reach

148

The Trahe Chronicles

Midnight's home. The pegasi slowly descended to a bay off the sea. They landed softly on a beautiful white beach. The bay was surrounded by high cliffs on all sides, except south where the ocean lay. On the bottom of the cliffs were large rocks. Smaller rocks were found at the edge of the beach. There was some tall grass for the pegasi to eat. Also, between the rocks and the beach, large coconut palm trees reached toward the blue sky.

"This is perfect," said Grandpa. "A perfect spot to camp for the night."

"Camp for the night?" said Brandon. "It isn't night yet. We have plenty of daylight hours. Why don't we just keep going to Midnight's home?"

Dale pointed his head toward the sea. "Because it is too far from here. It will take us an entire day's worth of flying, without stopping, to get there."

"Oh." Brandon's shoulders slumped.

"A whole day of flying without stopping?" asked Brooke.

Hachmoni nodded. "So we might as well enjoy the rest of this day on land. Stretch our legs, rest, and eat well. Tomorrow will be a very long day."

Jereco looked at the sea. He was looking forward to tomorrow. They would be flying over the ocean all day. He might be able to see some more water people. "Any one up for a swim?" he asked.

Everyone was up for a swim in the wonderful waters of the ocean. They set up camp first and then ventured into the sea. Jereco was the first to dive in. He felt more at home in the sea water than he ever did back home on Earth. As Jereco dove deeper into the depths of the ocean, his eye caught something softly glowing green. He looked back to see that it was the new green tattoo on his ankle. Jereco freaked out and came up to the surface.

As he looked around, no one else noticed. He wiped his face and calmed himself down. He checked the rest of his body to make sure he did not have any more tattoos. Nope, he was fine. In fact, he felt better than fine. He felt really good. He felt energetic. He decided that there must be a connection with his tattoo and the sea water. *Or the water people*, he thought.

Jereco dove back into the water. Once he decided that he was fine, he enjoyed himself by exploring the sea. He found a small reef that had an abundance of sea life, including coral, urchins, and a variety of sea fish. The sea fish did not seem to be afraid of him. In fact, they swam right up to him. Jereco felt safe and comfortable with them. Jereco was enjoying himself so much that he did not realize how far he had swum. He came across a dark cavern. A large movement in the cave caught his attention. The friendly fish he had been swimming with scattered away.

Jereco tried to follow them, but when he turned, something grabbed his right ankle. He turned, thinking a water person had grabbed his leg. But it wasn't. It was a monstrous sea arm that reminded him of an octopus tentacle. The calmness Jereco had felt earlier was gone. He panicked. He was going to be killed and eaten by a sea monster. Or drown!

He needed some air. He tried to kick the sea monster's arm off his leg, but it did not work. The monster's arm tightened around his ankle. It was at

149

Book One: The Chosen Ones

that moment that Jereco noticed his tattoo glowing again. The green mark shined stronger than ever, shining around his ankle and underneath the monster's arm. The monster did not seem to notice.

His knife. Jereco went to grab his knife and then realized he didn't have it on him. He had left it on the beach when he changed his clothes to go swimming. *Now what? God, now what?*

And that was his answer. He did a quick prayer to the Creator of Trahe and tried to pull the monster's arm off his leg. He was pulling with all his might when another arm came up toward his head. *I am going to die,* he thought. *I should be dead already. Why wasn't I dead?* That was one of the last thoughts he remembered before hearing the sound of familiar music. The sound of whales singing. He slowly lost consciousness as a blur of large fish swam toward him and the monster.

Cough, cough. Jereco was coughing up water. He gasped for air, and he heard familiar voices trying to calm him. He felt the water beneath his shoulders. His head was above the water. He was breathing. His panic subsided, and then he drifted out of consciousness.

The Trahe Chronicles

PART FOUR

Mermaids and Unicorns

The war of man is sad.
The death of the innocent is painful.
The destruction of evil is necessary.
Follow the Creator and the Light shall prevail.
- Prisca, the Unicorn

Book One: The Chosen Ones

Riding Horseback in the Air

Flames flickered in the darkness—orange, red, yellow, green, blue, and white. Jereco saw white in the flames. As his tired eyes focused on the light, he saw flashbacks from his past. His past on Earth. Being so young, the past was brief. It ended the day he drove to the farm field to find an aircraft like no other.

The thoughts ended. The dreams began. Dreams of crashing, snakes, trees, fish, and water. Lots of water. Turbulent water. Dangerous waters. Waters drowning him. Drowning him. Or at least the waters tried.

Was it the waters? No. It was a monster. A monster that dragged him under until he remembered no more.

Then there was the sound. Music. The sound of music drowned out by the sound of breaking waters. The sound of water. No, waves. The sound of ocean waves echoed through his ears. The sound slowly put him at ease. Put him back to sleep.

It was a slight tickle on his face that brought him back. As his hand tried to brush the tickle away, something wet licked his cheek. His eyes opened up to see a black and white face staring back at him. The face had green eyes and whiskers. Whiskers that tickled him. Cleo.

He reached out to pet her.

"Welcome back, Jereco," said Cleo.

Jereco smiled as he lay there. "It is good to be back."

Cleo stood up and stretched. As she did so, she meowed something to the creatures stirring around her. Jereco noticed flames flickering in the background. Fire. A fire that danced against the dark background. Nighttime. *It must be nighttime,* he thought.

Jereco rubbed his eyes and tried to sit up, but a hand pushed him back down. "Take it slow."

Jereco looked up to see Hachmoni had taken Cleo's position.

"How are you feeling?" Hachmoni asked.

"Fine."

Hachmoni eyebrows shot up. "Really?"

"Well, I feel a little tired and achy." Jereco rubbed his stomach. "And hungry."

"Good. Hunger is a good sign. We have a kettle of soup prepared. I will go get you some. Plus, you have some family members anxious to see you."

After a signal from Hachmoni, Jereco's family surrounded Jereco. They asked a lot of questions at once. Jereco did not answer any of them and started to rub his head.

It was not until Hachmoni came back with the soup that everyone stopped talking.

"What happened out there?" Hachmoni asked Jereco.

Jereco told them what had happened in the sea.

152

The Trahe Chronicles

"By the description of the monster," said Grandpa, "I would say it was a giant octopus."

"Or the Kraken!" offered Brandon.

Grandpa shook his head. "There is no such creature."

"Sure, there is. Or could be. Haven't you noticed that we are traveling on pegasi? Anything can happen here."

Grandpa finally admitted that Brandon could be right. It was also decided that there would be no more swimming in the deep depths of the sea here. Besides, it was time for everyone to get a good night's sleep. They wanted to leave very early in the morning.

Jereco's body wholeheartedly agreed. He felt exhausted, and the last thing he remembered was watching the flickering of the flames and listening to the sound of the sea.

The morning came quickly. They ate, packed up camp, and were ready to leave before the sun's rays hit the beach. As they were mounting the pegasi, Brooke expressed concern about flying all day without breaks. Midnight reassured them that there were small islands in between the mainland; the islands could be used for brief rest stops.

It was around high noon when they stopped at one of the islands for a lunch break. These small islands turned out to be very small, indeed. Basically rock, beach sand, some small shrubbery and a few palm trees, which gave very little privacy. However, the island was still big enough to act as a momentary resting place. As Jereco leaned against a palm tree, he looked out at the ocean. He realized that he looked at the water much differently now than he had back home.

In his home state of Michigan, summertime was very short. He would squeeze as much time as possible on the small lake near his home. He would spend the summer days, driving his ski boat across the waters. His favorite sport was water boarding across the lake as fast as he could and coming up with fun and extreme stunts. He never gave the fish or creatures in the lake much thought until now. Maybe when he got back home, he would take up snorkeling or scuba diving and venture into the depths of Lake Michigan. He was curious to explore deeper waters and see what type of marine life he could find. Jereco's thoughts were interrupted as Midnight announced that the break was over, and it was time to move on.

They flew for hours over the ocean and had lost sight of any islands or signs of any other type of life. Everyone was starting to get tired of traveling again, but there was no place to stop. The pegasi continued to fly steadily in the air.

Brooke and Diana were flying Midnight's back. "I am getting tired of flying, Brooke," said Diana.

"I know, so am I," said Brooke. "But can you imagine how tired Midnight and the rest of the pegasi must feel?"

Diana nodded.

Book One: The Chosen Ones

"Why don't you take a nap while we fly," said Brooke. "I can hold onto you."

Diana shook her head. "If the horses have to stay awake, then I will too."

Brooke smiled at her determination. However, within thirty minutes, Diana was fast asleep in her arms. Brooke was trying very hard not to fall asleep too. Brooke tried to concentrate on watching the rest of the group or the ocean waves. But after awhile, the noise and movement of the waves was making Brooke drowsy. She tried to make conversation with Midnight or anyone of her group, but it was too hard to hear each other over the sound of the great pegasi wings. Brooke's head drooped as she started to nod off. *Just a few minutes*, she told herself. *Just a cat nap. I can hold onto Diana and Midnight. Just for a few minutes.*

"Brooke!"

Someone screamed.

Brooke woke up with a start, disoriented.

"Hold on, Diana," yelled Midnight. As Brooke woke up, she took in the scene.

She must have fallen asleep and slumped over to the left where Diana was hanging over Midnight's side. Diana had grabbed on to Midnight's mane and was holding on as best as she could. Midnight dipped to the right, so Diana fell onto Midnight's side. Brooke reached over and tried to grab Diana's arm. She couldn't quite reach it.

"Hold on, Diana," Brooke yelled. She slid her right leg over the saddle, so she could balance on the left side of the saddle. Hanging on to the saddle and dipping down, she was able to reach Diana. She hooked her arm around Diana's waist. "I am going to push you back into the saddle. Okay?"

Diana nodded.

"On the count of three: one, two, three!" Brooke pushed with all her might to get Diana back into the saddle. "Got it?"

Diana nodded. She was safely in the saddle. "I made it!" yelled Diana.

Brooke breathed a sigh of relief and was just about to raise herself back in the saddle when Midnight tipped back to the left. The tip was just enough to throw Brooke off. She plunged toward the sea.

Screams from both girls had caught everyone's attention. Archelaus, who had been watching the scene from behind, quickly went into action. Riding Stal Lion, Archelaus flew after Brooke.

Brooke had mentally braced herself for the plunge into the deep sea. Years of lifeguard training back on Earth had paid off. She did not panic and was quickly swimming up toward the top of the water as soon as she could. It was taking all her strength to fight the ocean waves. As she broke through the water, she noticed something dark looming overhead. She could barely see the shape of a pegasus flying above her. The sprays and churning of the ocean was pulling her under.

This sea is not taking me, she thought. After all these years of rescuing other

154

The Trahe Chronicles

people from the waters of Lake Michigan, she was not going down in a sea far away from home. Far away from her own planet. And goodness knows what was in this sea. With as much determination as she could muster, she kept her head above water. She spotted the rope that was being lowered down to her. She knew it would be tough hanging onto a wet leather rope. She waited for the right timing of the waves and threw herself up toward the rope. She missed the first time and several times after that. She was getting exhausted and losing her strength. She said a silent prayer to the Creator. She asked for strength and help. Then she felt something grab her leg.

Brooke screamed. Her first thoughts were of the monster Jereco had encountered. She started to panic. But before she got a chance to fight the creature, the creature lifted her up and out of the water. The creature was actually pushing her toward the rope.

Brooke was able to grab the rope this time and quickly wrapped it around her right arm before she could be dragged back underwater. She was able to get both hands on the rope and felt herself being pulled out of the water. As she cleared the water, she tossed her head, trying to shake some of the water from her face, so she could see what she was doing. She looked down into the water but did not see any signs of the sea creature that had helped her. Brooke said a silent "thank you" to the Creator and the mysterious sea animal.

Then she looked up and saw Archelaus. He was above her on Stal Lion. They were pulling her up. He was shouting something to her, but she had a hard time hearing it over the sound of the waves and Stal Lion's wings. She knew that Stal Lion could not get too close to the water without putting himself in danger of being swept into the sea. She grasped firmly onto the rope and yelled, "Pull!"

She could see on Archelaus face that it was taking a lot of strength to pull her up. He was fighting the sea and the motion of being on Stal Lion's back. But he kept it up.

Archelaus heart was beating fast. He was trying very hard to pull Brooke up without her slipping back into the sea. When he first saw her plunge into the ocean, he thought time had stopped. He was determined not to lose her to the raging sea.

Archelaus pulled with all his strength. He almost had her all the way up. As Brooke got closer, she swung her right leg toward Archelaus stirrup. Once her foot was in, Archelaus was able to pull her up more easily. He pulled Brooke into his lap. She was shaking and soaking wet.

"How's Diana?" Brooke asked weakly.

Archelaus looked over to Midnight. "She is fine." He gave Diana thumbs up—a signal that Brandon had taught him.

"Stal Lion, I got her," Archelaus said. "Go over to Midnight to make sure Diana is fine, flying alone." Stal Lion flew toward Midnight.

"Can you hang on by yourself?" yelled Archelaus.

155

Book One: The Chosen Ones

Diana nodded with a look of concern on her face. "Is Brooke okay?"

Archelaus nodded, and then Brooke looked over at Diana. "I am okay," she yelled.

Brooke looked up at Archelaus. "Thank you."

He simply replied, "You're welcome." He held her tighter.

Brooke didn't admit to Archelaus that he had additional help in rescuing her. She glanced back at the water one more time, looking for the sea creature that had lifted her out of the water. She saw only the waves of the sea.

"Brooke," said Archelaus. "I don't see an island in sight and you need to get warm to prevent a chill." Archelaus pulled a light coat out of his saddle bag. "Put this on."

Brooke pulled her gaze away from the sea. She hesitated about wearing Archelaus jacket. The last time she accepted his coat, they almost kissed. But her survival skills told her that he was right.

Archelaus played the card that he knew would work. "Brooke, you can't get sick. Diana needs you."

Brooke already felt like she failed Diana by falling asleep while flying. It was her fault that Diana had slipped off Midnight and that she herself had plummeted into the great sea. She could not fail Diana or the rest of the group by getting sick now. "Okay" she said in a trembling voice.

Archelaus proceeded to wrap the opening of his coat around Brooke the best he could. He could feel her wet garmets through his own layers of clothes. Hopefully, the combination of his coat and body heat would help keep her warm.

They flew like this for hours. Archelaus warmth slowly crept into Brooke's body. Once again, her eyelids failed to obey. She was so exhausted.

"Go to sleep," Archelaus told her. "Rest. We will watch over Diana. In fact, Cleo is riding with her. Jereco will ride nearby to keep an eye on her too." With that said, Brooke nodded off to sleep.

After watching Diana's and Brooke's falls, Jereco and Brandon decided they could not take their chances either. They were both totally exhausted and did anything they could think of to keep awake. Perhaps it was the weariness that kept them from noticing the white spots in the sky.

Brandon was deep in thought when he brushed something away from the back of his head. The first time was subconscious, but the second was more urgent. He finally snapped out of his thoughts. "What the —" He looked back. "Whoa!"

A bird had been tickling the back of his head.

The bird flew to Jereco next. Then Brandon noticed that there were tons of white birds flying behind them.

"Jereco, birds!" yelled Brandon, pointing. "Birds — birds! Oh my gosh, *birds!* That means there is land nearby!" Brandon could tell that Jereco understood what Brandon had said. Jereco started to frantically look around

The Trahe Chronicles

for land.

Splash!

Something splashed below Jereco. Jereco looked down. Dolphins jumped out of the water below him. "Dolphins!" Jereco yelled. "Brandon! Dolphins! Look!" He pointed down.

The scene developed around them. White seagulls flew in the air beside them with dolphins swimming below. Now the entire group was aware of their new company. There were shouts of astonishment and enjoyment.

Even Brooke had awakened to the wondrous scene. She pointed toward the birds. "There must be land nearby."

"Yes," said Archelaus, "I believe it's to the west of us."

The sun was shining beyond a beautiful mountainous island. The island was green and lush. It reminded her so much of a Hawaiian island back home. Her thoughts were interrupted by a big splash and some laughing. She looked over, just in time to see Jereco get sprayed by a giant whale.

"Awesome!" exclaimed Brandon. The pod of dolphins had been joined by a pod of whales. The scene below was incredible. The pegasi flew closer to the water to enjoy the spray of water squirted by the whales. It was refreshing, indeed.

As they flew low over the ocean, Brooke noticed the waves had become calmer. The waters looked more blue and green. She was close enough now that she could hear the dolphins and whales singing. Speaking. Perhaps, they were speaking to the pegasi and welcoming them back home.

As everyone enjoyed the scene and the refreshing water sprays, Jereco kept his eyes out for any water people. He was so sure he would see some during their trip over the ocean, but he had not. He thought he saw a glimpse of one while Brooke was in the water, but he was not sure. When the dolphins and whales appeared, he had high hopes that he would see the water people swimming below, but there was still saw no sign of them. He began to lose enjoyment of the scene taking place around him as he searched for his beloved new friends. As if reading his thoughts, a dolphin jumped up nearby and sprayed water in his face.

Frustrated, Jereco wiped his face and looked where the dolphin went. He was just about to yell something unfriendly when he noticed baby dolphins jumping out of the water beside him. Jereco smiled. It was as if they were showing off just for him. Jereco looked around and noticed that only the dolphins and whales were swimming near him. Hachmoni and Grandpa were flying to the left of him, and there were no signs of the sea animals below them. It might have been a coincidence, but Jereco knew in his heart that the sea animals surrounded him because they knew who he was. He was the Water Guardian.

The Water Guardian then noticed another thing. Most of the white seagulls were flying around Brandon, as if they knew he was the Forest Friend and had a special gift for talking to trees. He looked over at his sister,

157

Book One: The Chosen Ones

who was enjoying watching all the animals with Cleo. Diana was the Vision Keeper, and perhaps it was a dream that had made her fall into a deep sleep that caused her to lose her balance off Midnight earlier in the day.

Jereco glanced at Brooke, who was flying with Archelaus. What was Brooke's role in all this? Did she have a special reason for being here? Was Archelaus the reason? Jereco was not sure about that thought. He was protective of his cousin. He would have to keep an eye on the relationship developing between Brooke and Archelaus.

Water shot up at Jereco. A large whale had swum up under Jereco and squirted water with his spout. Jereco wiped the water off his face and looked down again. *Wow,* he thought. He would never get this opportunity back home—to fly on a back of a pegasus and be so close to whales and dolphins. This was incredible! Jereco decided to enjoy the moment and rest his thoughts.

This moment was fantastic. They all were flying above beautiful waters, with white seagulls, and now colorful tropical birds had joined in the procession. They all laughed and watched the great animals around them. As they drew near to the island, the setting sun shot rays of orange, red, and yellow across the land and sea. It was a picture postcard moment.

Jereco, for the first time in a long time, wished he could use something electronic. He wished he had a camera, so he could capture this moment in time. *I wonder,* he thought. He dug deep into one of his bags. He grabbed his cell phone that he was not supposed to use here. He said a slight prayer, aimed his camera phone toward the island, and snapped. It worked! *Unbelievable.* His cell battery was almost dead, and he still got a picture. He smiled, tucked the phone away, and did not dare look at Cleo, knowing he would be reprimanded for using modern technology on Trahe. With any luck, he would at least bring back one picture to Earth.

The Trahe Chronicles

The Island of the Pegasi

The reflections of the blue sky glimmered on the ocean waters. It made the sea look so blue. As the travelers approached the island, they saw how clear the water really was. The whales, dolphins and other tropical fish were more visible. Ahead of them, a huge island sprawled across the sea. It was lush and green with tall mountains that reached up into the clouds. The setting sun continued to play tricks of color onto the scenic view.

"It is so beautiful," whispered Brooke. "It looks like it should be a Hawaiian island."

"Hawaiian island?" asked Archelaus.

Brooke did not realize that she had spoken loudly enough for him to hear. She looked at him and nodded. "Hawaii has a chain of the most beautiful islands. Our families vacationed there once. It is my favorite vacation spot. I have always wanted to go back." She nodded toward the island in front of her. "This looks so much like it, without the buildings, boats, and sea planes."

"Sea planes?" asked Archelaus.

"I'll explain later," she replied and looked back toward the island.

Archelaus didn't pursue his question because he was enjoying the look on Brooke's face. She looked so happy and excited as she took in the view in front of them. He imagined she was reminiscing about her family vacation at the place she called Hawaii.

Midnight slowed his pace and flapped his grand wings in midair. The rest of the pegasi followed his lead. Midnight spoke in Trahe and used his deep voice to bellow toward the waters. "Thank you, my friends. Thank you for your grand welcome and escorting us back to my homeland. I appreciate your friendship and your loyalty as you guard these ancient waters that surround our island. May the Creator bless and protect you."

As an answer and salute, musical sounds came from the whales and the dolphins. Flying fish jumped out of the water. Sea gulls flew above, calling out, "Bless and protect the ancient waters. Bless and protect the sea animals. Bless and protect the great leader Midnight."

The dolphins then jumped out of the water as high as they could. Whales flipped their fins and tails out of the sea, creating great waves. For the finale, a large magnificent whale jumped out of the water and landed just beneath Midnight. Afterward, the other whales and dolphins followed the large whale back out to the sea, away from the island. Schools of colorful fish swam away. The seagulls split off, heading in different directions. Finally, the colorful tropical birds made a line toward the island. Midnight neighed something in his language and followed the colorful birds.

As they flew toward the island, they saw the figure of a horse standing on top of a mountain, outlined by the setting sun. One by one, the pegasi landed on the sandy beach. They spoke to each other in their own language and then spoke to Hachmoni.

159

Book One: The Chosen Ones

Hachmoni nodded in agreement and turned toward the others. "The sun will completely set soon. It would be faster for the pegasi to unload and fly into their valley without us. This will also give them some quality time with their herd before introducing the Chosen Ones. We will camp here for the night and go into their valley in the morning."

Out of respect for the pegasi, everyone unloaded his stuff quickly, and soon the pegasi were off in the air after saying a quick goodnight. The men staked and lit torches as night fell. They were blessed with a full moon that evening, which also helped light up the sky. A fire was made on the beach, and the girls, who were used to setting up camp, did it quickly. They were soon sitting around the fire, eating dinner. After an exhausting trip in the sky, it felt good to finally enjoy the comforts of land.

Brandon broke the silence. "Why didn't we fly straight into the valley? We have flown in the dark before."

"This island has not been visited by many outside creatures," Hachmoni answered. "The youngest of the herd have never seen a human. This will give Midnight time to explain who we are and prepare them for our arrival tomorrow."

"So what creatures are on this island?" asked Diana.

"Well, there are the Pegasi and the Unicorns, of course," replied Hachmoni. "There are some exotic birds, lizards, and other small creatures."

Brooke, who now had warmed up by the fire and was much more alert, asked, "What about snakes? Are there any overgrown snakes? Any other dangerous wild animals?"

Hachmoni shook his head. "No snakes. The treacherous creatures are on the opposite side of the island."

Archelaus looked up from his food. "None on this side of the island?"

Cleo jumped in front of Hachmoni. "There are some dark creatures on the other side of the island. That is why the pegasi landed here. It is safe on this beach. The unicorn's powers help protect this part of the island. However, it has been a long time since I have visited this place. I will stand guard for the night as a precaution." Cleo stretched her body. "I might even do a little night hunting." She purred.

Brooke made a face as she thought about Cleo catching a rodent for her evening meal. "Well, that is my cue to hit the sack. Come on, Diana. We need a good night's sleep." Brooke reached for Diana's hand, and the girls said goodnight to everyone. As they approached Archelaus, they both thanked him for his heroic actions from earlier that day, and each placed a kiss on his cheek. If it wasn't so dark outside, they would have seen him blush.

As they turned to walk away, Brooke made eye contact with Jereco and motioned him to follow them. When they reached the girls' tent, Brooke ushered in Diana and said she would be in the tent momentarily. Diana wished them both goodnight and went into the tent. Brooke turned toward Jereco.

The Trabe Chronicles

She nodded toward the sea. "I just wanted to let you know that I think a water person helped saved my life out there." She proceeded to tell him how she felt something or someone lift her up out of the water when she was trying to grab Archelaus rope.

Jereco looked at the sea. Somehow, knowing that a water person may have saved Brooke made him feel better. He no longer felt depressed about not seeing one himself on their journey to Pegasi Island. "Thank you, Brooke."

"You're welcome. Goodnight, Jereco."

"Goodnight."

After Brooke went into her tent, Jereco walked to the edge of the water. He sat on the beach and felt the waves lap at his bare feet. He ran water and sand through his fingers and toes. It calmed him. Feeling and listening to the sea helped relax him. He sat there for a very long time until he finally went to bed in the tent he shared with Brandon.

Everyone slept well that evening. They were exhausted from the long flight and felt comfortable being guarded by Cleo. So it was not surprising that most of them slept solidly through the night and into the late morning.

Brandon woke before anyone else. The sun was just starting to peek above the ocean when Brandon decided to get up and find a secluded place to wash up in privacy. "Good morning, Cleo." Brandon noticed the remains of what might have been a mouse. "I see you found a late night snack."

"Yes," Cleo responded as she licked herself clean, "and breakfast too."

"You might want to get rid of the evidence before the girls get up," suggested Brandon. "It grosses them out for some reason."

Cleo just nodded and continued to clean herself with her tongue and paws.

"Is there a freshwater stream near here?" Brandon asked.

Cleo nodded her head toward the southwest.

"I will be back soon," Brandon said as he walked away.

Cleo just nodded.

Brandon found the stream easily enough, but he decided to wait until the sun came up a little higher before going into the water. He wanted to make sure he could see into the water. On the other hand, if there was any danger, Cleo would have told him. He shrugged and picked a spot to put his stuff down. He was just about to remove his shirt when he heard something in the woods behind him. His hands froze. He listened intently. Nothing. He swore he had heard something. He concentrated, and he felt a chill go up his back. He knew for sure now that something was nearby. He slowly pulled out his knife from its sheath. In slow motion, he turned his body, listening to the trees.

Behind you, came a thought through the light tropical breeze. *Something large behind you."* Brandon continued to turn slowly, and before he had a chance to

161

Book One: The Chosen Ones

complete his turn, a creature was charging him. It made an awful squealing noise. It was big and charged right toward him. Instinct took over, and Brandon thrust his knife into the creature. The creature let out a great squeal but continued to charge at Brandon. "Great, all I did was made him madder."

Something sharp pierced Brandon's arm. "Ouch!"

The pain caused him to let go of his knife. Brandon lost his footing and hit the ground. He feared the creature was going to trample him, so he rolled, trying to get away from the creature. The creature was smart and fast. Brandon could not get up quickly enough. He could only continue rolling, trying to avoid being trampled. "Help!" he shouted, hoping that Cleo would hear him.

The sun had come up, and Brandon finally could see his attacker. He saw two large tusks coming at him. "A pig! It is just a giant boar!" He made a fist with his left hand. He was just about to punch the attacker in the nose when something huge pounded down on the wild boar.

The newcomer was dark, fierce, and had a sword. He kicked the boar like it was a football. The boar flew through the air, squealing, until there was one final thud. Then silence.

Brandon rolled onto his stomach. The boar with tusks was lying on the ground, dead. Brandon studied the creature that was looming over the deceased. The creature was dark brown and had great massive wings. A pegasus! The creature's wings pulled back to its sides, and it began to turn toward Brandon.

Brandon sighed with relief. His rescuer was a pegasus—an ally. Brandon stood up, brushed himself clean, and bowed out of respect, thanking the pegasus.

As the pegasus turned, Brandon could not keep the look of shock off his face, for the pegasi had a horn on his forehead. The pegasi looked at Brandon, narrowed his eyes, and made a neighing sound like a horse, as if daring him to make a comment about his horn.

Brandon looked at him, confused. Brandon took a moment to think. Did he just thank the pegasus in Earth English or perhaps Willow tree talk? He switched gears, concentrated, and spoke in the Trahe language.

"I am Brandon. I am the Forest Friend. I am friends of the great Midnight, Dale, and Clyde." The pegasus stepped forward, looked at Brandon intently, and walked around him. Brandon noticed blood dripping from the horn. The pegasus must have used it on the pig. The horn was the sword that Brandon thought he had seen stabbing the pig.

The pegasus then looked into Brandon's eyes, nodded, and kneeled. "You are the Forest Friend. Son of the Creator. Blue eye. Green eye."

Brandon smiled. "Yes, I have one blue eye and one green eye. And you are?"

The pegasus spread his wings and proudly said, "I am Buster. Son of Midnight."

162

The Trahe Chronicles

"Son of Midnight," replied Brandon. "I did not know Midnight had a son." Brandon immediately regretted what he'd said.

Buster flinched with that comment and looked hurt.

Buster turned away and said, "I was sent to lead the way to the valley."

Why would Midnight send his son to get them? thought Brandon.

As if reading his thoughts, Buster replied, "I was sent because I am one of the few who knows of the two-legged creatures."

Brandon pointed toward the pig. "What about him?"

"What about him?" replied Buster as he started to walk away. "Other creatures will eat him."

Brandon looked at the pig and thought about the last time he ate meat. He could not remember. Too long, he decided, so he walked back to the pig and started gutting it with his knife.

Buster stopped and turned. "What are you doing?"

Brandon continued the grueling job, without looking up. "It has been a long time since we ate meat. I am bringing it back to the camp. It will make a good breakfast."

Buster nodded. "Yes, I forgot that you creatures are barbaric animals."

Great, we are off to a wonderful start, thought Brandon. But he kept up the job and replied, "It will provide us with much needed protein."

Buster just stood there, watching Brandon.

The sun had fully risen, so Brandon could see Buster clearly. The pegasus was smaller than Midnight. He was brown instead of black. He had a white streak on his forehead, a white streak in his mane, and a white streak in his tail. Then there was the horn. The horn was made out of thick bone and hair. It spiraled out of the pegasus's forehead. Brandon knew that this was a fierce weapon. *What power,* he thought.

Brandon looked into Buster's eyes. There was something about his eyes. Brandon stood up and approached Buster. Buster shifted uncomfortably, thinking that this human was staring at his deformed forehead.

"It is your eyes," Brandon said.

Buster looked confused.

"Your eyes," Brandon continued. "The color of your eyes. You have one green eye and one blue eye, just like me."

A look of shock crossed Buster's face. Brandon looked at the freshwater stream. The light was just hitting it right. "Come on." Brandon motioned Buster over to the water. Brandon kneeled by the water and looked into it. He could see the reflection of his face. The first thing he noticed was that he needed a bath, and the second thing was how long and curly his hair had gotten. Then Brandon studied Buster's reflection.

"Look down into the water," said Brandon. "See? See our eyes? One green and one blue. Oh my gosh! Even the same ones are the same color. What a coincidence!"

They both just stared into the water and then at each other.

Book One: The Chosen Ones

Buster plunged his horn into the water. He rubbed his horn against the rocks, scrubbing it clean of the blood. When he pulled it out, he said, "No one sees my eye. Not past this deformed head."

"Deformed head?" Brandon looked at the horn. "Your horn is not deformed. Your mom is a unicorn. Doesn't she have a horn?"

"Yes, but she is a full blooded unicorn," replied Buster. "I am not."

Brandon could see the once proud Pegasus, who just saved him moments ago, slipping away. "But you are part unicorn and part pegasi." Brandon stood up and spread his arms. "Man, you have the best of both worlds. You can fly, and you can kill a pig with your horn! Who can do that? Is there any other like you?"

Buster shook his head.

"Then that makes you special," said Brandon.

"You are just being kind because I saved your life," said Buster.

"Yeah, you saved my life!" Brandon pointed at the horn. "And you saved it with that." But Brandon could tell he wasn't being convincing, so he tried another approach. "Have you heard of the Vision Keeper? Have you heard of her?"

Buster stood tall. "Of course, I have heard of her. There is a great legend about her that has been told throughout our generations." He looked around and brought his head closer to Brandon. "I am told she is here," he whispered. "With you?"

Brandon nodded. "Not only is she with me, but she is also my sister. She has a disease. It is called epilepsy. Back at our home in our valley, she is not looked at as the Vision Keeper. She is just a child who is sick. Yet she is the Vision Keeper and is special. Just like you!" Brandon could tell that Buster was starting to think about it, but the pegasus was still not convinced.

"Look, help me get this pig back to camp," said Brandon. "I will introduce you to the Vision Keeper. If she thinks you are special, will you believe me?"

"The Vision Keeper will not think of me as special." Buster put his head down. "I am a disgrace to our herd."

Brandon knew that Diana would freak out about seeing a unicorn-pegasus and would probably squeal with delight. He was convinced his plan would work. "Well, there is only one way to prove who is right."

Buster agreed and helped Brandon with the pig. They walked back to camp.

Once the group got over the initial shock of Brandon bringing back an oversized dead pig and a pegasus with a horn, they all were enchanted with Buster, especially Diana, who exclaimed with delight, as predicted.

Brooke tried to keep Diana from running her hands all over the pegasus, but Brandon pulled Brooke back and explained the situation. Brooke then joined in, proclaiming how magnificent Buster was. In fact, the girls insisted

The Trahe Chronicles

on riding Buster back to his valley, and Buster decided it was a great honor to fly the Vision Keeper on his back.

Jereco was just asking how the rest of them were supposed to get to the valley when he spotted some pegasi flying over the island mountain.

Buster explained that he was sent first to get them ready for their departure. Midnight wanted to give his herd some time with their families before sending them to pick up the humans. They decided to pack up the pig and roast it for the dinner feast, and soon they were in flight.

The scenery of the mountains was breathtaking. It was lush and green with tropical plants, waterfalls, and rivers. Soon, they were descending into a massive and beautiful valley surrounded by steep, rugged mountains on all sides.

The pegasi took their time flying down, circling above the herd below. There were herds of pegasi and unicorns running in groups, almost like a dance in unison. Then the herds stopped in front of a great tree. The tree was similar to a banyan tree that the kids had seen in Maui.

As they touched down, they saw Midnight and a white unicorn standing next to the tree. The group landed between the tree and the herd. The Evadeam kids noticed how quiet it was when they landed. All they could hear was the whisper of the tropical wind. They quietly dismounted. Clyde, Dale, and the other pegasi walked over and stood to the left of the white unicorn. Buster stood to the left of Midnight. The Evadeam family followed Hachmoni and Archelaus; they stood in front of Midnight.

In the Trahe language, Midnight bellowed so all of his herd could hear. "The great Creator has brought forth the Chosen Ones. They stand before you now." Midnight walked in front of each Evadeam child and announced them to the herd. He stood in front of Brooke. "The Protector," he said. This was the first time Brooke had been called by her Trahe name. She was not sure what the name meant, but she didn't want to ask while Midnight was performing introductions.

Midnight rubbed his nose against Diana's hand. "The Vision Keeper."

Diana smiled and petted his nose.

Midnight stood in front of Jereco. "The Water Guardian."

Next was Brandon. "The Forest Friend."

And Grandpa was "The Returner."

The kids looked at Grandpa, then each other, for this was also a new name to them.

Midnight moved on to Cleo. "Cleopatra, the Guide and Protector." At this point, many of the herd bowed down.

Midnight continued. "Archelaus, leader of the Evadeam tribe." The herd neighed and stomped their hooves. They were clearly surprised and happy that the great leader was before them.

"Hachmoni." The elders of the herd bowed down at the calling of Hachmoni's name. Clearly, they honored him.

165

Book One: The Chosen Ones

Midnight moved back in front of the Evadeam family. They stood still, waiting for the herd to quiet. "Great legends had proclaimed a time—a time when descendents from the great Evadeam tribe would come back to us. A time when our world would be on the brink of danger. Of great perils. A time when peace would need to be restored by the Creator. A time when the Creator would send the *Chosen Ones!*"

A great roar came from the crowd. There was a mix of horse language and Trahe language, stomping of hooves, and birds singing above. Midnight reared and unfolded his massive black wings. He jumped into the air and took flight, followed by Buster, Clyde, and Dale. Then, one by one, the pegasi flew into the air, following Midnight. They circled above as a great herd, and as they did so, the great white unicorn reared and led the unicorn herd into the same pattern on land. It was a spectacular sight.

Both herds met back at the front of the banyan tree. Midnight and the white unicorn bowed, and the rest of the herd did the same. "It is the dawn of a new day. Let us thank the Creator for all that he has given us. Let us thank the Creator for all that he has taken away. Let us thank the Creator for this great day!" This time, there were no cheers. All heads bowed in complete silence.

Midnight lifted his head. "Let there be a celebration tonight!" Cheers rang through the crowd. Then slowly, the herd dwindled. Many went on their way while others stood around talking and looking at their guests.

Midnight walked up to the Evadeam family and their friends. "I believe you have not had a proper introduction to my mate." Midnight bowed his head toward the white unicorn. "This is Prisca."

Prisca bowed her head. "It is a great honor to meet those of great legends."

"The honor is all theirs, I am sure, Prisca," said Grandpa as he walked up to her. "My Prisca," he whispered and gave her a big hug around the neck.

The kids looked at each other with slight confusion on their faces.

Cleo interrupted the moment. "I think we should set up camp. The humans will want to freshen up before dinner." Cleo glanced over at Brandon.

Brandon remembered that he never did get his bath that morning with the interruption of the large pig.

"Do you have a place for them to rest, Lady Prisca?" asked Cleo.

"Yes, come follow me." Prisca looked over her shoulder at Grandpa. "I think you will be pleased." She led them past the banyan tree and into the jungle woods. Not far from the edge of the clearing were some huts made out of bamboo, trees, and palm. The huts blended nicely with the jungle.

"Wow," Grandpa said as he looked around. "After all these years, it looks the same. No, I take that back. I think it looks better. How could you have kept it up?"

Prisca looked up into the trees. "We had a little help."

166

The Trabe Chronicles

Grandpa looked up. "No! It can't be. Not from them."

The rest of the group looked up and did not see anything.

"The birds?" asked Diana.

Prisca shook her head, and it looked like she was smiling.

"I know," said Brandon, thinking of Willow. "It is the trees, right?"

Hachmoni laughed. "No, but that is very clever thinking, Brandon."

"Snakes?" asked Brooke with a slight quiver as she looked around.

"No, dear Brooke," said Grandpa. "There are no snakes on this island." He looked at Prisca. "Or at least there weren't any here before."

Prisca shook her head again.

At that moment, the trees above started to shake. Then there was a squeaky sound that sounded like laughter.

Grandpa laughed. "Well, I don't believe it. Aren't you a sight for sore eyes?"

Something came swinging out of the trees and landed on Grandpa's shoulders. Everyone jumped, except for Grandpa, Prisca, Hachmoni, and Cleo. Sitting on Grandpa's shoulders was a monkey.

"You are looking a little gray around the edges," Grandpa said to the monkey.

The monkey chattered something back with displeasure.

"Yes, I suppose I do too," replied Grandpa. "It has been a long time, my friend."

The monkey chattered something back, and Grandpa laughed again. "Yes, I would call you a friend, after all that we have been through."

The monkey said something that brought tears to Grandpa's eyes.

The Evadeam kids shifted uncomfortably because they did not see Grandpa cry often.

It was Brandon who broke the silence. "It looks like they did a nice job on the huts."

That brought Grandpa's attention back. "Yes, yes, indeed. Good job, Larry."

Brooke's eyebrow shot up at the mention of her dad's name. She did not get a chance to question Grandpa because the monkey was chattering something. Grandpa translated. "He said, 'thank you and that he's very proud to clean up the huts for the Chosen Ones."

"How is it that you can understand the monkey's language?" asked Archelaus.

Grandpa shrugged. "I guess it just came naturally after being around them."

"Is it like how Brandon can talk to trees?" asked Diana, "and how Jereco can talk to the water people?"

"Yes, I guess it is, Diana."

Diana thought for a moment. "I think I would like to learn the monkey's language."

167

Book One: The Chosen Ones

"Well, I do not know if it is that simple," Grandpa said.

"Wait a minute," Jereco said. "Am I the only one who has noticed something strange about all this?"

They all looked at him.

Jereco had a look of frustration on his face and threw up his arms. "How does Grandpa know Prisca? How does Grandpa know monkey language? How come Grandpa is friends with a monkey that he has never seen before?"

Brooke looked from Jereco to Grandpa. "Yeah, and how is a monkey named after my dad?"

Everyone got quiet.

The monkey chattered something that sounded a lot like "Oh, oh," and he flew back into the trees. Grandpa scratched the top of his head and then rubbed his hands together. "I guess you got me, kids. You are too smart for your own good, but then again, you are my grandkids."

All four of his grandkids were staring at him with folded arms across their chests. Grandpa shrugged and opened his arms. "I am sorry, but I was told to keep it from you."

He looked down at Cleo, who licked a paw and said, "Anyone hungry?"

Brooke stepped forward. "So you have been to Trahe before! You have been here before, and you did not tell us? You did not warn us about everything that we ran into? You could have shared something with us."

"Brooke, I swore not to say anything. Plus, this place is the only place where I have been on this planet."

Jereco stepped up. "That is not true. You have been to Willow before, haven't you?" Before waiting for an answer, he said, "You have. I can tell. There were too many signs. Too many hints. There was too much that you knew."

Grandpa rubbed his chin. "Oh yeah, I forgot about that one time."

"That one time?" asked Brandon.

"How many times have you been to Trahe, Grandpa?" asked Diana.

Grandpa looked down at Diana. "When you get to my age, you sometimes forget things. You see, I was just starting to think that all my time in Trahe was just a dream. Then I got shipped back here." He shook his head. "I just lost track of time. So many memories lost."

Prisca stepped forward. "I think it is time for everyone to unpack and get settled. We have a pig to cook for you humans, and from what I understand, that could take awhile. Your grandpa needs some rest."

Because these words came from Prisca, no one argued, and the subject was dropped for the moment.

The huts were dry and comfortable enough. There was a small freshwater stream that ran behind the huts and then back out to the meadow. The Evadeam kids took their time unpacking what they needed. They were used to keeping most of their items packed in their bags for quick departures.

168

The Trahe Chronicles

They took turns freshening up in the stream. They needed this time to think about their new discovery about Grandpa.

Brooke and Jereco seemed especially angry about Grandpa's lies or "untold stories," as Diana had put it.

Brandon broke the silence. "If he was told by Cleo or the Creator or God not to tell us, then he couldn't. I understand that. It is kind of like being in the military or an undercover cop. If you have a secret operation, you cannot tell anyone about it, not even your family. You should know this, Brooke, since your dad was in the military."

Brooke did not say anything, but the look on her face told everyone she was still mad at Grandpa.

Archelaus walked up to the four kids. "Look, I know you are mad at your grandpa. Believe me. I understand. I was mad at Hachmoni about lying to me about my sister and brother still being alive. But we are all on the same mission, and we have to pull together. We have to have faith that each of us is told to do something for a reason."

"So if the Creator tells you to jump off a bridge, would you?" Brooke asked in defiance.

Archelaus folded his arms. "Yes, I would."

"Oh bologna!" Brooke said with frustration.

"Bologna?" asked Archelaus.

Brooke just rolled her eyes and turned her back. But Archelaus would not let her walk away. He grabbed her arm. "Yes, yes, I would do whatever the Creator tells me to do. The point is that I trust him. He is a good god and would never ask me to do something that was not for my own good. Chances are, he would not ask me to jump off a bridge. Bologna!"

Diana started laughing. "Bologna isn't used that way."

They turned toward her, realizing what Archelaus had said. Even Brooke broke out with a smile.

"Besides," Diana said, "I thought Grandpa had been here before too, and I was not mad at him."

Brooke gave Diana a questioning look. "Why did you think Grandpa was here before?"

Diana shrugged. "In my dreams. I had dreams before about him being in another world, but kind of like Grandpa said, I thought they were just dreams."

No one questioned her dreams anymore, so Brooke knew now they must be true. "I still don't understand why Grandpa didn't say something once we landed on Trahe."

"Maybe because he did forget," said Archelaus. "I remember when I was younger, some of the elders would have forgotten memories."

"Yeah, they do on Earth too." replied Brandon. They all thought for a moment.

Archelaus rubbed Brooke's shoulders. "Remember what you told me

Book One: The Chosen Ones

about forgiving Hachmoni?"

Brooke nodded and let out a sigh.

Thump! A monkey landed right next to Brooke. He looked up at Brooke and chattered something.

Brooke bent down. "Larry, right?"

The monkey nodded.

"So I wonder if you were named after my dad, or if my dad was named after you?"

"Neither," said Hachmoni from behind them. "Larry, the monkey, is named after your grandpa's brother. Your dad is also named after your grandpa's brother."

Brooke's eyebrows came together. "Grandpa does not have a brother named Larry." "Yes, yes I did," said Grandpa as he walked up. "And he lived here." He gestured at the huts. "And he died here."

The Evadeam kids stood there in shock.

Prisca walked up. "The feast is about to begin, and Midnight wants to know if the honored guests are ready?"

The kids really did not want to leave during the middle of their conversation, but they could not refuse Prisca and Midnight. So the subject once again was dropped for the moment.

They walked out to the clearing near the banyan tree. The sun was setting, spreading beautiful colors into the valley. Tables and chairs for the guests were made out of fallen logs. A small fire was lit nearby. The kids assumed it was the monkeys who had helped. Besides themselves, the monkeys were the only ones with hands. The feast was small since they were the only humans to eat the roasted pig.

The pegasi and unicorns ate grass. The monkeys ate small bugs and fruit, and the birds enjoyed diving down to steal some of the bugs from the monkeys. As everyone enjoyed the dinner feast, it soon grew dark. Most of the animals said their goodnights and went off to their lairs.

Soon all that was left was the Evadeam family, Hachmoni, Archelaus, Cleo, Midnight, Prisca, Buster, and a few monkeys. The sky was dark and lit up by many stars. The air was warm and was starting to cool down from the island breeze. The island's natural sounds could be heard, instead of the cars that Brooke might have heard back home. The silence and thoughts were interrupted by Grandpa's low voice.

"I remember being fourteen years old." Grandpa looked up. "In fact, Diana, I believe that you are the youngest Evadeam family member to come from Earth."

Cleo nodded in agreement.

"My first time here, I was too young. Too young." He shook his head back and forth.

No one dared speak a word. They did not want to interrupt his story.

"There was so much war on Earth. I wanted so badly to get away. To

The Trahe Chronicles

come to another world. I was taught the Trahe language. I wanted to believe it. At night, I would sneak downstairs and hear my dad and uncles talk about Trahe. I would listen on the stairs for hours until a black and white cat would come and close the stairway door." He looked at Cleo.

"Then it came. The calling. Some older cousins and my older brother were ordered into the military. Everyone was told that they were going off to war on Earth. But I knew the truth. That they were going on a grand adventure to another world called Trahe. I was so excited, and I wanted to go. All the planning and preparation did not prepare them for a stowaway."

Grandpa looked up and seemed to stare beyond the fire. "I stowed away in the spaceship." He laughed. "I strapped myself down in the supply closet. It was a bumpy ride, but being fourteen, I did not mind. It took longer than I had thought. I needed to eat. I needed to use the bathroom, so I finally snuck out, only to be caught by my cousin. Luckily, they found me before we left Earth's atmosphere, and they put me in a capsule."

Grandpa shook his head. "Boy, was my cousin mad. He threw me at my brother, Larry, and said that he was in charge of me. Larry was not happy, but later, he confided that he would have done the same thing. He had also been waiting his whole life for this trip. Some Evadeam family members never got the chance to come to Trahe, even after years of studying and waiting. What a shame—never have that opportunity. Knowing that made me feel a little better about hiding in the ship. Of course, later, my dad let me have it for worrying my mother to death about my disappearance."

Grandpa looked at all the kids to get his meaning across. "Nothing prepared me for my arrival into Trahe for the first time. My dear grandkids, you have been pretty lucky on this journey. Back then, I had left a country in war to land in another country in war. It was terrible."

He ran his hand through his hair. "The Madeave were at the beginning of their war of revenge. They were killing and destroying anything that was not Madeave. They killed women, children, and animals. We were stuck right in the middle of it. At first, we were just surviving, and we really wanted to get right back on the ship. But then something remarkable happened. We discovered why we were sent to Trahe."

Grandpa paused. "I know you don't understand why you are here—why we have not found your parents yet. You do not understand the Trahe prophecy. Your time will come when you know why. Ours did for that trip. You see, all of this may seem very primitive to you: no cars, no malls, no phones, and no bathroom facilities. But this is nothing like it was when I first landed here. It was extremely primitive. There was hardly any medicine. So almost everyone who got hurt during these Madeave wars died. My cousins and brother were trained in the medical field. We had no modern medicine with us, but they knew enough. Even I knew some medical basics from helping out Dad on the farm, so we starting helping and healing the Evadeam people. We were saving them. We kept the Evadeam tribe from becoming

171

Book One: The Chosen Ones

instinct."

There was a moment of silence as Grandpa reminisced.

This time, it was Jereco who broke the silence. "How long were you here?"

Grandpa looked up. "Two years. I was sixteen when I finally went back home."

The kids looked at each other, all thinking the same thing—they thought they would only be gone for a few weeks. How long had it been already? Would they be gone for two years too?

"I know what you are thinking, but each trip is different, like why you are here and for how long. Besides, saving the Evadeam tribe on Trahe was one purpose. I believe there was another purpose. When it was time for us to finally leave, we came across some Madeave bodies on the way to the spaceship. We thought they were all dead. As I walked by one small body, it moved. After two years of helping people, my instinct told me to stop and help her. Yes, it was a she. She looked about my age, and she was the most beautiful girl who I had ever seen. My cousins and brother tried to help her, but the primitive medicine was not enough."

Grandpa looked up at Hachmoni.

Hachmoni nodded and Grandpa continued. "Hachmoni was with us and noticed a symbol on her right ankle. A green symbol wrapped around her ankle. Much like yours, Jereco, for she was a descendant of a Water Guardian. We did not understand at the time why she was lying among the Madeave bodies, left for dead, but we knew we had to save her. We knew what we had to do. It was decided that we would to take her with us, back to Earth. At the time I did not know what that meant until we were ready to board the ship. As we were getting ready, Larry said he would volunteer to stay behind because we were short one seat. See, our spaceship was not as good as it is today. We were lacking space to take back another passenger. I argued that I was a stowaway two years ago, so I should be the one to stay behind. However, Larry insisted on staying behind. I did not understand why at the time, but it was something he felt like he had to do."

"Did you ever see him again, Grandpa?" asked Diana.

"Yes, I did, Diana. Blessed by the Creator, I did. I was very fortunate to come back, and that was when I met Willow. That is also where I found my brother Larry. He was teaching the power of healing and modern medicine. At least, modern for this world. That was also when Larry met Koa, the tropical bird. Koa told him about a small tribe that needed medical attention on a remote island. Soon we were introduced to Luke Thunder, Midnight's father. He flew us to the island where Larry was able to help some of the islanders. He fell in love with a local, beautiful island woman."

"And they lived there, happily ever after?" asked Brooke.

Grandpa's face got dark. "Yes, I suppose he did for awhile."

"Yes, he did, Grandpa," Diana said. "He did. I saw it in my dreams. He

The Trahe Chronicles

lived happily ever after and had a baby. Well, until..." She bit her lip. "...until something dark came, and the baby died."

Grandpa looked at Diana. "You dreamed all of that?"

She nodded.

"And he was happy?"

She put her hand on Grandpa's. "Yes, Grandpa, he was."

"So was it on this island?" asked Brooke.

"No, an island south of here," Grandpa replied.

"But you said your brother found the monkey," Brooked pointed out. "Was that on this island?"

Grandpa nodded. "See, a disease had killed everyone on Larry's island, including his wife and child. The disease was something that he could not cure and something that he was immune to. He blamed himself, thinking he had brought the virus to the island. He burned all the bodies, and the whole island caught on fire. He wanted to die in the fire. He told me to leave with Luke Thunder, but I would not let him hurt himself. He would not come with us, so I knocked him out and threw him on Luke Thunder. Luke Thunder flew us to this island."

Grandpa shook his head. "Boy, Larry was mad at me. He wanted to die where his heart died back on that island. He was sad—useless—and I was running out of time. It was almost time for me to go back to Earth. Then one day, the Creator answered my prayer. He dropped—

literally dropped—a miracle out of the sky, or should I say, the trees."

Larry, the monkey, climbed onto Grandpa's shoulders. "Larry was a sick newborn monkey that dropped out of the trees. For some reason, my brother took an interest in this little monkey. He had a new determination to save this monkey, and he did."

"So now he lived happy ever after?" asked Brooke.

Grandpa sighed, and the monkey shook his head. "Larry died shortly after saving the monkey."

"And that is why you named him Larry?" whispered Brooke.

"Yes, that is why I named him Larry. For whatever reason, my brother was supposed to save this monkey. Maybe if only to save his own soul and heart."

Brooke got up and hugged Grandpa. "And you named my dad after him."

"That I did," Grandpa said as he hugged her back.

"And do you know who your grandmother is?" asked Prisca.

Brooke looked at Prisca and then at Grandpa.

"I know," said Brandon, jumping up. "It is the girl that you saved on your first trip." "Very good, Brandon," said Prisca.

The kids just looked at each other and Grandpa. They had forgotten why they had been mad at Grandpa. They were learning so much about Grandpa and themselves. Their eagerness to learn more was interrupted by Cleo.

Book One: The Chosen Ones

"It is time for bed," she announced. Protests were made, but Cleo won with the help of Prisca and Hachmoni.

As the children lay in bed, they thought of everything they had learned that day. They also remembered their parents. Parents who were still lost. Lost somewhere on Trahe. They prayed and hoped that they would find them soon.

The Trahe Chronicles

Brandon's New Friend

Brandon lay awake, unable to go to sleep. He looked over at his brother, who also was awake. Jereco lay curled up and was staring at the green mark wrapped around his ankle. As Jereco ran his finger across the green mark, he wondered if his grandmother had her mark until the day she died. He never remembered seeing it.

"I think it is cool that you and Grandma both have green marks," said Brandon. "Does it make you feel better that you are not the only one to be branded by alien water people?"

Jereco smiled at Brandon's frankness. "Yeah, it makes me feel better. We should get some sleep."

Brandon sat up. "I can't sleep. I am going to step out for a moment."

Jereco frowned. "It is dark out there, and we do not know enough about this island."

"I will only be a moment. The fresh air will do me some good."

Knowing he would not be able to stop Brandon without a fight, Jereco gave him five minutes to return to the hut.

"Fifteen," Brandon replied as he headed out the door.

Brandon took a deep breath as he stood outside. The air smelled good, like tropical flowers and an ocean breeze. Brooke was right; this place was a lot like a Hawaiian island. It was darker here though. There were no street lights, cars, or neon hotel signs. There was only the light from the huge moon and the stars above. Brandon grabbed a torch and lit it. He used the torch to light his way. He was not sure where he was heading. Jereco was right. He shouldn't wander far as he was not familiar with the island, unlike how familiar he had been with the city of Willow.

He sighed. He missed Willow. He yearned to hear her. To talk to her. He stopped and listened for the sound of talking trees. He listened to the night sounds, and soon, he was able to pick out the rustling sound of the island trees. He looked up and watched the gentle sway of the big palm trees looming above him. "I miss you, Willow."

"*Brandon*," spoke a gentle voice.

Brandon jerked his head and shined the torch toward the source of the voice. "Willow?"

"*Brandon.*"

"Mom?" As soon as he said it, he realized the voice could not be his mother's. But it sounded a lot like her. Just like it did when Willow first talked to him. Brandon felt anxious and started walking toward the sound of the voice. He was led to the huge tree that was in the clearing where they had feasted earlier.

The tree was not nearly as big as Willow, but it was quite massive, like a banyan tree. By Brandon's guess, the tree was old and ancient. He felt that he should respect and honor the tree. Brandon kneeled and placed his hand on

175

Book One: The Chosen Ones

the large trunk. He started to speak to the tree, and soon the leaves high above made a rustling noise.

The tree spoke. "Forest Friend, welcome. Welcome to the Island of the Pegasi. You have traveled far. We have waited a long time for your arrival. What brings you to me? Do you not desire sleep?"

Brandon sighed, relaxed his shoulders, and leaned against the tree trunk. "I miss Willow. I miss talking to the trees."

"Comfort, I bring thee. The Forest Friend will always find comfort with the trees. Do you not also seek answers?"

Brandon's eyebrows came together as he lifted his head up toward the trees. "My mom. I miss my mom. Do you know where my parents are?" He choked out a whisper. "Are they alive?" Brandon waited patiently as the ancient banyan tree's leaves rustled in the wind.

"The answer you seek is found in the ancient Evadeam City."

Brandon jumped up. He was just told where they could find their lost parents. He was so excited. He couldn't wait to go wake up the others.

But the tree stopped him; a tree branch blocked Brandon's way. "Answers will not be given if the path is not followed."

"What?" asked Brandon frustrated.

"Answers will not be given if the path is not followed," said another voice from behind the tree.

Brandon turned and raised his torch.

Standing before him was Buster. Buster walked toward Brandon and repeated, "Answers will not be given if the path is not followed." Buster nodded toward the tree trunk. "If you have not noticed by now, trees like to speak in riddles."

"You can speak the tree language?"

"Yes."

"So what does it mean?" said Brandon.

"I believe it means that you cannot take a direct path to the ancient Evadeam City. First, do you know where the ancient Evadeam City is located?"

Brandon shook his head. "No, do you?"

Buster also shook his head. "I do not, but I believe my grandfather or Hachmoni may."

Brandon turned to walk away. "Good. Let's go ask them."

The rustling of the leaves started again.

Brandon stopped and looked up. "Now what?"

The tree did not answer.

Buster stomped a hoof. "May I?"

Brandon gestured with his hands for him to go ahead.

Buster stood before the massive tree trunk. "How do we find the path?"

The tree answered, "The answer you seek is under the waters. The Water Guardian must find the symbols."

176

The Trahe Chronicles

"Great," Brandon mumbled.

A small tree branch came down and hit Brandon on the head. "Patience, Forest Friend. The Forest Friend must learn patience. The Forest Friend must learn from the Horned Wing One."

"Who?" asked Brandon.

"I am the Horned Wing One," replied Buster.

When Brandon turned toward Buster, he noticed Buster did not look to happy with his other name. "Horned Wing One?"

"Yes, that is my Trahe name."

Brandon thought about it for a moment. "So who named you Buster?"

"My dad."

Brandon decided not to pursue the name subject any further and turned back to the tree. "Why do we have to follow a special path to the Evadeam City?"

"There are others who must fulfill their prophecies and travel with the Chosen Ones."

"Like who?" said Brandon.

"The Horned Wing One, Midnight, Luke Thunder, and the other travelers who will be revealed in time."

"So now what?" asked Brandon.

As the tree leaves rustled, Buster replied, "We get some sleep and wait."

Brandon was frustrated again because waiting was not one of his best traits.

"I cannot believe that I get to leave this island," Buster mumbled.

"You have never left this island?" said Brandon.

Buster shook his head. "I have lived here all my life."

Brandon whistled and suddenly felt sorry for Buster. "Well, at least you will be able to leave now, and based on my experience so far, we will have some grand adventures."

Buster actually looked like he was smiling. Brandon looked at him and his gaze went to the unicorn horn. He wondered how creatures outside this island would react to a unicorn-pegasus.

Buster noticed Brandon's reaction. "Maybe I should not go."

"No, you must," insisted Brandon.

Buster hesitated and looked up. "I have always wanted to visit my mom's island."

"She isn't from this island?"

"No, Unicorn Island is several miles from here."

"So how did she get here, without wings?"

"That is a long story—one that the banyan tree loves to tell."

The tree rustled his leaves and shook his branches, agreeing that this was a story Brandon should know.

Brandon and Buster sat comfortably under the tree as the banyan tree began her story. Brandon was surprised to hear that his grandfather was one

Book One: The Chosen Ones

of the main characters.

"It began when Grandpa and his brother Larry came to the Island of the Pegasi," the tree said. "After Larry had healed the monkey, Larry's illness progressed. Grandpa was sitting next to Larry's bed when the monkey started to talk to Grandpa in the Trahe language. The monkey informed Grandpa that there might be a possible cure for Larry. The monkey told Grandpa about the legend of the unicorns and how their horns had magical healing powers. Grandpa took great interest since he had never seen a unicorn on Trahe. The monkey told Grandpa that Unicorn Island was only a few miles from this island. Surely, the pegasi could fly Grandpa and Larry there."

"Grandfather jumped at the opportunity. He persuaded Luke Thunder to take him to Unicorn Island. Luke Thunder, however, warned Grandpa that the magic from the unicorn horn must be freely given by the unicorn. Forcing, stealing, or killing a unicorn would release curses filled with evil. There was also no promise that the magic would work on Larry, but Grandpa was willing to take the chance."

"Luke Thunder's son Midnight volunteered to carry Larry to Unicorn Island. Horror lay before them when they arrived."

"The Madeave tribesmen and snakes had taken over the island. They had either slaughtered or imprisoned the unicorns."

"Luke Thunder and Midnight flew quickly out of sight. A seagull flew up to them and informed them that there was a hidden cavern on the other side of the island. There, they could safely rest. When they arrived, they were surprised to find some surviving unicorns. Mostly females and children. The surviving unicorns were led by a mare named Prisca."

Brandon's head popped up as he recognized the name.

The banyan tree continued. "Prisca had explained how the Madeave and snakes came on boats and attacked their island. It was the surprise of the attack and the numbers of the enemy that led to the unicorns' downfall. They had lived in peace for so long that they were not prepared for the evil that had pounced upon them. The attack had also just happened, so word had not spread to the other islands yet."

"Luke Thunder and Grandpa decided to go get help by finding the great Hachmoni, who was said to be currently visiting nearby. Midnight and Larry were to stay with Prisca and the unicorns to help them. Grandfather did not forget why they had come to the island in the first place and asked Prisca if there was a way she could help Grandpa's brother. She said she could, and with that reassurance, Luke Thunder and Grandpa were on their way."

"However, it was the last time your grandfather saw Larry alive. Larry was aware of the unicorn legend and knew that if Prisca gave a gift of life, she would weaken. As Larry looked at the other unicorns, he knew Prisca needed all of her strength to protect them. He insisted that Prisca not honor his brother's request and let him die. Larry convinced Prisca that he was ready to go to the Creator's world and see his beloved ones who had passed on before

The Trahe Chronicles

him. Prisca honored Larry's request, and he died peacefully surrounded by the creatures he only dreamed of—the unicorns."

There was a moment of silence before the banyan tree continued.

"Luke Thunder and your grandfather were successful in bringing back enough help to defeat the unicorn's enemies. During this time of war, Midnight and Prisca became good friends. They eventually fell in love and with the blessing of the Creator and Hachmoni, they became mates. Prisca decided to leave her herd and came to the Island of the Pegasi to live."

Brandon looked over at Buster. "And then you were created. See, you were meant to be. And tomorrow, we should start our new adventures together."

Brandon thanked the banyan tree for her story and said goodnight.

Buster walked Brandon back to his hut.

"Did the war ever happen on this island?" asked Brandon.

"No, this island is highly protected. The sea animals and water people protect the sea. The high, staggered cliffs protect the entire island. One can only fly onto this island."

Brandon recalled the steep cliffs that reached high above, overlooking the beach where they camped their first night.

Buster continued. "This island was once a mighty volcano. The Creator asked the volcano to go to sleep, so a new great, powerful creature could emerge and live in the volcano crater. The volcano was honored to become the home of the Pegasi. The volcano asked that her hot lava rocks be turned into green, lush gardens and the home of many creatures. That is how this island rainforest was created."

Brandon stopped and turned. "So the volcano was okay with dying for the pegasi?"

"Oh, she is not dead. She went to sleep. She slumbers deep under the planet's crust, waiting for the Creator to beckon her. I have heard the elders talk about how she stirs when evil is near. When the attack of Unicorn Island happened, the sea creatures said hot boiling waters were churning deep within the sea. She did not settle down to sleep again until after peace was restored." Buster lowered his voice to a whisper. "I hear talk that she is slowly waking up again due to the rise of the Madeave tribe and the monster snakes."

Brandon shuddered at the mention of the snakes.

"You have seen such evil creatures?" said Buster.

Brandon nodded. "One attacked our ship as soon as we landed on Trahe. Then others had attacked Mangus Village and destroyed it."

"Ship?"

They had now arrived at Brandon's hut, and Brandon decided that he would get in serious trouble with Cleo if he explained to Buster about spaceships, so he decided to change the subject. He stretched and proclaimed

Book One: The Chosen Ones

that he was tired. "We better get some rest. It sounds like we have our work cut out for us if we want to find my parents at Evadeam City."

At the mention of Brandon's lost parents, Buster decided to bid Brandon goodnight and wandered off to his own lair for the evening.

Brandon quietly entered his hut and crawled into bed. He noticed that his brother was fast asleep, and he thanked the Creator for not alarming Jereco that he had been gone for more than fifteen minutes.

Brandon said a small prayer to the Creator for his parents, the rest of his family, and his new friends. He then looked over at his brother. "Please give Jereco the wisdom and strength to help find the clues needed to help find our parents."

Brandon soon went to sleep as he listened to the sound of the island breeze passing through the large palm trees looming above.

The Trahe Chronicles

Abijam

Brooke and Diana slept in a nearby hut. As the sun rose, Brooke stirred. The first of Brooke's senses to waken was her sense of smell. The air was fresh, crisp, and clean. She smelled sweet flowers. She smiled as she breathed in the pleasant air. Then, came the sound. The sound of birds singing. It felt like a lazy summer day with wonderful smells and sounds surrounding her. Brooke slowly rise and watched Cleo try to wake Diana. Brooke smiled as she walked out of their hut. *She would let Cleo be the alarm clock this morning.*

Diana did not want to wake up, but a paw hit her face. Finally, irritated, Diana knocked Cleo's paw away. "Leave me alone," mumbled Diana.

Cleo was persistent. No matter how much Diana ignored her, Cleo continued to annoy Diana. Nothing was more annoying than a talking cat. "Diana, wake up! We must be on the move. Our time on the Island of the Pegasi is almost up. You must tell Jereco that Abijam beckons him."

Diana opened her eyes with a start. She remembered a dream. She had a dream that she stood in a field of very lush and long grass. She was surrounded by a tropical forest. First, she noticed the plentiful, beautiful flower bushes. They had white, pink, lavender, yellow, and red flowers. They were all so exquisite and smelled sweet. Their scent was better than any perfume. She picked one and sniffed. Yes! They were simply magnificent.

The beauty dulled, and the flower started to wilt. The smell of fresh flowers faded and was replaced with the smell of fish. Dead fish.

Diana felt very sad that the flower was dying. Diana began to cry. The tears in her dream flowed until water surrounded her and flooded the meadow. The field on the tropical island had turned gloomy. Dark and stormy. Diana's tears had flooded the island, and soon Diana was drowning in her own tears. Water swirled around Diana, and she tried to keep her head above the water. Diana screamed for help as she felt herself being pulled under the water.

Help came. A dark shadow pulled Diana out of the water. The shadow spoke. "Tell Jereco to seek Abijam for the answers."

Before Diana could ask who Abijam was, the shadow was gone. The water receded. The smell of tropical flowers filled the air once more.

Diana blinked as she remembered the end of her dream. She turned to Cleo. "Who is Abijam?"

"Abijam is the leader of the water people. He is very ancient and wise. Very few land people have seen him. Even fewer have been beckoned by Abijam."

"How did you know about my dream?"

"I had the same dream. Now come. We must be off at once." Cleo jumped off Diana's bed and proceeded outside the hut.

Diana dressed quickly. She walked out of her hut and looked at the surroundings. Diana saw the flower bushes. They were like the ones in her

181

Book One: The Chosen Ones

dream. She smelled the flowers, picked one, and put it in her hair. She looked around the tropical jungle. Hovering over the bushes was an assortment of trees. There were palm trees, coconut trees, and other tropical trees she didn't recognize. In those trees were the birds she had heard.

There were so many of them, and they came in an array of different colors. Some were all white. Some had many colors like red, yellow, blue and green. Some were all green. Some all blue. Some were even black with red beaks. And they all seemed to be chirping. No, now they seemed to be talking! They were talking at Cleo, who had walked up behind Diana.

The birds were telling Cleo things, like "don't think about eating us. Keep on walking. Do you know where you are at? What do you want here in our home?" Then suddenly, a few of them started to dive-bomb toward Cleo.

Cleo stopped, and Diana saw something that reminded her that Cleo was not a typical house cat. Cleo's eyes turned yellow, then white. Then a white glow surrounded the cat. She said in a very loud voice, "I am the messenger for our Creator; I am Cleopatra the Cat, I bring the Chosen Ones. Do you dare disrespect me?"

The birds landed, surrounding Cleo. They bowed and replied that they were at her service. Then they all flew up, flocking together, made a V-line, and headed east toward the rising sun.

Diana and Cleo followed the birds until they arrived at the banyan tree. Koa was perched in the tree. "Good morning," he squawked.

"Good morning," said Diana. "Have you seen Jereco?"

Koa's head cocked. "He is helping gather fruit for your breakfast."

Koa turned to Cleo. "Legends are dying. Legends are fading."

Cleo nodded sadly in agreement as she remembered the way the island birds had just treated her.

Diana and Cleo turned and walked toward the table that was set up for their meals. Everyone was slowly gathering for breakfast. The food for the land people consisted of fresh fruit, juice, and nuts. Diana thought it was very good. As she ate, she relayed her dream.

Jereco was excited that he had been beckoned by the leader of the water people. "Where will I find him?"

"In the sea," replied Hachmoni.

"But where in the sea?"

"I imagine that he will find you."

Luke Thunder had offered advice to start on the side of the island where there were some well-known water caverns. They agreed to venture out right after breakfast. Jereco, Brandon, Hachmoni, and Archelaus would be flown to that part of the island. The rest of their group would stay behind.

The party that would head to the caverns packed supplies. As Archelaus was tying his pack to Midnight, Brooke walked up to him. "Be careful and keep my family safe."

Archelaus nodded. "Why don't you get some rest? I have a feeling our

182

The Trahe Chronicles

visit on this island is short-lived, and we will soon be on our way."

Brooke agreed and quickly gave him a hug before she walked away.

Jereco was quietly watching the exchange between Archelaus and Brooke. He liked Archelaus, but he did not like what was developing between the two of them. He didn't want his cousin getting hurt. She always seemed to pick the loser guys who broke her heart. Of course, Brooke would never admit to it. Archelaus was not a loser, but he was of the Trahe world—

a world that they would be leaving someday.

Grandpa walked up and handed Jereco his pack.

Jereco nodded toward Brooke. "Grandpa?"

Grandpa held up his hand. "I know. Already noted. I will take care of the situation if there becomes one. You, on the other hand, need to concentrate on your task."

"Which is?"

"According to the conversation Brandon had with the banyan tree, you must find the written words in the water caves that will lead us to Evadeam City, which eventually will lead us to your parents."

"But I thought Hachmoni knew where Evadeam City is located."

"Apparently, time has changed the path, and we have not a moment to waste, trying to find it. Plus, there seems to be some other people who we need to pick up on the way. These written words that the banyan tree speaks of may lead us down the right path."

Jereco shook his head. "Riddles—the trees always speak in riddles."

Soon they were off in the air once more. Jereco admitted that he was going to miss flying on the pegasi when they returned to Earth. He looked over at Brandon, who was enjoying riding Buster. Jereco was sad to think how much Brandon was going to miss Buster when they finally did leave.

Brandon had said something about becoming a pilot when they returned to Earth. A pilot and a forest ranger. Jereco smiled. Brandon had never showed an interest in what he wanted to become when he grew up. Brandon was maturing fast on this trip to Trahe. *I suppose we all are,* thought Jereco. Jereco's thoughts shifted when he noticed the change of scenery below.

The lush tropical forest had been replaced by rocks and less foliage. It dawned on Jereco that they were heading toward the part of the island that was deemed to be more dangerous. That was probably why the girls and Grandpa were left behind. Luke Thunder assured everyone that they still would be safe on this part of the island.

Beyond the rocky side, the tropical forest was thicker, darker, and more dangerous. Jereco shuddered as he thought of what lived in that part of the jungle. He was told that there were no snakes, but something lurked there that no one seemed to talk about.

Soon the pegasi descended onto a black, sandy beach. This part of the island had signs of volcano lava that once flowed down from the island mountain into the sea.

Book One: The Chosen Ones

The small group of men dismounted from their pegasi.

"Now what?" asked Brandon.

"Now we eat lunch," announced Hachmoni.

"Eat lunch?" objected Jereco. "We just had breakfast." He was anxious to get under way.

"Lunch sounds good to me," said Brandon as he started to help Hachmoni with the lunch pack.

Jereco just shook his head and walked toward the seashore. He left the sunny side of the island and faced a dark and turbulent sea. It almost looked like a storm was brewing in the ocean. Even though the sea did not look inviting, Jereco had an urge to go into the waters. He quickly stripped down his clothes to his swimming outfit. He walked into the sea and was a little hesitant as he remembered the sea monster he last encountered. Jereco looked back at his friends. Jereco's eyes met Hachmoni's. Hachmoni urged him to go on. Jereco took a deep breath and dove into the sea.

The water was warm and inviting here. It was a salt water sea and easy to swim in. Jereco wished he had snorkel equipment to make it even easier. He then noticed his green mark on his ankle start to glow. As it did, a similar glow shined north of him. He decided that was a sign and followed the light. He soon swam up to an underwater cavern. He was hesitant about entering. As if to encourage him, some tropical fish swam around him and then into the cavern. Jereco followed. He would need air and was hoping there would be an air pocket inside the cave.

He continued to follow the fish and was losing hope. He needed air soon. He was just about to give up and turn around when he heard a familiar sound. The sound of the singing whales or singing water people. That gave him the boost he needed and he quickly swam ahead. He followed the tropical fish into a small hole that led into a larger room.

The cavern room was filled with rocks that had the same green glow that came from his green mark. A bright light shined above. Jereco swam up and out of the water.

He surfaced into a sea pool that sat in a huge room. Jereco took much needed breaths of air. He wiped his face and looked around. He was expecting to see a room filled with water people but was disappointed. The room was empty. It was a glowing green cavern of nothing but rock. Feeling discouraged, Jereco pulled himself out of the water. He decided to take a moment to rest on the rocky surface.

"Now what?" he mumbled.

As he lay on his back, he looked around the underwater cave. Maybe he had the wrong cave. But it seemed right, with all the glowing rocks that seemed to be the same color around his ankle. He sat up, wiped his face again, and looked around once more. He decided he'd better get up and explore. He decided that if there were any drawings, they would be on the walls. So he walked along the walls and looked closely. Nothing. The shining

184

The Trabe Chronicles

rocks provided light, but he didn't see any writings on the wall. He decided that he had been down there long enough, and it was time to move on.

Jereco went back into the water and continued to follow the lighted rocks north. He swam into another underwater cave. This cave was smaller, and he barely had enough room to move around. And once again, he did not find any writings on the wall. Frustrated, he dove back into the water and swam to yet another cave.

Again, there was no writing on the cave walls. He sat at the cave's pool edge, frustrated and now hungry. This task was not as easy as he'd thought. He would have to turn around soon to avoid being in the water after dark.

"This is all a waste of time," he mumbled. "It will be dark soon, and I have no modern equipment. I have no underwater flashlight, scuba equipment, or even writing tools. If I do find some writings on the walls, what am I supposed to do about it?"

Memorize it. That was Hachmoni's answer. Memorize it and repeat it back to him when Jereco returned. Brandon had encouraged Jereco by telling Jereco that he had the best memory out of anyone he knew.

Jereco kicked the water out of frustration. As he watched the rippling of the waters settled, he noticed the glowing rocks below. He wondered what made them glow. He had never seen the glowing substance on Earth. He looked at his ankle. He wondered if it was the same substance that made his ankle glow.

The scientific part of his mind took over. He grabbed his knife and decided to chisel out a glowing rock from the cavern wall. He had no luck getting any of it off the rock. He looked down in the water and decided maybe a rock would break free easier if it was wet.

Jereco went under the water surface and started to look against the cavern wall for a loose rock. As his fingers felt the wall, he noticed something in between the glowing rocks. He squinted under the water, trying to see well. Was that a picture?

Jereco came up, took a deep breath, and dove back in. He looked at the cavern and sure enough there was a picture. Several pictures, in fact. No, maybe hundreds. Jereco swam along the wall. How did he miss this?

The writings on the wall were not in the caves above the water but below. As Jereco continued to swim, he realized that there was too much. There was a lot to remember. Plus, he didn't understand it. The writings were in a language he didn't know. There were some pictures too, but none of it made sense to him. He wouldn't know where to begin.

Jereco followed the writings back to the first water cavern that he was in. He swam out of the pool, pulled himself out, and lay down on the cave floor. As he ran his hands over his eyes, he wondered what to do next. There was no way that he could remember all those writings, and it had to be getting dark outside. He would just have to go back and report his findings. Maybe Hachmoni would have some good advice.

Book One: The Chosen Ones

"I wonder who carved all of this into the walls?" Jereco mumbled out loud. "They must have been water people."

"Water Guardians," said a low, deep voice.

Jereco jumped up and grabbed for his knife, but he lost his balance on the slippery cavern floor. He stumbled and plunged into the cavern's pool of water. As he did so, a large green-looking hand grabbed him, preventing Jereco from hitting the underwater cave walls. The large hand pushed Jereco back out of the water. Jereco grabbed the edge of the pool and pulled himself back up. He opened his hands and noticed that he had dropped his knife.

A large splash came from the water, and Jereco saw a large fish fin dive underneath. "A water person," he whispered. Jereco felt relief and sank down to the ground. He took a moment to rest, but he only had a moment before the water person was once again beside him.

"Looking for this?" The water person handed Jereco his knife.

Jereco nodded. "Thank you."

The water person was huge and looked like a male. He was green, scaly, and older than the other water people that Jereco had seen. Jereco thought the water person looked distinguished. When the water person spoke, his voice was deep and bubbly. Like someone talking underwater. However, Jereco could understand every word.

The water person moved aside and pointed down to the written words. "Water Guardians carved the words. Water Guardians before you and your time."

"You know who I am?"

The water person looked Jereco up and down. "Yes, you are the Water Guardian of this time—a time when the Creator assigned a land person."

Jereco blinked and looked at the water person. "Water Guardians are not always land people?"

"Water Guardians are water people." The water person hesitated and then said, "Except where there are no more water people."

Jereco's eyebrows came together as he thought about what the water person had said. "But there are water people here."

The water person nodded. "But are there water people where you live?"

When Jereco didn't answer, the water person continued. "Who protects the waters at your home? Who protects the creatures of the water at your home? Where are the water people?"

Jereco looked into the eyes of this water person, and Jereco knew. He knew that there were once water people on Earth. Mermaids. The legend of mermaids were true. Legends from true stories. So what happened to them? As Jereco continued to look into the deep green eyes of this water person, another realization hit him.

He knew the truth and suddenly felt ashamed. Man. Man had killed them or perhaps destroyed their environment, just as they have destroyed the environment of the Earth's seas. The great waters and water creatures of

186

The Trahe Chronicles

Earth have been slowly dying due to man. Jereco recalled hearing the continued cry for help on television, on the Internet, and in a variety of different ads—ads asking for help to save the Earth's water creatures. He had ignored them, thinking he was too young, too inexperienced, and too poor.

As Jereco's shoulders slumped, the water person put his hand upon him. "It only takes one. One to be great. One to make a difference. Save what you can."

Jereco wiped the water from his eyes. "I will. I promise."

The water person nodded in satisfaction and started to head back into the water.

"Wait!"

The water person hesitated.

"What do I call you?" Jereco said. "Your name?"

He smiled slightly. "I am Abijam."

Jereco jumped up. "Abijam! You are Abijam?"

Abijam nodded.

Jereco wiped his hands on his wet legs and held out a hand. "I am pleased to meet you, sir. It is an honor."

Abijam shook Jereco's hand.

Jereco noticed that Abijam's hand felt like a dolphin's skin. Then it dawned on Jereco that Abijam was about to leave. "The Vision Keeper said that you were going to seek me out today," Jereco said.

Abijam nodded. "I did." He bent over, and his face came closer to Jereco's. He looked directly into Jereco's eyes. "Abijam always seeks the Water Guardian. To warn him and to guide him. For you, it is not only about our world, but it is also about yours. Remember what I have told you on this day." He turned slightly and hit his large spear on the cavern ceiling. The ceiling sparkled in a glistening green. He waved his hand above him. "The answers you seek."

Jereco looked above. There were drawings on the ceiling wall too. There was a plant that looked like a cactus, followed by a winding river. Then a shape that looked like a mountain. The last two pictures were not complete. One was of an animal that he could not make out. The other looked like a beginning of a snake's head, which gave him goose bumps. The green glow faded.

Jereco turned to Abijam. "That is all? Isn't there more?" He was still confused. He touched his stomach as it rumbled. He was confused and hungry.

Abijam shook his head. "You must eat. I will lead you back to Luke Thunder. He will understand the pictures. Also, tell Luke Thunder that he must lead you on this quest. It is his time."

Jereco nodded with agreement and wondered if he was too weak to swim back. But he soon discovered that he did not need to worry about the swim. As Jereco followed Abijam back into the water, they were escorted by several

Book One: The Chosen Ones

water people and sea creatures. Abijam had requested assistance for Jereco, and he was swept away through the underwater caverns.

The swim was fast, and when Jereco resurfaced, he was near his friends. He noticed that he was correct when he thought dusk was upon them. The sun was already starting to set. No wonder he felt hungry; he had skipped lunch, and now it was dinnertime.

As the water people and sea creatures dived back into the sea, Jereco turned to Abijam. "Thank you."

Abijam nodded and put his right hand on Jereco's shoulder. He looked Jereco in the eye. "Save your waters as I try to save mine. Until next time, Water Guardian."

Before Jereco had a chance to reply, Abijam dove into the waters. Jereco silently watched the ripples in the water. It occurred to Jereco that the turbulent sea waters earlier might have come from Abijam. The sea was calm now as Abijam swam into the darker and deeper waters.

Jereco lingered on Abijam's last words. Jereco felt some comfort knowing they would meet again. He turned toward the shoreline and his friends.

During dinner, Jereco briefed everyone on his encounter with Abijam. Luke Thunder did seem to know the place Abijam had mentioned.

Jereco also repeated Abijam's message to Luke Thunder about him going on this quest. Luke Thunder nodded and looked up into the stars. "As it is written."

They camped for the night and would return to Pegasi Valley the next morning.

They reported their adventures to Cleo. She and Luke Thunder identified the desert that was drawn on the cavern walls. Cleo nodded. "It is obvious from the grand river and the mountain pictures that we are to head toward the Great Rock Mountains. The quickest way there is to fly over the desert northwest of here. We will leave in two days. That will give everyone time to rest and pack."

Jereco was going to miss the sea. They were flying toward a desert where there would be no water people. He found comfort remembering Abijam's words—*until next time, Water Guardian.*

He hoped that meant they would be coming back here after their journey ended. Jereco did not sleep well during their last nights on the island. The worst was the night before their departure. A storm had come off the sea, leaving him with nightmares of snakes, glowing dark tunnels, and scary aliens.

In another hut, Diana also had nightmares. Diana's eyes snapped open. She lay there in soaking wet pajamas. Did she have another seizure? She had sweated so much in her sleep. She was too weak to get up or reach over and wake up Brooke. So she just lay there and thought about the last vision in her nightmare.

A storm had come off the sea, and lighting had flashed across a mountain

188

The Trahe Chronicles

on the other side of the island. As the lightning flashed across the dark skies, it revealed a figure standing in a cave opening. The figure was pale-skinned with dark hair and dark eyes. The wind from the storm blew the dark hair around the head of the lone figure. Or maybe she wasn't alone. Then there was a scream—a scream mixed in with the sounds of the thundering storm.

Book One: The Chosen Ones

PART FIVE

Bears, Caves, and Dragons

They will soar on wings like eagles in the sky.
Some will fly with the Creator.
Some will soar down into darkness.
And for others, survival is the only purpose.
- Methuselah, the Grizzly Bear

The Trahe Chronicles

Friends and Foes of Great Rock Canyon

Brooke awoke to find Diana looming over her. "What is wrong?" Brooke asked with a voice sleepy.

"I had a bad dream," Diana said, tears in her eyes.

At that moment, lightening flashed outside and shadows danced inside their hut. "It is just a storm." Brooke reached for Diana. "Come lay next to me. It will be okay."

Thunder rolled across the sky, followed by a cat's meow. Cleo came running into the hut and jumped on the bed.

The girls let out a shriek.

"You scared us!" scolded Brooke.

"Are there monsters out there?" whispered Diana.

"No," said Cleo. "There is only bad weather. My hunting for the evening is over." She started to shake the rain from her wet fur.

Brooke kicked at her. "Don't you dare! Not on our bed."

Cleo's ears bent backwards as she scowled, but she obeyed and jumped to the hut floor. After shaking off the excess water, she jumped back onto her blanket at the end of the bed.

Brooke looked at Diana. "See? It is just a bad storm. You can go back to sleep now."

Cleo stopped licking herself and paused to look at the girls.

"Diana had a bad dream," Brooke explained.

"Are you all right?" asked Cleo.

Diana nodded. "Just scared. I have a bad feeling."

Brooke's eyebrow shot up. She knew that Diana's bad feelings could mean something.

"I will stay here for the rest of the night," replied Cleo. "Go back to sleep. I will stand guard."

Diana burrowed back under her blanket and snuggled closer to Brooke and Cleo. Brooke looked over at Diana, and gave Cleo a questioning look. Cleo gestured for her to also get some sleep.

Brooke had a hard time sleeping with the storm brewing above in the island skies. She also was a little nervous about Diana's bad feelings. Finally, she drifted to sleep and woke the next morning after the storm had passed.

As she walked to the breakfast table, Brooke saw the storm's aftermath outside. Broken branches and debris lay on the tropical floor. Some hut roofs were whisked away. During breakfast there was talk about delaying their departure. The Evadeam children wanted to stay and help clean up the island. But Luke Thunder assured everyone that this had been a mild storm compared to what was due to arrive in the upcoming storm season. So they continued to prepare for their journey according to their original plan.

Weeks passed. They had been traveling in a desert somewhere north of

191

Book One: The Chosen Ones

the island and ocean. Brooke was missing the safety and security of the Island of the Pegasi. She would give anything to be back in the tropical paradise. It has been days since they last stopped at a water oasis. They were starting to run out of food and water. Everyone was rationing the best they could, but it made them weak. They were tired, dirty, and longed to see any other signs of life. They had been riding in a rugged, hilly terrain that was a barren desert.

The days were hot from the raging sun, and the nights were cool and dark. They decided it was best to travel during the dusk and dawn hours. During the hottest part of the day and the coldest of the night, they staked coverings as best they could to make a miniature tent house to rest in. When they were traveling, the humans often walked beside the pegasi to help save the pegasi strength. The days were getting quieter; they hardly talked as they all were getting tired and slightly concerned. No one dared question Jereco, Archelaus and Hachmoni's directions, so they kept to themselves, deep in thought. Even Cleo had not been saying much the last couple of days.

It was on the third day after their last oasis stop when Brandon noticed something in the distance. They were walking during the early morning dawn, and Brandon swore he saw something far off. He shook his head, rubbed his eyes, and looked again. He knew that the sun in the desert could play mean tricks on his mind. But when he looked again, he still saw something. What was it? He decided to keep the discovery to himself a little longer. He did not want to embarrass himself in case he was wrong.

A few hours later, the wind started to pick up. *It felt refreshing*, thought Brandon. The wind was light enough to kick up a breeze without blowing sand into their eyes. As they walked on, Brandon smelled something. He stopped as the others kept moving. He looked over to the northwest.

Buster had noticed that Brandon was no longer walking. "Do you need some water?" Buster asked.

Brandon nodded, thinking this would be a good idea. Maybe having a little water would help him see and think more clearly. He grabbed his canteen from his pack that was on Buster's back. He drank a little water and then decided to splash some on his face.

"Brandon?" said Buster. They were rationing the water, and he did not think it was a good idea for Brandon to waste it on his face.

Brandon just held up his hand to signal to Buster to be quiet. Then he handed the canteen to Buster. "Drink," Brandon suggested.

Buster shook his head.

Brandon turned to Buster. "I think I see something to the northwest, so I want you to drink and verify it for me."

Buster turned his head to the northwest and squinted. "Maybe," he whispered. Brandon lifted the canteen up to Buster's muzzle. Buster took a good swallow and then shook his head. He looked into the distance and turned to Brandon. "Get on. Let's take a look from above."

Brandon nodded and jumped onto Buster. They flew into the air and went a little northwest. They were careful not to travel too far from the rest of the group in case the desert winds picked up and blinded them.

"Trees!" Brandon yelled. "They are trees, Buster!"

"Yes, I see them. I see them too, and look beyond the trees." Buster flew a little closer and higher up.

"What is it?" asked Brandon. "All I see is something dark. Dark clouds?"

"No, those are mountains! Very big mountains!" Buster flew back to the group, who had stopped traveling when they noticed that Buster and Brandon were no longer following them. Before anyone could ask, both Brandon and Buster excitedly rattled about the mountains at the same time.

"Whoa!" said Grandpa, wearily. "One at a time."

Brandon and Buster looked at each other.

"You go ahead since you discovered it first," said Buster.

Brandon nodded and turned to the group. He pointed over his shoulder. "Over to the northwest, there are some trees and some large mountains in the background."

They all looked over.

"I don't see anything," said Brooke. "Are you sure you are not imagining things?"

"No," replied Buster. "I saw them too, Brooke."

They all looked again.

Hachmoni stepped forward, gazing into the distance. He put his hand over his forehead, trying to shade out the sun. "It could be."

"It is," insisted Brandon.

"But we need to be positive before we change direction," suggested Archelaus.

Hachmoni turned to Brandon. "There is a way to be sure that those are trees—"

"I can talk to the trees," cut in Brandon. He jumped off Buster. He tilted his chin up and looked toward the northwest. The wind was coming from that direction, so his voice would not carry. He looked around, trying to decide what to do. How could he communicate with those foreign trees way off in the distance?

The others just stood there waiting and watching Brandon.

So much pressure, Brandon thought. He rested his head in his hands. He had to think. He could hear the slight wind and a pounding. Pounding of his ears … blood rushing into his head … no, it was a different kind of pounding. He looked up and saw that the pegasi were pacing. Their hooves were pounding the desert floor. That was it. The floor, the ground! Tree roots would be in the ground.

He grabbed his blanket off Buster and walked northwest, away from the group. He put the blanket down on the ground and lay on top of it. He put his ear to the ground and closed his eyes. He started thinking of Willow, and he pulled together all his thoughts to communicate to the trees. He

193

Book One: The Chosen Ones

whispered the thoughts into the air and into the ground. He listened. He just lay and listened. He heard noises, but he had to determine which noises were coming from the tree roots.

The wind picked up a little, and Brandon almost went into a trance. He thought he could hear Willow talking to him. Willow? How was that possible? She was so far away, but he listened anyway. A smile touched his lips, and he remembered her sweet voice. He missed Willow. Then he heard a rougher voice. It seemed sharper like prickles. His eyes flew open. He knew he was hearing the desert plants and perhaps the far off trees.

Finally, Brandon got up and carried over his blanket to Buster. The others stood in silence while he packed his blanket away. He turned toward them. He knew what he saw, and he now knew what he heard. His confidence was unmistakable by the look on his face and the sound of his voice. "If we ride hard, we will hit a plateau that has cactus with milk and some food. It will take some time before we hit the mountains, but at least, we will be leaving the desert and heading for the foothills."

Without replying, everyone looked at Hachmoni for final approval. He nodded and turned toward Midnight. "Are you up for this?"

Before answering, Midnight spoke to the rest of the pegasi in their pegasi language. They replied and stomped their legs. "We are ready," he told Hachmoni, and then he turned toward Buster and Brandon. "You two will lead the way."

Brandon nodded, but Buster was surprised. It was the first time that his dad had given him a job requiring leadership. He secretly hoped Brandon was right, and they did not mess this up.

"Everyone, mount!" said Midnight. And so they did.

The girls were especially ready to ride again as they were getting tired of walking. They all took drinks of water before they took flight. Then Diana turned to Brandon. "Good job." She smiled.

They flew hard that day. It was difficult because they were flying into the wind and the sun was beating down on them. Nevertheless, they were determined to move on, now that they had hope for some food and water ahead.

Brandon focused on the vision ahead. Now and then, he would ask Buster if he still saw it. They kept each other in check. But as the sun started to go down, doubt lingered in the back of Brandon's mind. What if he was wrong, and they were heading in the wrong direction? He shook his head, trying to clear away the thought.

Buster slowed down.

"Buster?" Brandon asked.

"Do you smell that?" Buster asked.

"Smell what?" Brandon took a sniff. "I don't smell anything," he answered.

"Well, I do," said Buster, flying harder. "It smells like grass. You are right,

The Trahe Chronicles

Brandon. We are heading in the right direction."

Brandon relaxed a little more. If Buster smelled grass, then they had to be close. Brandon looked at the sun. It was getting low, and when it set in the desert, it would go down fast. He followed the rays of the sun that spread across the desert, and then he saw it. The plateau! "Look!" he shouted, pointing straight ahead.

The others also saw it, and there were cheers of delight. They had just reached the plateau when the sun was starting to set, casting brilliant colors over the rocky terrain. As the others started to fly downward, Buster kept on moving.

Brandon looked down. "Buster, where are you going?"

"I smell grass," he replied. "Not here. This way."

"But we are losing the sun," argued Brandon.

"Trust me," said Buster. "Trust my nose."

Brandon thought Buster wasn't a bloodhound, but he kept that thought to himself for the time being. Brandon looked over to the west and watched the sun. He was getting a little nervous about where his friend was going when suddenly Buster started to descend. Brandon peered over Buster's shoulders. "Whoa!"

Buster landed at the edge of the plateau. "That is what I am talking about." Buster stomped his hooves. Sprawled in front of them was a massive canyon. The sunset tossed all kinds of colors and reflections into the canyon. At the very bottom was a river flowing through the canyon.

Brandon could barely see it, but he was pretty sure there was some desert grass growing next to that river. He patted Buster's neck. "Good job. I should have never doubted you, my friend."

Buster lifted his head and let out a thunderous neigh that echoed through the canyon. Soon the other pegasi and their passengers landed next to them.

"Wow!" exclaimed Diana.

"It's just like the Grand Canyon," said Jereco.

They all looked at him and then back at the canyon. The canyon was cut out of mountain rock with different shades of red, brown, beige, and black. The rocks made the canyon jagged and rough. Foliage sporadically grew inside the canyon, accenting the rocks with a variety of greens, yellows, reds, and blues.

"Oh my gosh, Jereco," said Brooke. "You are right. It is so much like the Grand Canyon, or at least, like the parts I have seen."

"You have a canyon as big as this on Earth?" asked Archelaus. The canyon before him was huge. He could not even see where it began or ended.

"Yes, and it is just as beautiful," replied Brooke.

They all turned back to the canyon and took in the sight.

It was Grandpa who broke the silence. "Well, I have stayed at our Earth's Grand Canyon. It is picturesque with plenty of food and water, but it can also be deadly at night. This sun is going to set quickly. I suggest we get down

Book One: The Chosen Ones

there and set up camp by the water."

They all agreed and took flight spiraling toward the river. By the time they arrived, darkness was enveloping the canyon. They dismounted and quickly set up camp. Torches were set up around the camp perimeter.

The pegasi and men went down to the river to fetch water while Grandpa, the girls, and Cleo stayed behind to finish setting up the bedding inside a makeshift tent. It was decided that while traveling in unfamiliar territory, everyone would sleep under one big tent. Blanket dividers were hung between the girls' side and the boys' side. The girls longed to bath in the river, but they decided to wait until morning when it would be less dangerous. They also decided to not build a fire because it was too hard to find dead tree limbs in the dark. They ate what leftover food they had, knowing they would be able to find more food in the morning.

Brooke thought the evening had gone by too fast. The morning sun was already heating up the tent. Brooke looked over at the divider that separated the boys from the girls, and she wondered if Archelaus was awake yet.

Diana, who had slept closest to the divider, was already awake. She was sitting up and talking to herself. Or at least Brooke thought she was talking to herself. Brooke's eyes narrowed as she sat up. "Diana, who are you talking too?"

Diana turned her head toward Brooke and smiled. "Good morning." Diana gestured at an empty spot on her bed. "Brooke, meet Nicolas. Nicolas, meet my cousin, Brooke." Then she covered her mouth and leaned toward Brooke. "Isn't he cute? I told him that he would be cuter if he took a bath."

"Are you feeling okay?" Brooke asked Diana as she looked at the invisible Nicolas.

"Yes. Why?" Diana turned her head back toward the spot where Nicolas was supposed to be sitting. Diana frowned and then turned back to Brooke. "Nicolas says that you do not see him."

"Diana, is Nicolas your new imaginary friend?"

Before Diana had a chance to answer, a wind shook the tent. Brooke jumped out of bed. "Whoa! What was that?" Under normal circumstances, Brooke would have thought the sudden wind was coincidence, but she had learned that nothing was normal on Trahe.

"Nicolas, stop!" replied Diana. "It was Nicolas."

"Okay. Can you please ask Nicolas what he is?"

Diana looked confused, so Brooke elaborated. "Is he an alien?"

Diana giggled. "No, he is a boy."

Brooke was frustrated and in need of some coffee. "Then ask Nicolas why I cannot see him."

"Um ... he said he will explain later. But if we want to eat breakfast and wash up at the river, we need to do it now because we will have company soon."

The Trabe Chronicles

"What?"

Diana looked at the empty spot on her bed. "He is gone now."

Brooke let out a sigh. "Where is Cleo?"

"She has not come back from her nighttime hunting yet."

Believing in Diana's visions, Brooke decided to take invisible Nicolas's advice. Brooke took Diana down to the river to bathe. Buster, the pegasus, volunteered to be on guard duty while the girls washed up.

Afterward, Brooke and Diana quickly fixed breakfast for everyone, and Brooke informed them about Diana's new vision.

"It wasn't a vision!" Diana exclaimed. "He was real."

Brooke had more patience now that she had her cup of pan-brewed coffee. "If the boy was real, then I would have been able to see him."

"Is Nicolas here now?" asked Hachmoni.

Diana looked around and shook her head.

"What did he look like?" Hachmoni continued.

Diana described him as being a boy about Brandon's age. Nicolas had big blue eyes and sandy brown hair. Diana crinkled her nose. "And he was very dirty. He needs a bath."

"On guard!" said Cleo as she came running out of the brush. She leaped onto Diana's lap.

"Nicolas?" asked Brooke.

"No," replied Cleo. She switched to speaking in her native cat tongue. As if on cue, the pegasi hid behind the largest boulders they could find. Hachmoni whispered something to Archelaus and then told the others to follow Archelaus's lead. Hachmoni also hid.

Before anyone had a chance to ask what was going on, a coyote howled. Within minutes, a very large gray coyote walked into their campsite. He looked mean and hungry. He bared his teeth and growled at the small group around the campfire.

Cleo jumped off Diana's lap and hissed back at the coyote. When Cleo hissed, the hairs on her back stood up, and her eyes glowed. The coyote did not retreat. He hesitated, barked very loudly, and took only a few steps back.

Cleo hissed again and then meowed something very loudly. Her tail started to swish in a defensive motion.

Brooke had an instinctive feeling that Cleo was talking to the pegasi. Brooke slowly stood up and grabbed her knife out of her boot. She also motioned to Diana to get up when she heard the sound of boots stepping on rocks behind her. Brooke looked over her shoulder to see four men standing behind her. She did a quick visual assessment. There were four men of different sizes each carrying swords, knives, or both. She also noticed the ropes hanging from their belts. *Curious, but no problem,* she thought.

"I keep on telling you to replace those noisy boots for some soft shoes," said a deeper voice. Brooke swung her head the other way to find three more men standing behind the coyote. The voice had come from a tall and bulky

Book One: The Chosen Ones

man. Most of his face was covered by a huge cowboy hat. His eyes looked dark.

The men who were standing behind Brooke started to step forward. Brooke swung her knife at them.

The man who seemed to be in charge signaled for them to put their weapons down. "No need for weapons. We were camping over yonder, saw your fire, and decided to investigate."

Archelaus spoke up. "We were just cooking breakfast. Would you like to join us?"

"If there is plenty?"

Archelaus gestured at the men to take a seat. "Yes, please join us."

So they did. They ate and were very polite, but Brooke was still suspicious of them. She looked at the coyote that lay on the ground, chewing some meat. The coyote paused for a moment to look Brooke in the eye. A chill went down Brooke's spine, and she decided she was right not to put her guard down. At that moment, Diana also got the chills.

Brooke looked down at Diana, who leaned into Brooke. Diana whispered, "Nicolas said these are bad men."

The coyote's head popped up, and he growled something to the men's leader. This caught everyone's attention. This meant the man had the gift of understanding the coyote, who was not speaking in the universal Trahe language.

The big man paused from eating and looked over at Diana. "So you have met Nicolas?" He put another spoonful of food in his mouth.

Diana did not say anything and just looked down.

"So who is Nicolas?" asked Archelaus.

Brooke shot him a nasty look. *What is he doing?* she thought.

Archelaus ignored Brooke, but the big man did not.

"It is okay, my lady. Everyone around these parts has heard of Nicolas."

"So who is he?" asked Jereco. Jereco had been very quiet about his sister's new friend. Everyone was aware of her gift that had given her the title of the Vision Keeper. However, he was not sure if they were aware of her other gift. This man might confirm Jereco's suspicions. Jereco also noticed that no one had formally introduced themselves. Names had not been given. He decided that both parties of people had not wanted to reveal who they really were.

"Nicolas *was* a boy that lived in a town over that ridge." The man pointed at Brandon. "He was about your age when he died."

Brandon also had been quiet and on guard since the men's arrival. For once, Brandon did not say anything. He was trying very hard to talk to the trees subconsciously but was not having any luck.

"What happened to the boy?" asked Archelaus.

The man shook his head. "A sad story. The town was raided by the Madeave, and everyone died."

"Everyone died?" asked Jereco.

The Trahe Chronicles

"Yes," the man replied as he put another spoonful of food in his mouth. Jereco wanted to know more. "So Nicolas is a—"

"The man is a liar!" interrupted Diana.

Everyone turned to look at her. Diana, who was usually a very quiet and easygoing little girl, looked very mad. She was standing now, her hands balled into fists. Diana's anger also freaked out Jereco because he did not want his sister so upset that she might trigger a seizure.

The man paused and looked up at Diana. Then he turned to Jereco. "Yes, Nicolas is a ghost." Then he looked back at Diana. "And what is that little devil telling you?"

Before anyone could stop Diana, she blurted, "He said that you are lying and that you were one of them. You helped lead the raid. You helped kill many people, including his parents and an older brother." Diana started to cry, but she went on. "He said that you kidnapped young women and children." She took a deep breath and took one step forward. "You killed Nicolas! You killed him when he tried to stop you from taking his sister."

"That was an accident!" he growled. Then he silenced himself, realizing what he had just admitted.

"Yes, it was an accident," said Diana. "Nicolas tried to stop you, so you pushed him down. He landed on the ground, and his head hit a rock. He died instantly."

The man gathered his composure. He casually put down his plate and spoon. He took a drink, wiped his mouth, and stood. "Then he did not suffer. Good."

Diana took another step closer. Brooke grabbed for her, but Diana shrugged her off and continued talking. "Nicolas wants to know where you took his sister."

The man laughed. "Oh, he does? Well, I do not remember. It was so long ago, you see." The man rubbed his chin, looking like he was deep in thought. He looked down at Diana. "Wait. I do seem to remember. The same guy who bought Maria would probably buy a very gifted little girl."

Suddenly, Hachmoni, riding atop Luke Thunder, flew in out of nowhere and yanked Diana into the sky, out of harm's reach.

Brooke watched the scene unfold in front of her eyes. She knew they were in trouble the moment Diana started talking about Nicolas. Apparently, so had Hachmoni.

The surprise was enough to give them time to arm themselves from an inevitable attack. Brooke decided that Nicolas, the ghost, was correct about these men.

The strangers recovered quickly and attacked. Two men went after Brooke. One tried to disarm her and the other tried to kidnap her. At least that seemed to be their plan, but they were not prepared for how well Brooke could fight. She took care of one man herself while Archelaus quickly disarmed the other. *Two down and five more to go,* thought Brooke.

Book One: The Chosen Ones

She turned to see Cleo's front paw slash at the coyote's snout. Brooke thought she saw Cleo's claw emit light, but it happened so fast, she wasn't sure. The coyote yelped and ran away. Another one down.

Grandpa was fighting one man. Jereco and Brandon together were fighting another man. Two more men were ransacking the camp and stealing whatever they could find, including the pegasi. The pegasi were mean, fighting creatures! They flew up in the air and then swooped down for the kill. But before the pegasi had a chance to stomp the men to death, a large roar echoed in the canyon. The roar startled everyone, especially the strangers when they saw what had made the roaring sound. Standing on a large rock was Skylar.

The huge white tiger roared one more time, and a man standing next to the tiger followed with his own yell. The big cat and man leaped off the rock. Brooke watched as Silver Kat ran after one of the men. Silver Kat had a knife in one hand and a rope in the other. She watched as Silver Kat easily lassoed the man and tied him up.

Brooke decided to follow Silver Kat. They chased down two other men. Silver Kat roped up one of them while Brooke tackled the other man, football-style. Brooke put her knee into the man's back and kept him pinned down while she quickly tied his hands with a leather strap that had been attached to her jeans.

"Who are you?" asked the man, his face pressed into the hard and rocky ground.

Brooke bent down and looked into the man's eyes. "I am your worst nightmare. I am The Protector!" She pulled the man up onto his knees. "And your boss made a mistake, trying to kidnap my cousin. You should have chosen to be friends instead. Now you just made enemies with the wrong people." Brooke brought the man to his feet. She pointed toward the white tiger.

Their breakfast had been shared with seven strange men and a coyote. Now they shared their lunch with four tied-up men. The other three men and the coyote had escaped. Hachmoni had returned with the one who was the ring leader. Brooke had been surprised; she thought that he would be the one to get away. She looked at Hachmoni in a new light, thinking he must have special hidden talents.

"So," said Hachmoni, "do any of you care to share the location of this missing Maria?" The men shook their heads and did not say anything.

Silver Kat, who was sitting right in front of them, jabbed his knife into a piece of meat on his tin plate. He nodded at the white tiger lying next to him. "My friend Skylar here is really hungry for some fresh red meat."

Jereco looked up. He was not surprised to see the men turn pale, but he was taken aback when Silver Kat revealed Skylar's name. Skylar was far away from her homeland, but maybe they had heard of the legendary Evadeam

The Trahe Chronicles

white tiger. Or maybe the men paled because there was a five-hundred-pound tiger licking her paws and claws in front of them. Jereco shuddered. He was glad Skylar was on their side. Back home on Earth, a tiger this size could bring down a large man in a single swipe and eat him for lunch before the man could yell for help.

Similar thoughts might have come to one of the men because he started speaking as fast as he could. The other men yelled at him to be quiet and tried to kick him, so Silver Kat and Hachmoni dragged the talking man to the tent. They must have been satisfied with what he said because moments later, the stranger walked out of the tent, untied.

Hachmoni looked at the other three men and spoke in a deep voice. "I am feeling generous today. Each of you has an opportunity to speak to me privately in the tent. After that, we will set you free." He paused for a moment. "Or you can stay tied up here with the pussy cat."

Skylar looked up. "*Pussy cat?*" she said in Trahe tongue.

"I am taking my chance with the cat," said the ring leader with the cowboy hat. "Besides, we have more men on the way, and you will not win this time."

Hachmoni looked over at Silver Kat, who simply nodded. "Do we have time to break camp and be in the air before they get here?" he asked Silver Kat.

Silver Kat nodded again and cleaned off his knife. Then Skylar stretched and stood as tall as she could.

Hachmoni turned to the freed man. "Since you were kind enough to share some information with us, we will give you an airlift far away from your boss. Hopefully, you can start a new life."

"Joining forces with the Creator would be a good start," added Archelaus.

The man simply nodded in appreciation.

Hachmoni turned back to the other tied up men. "You can choose the same fate as your friend here, or you can stay tied up, waiting for help." Hachmoni gestured at the tiger. "And might I add that Skylar cannot fly on a pegasus, so she will be following on the ground. She might stay behind and eat a good hearty meal before her long run."

The cowboy spoke up. "Why would I believe you would not feed me to the tiger after we give you information?"

Hachmoni bowed. "You have my word."

"Huh. Your word means nothing to me. I will take my chances with my boss and this tiger!"

Diana, who was brought back to the campsite on Luke Thunder, approached the men. "You have my promise and Nicolas's promise."

The man looked at Diana. "Sorry, kid. The promise of a weird little girl and a ghost is no better."

Jereco wanted to pounce on the guy for calling his sister weird. Cleo felt the same way. She hissed and glowed at the same time. "If I were you, I

Book One: The Chosen Ones

wouldn't take my chances with this little cat, either."

To Diana's surprise, the man didn't change his mind. However, the other two did. Hachmoni was satisfied with the information he had gathered, and soon they were flying away from the campsite. As Diana looked down, she wondered what the man's fate would be as he continued to sit, tied up next to Skylar. She decided she did not want to know.

Diana was worried about Skylar, but Silver Kat assured her that Skylar could take care of herself and would meet up with them soon. Silver Kat figured the men would try tracking Skylar to find all of them, so Skylar was left with instructions to take them on a detour until she had lost them. Diana did a little prayer for Skylar's safety, and for added measure, prayed for the man who had made the wrong choice and stayed behind.

Silver Kat led them to a formerly abandoned town that had been destroyed by the men and the Madeave. Several days earlier, a message had been sent to Silver Kat that the Chosen Ones were at Great Rock Canyon. While seeking them out, Silver Kat and Skylar came across this town. They discovered it was no longer abandoned. The town was now a military post for the Evadeam and their allies. The Madeave had stayed away because they had heard stories of the town being haunted.

And the town was haunted by many spirits who died the same day Nicolas had died. Nicolas was one of the few spirits who had gained the strength to leave town, for his spirit would not rest until he found his sister.

Word had already spread into the region that the Chosen Ones had arrived into the world of Trahe, and the town's leaders and their soldiers welcomed the legendary Hachmoni and his friends. The townspeople took the three men and promised to give them a second chance to redeem themselves. However, they could not promise how the spirits of the town would react to them.

After a good dinner, everyone was given a room in the town hotel and went to bed. Diana tried to sleep, but she was constantly awoken by a spirit. Nicolas tried his best to keep them away, but before the sun had risen Diana was overwhelmed.

Brooke rushed to Silver Kat's room when she found Diana barely asleep, her clothes soaked with sweat. Silver Kat decided it was the spirits' presence that was making Diana sick. "She is too young and not strong enough to handle all the spiritual presence in this town. I will give her some herbal medicine, but we need to leave this place immediately."

And so they did. After packing their stuff and thanking their hosts, they mounted the pegasi. *Here we go again,* thought Brandon. "So where are we going now?" he asked Hachmoni.

"According to our calculations and the information provided to us, we are going to Bethemek."

"Bethemek?" said Jereco. "Will we find Nicolas's sister there?" He was

The Trahe Chronicles

concerned about Diana. Silver Kat had sedated Diana, so she could get away from the spirits and sleep on their flight. But once she woke up, she would ask about Nicolas and Maria.

"I do not know, Jereco," replied Hachmoni. The soldiers here were given the information and will also try to find out what happened to Maria. But our journey must continue the way of the signs."

Jereco knew not to argue with Hachmoni. They had learned from their three captive men that the women and children from this invaded town were kidnapped and sold into slavery. The slave trade had been introduced during the last outbreak of war between the Madeave and the Evadeam. The Evadeam and their allies were breaking up the slave trade business as fast as they could, but it still was not fast enough. Some slaves had been tracked down while others were still missing, and no one seemed to know where the majority of the slaves were being sold and kept. However, the new leaders of the town informed Archelaus that many freed slaves had made the journey to Bethemek.

"So that is another reason we are going to Bethemek," explained Archelaus. "Maybe with some luck, we will find a freed slave who knew Maria or is Maria."

This satisfied Jereco, and soon they were in the air flying over the same river that cut through the Great Rock Canyon. The river continued to wind toward the north. Jereco watched the river and realized he barely had a chance to enjoy it. As he continued to watch from above, he saw a small white blur running along the river. "Hey!" he yelled at Silver Kat, who was flying on a pegasus named Pinto Dreams.

Silver Kat looked down and nodded. He gave Jereco thumbs up. Jereco had to smile because this was a signal that Jereco had taught him.

They continued to follow the river until dusk approached. As the setting sun cast light on the canyon, they landed on the river shore where Skylar was waiting for them.

No one asked Skylar what happened to the fourth man that was left with her. But later that night, while Diana leaned against a rock eating some soup fed by Brooke, Skylar walked up to Diana and whispered something in her ear. Diana smiled, stroked Skylar's fur, and continued to eat her soup.

Brooke smiled knowing that Skylar did the right thing—maybe not a tiger choice, but a good choice for Diana.

Book One: The Chosen Ones

Thou Shall Not Kill a Talking Beast

Diana recovered, and days later or maybe it was weeks, they were no longer in the desert. Diana was cold, bundled in layers of clothes, as they flew north into a mountain region. "Behold." Hachmoni motioned to the valley below them. "Bethemek."

The valley was beautiful. It had an abundance of trees broken up by rock and running water. "This picturesque landscape is rugged," said Hachmoni. "If the terrain doesn't slow us down, the wild animals will. It is the surroundings that make Bethemek a safe haven from Madeave attacks. If the Madeave were lucky enough to get close to Bethemek, they would have to get past the archers camped high in the trees. Bethemek is surrounded by a high wall made out of rocks. There are archers stationed within those walls."

The kids looked down into the valley and could barely make out the village of Bethemek, but they knew it was there based on the slightest sign of smoke blowing upward into the sky. "It is a breathtaking view from up here," observed Brooke. "Hachmoni, if you didn't point out Bethemek, I wouldn't have noticed it."

Hachmoni nodded. "Another reason it has been safe. Not many people are aware of its existence. Many that have traveled this way would have not have noticed the village below. It is well-hidden, camouflaged by its surroundings. Plus, it's very difficult to get to if you do not know the way. It will take us almost two days to reach the main gate traveling by foot. We will ride until night fall, break camp, and start early in the morning again."

"Why don't we just fly down there?" asked Brandon. "Wouldn't it be quicker?" Midnight shook his mane and looked back at Brandon. "We have not been to this part of the country before."

"Pegasi are just legends here," Hachmoni explained. "We don't want to take a chance that one of their archers tries to shoot us down. They do not know that we are friendly and might mistake us for a dragon."

Diana looked around nervously. "Dragon?"

"Do not worry," said Luke Thunder. "I do not smell any dragons."

"Come." Hachmoni started to take an unmarked trail. "I know the way."

"So there are dragons in this world?" Diana asked Cleo, who was sitting on her lap. Brooke, Diana and Cleo rode upon Midnight.

"Yes, but no need to worry." Cleo twitched her nose. "Luke Thunder is correct. A scent of a dragon is not in the air."

"What does a dragon smell like?" asked Brandon.

"A big, nasty lizard."

"Have you seen a dragon?" asked Brooke.

"Yes," Cleo replied without supplying any further information.

The conversation had to come to an end so everyone could focus on navigating through the forest. The forest was dense, and there was not much room for the large pegasi to walk through. Their passengers had to keep alert

The Trahe Chronicles

and duck from many large tree limbs and the overgrown brush. However, none of them complained. It was much cooler in these woods compared to the desert. A soft breeze brought the scent of fresh woods, flowers, and pine to their noses.

"This reminds me of home," Brooke said.

The others nodded in agreement.

"This forest is much thicker," continued Brooke, "but it reminds me of some of the state parks back home in Michigan. Remember when we used to go camping?"

The Evadeam kids' thoughts were being brought back to a time they could barely remember. They had all agreed to talk about home to remind them of where they had come from. By now, they had lost track of time. They were not sure how long they had been gone. Longer than any of them had thought they would be. They tried not to think about their families and how worried they must be.

"Brooke," said Brandon, "do you remember when I used to go deer hunting with your dad and Grandpa?"

Brooke just nodded. Brooke was really close with her dad and missed him terribly. "Hey, Grandpa," said Brandon, "Do you think we can hunt some deer in these woods? I am craving some meat."

Since there were talking animals on this planet, they all had steered away from eating a lot of meat. They'd been eating mostly fish that they had caught from the streams or had eaten fruit from the trees. But as Brandon traveled through the woods and memories overcame him, he began to crave cooked venison.

Before Grandpa could answer, Diana protested. "We cannot kill a deer. What if it is a talking deer?"

Brandon just shrugged. "We will ask it first, like we've been trained."

Jereco, who had been very quiet, pointed out that if they tried to talk to the deer first, it would just scare it away.

Brandon looked frustrated. "Well, there has to be a way."

"Yes, there is a way," exclaimed Diana. "You just don't eat meat!"

Silver Kat, who chose to walk whenever they were not flying, jogged up to Brandon. Silver Kat looked up at Brandon. "Skylar is also in need of protein that is found in the great stags of these woods. Come down from your ride, and we will hunt for dinner."

"I can't keep up with you on foot," said Brandon. "I will just slow you down.""Nonsense," said Silver Kat. "You are in much better shape now than when I first met you."

Archelaus rode behind them. "I will come along. You will be able to keep up with me."

"Jereco, come," ordered Archelaus. "You will need to learn how to hunt something besides fish."

Jereco just nodded his head. He never did hunt back home and didn't

205

Book One: The Chosen Ones

have the desire to do so. However, he eventually gave in, not wanting to deny the order from the leader of his people. Plus, Hachmoni has taught them to learn everything they possibly could in this world.

Dale and Clyde stretched and enjoyed having the extra load off their backs while Silver Kat ran ahead to let Hachmoni know of their plan. Silver Kat and Skylar also knew their way to Bethemek, so they agreed to meet up at a bend in the river that they were all familiar with.

"Don't worry, Jereco," whispered Brandon, as he adjusted his bow and arrows. "You can just hang back and let me do the hunting."

"Thanks for the offer," replied Jereco, grimly, "but this is something we need to do. Besides, I need the practice."

As Silver Kat, Skylar, Archelaus, Jereco, and Brandon headed down the path, Brooke called from behind them. "Wait for me!"

Archelaus raised an eyebrow. "You are coming along?"

Brooke looked at him. "Do you have a problem with that?"

Archelaus shrugged. "You should stay with Diana."

"Cleo, Hachmoni, and Grandpa are going to watch Diana. Plus, there are seven very large pegasi standing guard."

Archelaus looked at the other men. "But—"

Jereco shook his head as a warning.

Unfortunately, Archelaus didn't get it. "But you are a woman."

Brooke put her hands on her hips. "So?"

Archelaus stood tall. "It is the man's job to hunt."

Jereco walked by and brushed Archelaus's shoulder. "Big mistake," he whispered. "I warned you."

Archelaus followed Jereco. "What? Do woman on Earth hunt?"

Jereco stopped and looked at him, dumbfounded. "After all this time, haven't you learned anything?"

Archelaus looked frustrated. He looked back and forth between Jereco and Brooke. "It isn't safe for her to go with us."

Brooke laughed. "Are you kidding me? This whole entire trip— adventure—or whatever you want to call it hasn't been safe for me. Now come on, we are wasting time. Besides, the rest of the party has left without us."

Archelaus looked back and realized she was right. The pegasi were already out of sight. He sighed, realizing he had lost another battle with the Earth woman.

They had agreed it would be better to spread out and cover more of the woods. To prevent them from getting lost Silver Kat and Skylar took the ends while everyone else stayed in the middle. Archelaus insisted on staying close to Brooke.

They quietly marched deeper into the woods. Now and then, they heard branches break, leaves rustle, or a thump against the forest floor. They heard all of nature's sounds, from the squirrels, to the chipmunks, to the birds and

The Trahe Chronicles

other creatures of the woods. Yet, there was no sign of deer or anything large enough to kill for their evening meal.

Brandon was convinced that they would never get a deer. The hunting party was too noisy and did not smell like the woods. Only Silver Kat and Skylar who made no noise were truly ghosts of the woods.

Brandon stopped in frustration, took a deep breath, and looked around. Trees were everywhere, as far as he could see. He looked up. The trees were so tall that they looked like they could touch the sky. Trees. Trees! Why didn't he think of that before? He had an advantage over the others. He could talk to trees. He wondered if he could talk to these old woods. He looked for the oldest-looking tree he could find. He then leaned against it and sent his thoughts out.

Jereco was the first to notice what Brandon was doing and motioned the others to stop. He did not want to leave Brandon behind.

Brandon slowly moved down to the forest floor and listened. He heard running water very, very faintly. Then, he heard footsteps—soft steps. Yes, the trees were talking to him. The wind blew. Brandon's eyes snapped open. The wind was blowing the opposite way, so their smells would not be brought in the direction of the hunted. Brandon got up and waved everyone to follow him. He broke out in a jog and moved as quietly as he could. They jogged a few yards and then Brandon stopped. He held up his hand and squatted to the ground. Everyone followed suit, trusting his judgment. Trusting the trees.

They crawled to an edge of a small ravine. Brooke gasped. Straight down below was a herd of deer standing in a stream.

Archelaus slowly pulled out an arrow.

At this point Silver Kat took over. He raised his hand and waited. Skylar crept closer. At Silver Kat's signal, everyone shot arrows at the herd. One down, two down. The herd was off, and the chase began. Skylar leaped upon them and brought another one down. More arrows went flying and one bigger doe went down. The hunting party ran down the ravine. By the time they got to the stream, the rest of the herd was gone. Four does were killed. Three by arrows and one by the jaws of Skylar. Skylar was enjoying her kill. Jereco and Brooke had to look away. No matter how much time they had spent with Skylar, they still could not get used to seeing her eat fresh kill.

The sight of the blood was making Brooke and Jereco a little nauseated. They must have looked piqued because Silver Kat, Archelaus, and Brandon offered to gut the deer. Jereco and Brooke looked for fallen tree limbs to tie and carry the dead deer.

The small hunting party had to be careful about the scent of fresh kill. They still had to travel to meet up with the rest of the party, so they took a quick break to freshen up, quench their thirst, and wash away the blood.

As they gathered up their arrows, including those in the deer, Archelaus raised a hand to shake Brooke's. "You have proven me wrong. Earth woman

Book One: The Chosen Ones

can hunt." He presented an arrow to her that bore special markings, indicating the arrow had come from Brooke's quiver. "Your arrow brought down the second largest doe."

Brooke smiled smugly. "You're welcome." She paused and whispered "I had a good teacher—my father."

Brandon pulled an arrow out of the third deer and brought it to Jereco. "Good shot! I did not know you could shoot that good."

Jereco shrugged and looked at Brooke. "I had a good teacher." He smiled as he remembered his uncle.

Brandon just shook his head. "I do not get it. The two who don't like to hunt got the deer."

Brooke slapped Brandon on the shoulder. "What can we say? If we got it, we got it." Brandon didn't look very happy.

"What is wrong, Brandon?" asked Brooke. "Don't like a girl beating you out on deer hunting?"

Brandon shrugged. "It's not that. I know that you were taught by your dad, the military woodsman. I just wish I would have landed a deer. I do not know what happened."

Silver Kat walked up. "But you did get us the deer." He pointed at the trees. "If it weren't for you and the trees, we might not have found the herd. Good tracking."

Archelaus walked up to Brandon and shook his head. "Yes, Silver Kat is quite right. There is no reason to be down on yourself. You did a great job of leading us right to them." Jereco also agreed. "You have an amazing gift, and you used it wisely, as Hachmoni might say. Besides, my arrow might have brought down the doe, but I have no desire to gut it or eat it. That is your job." Jereco made a face.

"Eat it! You have to eat it," said Brandon. "Wait until you smell it cooking. You won't be able to resist."

Brandon was right. After they met up with the rest of the group, they made camp and cooked the deer. No one could resist the smell. It had been so long since they had eaten some good meat. Even Diana had a little bit, but she proclaimed that she only ate some because she did not want to offend the hunters. After all, they went through so much trouble to find, hunt, clean and cook the deer.

Skylar ate a whole deer, but there was no way the rest of them could eat the remaining two deer themselves. After all, the pegasi were vegetarians. They agreed to wrap it up and bring it into Bethemek for trade. Silver Kat knew how to package the meat without it spoiling. They hung the meat up high in the trees. Skylar agreed to watch over the carcass to make sure nighttime critters did not consume it.

Silver Kat offered everyone a hot drink mixed with herbs that would help settle their stomachs. After all, it has been awhile since they'd eaten red meat; he did not want anyone to be sick. Hachmoni reminded them it would be an

208

The Trabe Chronicles

early morning for them the next day, so they all went off to get a good night's sleep.

The next morning, a mist lay over the valley. The smell of dew on the trees filled the air. Slowly, the woods became alive with sounds of critters snapping tree branches and birds singing a welcoming dawn song.

Brooke awakened to the sounds of daybreak. She rubbed her eyes, remembering her dream. During the night, she had dreamed of her dad and the hunting and the camping trips they used to take. Listening to the sounds in the woods reminded her of those trips. As she lay in her bed, she was feeling more like she was at home on Earth. At that moment, she felt like she was on their family camping trip in the Smoky Mountains. Those were good times, good memories. She lay there, wondering if they would ever have family trips again. Would she ever see her dad again? She missed him. She missed home. She missed Earth.

She glanced over to Diana, who was still sleeping. Cleo was lying at Diana's feet. Cleo usually stayed up all night, guarding them during the night watch. But lately, Cleo had been turning in just before dawn for a few hours of sleep.

Brooke smiled. At least she was with some family on this planet. She could not imagine not being here with her cousins, Grandpa, and Cleo. She looked over at Diana again. What made her the Vision Keeper? What made her see ghosts or spirits? She had not been able to figure that one out yet. Yes, Diana had visions, but it seemed like there should be more to it than that.

What about herself? Diana, Jereco and Brandon all now had discovered their special gifts in this world. Did she have a special gift? She didn't feel like it. However, she did have a special urge to protect her cousins. She was after all named The Protector by Midnight. Maybe that was all she was meant to do—protect and watch over them while they were on this adventure. Brooke sighed and saw Cleo open up one eye and look at her. Well, at least she had Cleo, Archelaus, and the rest of them to help.

Archelaus. Brooke sighed again and looked away from Cleo. When they did finally return to Earth, she would be leaving Archelaus. She was having a hard time accepting that. She wished he could come back with her, but she knew that was impossible. Or was it?

Cleo meowed and Brooke looked over at her. Cleo just shook her head.

"What?" ask Brooke. "You read thoughts now?"

Cleo just meowed again, stretched, and kneaded a new spot on Diana's bed. She lay back down.

Brooke just shook her head. It amazed Brooke how Cleo often acted like a normal house cat. Sometimes, Brooke wished she could go back to being a normal teenager where her biggest worries were school grades, what outfit to where to school, and which boy might ask her to the school dance. She

209

Book One: The Chosen Ones

wondered if Archelaus danced.

"Meow."

Brooke looked up and watched as Cleo ran out of the tent. Brooke sat up. A chill ran down her back; she knew something was wrong. She grabbed for her knife and looked over at Diana, who had just awakened.

Diana whispered, "Bear."

Based on the experiences on Trahe, Brooke knew not to question Cleo's senses or Diana's visions. If Diana said there was a bear outside, then it was true. Plus, her own senses were hyper alert. Her camping experience with her dad had taught her many things, including being in a tent while a bear is in the campsite is not a good idea. A tent offered no protection from a large and hostile bear. Luckily, the girls slept in their clothes, so they were ready to dash out of the tent. Brooke motioned Diana to quietly put on her shoes. Brooked grabbed her weapons quickly and quietly while keeping an eye out for any bear shadows that might appear on the tent walls. She also listened intently. She was hoping that Cleo had reached the bear first.

Their tents were not modern with zippers. Brooke would have preferred a zipped up tent for warmth, but now she was glad for the lack of noise when she slowly peeked outside. She had a knife in hand, with Diana close behind her. Nothing. No bear. Not even any movement or sounds from the rest of the tents. Brooke listened. Still no sound. *Odd*, she thought. Even the pegasi should be stomping around if there was a bear in the area.

Brooke cautiously stepped outside, looking around with Diana behind her.

"Over there," whispered Diana, pointing toward a cluster of white birch trees. "We need to go that way. I saw it in my dream."

Brooke shook her head. "I am not going away from camp."

Diana passed Brooke and hurried ahead. "But we must. We do not have much time."

"Diana! Diana!" whisper Brooke in a hushed voice. "Come back here." But Diana was already running into the woods. "Diana!"

Oh great, thought Brooke. She decided there was no sense in whispering now so she yelled back to the tents. "Archelaus, Hachmoni, help!" Then she ran after Diana as she still had her in sight. As she was running, she wondered why she didn't wake up the guys before they left the tent. But it was too late now. She ran faster.

"Diana! Wait for me! Right now, young lady! *Diana Lorraine Evadeam!*"

Diana finally stopped. No one had called her by her full name since they landed on this planet. Back home, if the adults had to call out her full name, then she knew she was in big trouble.

Brooke got the reaction she was hoping for, which was Diana's immediate attention.

She caught up with Diana and grabbed her arm. "Don't you ever take off like that again!"

The Trahe Chronicles

Diana started to say something, but Brooke cut her off. "We are in a strange place, a strange country, a strange planet, and I am in charge of you until we get back home. An adult has to be with you at all times. You know that there are people after you. You know that if you disappeared here, we may never see you again. So don't ever, ever leave like that again."

Diana could see that Brooke was more than just mad. Brooke was scared; her voice was shaking. Diana knew they had to keep moving. She slowly continued walking as she listened to Brooke vent.

Growl!

The girls stopped walking.

Then they heard a loud whimper ring through the woods. They looked around, but could not see anything.

Brooke whispered to Diana. "Which way are we supposed to go?"

Diana looked around again, trying to get her bearings. She was no longer sure.

They heard a noise from above and saw the largest bird they had ever seen. A huge bald eagle landed on a large branch. It cocked its head and looked down at them. Its eagle eyes seemed to narrow at Diana. "This way," he cawed and then flew off the branch. His wingspan was enormous, and the girls had to duck when he flew above them and off into the woods. Brooke looked at Diana.

"The eagle was in my dream too," said Diana. "Come on." She grabbed Brooke's free hand and pulled her along. The two ran after the eagle, trusting it, but Brooke still stayed alert for anything that might attack them. Suddenly, the large eagle landed in front of them. They were deep in the thick of the woods. The eagle looked back at the girls and pointed one of its wings to something in front of them. The girls slowly went around the eagle. Brooke had her knife in hand and stayed Diana behind her.

A big black bear was lying on the ground, and Cleo was crouched down beside the bear's head. She seemed to be talking to it.

"It's her," said Diana. "The bear in my dream."

The bear looked over and growled. It managed to stand up on all fours, but obviously, it was hurt. Brooke saw that its hind leg was caught in a steel bear trap. Confused, Brooke looked over at Cleo. Brooke didn't think that there were steel traps on this planet. Weren't they too modern? Plus, trapping a bear or any animal was against the law because one could accidently trap a talking animal.

Diana saw the trap and gasped. "Who would do such a thing?"

"*Man,*" growled the bear. It snapped at the girls. They jumped back. The eagle spoke in a deep voice. "Arcturus, these are not the daughters of the man who set this trap. These are the daughters of the great Evadeam tribe. They are here to help you and your cubs."

The bear looked at the eagle and the girls with skepticism in its eyes.

Cleo stood up and walked to Diana. Cleo turned around and faced the

211

Book One: The Chosen Ones

bear. As she started to speak, a light glow came from her body. "As the great eagle Aquila said, these are the legendary daughters of the great Evadeam tribe that brought forth Skylar, the legendary great princess of all time, who befriended the great white cat, Bright Eyes. Cleo jumped into Diana's arms. "This is the Vision Keeper. You owe her thanks for finding you. It is her vision that brought the Protector to help save you."

"Vision Keeper?" growled the black bear. "She is just a mere man child. Protector? I do not see the great legendary Protector."

"It is your pain that distracts you from the truth," said a voice from behind the girls. Everyone turned to see Silver Kat standing there.

He had walked up so quietly that no one knew of his presence until he had spoken. He walked over to the great black bear. Silver Kat put his hand on the bear's shoulders as a respectful gesture.

"Silver Kat?" The black bear smelled him. "It has been a long time, Silver Kat."

"Yes, Mother Arcturus it has been a long time. You have aged well."

Arcturus shook her head. "No, if I had aged well I would have spotted this man trap before stepping in it. I am getting old, dear friend."

Silver Kat nodded. "Not too old to birth cubs, I hear. So where are these cubs?"

Arcturus looked over at the girls and Cleo. "Is it true, Silver Kat? Is this the Vision Keeper and the Protector?"

Silver Kat nodded. "Yes, it is true. The time is finally here. It is the reason we have been brought to your woods. We are fulfilling destiny." He pointed toward her foot. "And it is time to fulfill another." Silver Kat motioned Brooke to come over. "I have not seen one of these before. Do you know what it is, and how to remove it from our friend?"

Brooke had noticed that Arcturus had not answered Silver Kat about her cubs. Instinct told Brooke that Arcturus still did not trust her and Diana. Brooke didn't blame her when she looked at the bear's foot that was caught in the trap. Yes, Brooke had seen similar traps like this back on Earth. She remembered the first time she came across one. She almost stepped in it herself. Her dog prevented her from doing so by pushing her aside, but he got caught in the trap. She was a young girl and became hysterical when it happened. They were camping deep in the mountains with her dad, and she had wandered off after being told not to.

It was ironic that she had yelled at Diana earlier for doing the same thing she had done many years ago. Her dad had eventually found them. He showed her how to release the trap and made Brooke tend to her dog's wounds. The dog survived, but he had a slight limp. Now he was home, old and graying like this bear. Brooke felt sympathy toward the bear.

She looked at Silver Kat. "Yes, I am familiar with this type of trap." Brooke kneeled in front of the bear and suppressed her fear. "Great mother black bear Arcturus, will you please do me the honor of letting me remove

212

The Trahe Chronicles

this terrible iron man trap from your paw? I will tend to your wound."

The bear looked deeply into Brooke's eyes and then the bear closed her own eyes. She drew in a great breath through her nose. She smelled Brooke's scent and perhaps relied on animal instincts. After a moment, the bear sighed and said, "Silver Kat believes you are the Protector of the Chosen Ones. My instincts tell me it is so, but my senses are failing me." She turned her head toward her trapped paw. She turned back to Brooke. "If you can save my paw, save my cubs, and bring to me the man who traps, I will believe you."

Brooke knew that was a lot to ask, but the bear was running out of time. "I will do more than that. I will save more than just your paw. I will save you too."

"Then do what you must," said Arcturus, giving her permission to touch her.

Brooke took a deep breath as she stood, said a silent prayer in her head, and thought of what her dad would do in this situation.

She turned to Cleo. "Please go back to the camp and inform everyone that we are bringing back a new friend who will need food and water."

Cleo nodded and was off.

Then Brooke turned to Silver Kat. "I need help prying open this trap."

She turned to Diana. "Stand behind Arcturus and try to keep her still and calm."

Diana, who had no fear of Arcturus because of her dreams, eagerly started petting the bear's fur coat. Diana told her about her dreams and noticed Arcturus's ears perk. She was listening to the child.

Brooke and Silver Kat had the trap open in no time, and then they continued to take it apart as much as possible. Brooke decided to take it back to show Archelaus. She figured the law needed to find whoever had set this trap.

Since Brooke had no modern Earth medicine, she discussed possible herbal treatments with Silver Kat. The two of them came up with ideas on how to treat Arcturus's wound. Silver Kat made a loud call that sounded like a cat, and soon Skylar came plunging out of the trees.

Arcturus did not look surprised. "Skylar, you are losing your touch. I smelled you before Silver Kat revealed himself."

Skylar growled. "Ancient one, perhaps I revealed my presence on purpose—to prove that the Protector is here."

Arcturus growled right back. "Who are you calling ancient? You are at least a hundred years older than me, ancient white tiger."

"A hundred years?" growled back Skylar. "I think you have been stuck in these woods for too long and forgot how to count the days of the sun and the nights of the moon."

As the two beasts exchanged words, Diana and Brooke stepped farther back, afraid that a fight might break out between the two. But Silver Kat assured them that the two ancient animals were good friends. This was their

Book One: The Chosen Ones

way of saying hello to each other after being apart for many years. As they headed back to the campsite, the two animals sent insults back and forth during the walk. Brooke noticed that Skylar had slowed her pace down as she walked next to the bear, who was struggling to walk on three legs. Skylar would pretend to fall onto the side of the bear to help hold the bear up when needed. Brooke decided that Silver Kat was right; these two beasts had a strong bond which years and miles apart could not break.

Once they got back to the camp safely, Silver Kat and Skylar went back into the woods to find nature's medicines that would help heal Arcturus's paw.

Archelaus was furious when he saw the trap. He blamed the Madeave. Archelaus had thought no one would have dared try to trap an animal for fear of breaking one of the main laws. They wondered if the trappers were in the mountains or in the town of Bethemek.

As they were discussing this over breakfast, Diana piped up. "What about the cubs?" Everyone got quiet.

"What cubs?" Hachmoni asked.

Brooke looked over at Arcturus, not wanting to reveal anything without her permission. Arcturus paused from her meal. "I had two of my cubs with me when I fell into the trap. I

sent the cubs away for fear that man would return and take the cubs."

"Away?" asked Hachmoni. "Where?"

Arcturus looked at Aquila. She growled something to the great eagle. Aquila looked at Hachmoni and spoke in a bird language. Hachmoni nodded in agreement and then looked at the others. "Aquila led the cubs far up into the mountains for safety. Aquila assures me they are safe. To protect them, she will not reveal their location."

"Why would trackers hunt for cubs?" asked Archelaus.

Hachmoni hesitated, and it was Aquila who spoke in the Trahe language for them to understand him. "There are some evil men who are caging up the bears. They feed them and let them grow until they are big enough to kill for their meat and fur."

"That is awful!" Diana cried.

Brandon shook his head. "I do not understand why they would take a chance on doing that with the talking bears."

"They are nonbelievers," replied Aquila. "They only look at the animals as beasts, not equal to men."

"I believe that," said Jereco. "We have people back on Earth who hunt animals just for fun—just like a prize in a game. Those animals do not even speak our language. Animals on Earth are less superior, but they should still be respected." Jereco sadly shook his head. "Yet they are not."

Archelaus looked over at Hachmoni. "Hachmoni, when I was a child, my mother told me stories—stories about great legends and prophecies. Some of these stories are unfolding before my very eyes." He pointed at the kids.

214

The Trahe Chronicles

"The Water Guardian, the Forest Friend, the Vision Keeper and the Protector. In one of these stories, there was a story about a bear that helped the Vision Keeper and Protector fulfill their quests. A bear with a special marking. A bear with a silver paw."

They looked over at Arcturus, who had stopped eating and was now listening intently to Archelaus. Even though Arcturus has some silver hairs growing throughout her fur, she had no silver paw. She slowly got up and limped over to Brooke. "Protector, you have done as I had asked. Even though I am still in great pain, I have quenched my thirst, fed my belly, and am now more alert. The spirits are telling my senses that you are who Silver Kat and Cleo say you are. It is true. I have two cubs, and one of them has the silver marking Archelaus speaks of. The spirits will guide you to protect my cubs until the day comes when they protect the Vision Keeper."

It was at the moment Brooke knew who she truly was. She had been named and she bestowed no great power or gift like her cousins; yet she knew that a great responsibility had been bestowed upon her. Tears formed in Brooke's eyes as she stood up in front of Arcturus. The great bear towered over her, but Brooke no longer feared her. She looked into Arcturus's eyes and promised that she would try her very hardest to protect the cubs. Arcturus licked Brooke's right hand. Brooke knew it was a gesture of affection, like a kiss. Her pets back home often licked her with great love and affection. However, the kiss of the bear seemed different somehow. Her right hand felt tingly, and the feeling went up her right arm into her shoulder. Brooke subconsciously took her left hand and reached to the backside of right shoulder.

"Brooke!" shouted Jereco as he jumped up. Everyone looked at him as he ran up to Brooke. "It just dawned on me. When we used to go swimming, I would dunk you from behind."

"Dunk Brooke?" Archelaus asked.

"Never mind that," replied Jereco. "What is important is what I noticed on your shoulder. Brooke, remember what I used to tease you about when we were little?"

Brooke looked at Jereco and slowly replied as if she was remembering the moment. "As you dunked me underwater you used to say 'Bobbing Brooke's birthmark!'" Brooke removed her coat—tugged out her right shoulder from her shirt. "Hachmoni, look at the top of my right shoulder. What do you see?"

Hachmoni looked at the shoulder. "A birthmark. *The* birthmark." He stepped aside so Archelaus could see it.

"I've seen this before," said Archelaus. "It is a picture that my mom drew on a cave wall when I was a small child." He pointed toward the top of the birthmark. "She said that this is the hand of the Protector." He pointed toward the bottom. "And this is the silver bear. She said that someday, the hand of the Protector and the Silver Paw will bring together the Chosen

Book One: The Chosen Ones

Ones' destiny."

Brandon stepped up behind Brooke. "Weird. I never noticed it looking like a hand and a bear until now." He turned toward Hachmoni. "What does it all mean?"

"It means that Brooke has now found her destiny in this world," replied Hachmoni.

Brandon still was not satisfied. "Yeah, but what does it mean? What do we do now? How are Brooke and this bear going to help us?"

Hachmoni shook his head and walked away. "I do not know. In time, I am sure we will find out."

Brandon shook his head in disgust. "Riddles. Just riddles and no answers."

Brooke shrugged her arm back in her shirt. "No, Brandon, but we do know. We now know how I fit into this puzzle. Don't you see? We have all been named now. I am the Protector. I am the final piece of the puzzle. It is all coming together, and we must be that much closer to the answer—why we are here in the first place. And we are that much closer to finding our parents."

"Brooke is right," said Jereco. "Everything is coming together now. I am remembering stories I have not thought about in a long time. Between these stories and the information we do have, we must be able to figure out what it all means and understand what we are supposed to do.

"Based on the information I found in the caves back on the island," continued Jereco, "we need to find the ancient Evadeam city in the mountains." He looked at Aquila. "Didn't you say that you hid the cubs in the mountains?"

Aquila nodded.

Jereco turned and walked to the small ridge that looked over the town of Bethemek. He pointed beyond the valley to a far-off ridge of rugged mountains. The tops of the mountains were so high up that it looked like they were reaching up into the clouds. "Did you by chance take them to those mountains?"

Before Aquila could answer, Brooke spoke. "That is impossible. Arcturus has not been trapped long enough for Aquila and the cubs to get to those mountains before Aquila got back here."

Hachmoni stepped up and looked at Aquila. "Who is taking those cubs into the mountains and protecting them?"

Aquila responded. "Someone who can be trusted. Besides I fly fast and have been keeping track of them."

Hachmoni narrowed his eyes at Aquila. "Who can be trusted more than yourself?" When Aquila didn't respond, Hachmoni looked over at Arcturus. "Who else could you have possibly trusted with your cubs?"

Arcturus let out a slow growl. "Methuselah."

"What? Methuselah? Can't be!" said Hachmoni unbelievably.

216

The Trahe Chronicles

"Who is Methuselah?" asked Brandon.

"Legend speaks of a Methuselah who was an ancient grizzly bear," said Archelaus. "He lives in the same mountains as the ancient Evadeam city. Again, it is only legend. If he really did exist, he would not still be alive."

"Why not?" asked Brandon.

Silver Kat quietly spoke. "If Methuselah was still alive, he would be over nine hundred years old."

"Nine hundred years old!" the kids said in unison.

Silver Kat turned to Arcturus. "You should get off that foot. Come and let us tend to it." Silver Kat and Brooke mixed up more ingredients and put the paste on Arcturus's paw.

"We really should stitch this," said Brooke. Silver Kat agreed but wanted the medicine to work its magic by killing off any infection first. It was decided that they would have to stay at the campsite until Arcturus's paw healed.

Brooke and Silver Kat tended to Arcturus's wounds while Aquila, Skylar, and Silver Kat tried to convince everyone that Methuselah did exist. Skylar admitted to seeing him once. However, Hachmoni still could not understand how the old, legendary bear could be alive. Around the campfire, Diana brought up a good point.

"Why can't Methuselah exist?" said Diana. "We exist. My brothers and cousin were just a legend here, but here we are from Earth. Hachmoni, you are really old, and here you are too. Skylar and Arcturus are really old, and here they are."

Archelaus laughed. "Yes, Hachmoni, you are really old and here you are."

Hachmoni gave him a dirty look.

Diana continued. "My mom used to say that just because you cannot see it, does not mean it does not exist. Just like God on Earth or the Creator here."

Hachmoni agreed with Diana. "You are right, my child. That is called faith. We must have faith that the Creator is leading us down the right path. The path of light. The light that will shine upon the Evadeam tribe once more. A light that will bring peace and justice back to this world."

They were quiet for a moment until Brandon broke the silence. "So what does an old grizzly bear have to do with bringing peace back to your world?"

"If anyone can protect the cubs, it would be Methuselah," replied Skylar. "And protect, Methuselah will."

"Perched at this camp for the past few days," said Aquila, "I have noticed that you are not prepared to go into the mountains. The winds will blow in the white in a few weeks. You will need to go into Bethemek soon. I will send word to Methuselah and then lead you to him."

"Winds will blow in the white?" asked Jereco. "Please do not tell me that is snow." They had left their home in the winter time. The air here now felt the same as autumn back home. On the faraway mountains, white capped the

217

Book One: The Chosen Ones

peaks. He guessed the white was snow. Large, thick white clouds with a hint of grey nestled on the mountain range. *Snow clouds*, he thought.

Silver Kat nodded. "When winter approaches, the mountains can be rough. Aquila is right. We need supplies before we can continue into the mountains. I will stay with Arcturus. I can gather supplies from the woods. I also think it is time we became the trackers. Skylar, Arcturus, and I will track down the ones who set these iron traps. We will meet you in the mountains after you visit Bethemek."

Hachmoni agreed. "I think it would be best if we keep the children and Skylar away from the town. We do not know who and what is down there. It has been a long time since I have been to Bethemek, and some things have probably changed. I do not want to take any chances of revealing who the identity of the children."

"I think it would be a good idea if I go," said Archelaus. "The people in Bethemek need to see a leader of the Evadeam people. I could tell them that all of you have been traveling with me, and we have arrived to warn them of the Madeave movement. We might be able to find some allies in Bethemek."

They agreed to leave for Bethemek the next day. No one liked the idea of getting caught in a mountain winter snowstorm.

The Trahe Chronicles

Talking Sheep in Bethemek

Brooke could see her breath turn into a cold cloud before her. It was a cool, crisp, and sunny day when they headed down to Bethemek. Brooke was thankful for the warm rays that came from the sun above. She listened as there was much discussion about how to enter the village. Hachmoni wanted to hide their true identities, and Archelaus insisted that he present himself as who he truly was, a leader of the Evadeam tribe.

Brandon and Jereco thought it would be a good idea to wear disguises. Diana wanted nothing to do with lying. The boys tried to tell her that this would be like a make-believe game, and she just needed to pretend. However, she wasn't buying it. With her arms crossed, she refused to play along.

It was Brooke who finally stepped in and suggested a plan that would not require lying. Archelaus would present himself as himself. Brooke also thought it would be best that Hachmoni was himself—the ancient, wise man who all true Evadeams would respect. The children and Grandpa would be distant relatives of Archelaus who were looking for their own relatives of the lost Evadeam tribe. All of it was true, so Diana agreed.

Hachmoni led everyone down the twisted, rugged mountainside. As they approached the village, Hachmoni signaled up toward the trees, reminding the small group to keep their eyes open for the archers. Archelaus wore his tribal cloak. He distributed flags to the group that bore his tribe's markings. Not long after that, the first archer made his presence clear.

An arrow landed right in front of Hachmoni. He stopped and put his arm up as a warning to the group and as a sign of peace for the shooter. Jereco, Brandon, Brooke, and Grandpa nervously surveyed their surroundings.

"Who goes there?" shouted a loud voice.

Hachmoni responded with a very formal tone. "You have shot an arrow at the former leader of the Evadeam tribe. Before you decide to raid our party for any riches, let me warn you that we have none among us. Let me also remind you that it is unlawful for you to attack and not show respect to a leader of the Evadeam tribe."

Six more arrows landed by the rest of the group.

"Good shots," murmured Jereco.

The booming voice rang out again. "We know of our laws. You must prove your claim. You could be imposters."

Hachmoni responded loudly. "If you truly know your leader, you know that he often travels with the great Hachmoni. I am Hachmoni. Show yourself, look into my eyes, and see the truth."

There was silence, and then out of nowhere, a man landed in front of Hachmoni. He had a knife in one hand. A bow and a quiver filled with arrows were attached to his back. He was short, skinny, and dressed in camouflage. He looked into Hachmoni's eyes.

Jereco noticed the feathers on the man's arrows matched the first arrow

Book One: The Chosen Ones

that had landed in front of Hachmoni. He also noticed the different feathers of the other six arrows that had landed by them. There were at least six more archers in the trees. With his hands, he conveyed this information to Brandon. Brandon nodded his head as though he understood and then motioned to Jereco that he was going to try to talk to the trees. Jereco nodded and stayed on high alert while Brandon meditated.

"Hachmoni is only legend in these parts," said the small man. "We have never met him as he comes from ancient times. He rests in peace with our ancestors." He pointed at Hachmoni. "You could not possibly be the Hachmoni whom we fear and respect."

Hachmoni pushed his cloak back from his head and stood straighter. "I am Hachmoni; why would you think that I am no longer part of this world?"

The man looked confused for a moment. "Because if you were Hachmoni, then you would be—" His voice trailed off as he started to count in his head how old Hachmoni would have to be if he was indeed alive.

Archelaus laughed at the expression on the man's face.

The man turned his knife on Archelaus. Instantly—Jereco, Brandon, Brooke, and Grandpa drew their weapons.

Archelaus raised his hand. "Halt. No need for the weapons and for any unnecessary bloodshed. I only laugh because no one really knows how old Hachmoni is, and it would take a very long time for anyone to add up the years."

The man seemed to relax a little.

Archelaus signaled to Midnight who unfolded his grand wings. He snorted loudly and stood up to full height. "I am Midnight, leader of the pegasi. Our tribe has joined forces with Archelaus, leader of the Evadeam tribe, and all his allies to fight the Madeave."

Archelaus bowed in his saddle. "Let me properly introduce myself. I am Archelaus of the last and true remaining tribe of the Evadeams."

The man lowered his knife a little. "I am Zacchaeus, leader of the woodsmen. I confess that I have never seen such a creature as grand as you. I have only been told of the legends since I was a child. Seeing with my own eyes, I want to believe that you are who you say are, but my job must come first. I must protect these woods from predators. I still have no proof that you are Archelaus, leader of the Evadeam tribe."

As if on cue, Aquila flew in and landed between Archelaus and Zacchaeus. Zacchaeus, who was as surprised as everyone else, immediately gained composure and bowed down to the great bald eagle. "Aquila, king of the sky."

Aquila acknowledged, "Zacchaeus, leader of the woodsmen of Bethemek, job well done. You continue to protect the woods that surround Bethemek. However…" The eagle sadly shook his head. "…the higher and deeper woods are left unprotected as man traps innocent talking animals."

Zacchaeus looked upset. "Traps? There are more traps?" His voice was

220

The Trabe Chronicles

angry. "*Again?*""Yes, just days ago a black bear mother was trapped in iron." Aquila raised his voice so the archers in the trees could hear. "We are so fortunate that the legendary Vision Keeper and the Protector had found mother Arcturus before she passed to the other world."

Brooke and Jereco looked at each other, both thinking the same thing: so much for hidden identities.

There was silence as Aquila's words sank in for Zacchaeus.

It was Brandon who interrupted the silence. "Excuse me, Aquila, but the trees are saying that someone else in the air is seeking you."

Aquila turned to Brandon. "Zacchaeus, this is—"

"This would be the Forest Friend," finished Zacchaeus. "He who speaks to the trees." Zacchaeus bowed toward Brandon and then turned to Jereco. He looked directly into his eyes. "And this would be the Water Guardian, he who speaks to the water people." He bowed.

When he came back up "Tell me, is there such thing as people who live in the water?"

Jereco smiled. "Yes, and they are quite beautiful." Zacchaeus smiled and had a wistful look on his face.

A slight cough came from behind him. He looked and saw Diana. "Ah, this must be the Vision Keeper."

Diana held out her hand. She was pleased that they did not have to pretend to be someone else. "How do you do?"

Zacchaeus took her hand and kissed it. Then he glanced up at Brooke, who had been riding with Diana. "And this must be the Protector, yet she cannot be. You are much too beautiful to protect anyone. May I?" He gestured to her hand that was resting lightly on her knife sheath.

Brooke stole a glance at Archelaus, who was watching the exchange very closely. Brooke smiled and held out her hand as he kissed it.

Cleo jumped off Diana's lap. Zacchaeus was taken by surprise as he had not noticed Cleo. He immediately bowed down to the cat as Cleo said, "Precious time is being wasted. After all, someone is trapping the speaking animals."

Zacchaeus stood. "And I vow and promise to find whoever is breaking one of the Creator's laws." He made a bird-like sound. A moment later, a man with red hair jumped out of the trees. "This is my second in command." Zacchaeus made quick introductions and the red-haired man bowed to all of them, especially Archelaus. Zacchaeus pulled him aside and gave him firm, clear orders. The red-haired man nodded and bowed back to everyone. Then he pulled on a vine and swung up into the trees. The sound of bird calls rang in the air. Before long, many men were swinging in the trees and flying away, deeper into the woods.

Zacchaeus bowed to Cleo. "I give my word that we will find whoever is breaking the law; justice will be served. My men will find answers by nightfall. I will personally guide you down to Bethemek."

221

Book One: The Chosen Ones

As they approached the village of Bethemek, Aquila flew ahead of them. Another smaller bird flew up to Aquila and started circling him. Everyone watched as the two circled each other. The Evadeams were not sure if they were friends or foes. Finally, the two birds flew toward the group.

Aquila landed in front of them, but the smaller bird, a falcon, landed on the shoulders of Zacchaeus. The bird spoke to Zacchaeus in its own language. Zacchaeus seemed to understand him and nodded. Aquila spoke to the rest of them as he pointed to the falcon. "This is Zippor." Surprisingly, the falcon spoke the Trahe language. It was broken and a little hard to understand, so they had to listen intently. Zippor introduced himself as an ally of the Evadeam tribe. He was honored to meet all of them and that his trusted friend Michael had been anxiously awaiting their arrival.

"Michael?" Archelaus asked.

With a slight smile, Zacchaeus looked over at Archelaus. "Michael is one of our trusted and honest leaders. He, along with the rest of us, was informed days ago of your arrival."

"You have known for days that we were here in the mountain?" Grandpa asked.

Zippor spoke up. "I knew you were coming. I knew you were coming." Zippor then flew off toward the village.

"Good thing Zippor is an ally." Brandon said. They nodded in agreement, thinking the same thing. If Zippor was a friend of the Madeave, they would have been attacked by now.

When they arrived at Bethemek, they noticed the rock wall was heavily armed with guards. Archelaus and Hachmoni both made comments about how the village had changed and seemed more secure. The location alone was all the security the city needed years ago. Zacchaeus explained that they had one major attack on the village about five years ago. Many innocent people, including some women and children, were killed. After that attack, they built the wall higher and stronger. They added more guards on the wall and increased the number of woodsmen outside of the village. The Madeave were unwise and killed some talking animals. That helped unify the animals with the villagers. But now with the news of someone trapping animals in the mountains, Zacchaeus was concerned that maybe they had not captured or scared away the Madeave completely.

As they entered the stone fortress village, they were greeted by a small crowd. Most stood back and eyed them warily, especially when they noticed the pegasi.

A dark-skinned, blond-haired man with green eyes walked forward from the crowd. He was less than six feet tall and had a stocky build. Zippor landed on his shoulder and spoke to him in his bird language. "I am told that the great Hachmoni and Archelaus are among us," the man said. "I will know if this is true. If you are not who you say you are, beware of the

The Trahe Chronicles

consequences." The man stepped closer, and Archelaus jumped off Midnight.

"Michael?" said Archelaus.

The man looked Archelaus up and down.

"Here is your proof." Archelaus started to take off his shirt.

Brooke whispered under her breath. "What is he doing?"

No one answered as Archelaus stripped off his shirt and turned his back to the man. The man examined his right shoulder. Archelaus turned around and gestured to the man to do the same. Surprisingly, the man did, and then Archelaus examined his back. Soon afterward, they embraced each other.

The kids just looked at each other, confused. After the two men put their shirts back on, Archelaus turned and introduced the man as his cousin Michael. The children learned that if something ever happened to Archelaus and his immediate family, Michael would be next in line to be the leader of the Evadeam tribe. This led to many questions from the children, but they were told the answers would come in due time.

Michael insisted that they stay with him at his home. He explained that his family relocated to Bethemek after the fall of the great Evadeam tribe many years ago. They walked to his house which was located at the back of the village. It was situated against the rocky mountain wall. Michael informed them that his home had a hidden passageway into the mountain.

The pegasi were brought to the horse stables and were given the royal treatment: grooming, food, and water. Likewise, the humans and Cleo were given the chance to freshen up in their own sleeping quarters. Everyone changed into some clean clothes and met in Michael's dining room.

Michael invited Zacchaeus to join them for dinner. Zacchaeus and the others informed Michael about the trapping of Arcturus and possibly other animals. This caused great concern, and he whispered something to Zacchaeus and Hachmoni.

The subject turned to Archelaus. Archelaus shared with Michael that his own brother and sister might still be alive. Michael was not surprised. He said it made sense that they were in hiding to help ensure their safety. By now, Archelaus had forgiven Hachmoni for keeping this secret about his siblings from him; he just wanted to concentrate on finding his family. Archelaus believed it was time to reunite the Evadeam family. He believed the arrival of the Evadeam tribe from Earth was a sign. Archelaus explained who Brooke, Jereco, Brandon, Diana, and their grandfather were and told Michael about the adventures the family had had on Trahe. "And that is how we were led to Bethemek," ended Archelaus.

Archelaus told Michael about the information they had gathered about the slave trade. Michael confirmed that some escaped slaves had made it to Bethemek. Diana asked him if a girl named Maria had made it to the village.

"I do not recall, but I will investigate that for you," he promised.

Diana smiled and decided she liked Michael very much.

While the conversations took place, Brooke wondered what Michael and

Archelaus had shown each other on their backs, but she did not think it was an appropriate question for her to ask. She looked over at Brandon, whom she usually could count on to ask anything.

Brandon knew exactly what she was thinking. "So what was the deal with the strip show earlier?"

Jereco coughed up his drink. "Brandon!"

"Come on," replied Brandon. "Aren't you curious?"

Before Jereco could answer, Brandon continued. "Then what is the deal with the backs? We are Evadeams too, you know. What if it is something we need to know?"

Michael looked over at Brandon and started laughing. "He has a point, Cousin." Michael stood up and started taking off his shirt.

Brooke protested. "There is no need to remove your shirt."

Michael gave her a wide smile. "Oh, but you need to see it to believe it." He stripped off his shirt and turned his back to them. On his left shoulder was a mark that looked like a star.

"We both have one," replied Archelaus. "Mine is on my right shoulder. We were born with the mark."

Grandpa swallowed his food, "It seems we have something in common with the Trahe Evadeam tribe. You see—we have similar birthmarks."

Needless to say, Archelaus, Michael, and Hachmoni were surprised by this news. "So where are these star markings?" Michael asked.

Jereco was the first to show his birthmark located on the bottom of his right heel. Brandon's was located on the left heel. Diana pulled back her hair to show her small star behind her right ear. "That is why I always wear my hair long—to cover it up."

Archelaus looked over at Brooke. "Well?"

Brooke placed her hands in her lap and looked into Archelaus's eyes. "That's none of your business."

Archelaus eyebrow shot up. "Really?"

Brooke shot him an angry look. "You will have to trust me that I have one."

Archelaus grinned, ear to ear. "Oh, I don't know if we can trust you with something this important. What do you think, Cousin?"

Michael took a bite of his food, gesturing that he could not speak at the moment. He was obviously staying out of this argument.

Brooke, who was turning red in the face, looked over at Hachmoni. She pleaded with her eyes to stop the teasing.

"Even though I do trust you, Brooke," said Hachmoni, "We do need someone to verify the marking."

"I can tell you that she has the star," volunteered Diana.

Everyone looked over at Diana.

"That is right. Diana has seen my mark, and since she is the Vision Keeper, her word should be good enough." Brooke smiled when she saw

The Trabe Chronicles

Hachmoni and Archelaus look over at Diana, knowing they did not dare question her.

However, Michael, who had just met Diana, was not completely convinced. He was not afraid to question her. "So exactly where is Brooke's star, Diana?" he asked.

Diana shrugged. "It is over her belly button. I don't know what the big deal is. You can see it when she wears a bikini."

Michael looked confused. "What is a bikini?"

"One of the best things man has invented on our planet," Jereco replied.

Brandon looked up. "No, it's not. It's pizza. Pizza is the best thing." He looked down at his plate. "I sure could go for pizza right now."

"Pizza?" Michael asked. The boys explained what a bikini and a pizza were on Earth. The bikini swimsuit shocked Michael, and the pizza sounded intriguing.

Brooke was happy the conversation had shifted away from finding a star on her body. Later that evening, after everyone went to bed, Brooke lay in bed awake. All these years they thought they had abnormal birthmarks. She always thought it was a curse to have a star outlining her belly button. But now, it meant something more. It was a mark that represented something important on this planet. So was she now considered a cousin of Archelaus? If that was the case, a relationship might be out of the question. Brooke sighed. It did not matter anyway. Someday, they would go back home to Earth, and she may never see Archelaus again. She closed her eyes. That evening, she dreamed of stars.

The next day, there was no more talk about birthmark stars. Michael showed them the village. It was quite impressive. Everything was made out of stone or fallen trees. Nothing was made out of fresh cut trees. Brandon was really happy to hear this. Michael had only heard of the legendary Willow, so he was happy to hear Brandon's stories about his experience with her.

As they walked around the town, Archelaus noticed how well the village was protected. The village was surrounded by stone walls, a face of the mountain, and a raging river.

The girls found the people to be so friendly. It was nice to see people who looked like humans. "Look, Brooke!" said Diana. "They have stores."

Brooke smiled when she saw a row of stores made out of stone. The stores were located on the main street.

"Oh, I wish we had some money," said Diana. "I want to buy something."

Brooke wistfully looked at the stores too. "Even if we had some of our money, it would not be any good here. I wonder how they do pay for things."

Michael had come up behind the girls. "It sounds like you girls have not had the pleasure of shopping in a while."

Brooke faintly smiled. "It has been a long time."

225

Book One: The Chosen Ones

"Come then. We cannot deprive ladies of some fine shopping before they are dragged into the rugged mountains." Michael walked between the two girls and nudged them toward their first store. It was a clothing store. He laughed as both girls' eyes lit up, and a sound of glee came from their lips. The clothing was different from the clothes on Earth. They were made of a rougher cloth that looked like wool. There were cloaks, coats, hats, gloves, dresses and even shoes. The store owner came to the front as soon as he saw Michael walk in. Michael introduced the ladies as distant cousins. He told the store owner they were to have anything they wanted, and the charges could be put on his account. The girls kissed his cheek and thanked him.

The men and boys also needed to do some shopping. Hachmoni insisted that they would need some supplies for their mountain trip. However, they did not take as long as the girls. They once ran into the girls during their shopping spree, and Grandpa kindly reminded them that they would not have a lot of room to carry too many purchases. Michael just laughed and said, "We will make room." And so the girls were off to another store, arm in arm with Michael.

Grandpa looked over at Archelaus. Archelaus had a little jealousy in his eyes. "Come on, my boy," said Grandpa. "It is time for lunch." Archelaus simply nodded, and the men went to the local hotel restaurant, which was more like a tavern that served food.

"Cool!" exclaimed Brandon. He felt like he was walking into a western movie. The restaurant looked like a good ole western saloon, but it was a little nicer and not as smoky. Both Jereco and Brandon enjoyed the atmosphere. "This is great!" exclaimed Brandon again, with a mouthful of food.

They were enjoying their meal until five rough-looking men walked into the saloon. Jereco noticed the voices in the restaurant dropped to low whispers. The men wore large hats that covered their heads and shaded their eyes. They did not remove their hats; Jereco thought that was rude. He shrugged. *Whatever.*

"Who do you think they are?" asked Brandon.

"Probably the bad men of the town," replied Jereco.

One of the men wearing a brown leather hat looked up at Jereco. Jereco just stared right back at him and nodded. After traveling with a large white tiger, Jereco was not easily scared. He could tell that the man was impressed by Jereco's boldness. Then the man looked down and went about his business.

Before the boys finished their meal, Brooke, Diana, and Michael came walking into the saloon. Their arms were full of packages, and they were all laughing. Michael's laugh suddenly stopped when he saw the rough group of men.

The man who had looked at Jereco talked to Michael. "Good afternoon, Michael."

Michael nodded and kept on walking.

226

The Trahe Chronicles

"Look at all the stuff Michael bought for us," said Diana, excitedly.

"Yes, I see," replied Grandpa. He glanced up at Michael. "But I am not sure how the pegasi will be able to carry all this stuff."

"We will make it work," replied Brooke as she put her packages down. She grabbed a fruit off of Grandpa's plate. "Yum. Food. I am starving."

"Yes," said Brandon, "shopping sure can work up an appetite."

Brooke ignored him and Michael waved over a waitress, so she could order food.

"Well, I am done," announced Brandon. "Who wants to go explore the town?"

No one said anything, so Jereco volunteered to go with Brandon.

"Just stay close to the center of town," ordered Michael. "Stay away from the outskirts."

Brandon asked why, but Jereco nodded and pushed Brandon toward the door. As they stepped out, Brandon took a deep breath. "It smells so good here. Fresh air. The smell of pine trees."

Jereco simply nodded in agreement. Jereco knew that Brandon was happy to be in the middle of some great towering trees. He knew Brandon missed Willow as much as Jereco missed the water people.

Brandon and Jereco explored the town. A lot of people were friendly, and then there were some that were not. As they were walking behind the row of shops, they heard a voice. "Beware, beware." The boys stopped, looked around, and did not see anyone who might be talking to them. "Beware. *Baa, bea*. Beware," said the voice again.

Brandon looked toward the back of the wool clothing store that the girls had shopped in earlier. "Could it be?" he whispered. "Come on, Jereco." Brandon walked over to a large fenced yard. Within that yard were wooly sheep.

At the edge of the fence was a very large sheep saying, "*Baa*. Beware," in the Trahe language.

"Beware of what?" asked Brandon.

The sheep did not answer.

Jereco reached out and carefully touched the sheep's head. He started scratching it.

The sheep seemed to really like this.

"Beware of what?" Jereco asked.

This time, the sheep started to answer, but he was interrupted by another voice coming from behind the boys.

"Talking to the sheep, boys?" said one of the rough-looking men from the saloon.

"Yeah, what's it to you?" replied Brandon.

Jereco elbowed Brandon.

"Ow!" mumbled Brandon.

One of the other men laughed. "Putting in a request to have a wooly dress

Book One: The Chosen Ones

made for you?"

Jereco grabbed Brandon before he could react.

Likewise, the man who had stared down Jereco in the saloon put his hand up. He ordered the other men down. "Come on, boys," he said. "Stop acting like children. We have worked to do."

The other men shut their mouths and followed the man in the brown leather hat. Jereco concluded that he was the leader of the pack. When they walked by, Jereco noticed the leather strap on the leader's hat had something that looked like a big animal claw on it.

The sheep spoke again. *"Baa. Baa.* Bad two-legged."

The men did not seem to notice and kept on walking.

After they were gone, Jereco turned to Brandon. "Those men must not speak Trahe."

Brandon nodded in agreement.

Jereco turned back to the sheep. "So what can you tell us about these bad two-legged creatures?"

Later, Jereco and Brandon were running through town, trying to find their group. They finally found everyone.

"Where have you been?" demanded Diana, placing her hands on her hips. "We have been ready to go, and we could not find you."

Michael looked down at the boys' boots. "By the looks of it, you have been at the edge of town where I told you not to go."

"Yes, but we can explain," said Brandon, who was a little out of breath. The mountain air was weakening his lungs.

"You can explain back at Michael's home," suggested Grandpa.

Brandon started to object. "But—"

"Not here in public," interrupted Hachmoni. Then he looked around as if someone might be watching them.

Jereco put a hand on Brandon's shoulder. "They are right, Brandon. There are too many people around who could hear our conversation. We need to talk in private."

Brandon's shoulders slumped, but he agreed to wait.

As soon as they walked into Michael's home, the boys started talking. Michael put his hand up. "Whoa! One at a time."

Jereco let Brandon do the talking—knowing his little brother could not stand it any longer. "We know who is trapping the talking animals!"

Michael's eyebrow shot up. "Oh?"

"Yeah, those nasty-looking men from the saloon have been doing it," said Brandon, proudly.

"Oh," said Michael, unsurprised.

Jereco and Brandon looked at each other.

"Oh?" said Brandon, disappointed. "That is it?"

Michael shrugged his shoulders. "We had our suspicions about them for a

228

The Trahe Chronicles

long time, but we have never been able to prove it. We broke up a trapping ring a few years back, but the men we did capture never implicated the others."

"So why have you not been able to prove it?" asked Jereco.

"We need to catch them in the act or, at the very least, catch them with the dead animals before they strip them down for sale. We have never been able to find their workshop."

"So what if I can tell you where they take the captured animals?" asked Jereco. "Would that help?"

That caught Michael's attention. "Yes. How would you know that?"

"The sheep!" said Brandon. "Haven't you ever talked or listened to the sheep?" Michael just looked confused. "The sheep?"

The boys told him about the talking sheep behind the wool clothing store.

"Well, I'll be," said Michael. "I walk by there all the time. They always seem to get real noisy when I walk by, but they never say anything to me."

"Maybe it is because you haven't been really listening," suggested Brandon.

Michael did not like that comment very much, so Jereco stepped in. "Anyway, the sheep gave us directions to some mountain caves outside of town."

'How did the sheep know?" asked Brooke.

Jereco just shrugged. "Other creatures. Other traders. The bad guys themselves. The sheep are a captive audience in that fenced-in yard. I guess they felt bad for the other talking animals that have been killed. The sheep do not have to die to contribute their wool."

"So when do we get started?" asked Brandon.

Hachmoni spoke up. "I think Michael, Zacchaeus, and their men can handle the situation from here. We have other things to concentrate on, including leaving soon to find your parents."

Brandon had started to protest until the words *your parents* were spoken.

"Hachmoni is right," said Michael. "We can handle it from here, boys, but we do appreciate the information. Thank you for the hard work."

The boys smiled a little, but they were disappointed that they would not be present for the bust.

"Besides," continued Michael, "the winter storms will be approaching the mountains soon. We need to pack and plan the best route to Evadeam Mountain."

"We?" asked Archelaus.

"Yes. I have decided to join you on your search. After all, I am an Evaceam and have decided it is my duty to help the Chosen Ones."

"So you are going with us?" asked Brooke.

Michael nodded, smiling.

"Oh joy!" exclaimed Diana.

Brandon was not thrilled. "Yeah, packing and traveling again sounds way

Book One: The Chosen Ones

more exciting than helping bust some bad guys who are killing the talking animals!"

"Well, I am excited," said Brooke, "because then I can wear my new winter coat."

"And I am sure you will look beautiful," commented Michael.

Archelaus gave him a dirty look. "Here. I will help you girls with your packages."

Brooke smiled as she led Archelaus the way.

The Trahe Chronicles

Ancient Methuselah

"That is the last of it," said Brooke as she packed up her stuff a few days later. By some miracle, she was able to pack up all her belongings and the stuff she bought while in Bethemek. The pegasi reassured the girls that they were able to carry the extra load and Michael. Michael was yearning for an adventure and was excited to leave Bethemek. Michael left Zacchaeus in charge. "Are you sure this is not too much of a burden for you?" asked Michael. "In addition to the woods, your responsibilities now include guarding the town."

"Not to mention the capture of the thieves," pointed out Archelaus.

"I will be fine," assured Zacchaeus. "I have the help of many good men. And do not worry. My wife and her friends will keep your home in good shape while you are gone."

With that, Michael joined the group.

They started out early the next morning. The smell of dew on the grass and trees lingered in the air. The sounds of birds making their morning calls filled their ears. They listened for any unnatural sounds from possible predators lurking in the shadows of the woods. It was decided to ride on land to avoid attracting attention. Soon they were at the foothills of the large mountain. They continued to ride quietly until lunch.

"We will stop for lunch around this bend," said Michael.

As they turned the corner, a magnificent sight awaited them.

"Wow!" exclaimed Diana.

Michael smiled back at the young girl. "Welcome to the Color River."

A large river flowed in front of them. The beauty of the river's surroundings was reflected in its waters.

"I can see why it is called the Color River," said Brooke as she dismounted from Midnight. Not only were the colors of the blue sky, trees, grasses, flowers and mountains reflected in the clear waters, but there were also colorful rocks and pebbles that lay at the bottom of the river.

"The water is so clear that I can even see the fish," Diana pointed out.

"Perfect," Brandon said as he dismounted. "They will be perfect for lunch."

Diana made a face at him, but she didn't say anything. She had learned that they needed to eat what they could pick, dig up, or catch, including the live fish. So the girls unpacked the supplies needed for lunch while the men caught fish. They cooked the fish over a small campfire and enjoyed a nice meal. Afterward, the guys decided to clean up and put the fire out while the girls went upstream to find a little privacy.

Brooke and Diana were washing their hands and face up stream when Brooke heard a loud crack coming from the woods behind her. Instantly, she grabbed her knife out of her sheath with one hand and reached for Diana with the other. She motioned Diana to be quiet and stay motionless. Even

Book One: The Chosen Ones

though she could not hear anything, Brooke knew something was in the woods. The chill that ran up the back of her neck was a warning sign that the creature was probably not friendly.

Brooke slowly turned to face the woods. She spotted a large, brown creature. Brooke squinted trying to determine what type of animal lurked in the trees. Brooke put herself between the creature and Diana. She motioned Diana to gather up their things. Diana quickly put their stuff in the bags. Brooke knew that they could not stand here for too much longer. She hoped that the guys would start searching for them. Brooke thought it would better if they started moving toward the camp, so she motioned to Diana to start walking backward.

Brooke constantly kept her eyes and ears open. She would much rather use the bow and arrow, but that had been left in her saddlebag on Midnight. She did not like using the knife because it required close contact. But if she had to use it, she would. And maybe it was that last thought that stirred up a little fear in Brooke. It was enough to get the creature's attention.

They heard branches break. Diana's eyes widen. She panicked and ran as fast as she could toward their camp. Brooke started after her and turned to get a glimpse of her attacker. It was a grizzly bear!

Grizzly bear? Grizzly bears here on Trahe? The large bear was dark brown with flecks of gray. Its paws were as large as Brooke's head.

"Oh, no—a bear." Brooke remembered everything her dad and Grandpa taught her about being attacked by bears. They were doing one of the things they weren't supposed to do—

running! They could never outrun a large grizzly bear.

"Diana!" yelled Brooke. "Stop. Freeze. Roll into a ball."

There was no way Diana was stopping; she was scared and running for her life.

The grizzly was almost upon Brooke. Brooke needed to protect Diana. Brooke summoned up all her courage and turned to face the bear.

Brooke roared at the bear at the top of her lungs. She threw her arms above her head, trying to make herself look taller. The sun shined down on her knife, and the reflection caught the bear's eye. The bear skidded to a stop, stood on its hind legs and let out a loud growl. Brooke decided that the bear was sizing her up. It was much larger and taller than she. She could not see behind her, so she was not sure if Diana had gotten very far. If the bear decided to push Brooke aside and go for easier prey, Diana could still be in danger. A thought came to Brooke.

She spoke as loudly as she could. "Do you speak the Trahe language?"

There it was—a flicker of comprehension in the bear's face. Brooke had been very careful not to look the bear in the eye until this moment. She was sure it understood the Trahe language now. In a much louder, huskier voice, she repeated herself. "Do you speak Trahe?" The bear did not answer, but it did come down to stand on all four paws. It smelled the air, sizing Brooke

The Trahe Chronicles

up. It rocked from side to side. However, it still did not answer Brooke.

Brooke kept her arms above her head. Her knife was ready in her right hand. She slowly started walking backward and spoke again. "If you speak the Trahe language, then you understand what I say. I honor and respect the law. I will not kill a Trahe-speaking beast. However, if you do not answer me, I will assume you do not speak the language. I will have to kill you if you come closer."

The bear let out a loud growl and then laughed heartily. "You kill me? And how dare you call me a beast!"

"So you do speak Trahe," said Brooke as she slowly moved backward. She was hoping that Diana was back to the camp by now and reinforcements were on the way.

"I do speak the ancient tongue," said the bear as he smelled the air again, "but I am ancient; you are not. I do not recognize your scent. How is it that you speak the ancient Trahe language? Is this a trick?"

"I am blood of the ancient Evadeam tribe," Brooke said. "The language has been passed down through my ancestors to me." As she spoke, she felt more confident that perhaps she would not be eaten by a grizzly bear today.

However, her confidence sank as the bear reared and roared. "Evadeam tribe! You are not of the Evadeam tribe! I would smell the Evadeam blood, and that I do not smell." The great bear dropped to all four paws again. He hesitated and started to circle to the left of Brooke. This forced Brooke into the water. "You do not smell of the Madeave," said the bear. "What are you?"

'I am of the Evadeam tribe," insisted Brooke. "I am the Protector!"

'Liar!" roared the bear. It swung its large paw at Brooke.

Brooke ducked and tried to move out of the water. As she did so, she swung the knife at the bear. They were now facing each other at the edge of the river. Brooke knew the bear would have the advantage in the river. But she also knew that if the bear wanted to hurt her, he would have already done it. His paw had missed her on purpose; she was sure of it. He was curious. He had not quite figured out what she was, so she hoped if she kept on talking, she would get somewhere.

"I am the Protector of the Chosen Ones," continued Brooke. "If you are an ancient one, friend, or foe of the Evadeam tribe, then you have heard that the Chosen Ones have arrived. My smell is of ancient and new blood. My smell is of legend."

The bear got too close for comfort, and Brooke swung her knife at it. This time, the bear easily knocked the knife out of Brooke's hand. Brooke's instinct took over. She rolled over backward and grabbed a large rock from the riverbed. She threw the rock as hard as she could at the bear's head. Right on target. It took the bear by surprise, giving Brooke a moment to spot the knife in the water. She ran for it, knowing she only had a split second. She grabbed the knife and turned around as fast as she could, not wanting to have

233

Book One: The Chosen Ones

her back to the bear for too long. Much to her surprise, the bear was not at her heels. He had stood up to full height. He roared the loudest grizzly bear sound that Brooke had ever heard.

Then he slowly dropped down to all four paws and walked toward her. "I will let you live a little longer—long enough to tell me what you know of the Chosen Ones. If you tell me the truth, then I will let you die fast. If you lie, then you will die a long, painful death."

Brooke yelled back at him. "You are the one who does not tell the truth! I have been telling you the truth, yet you do not believe me! You are not a friend of the Chosen Ones or the Evadeam tribe. You are an enemy to Archelaus, leader of the Evadeam people!"

The bear paused. "Archelaus? You know of Archelaus? What do you know of him? Is he alive, or is he dead?"

Brooke wondered if she had said too much. She had been sure this bear would be on their side since he spoke Trahe, but now, she was no longer sure of herself. Maybe the enemies also spoke Trahe. "I will tell you no more!" yelled Brooke. "You will not kill me, for if you do, the wrath of my dead Evadeam ancestors will be upon you!"

The bear seemed to hesitate for a moment. "Female of man. You have only your word. Prove to me who you are, for your fighting surely is not Evadeam."

Brooke could not think of anything. Proof? What proof? And where was everyone? As these thoughts ran through her head, she glanced over the bear's shoulders for any sign of help. Nothing. There was no one. Where was everyone? She looked away.

The great grizzly bear took that moment to pounce on Brooke. Brooke brought her hands up to cover her head, and she fell backward. Her shoulders hit the rocks below, knocking the breath out of her. The weight of the bear was enormous, and she was sure he was going to crush her before he sunk his claws and teeth into her. She kept thinking, *I need to roll up like a baby. Protect my head and face.* Her right hand still had her knife, and she gripped it hard. She tucked her head under her arms. Maybe with any luck, the knife would dig into some part of the bear. She did a silent prayer and hoped that Diana was safe. *Why am I not crushed by now?* She felt the bear's breath near her ear.

In a low growling voice, he said, "Tell me what you know of the Chosen Ones. Tell me what you know, and I will not tear you into little pieces." As if to prove his point, he put more weight on Brooke.

Brooke felt a claw start to dig into her rib cage. "Let me up, and I will tell you," she whispered.

"Liar!" He dug his claw into her a little more.

"Dear God, help me," she whispered out loud. "Help me now."

"Who is this God you speak of?" asked the bear. He adjusted his weight so she could speak.

The Trahe Chronicles

"My God, your God, the Creator!" she said louder.

"Tell me a law," he ordered. "A law from the Creator."

"I did! I did! I told you that I cannot kill a speaking beast—I mean, *animal*." She remembered the bear had been offended by the word *beast*.

"Tell me another!" growled the bear.

"*I will tell you another!*" boomed a voice. "*Talking animals are not allowed to harm Evadeam blood!*"

Brooke heard a loud roar. Then the next few minutes felt like a blur. The bear shifted his weight and looked up. A streak of white ran at full speed toward the bear. The bear quickly released Brooke and stood to fend off the new attacker. The white animal jumped right at the middle of the bear's stomach and brought him down into the river.

A huge splash of cold water spilled over Brooke. She quickly pulled herself out of the river. She ran toward the shore, but the pain in her side made her double over. She fell onto the shore's edge and tried to catch her breath. The sound of animals roaring brought her attention back to the river. She saw splashes of water mixed with grizzly bear and white.

Brooke squinted her eyes. *Skylar! The white tiger, Skylar, saved her.* Brooke started to cry. She looked at the sky. "Thank you, God! Thank you, Creator!"

Then she saw them. Pegasi in the sky. The pegasi were coming. She looked back toward the water and saw that the grizzly bear was now on top. His paw came down on Skylar.

"No!" Brooke cried. "Skylar!"

Skylar fell backward into the water, and the great bear stood up on its hind legs. It let out a great roar. Brooke knew what was coming next. The bear would try to crush Skylar, perhaps drown her.

"Skylar! Get up!" shouted Brooke as loudly as she could.

Then Brooke heard screeching. Aquila came swooping down in front of the bear and started circling it. The grizzly bear swung his paws at the eagle, trying to shoo it away.

"This is my battle," growled the bear.

The eagle kept swooping down and screeching at the bear.

"Go away, Aquila!" yelled the bear.

The bear knew Aquila? Brooke got up, and as she did, so did Skylar.

Skylar shook off the water and started growling at the bear. The bear snarled back. They circled each other, both walking on all four paws.

Brooke thought they were talking to each other as Aquila circled above cawing at them.

Another rumble came from Skylar. The bear stood up and then splashed his front paws back into the river.

Water spilled over Skylar. She stood her ground and let out a roar louder than the bear's and then shook off the water. They both just stood there looking at each other, and as if in agreement, they nodded and turned back toward the shore. It looked as though they had made up but still did not trust

Book One: The Chosen Ones

one another completely as they walked side by side. Aquila followed them from above.

Brooke felt wind brush against her back as Midnight came behind her. Archelaus jumped off before Midnight completely landed. Brooke noticed the look on his face. She had never seen him look so distressed.

"Brooke!" He ran up to her and lifted her into his arms. "Oh, thank the Creator above! You are all right!"

Brooke screamed in pain. She grabbed her side.

"You are hurt!" Archelaus ripped back her clothing and saw the blood and bruising. "Broken ribs?" he asked.

Brooke shook her head. "I do not think so. I think I'm just bruised."

"Let me see!" said a voice from behind Brooke.

It was Grandpa. "The next time you and Diana decide to go freshen up, we are sending an escort!"

Brooke looked up at her Grandpa and saw that he was deeply concerned for her. "I am fine Grandpa," she barely choked out.

"Spoken like a true Evadeam!" said Grandpa. "A true Protector!"

"Some Protector," she mumbled.

"Yeah, some Protector," he said proudly. "You protected Diana. She is safe and sound, thanks to you."

"She is?" asked Brooke. "She is okay? I was beginning to worry."

"Well, the poor little thing was tuckered out by the time she got to camp," mumbled Grandpa. "It took awhile to figure out what was going on."

Brooke looked more closely at Grandpa. He was hiding something. She could always tell when he was hiding something. "What's wrong?"

He didn't answer.

"Grandpa?"

Grandpa shrugged. "Nothing is wrong, but there will be a problem if we do not tend to your wounds."

Brooke looked around and did not see Jereco or Brandon. "Where are the boys?" she asked.

Again, Grandpa didn't say anything.

She gave Grandpa a dirty look and then turned toward Archelaus. "Archelaus? Is Diana all right? What is going on? Where is Jereco?"

Archelaus looked into Brooke's eyes and could not deny her the truth. "Diana is all right." He hesitated for a moment. "But when she got to camp, she was exhausted. She looked like she had just run a marathon while crying. Then she ... well, she had an episode."

Brooke was confused. "An episode?"

"She had a seizure," Grandpa said.

"A seizure? We have to get back to her."

Grandpa and Archelaus helped Brooke up to her feet.

The bear stopped in front of Brooke and then bowed down. "Protector." He hesitated and looked at Skylar, who nodded. The bear continued.

236

The Trahe Chronicles

"Protector, will you forgive me? I was doing my duty."

With that last sentence, Skylar let out a little growl.

The bear looked at Skylar and stood to full height on his rear legs. "I am Methuselah, Protector of the ancient Evadeam tribe." He dropped back to all four legs. "We seem to have something in common, Protector of the Chosen Ones."

Skylar growled again, obviously not liking his apology.

Brooke held up her hand to show it was all right. She stepped forward. "Did you say Methuselah?" She remembered Arcturus talking about the ancient Methuselah, who had brought her cubs to safety. She quickly relayed that story to Methuselah about saving Arcturus.

Skylar, much to everyone's surprise, invited Methuselah back to camp so the bear could see Arcturus. Arcturus and Silver Kat had come to camp with Skylar just before Skylar had run off to help Brooke. They should still be there, waiting for everyone.

Grandpa quickly reminded Skylar of Diana's condition; her seeing Methuselah right now might not be a good idea. Methuselah agreed to stay back in the woods out of the Vision Keeper's sight. Arcturus would be sent into the woods to meet up with Methuselah.

Midnight, Luke Thunder, Clyde, and Dale flew Brooke, Grandpa, Archelaus, and Michael back to camp. Skylar and Methuselah walked back with Aquila flying overhead. The two large creatures still had tension between them, but they had agreed on a truce.

When they got back to camp, Brooke insisted on seeing Diana before being treated. Diana was resting and awake. She looked pale, and all her energy seemed to be zapped out of her. Jereco, Brandon, and Silver Kat were beside her. Cleo lay at her feet.

Diana's eyes lit up when she saw Brooke. "You are okay?" she asked.

Brooke nodded, choosing not to talk about her injuries. "Yep. I am okay, sport. But what happened to you?" asked Brooke as she pulled off a cloth from Diana's forehead. She handed it to Brandon. "This needs to be cooled." He nodded and left to go dip the cloth in the cold river.

Tears welled up in Diana's eyes. "I ran as fast I could. But when I got here, I was so tired. I could not breathe. I tried so very hard to tell them to go and help you. It was like my body would not listen to my brain. Then I felt the seizure starting. It was awful, Brooke. I could not tell anyone about the bear attacking you. I tried to talk through the seizure. I really tried."

"Shhhhh ... it is okay, Diana," said Brooke. "It all worked out. It is not your fault. You got back here safely, and that is all that matters. I am supposed to protect you, not you protect me. Besides, I think your seizure was meant to be."

Diana looked up at her, confused.

"I have a thought. You have not had a seizure in a while. We even had to cut back your medicine to try to make it last, yet you were still seizure-free.

237

Book One: The Chosen Ones

But then you had one when you were trying to send the guys my way. If they had arrived sooner, the bear might have gotten killed by one of us, the more I think about it. The time it took for help to come gave me time to speak to the bear. I think for some strange reason, it was supposed to work out this way."

"What happened to the bear?" asked Diana.

"Do you remember Arcturus telling us about that ancient grizzly bear that is over nine hundred years old? The one called Methuselah?"

Diana nodded.

"Well, that bear is Methuselah."

Diana eyes got big. "No way! He is Methuselah?"

Brooke nodded.

"Are you sure?" asked Diana.

"Aquila flew in and said he is. If help had come sooner, the bear could have been killed by Archelaus or Michael before we found out the truth."

Brandon came back with the cold cloth. Brooke used it to wipe Diana's tears and then placed it on her forehead. "So, you see, it all works out for the best. Now you have to rest and start feeling better."

"It really is Methuselah?" asked Jereco. "He is still alive?"

"Methuselah?" asked Brandon. "Who is Methuselah? What did I miss now?"

Brooke quickly filled him in on what took place at the river.

"Wow! How cool is that!" said Brandon. "Can we see him?"

Brooke looked down at Diana. Her eyes were closed. "It is okay," Diana said. "He can come into camp now. I am not afraid."

Brooke smiled.

Diana, the Vision Keeper, was back.

Brooke felt something touch her side. She grimaced and pushed Jereco's hand aside. He was about to ask her what was wrong, but she put her finger up to her lips and looked at Diana. He understood to keep quiet and motioned her to leave.

As if reading his mind, Silver Kat stood up and motioned for Brooke to follow him. Silver Kat's father, grandfather, great grandfather, and the ancestors before them were medicine healers. Silver Kat followed their spiritual and medical path.

Silver Kat had attended to Diana earlier. He was now caring for Brooke, Skylar, and Methuselah's wounds. He applauded Brooke for her quick thinking and actions against Methuselah. Few had survived Methuselah's wrath and lived to tell about it.

Brooke felt better. She had felt like such a failure. She was sure she would have died if Skylar had not come at the right moment. Silver Kat said she had been very brave and was very smart to have lasted as long as she had.

Grandpa and Archelaus both lectured her for wandering too far away in the first place. They said that from that point on, she was to have an escort at

The Trahe Chronicles

all times. It did not matter if her title was the Protector of the Chosen Ones. In their eyes, she was still just a young woman, and the girls could no longer be out of their sight. Brooke reminded them that the girls needed private time without the supervision of men. It was then decided that Arcturus or Skylar would be at their side, since they were both female. Brooke agreed to this. She quietly knew that they were too close to real danger today, and next time they might not be so lucky.

Because Diana was too weak to travel, they decided to camp for the night. Around the campfire that evening, Michael brought up his concern about being stuck up in the mountains before the first snowfall. The crisp smell of autumn was in the air.

"The snow clouds on top of the mountain are looking closer," Jereco said. "but shouldn't snow be about two to three months away yet?"

"Very good, Jereco," replied Michael. Michael and Jereco had done a lot of talking while traveling. Jereco had learned that the seasons in this area were similar to Earth's. "Yes, in about two months, it will snow in Bethemek," said Michael. "But the higher we climb in the mountains, the sooner we will hit snow."

"It was snowing when we left home," recalled Brandon. The kids got really quiet as they each thought of the days before their departure.

A weak voice from behind said, "Christmas. It was just before Christmas. We missed it."

Archelaus stood up to help Diana. "Little one, you are up and walking."

Diana was slowly coming toward them while leaning against Skylar. Archelaus helped Diana sit down next to him and Grandpa.

"You should be resting," scolded Jereco.

"I was, but I wanted to be by the fire," said Diana.

Jereco knew she was warm enough, sleeping next to Cleo and Skylar, but she probably wanted some other company too, so he dropped the subject. They all would be going to bed soon anyway.

"So what is Christmas?" asked Michael.

Grandpa and all the kids smiled as they thought about Christmas.

"So?" insisted Michael.

"Well, it is religious celebration back home," explained Brooke. "It is a celebration of the birth of the Son of God, or the Creator, as you might call him or her."

Michael looked confused. "Son of the Creator? Don't you mean sons and daughters of the Creator? We are all sons, daughters, and creatures of the Creator."

Jereco shrugged. "It is kind of complicated. See, there are some back on Earth who believe that this one man was sent by God during a time when men were not being very good. God sent his son to remind people of God and to be good again. Good for God and all mankind. Some people believed and followed him, and some did not. The ones that do believe celebrate the

Book One: The Chosen Ones

son's birth on Earth. They call this event Christmas. It is one time of the year where a lot of different people all over the Earth celebrate this one major blessing. They celebrate with love and peace. This one time. Peace."

"And presents," piped up Brandon.

"Presents?" asked Michael.

"Yeah, presents and stockings," agreed Diana.

"Stockings?" Michael asked as he looked at his feet.

"And fancy dinners, parties, and new clothes," said Brooke as she reminisced.

"And food. Ham, pies, and chocolate candies," said Brandon.

"Candy canes!" piped up Diana. "And candy canes!"

Michael insisted that they explain what all of that had to do with Christmas.

Grandpa shook his head and got up to leave. When he returned to the campfire, Diana was telling them about all the presents she had gotten in the past. She got very quiet when she said she had asked for a new doll this year. "I wondered if Santa Claus brought it."

Michael's eyebrow shot up, and he looked at Jereco. "Santa Claus?"

Jereco shook his head. "Another story."

"Yes, that is another person," said Grandpa. "Another story. This is the story you should read, Michael." He handed Michael a book.

Brooke leaned over and looked at the book. "It is Grandma's Bible."

Grandpa nodded. "Yes, bless her soul. I do not leave home without it. Out of all the things we have lost on this trip, I feel blessed that I have not lost her Bible."

Brooke reached for the Bible. "May I?"

Michael, who was looking at it, said, "Of course, it is your grandmother's, after all."

Brooke took the Bible and flipped to a page. "This is what Christmas is really about." She read a passage from Matthew.

Everyone was quiet after the reading until Skylar said, "Look!" She was gazing up at the night sky. Bright lights were flying across the sky.

"Shooting stars!" exclaimed Diana.

"Comets," insisted Brandon.

Archelaus stood. "It is the great lights."

"It is a sign," growled Methuselah, who walked up slowly to the campfire. "Your God, our Creator is all the same. The Great One is reminding us—it is time for the Chosen Ones to return the Evadeams to their home. I will lead you there. We leave tomorrow morning."

"To our home?" asked Archelaus.

Methuselah nodded. "I am Methuselah. I have lived over nine hundred years. I have been friends of the Evadeams for all those years. I was instructed by the Creator to protect the Evadeams, for it is the Evadeams who will help bring peace to this world. It is the Evadeams who believe in the

240

The Trahe Chronicles

Creator and the laws of the Creator. The Evadeams are not to be terminated. I am to protect them at all costs, even if that means I must hide them from the Madeave."

Methuselah started to walk around the outside of the group that encircled the campfire. "I was told that a day would come when the Vision Keeper, the Protector, the Water Guardian, the Forest Friend, and the Returner would be brought back to this world. At that time, the ancient city would be revealed to them. The prophecy, as you know, says that the Evadeam will once again return and rule in the ancient city. The Lost Evadeam Times will end. The Believer Times will return. Be prepared for what is to come."

Confusion spread across the kids' faces, but none of them dared question the huge grizzly bear. Hachmoni stood up and bowed down to Methuselah. He pointed toward the sky with his walking stick. "The stars tell us this is the truth. We will begin our final journey tomorrow morning."

Everyone rose to go to bed.

"Wait," said Brandon. "Where exactly are we going tomorrow?"

Methuselah looked over at Brandon and walked over to him. Methuselah's nose almost touched Brandon's nose. Brandon stood his ground. He was not afraid of this huge grizzly bear. He should have been, but somehow having the talking trees on his side gave him some additional strength. At that moment, a wind blew in. The trees started to sway and creak.

Methuselah let out a hearty laugh. "So this little guy is the Forest Friend, you say?" Methuselah was not speaking to anyone in particular, but Brandon had a feeling he was talking to the trees. The wind picked up and leaves fell around Brandon and Methuselah. Methuselah stepped back. "It is foretold that I am to lead you to the ancient city in Evadeam Mountain."

"Evadeam Mountain?" Archelaus and Michael both asked in unison.

Methuselah nodded, and as he walked away, he said, "I advise all of you get a good night's sleep. We have some long day and nights ahead of us."

As Methuselah disappeared into the woods, Brandon turned around to Archelaus. "Where is Evadeam Mountain?"

Archelaus shrugged. "I do not know. It has only been a legend passed on through generations. I only know one person who has been there, and that is Hachmoni."

Michael spoke up. "History has said that Evadeam Mountain is where the Evadeam were first placed into this world by the Creator. They built a great city in the mountains."

Grandpa stood up. "If you kids studied the books I gave you before this trip, you would have read about it."

Diana spoke up. "Evadeam Mountain is where all the seven man tribes of Trahe met once a year to keep the peace. Evadeam Mountain is where the Madeave came to announce war against the Evadeam tribe. It is where our ancestor Princess Skylar married a Madeave man. She left Evadeam Mountain

241

Book One: The Chosen Ones

to live with him and help keep peace between the two tribes."

Skylar walked over. "Yes, it was my ancestor Bright Eyes who went with her. I was named after the Evadeam ancestor princess."

"So what happened?" asked Brandon. "Why is the city now hidden?"

Skylar sat by Diana and shook her head sadly. "After the death of Skylar and her husband, the wars between the Madeave and the Evadeam broke out again. Many decades of bloodshed fueled by the Snakes, the Madeave's ally, caused the Evadeam to stop the annual meeting between the seven tribes. The allies of the Evadeam vowed not to give the location of the Evadeam city. It is ancient and holy. It is said that over time, the Evadeam wandered out of the city. They had a thirst for adventure, to discover new lands, and to spread out. Some left to defend their outside villages from the Madeave. Over time, the city was abandoned and lost.

"Over time, it just became legend," continued Michael. "A myth—some searched for Evadeam Mountain and the ancient city but never returned. It became too dangerous. Even the most aggressive Madeave gave up searching for it."Jereco turned to Hachmoni. "So is it true? Is there a lost city? Is there an Evadeam Mountain? Is this where we are to go?"

Hachmoni nodded his head. "It is as Methuselah says."

Brandon spoke up. "The banyan tree. The tree on the Island of the Pegasi said that we would find answers we seek at the ancient Evadeam City."

Grandpa clasped his hands together. "Well then, we must be off to bed. A new adventure awaits us tomorrow."

Late in the night, long after everyone was asleep, there was the sound of a branch breaking. The grizzly bear's head shot up. He narrowed his eyes and looked into the deep woods. The moon was full and bright. Not much would be unnoticed under the evening sky's light. A creature came out of the woods and bowed down to Methuselah. "Methuselah," it simply said.

Both heads turned as another creature stepped out of the shadows. Hachmoni stepped forward.

"You are quiet for a two-legged creature," said Methuselah.

Hachmoni simply bowed and was interrupted by Aquila who flew down and landed before them. One by one, other creatures slowly came forward, including Skylar and Silver Kat. Soon, a small circle was formed.

The first that came forth was an old gray wolf. He spoke. "The time is here, Methuselah. It is time to bring the Evadeam back to the mountain, back to their home. I smell evil near. It is a greater evil than we had anticipated. I fear it is an evil that can only be stopped by the Evadeam tribe."

Methuselah nodded in agreement "It is foretold, and yes, it is time. Is he safe?" he asked the wolf.

"He is safe," he replied.

Hachmoni spoke up. "He knows."

They all looked at Hachmoni. "Archelaus knows now. He knows that his

242

brother and sister did not die all those years ago. He will want to search for them."

Methuselah shook his head. "It is not time yet. They will not stay safe if Archelaus seeks them out. You must make sure he stays on his path. His path is to the lost Evadeam city."

Hachmoni rubbed his chin in thought. "If he thinks that path will lead him to his lost family, I can keep him on that path. But I cannot lie to him. I cannot mislead him anymore." Arcturus spoke up. "You will not need to. His interest in the Protector may be the key to keeping him on the right path. Where she will go, he will follow."

Hachmoni looked thoughtful. "True, but is she to stay in this world? If not, will he follow her then?"

Methuselah looked at the sky. "Follow the stars, Hachmoni. Continue to follow the signs, and all will lead to the right path—destiny."

Archelaus had watched Hachmoni, Skylar, and Silver Kat silently go off to the woods. He felt disappointed that he was not invited, especially since he was the leader of the Evadeam tribe. However, showing up to a meeting, uninvited, with the great Methuselah did not seem like a very smart move. He was certain that Hachmoni would share what information he needed to know. He made himself feel better, knowing this was some sort of meeting of ancient beings. He was far from being over hundreds of years old. He was a youngster in their eyes.

Besides, he did not want to leave Brooke's side. He insisted on sleeping near Brooke and Diana for their safety, of course. He looked over at the tent Brooke slept in. Earlier, he had a horrible feeling in his gut when they realized she was in danger. When he flew on Midnight and looked below to see a big grizzly bear towering over Brooke; he had such a horrible feeling of despair.

What if something had happened to her? He did not care if she was the Protector. She was a young, beautiful woman whom he had developed feelings—deep feelings. They were on a mission that could end badly. But what if it did end well? Would her time be done in this world? Would the Creator send her back to her home on this place called Earth? Then what? He shook his head. He did not want to think about it. He looked away and up at the stars.

Ever since the invasion of his home village all those years ago, Archelaus had missions in his life. He was to find the missing Evadeams, kill the Madeave, and bring back the Evadeam empire. He had no room for a woman in his life. No room for love. Love? He shook his head. He still had no room for it. He looked up at the sky and watched the shooting stars. *A sign*, Methuselah and Hachmoni had said. Archelaus continued to watch the stars until his eyelids got heavy. The leader of the Evadeam people finally drifted off to sleep. He dreamed of a young woman with long brown hair and big brown eyes.

Book One: The Chosen Ones

The Living Rock

"This is the best color tour I have ever seen," yelled Grandpa. They had been traveling for weeks, and the season was changing right before their eyes. They were flying above the trees and the colors below them were spectacular. The trees' leaves had turned from green to brilliant colors of gold, red, orange, and yellow. Large green evergreen and pine trees dotted the landscape.

Brooke looked below and had to admit it was quite pretty. It looked like a painting from God, as her mom used to say. Her mom. Now and then, something would remind her of her home back on Earth, yet it seemed like a faraway dream.

They were riding high in the sky on the Pegasi, led by Aquila, while Skylar, Arcturus, and Methuselah ran below on the rough terrain. Methuselah knew the way and led the ground group. They met in the evening, somewhere along the Color River. Even though the terrain was beautiful, it was rugged. The girls were still healing from their first meeting with Methuselah, so they thought it would be better for them to fly on the pegasi. It was a smoother ride than galloping over the mountains. Methuselah also wanted to make sure they were not spotted. He thought it was best that they split up and meet only in the evenings.

It was on one of those evenings that evidence of winter was fast approaching. There was definitely a chill in the air. After dinner, they huddled close to the fire.

"I wish we were there already," complained Brandon. "I am tired of living outdoors. It is getting colder every day. What if it starts snowing? What if the river freezes up, and we cannot catch anymore fish? What are we going to do for food?"

"Freeze?" asked Diana as she pulled a blanket over her shoulders. "Are we going to get caught in a snowstorm and freeze to death?"

"No, we are not," said Brooke as she wrapped a scarf around her neck. "Brandon, stop scaring Diana."

Brandon shrugged. "I am just being practical and honest. We do not have enough food to get us through the winter, and we do not have much for shelter, except for our makeshift tents."

Brooke thought Brandon was right, of course, but she did not want to think about it. She did not want to deal with having to calm Diana.

"Do not worry, Diana," said Archelaus. "The Creator will take care of us."

Jereco—who typically was the silent one—could not agree with Archelaus. Maybe it was the chill in the air or that he was tired, but he could not keep quiet any longer. "How exactly is the Creator going to help us, Archelaus? We are in the middle of nowhere in the mountains, with old man winter knocking on our door. We do not have permanent shelter. Brandon is

The Trahe Chronicles

right. We do not have enough food to get us through the winter. If we do not find this ancient city soon, we are going to have to turn back to Bethemek and wait until spring."

"Turn back to Bethemek when I just got here?" spoke a voice that came from the woods. Everyone was startled and jumped up, armed with their weapons. By now, they knew each other's voices, and this was not a voice of anyone traveling with them. It was dark outside, and they had to wait until the creature that spoke stepped into the moonlight. He stepped out cautiously.

As soon as the light shined upon him, Diana squealed. "Sir Bolivar!" She ran to her four-legged friend. She gave him a big hug around his neck as everyone else put their weapons away.

Questions flew out of the kids' mouths.

Sir Bolivar laughed. "Wait a minute. One at a time. I sure am hungry. Have any food?"

Jereco smiled. "Funny you should ask about food."

Sir Bolivar looked at him, puzzled, but Archelaus waved him over. "Come and rest, my friend. We will feed you what we have, and then you should tell us how you came about meeting us in these mountains."

While Sir Bolivar ate, the kids filled him in on their adventures since they left Willow. "Wow," said Sir Bolivar, "what grand adventures you've had. Mine was not as grand. After you left, we secured Willow as our new home. The Madeave and the snakes have disappeared from the area. Koa had brought a message back to us that you were on your way to find the lost ancient city of the Evadeam. On his way back to Willow, he intercepted a message that some Madeave scouts were hot on your trail, and that they were now aware that the Chosen Ones had returned to Trahe. Koa also had gathered information that gave him the impression that there was something or someone bigger and more evil supporting the Madeave. He wanted to get this information to Hachmoni as quickly as possible through the birds. Bathsheba insisted that I come along and find you in case help was needed."

"Oh, how is Bathsheba?" asked Brooke.

Sir Bolivar smiled. "She is doing great. She wanted to come along with me, but I convinced her that it would be in everyone's best interest that she stayed in Willow. She does miss you girls very much."

Brooke and Diana smiled as they thought about Bathsheba and how they missed having a mother figure around.

"So here I am," said Sir Bolivar. "I have finally found you."

Jereco had a look of concern on his face. "If you found us this easily, then the Madeave are sure to find us."

Sir Bolivar shook his head. "No, I covered my tracks well and followed different birds along the way. We came across Madeave a few weeks ago and sent them in another direction, away from you." Sir Bolivar looked over at Hachmoni. "However, I think Koa is right. The Madeave are smarter than

Book One: The Chosen Ones

they used to be. I believe they are taking directions from something else. I cannot quite put my finger on who might be leading them."

Hachmoni nodded and rubbed his chin. He then turned toward Methuselah. "We need to take extra precautions so we are not followed."

Methuselah nodded in agreement. "And I will send word out to the other creatures that we need to find out the identity of all of Madeave's allies." He got up and walked into the forest.

Sir Bolivar let out a low whistle. "So that is Methuselah? I've only heard of the legend. He is even bigger than I imagined. I can't believe he is still alive! It is a good thing he is on our side."

Everyone nodded in agreement.

Cleo walked over to Sir Bolivar. "How tired are you?"

Sir Bolivar raised his eyebrow, but before he could answer, Cleo said, "We need to talk about some things." She turned to the others. "The morning will come soon enough. I predict some long days are coming, so I suggest you turn in for the night."

Everyone felt like that was more of an order than a recommendation. They meekly said their goodnights.

Diana did not want to go to bed without Cleo. Cleo always started the evening by climbing into bed with her, but Cleo assured her that she would there be shortly. Diana hesitated and then went to the tent with Brooke. As they lay in their beds, Diana asked Brooke what she thought Cleo wanted to talk to Sir Bolivar about.

"I am not sure," Brooke replied with a yawn.

Diana paused. "I sometimes wonder if Cleo does more than just hunt at nighttime after we go to sleep."

Brooke nodded. "Well, we know she watches over us during the night shift." *Especially since she sleeps all day*, Brooke thought to herself.

"Yeah, but I think she does something else," said Diana. "I think she talks to the Creator."

Through sleepy eyes, Brooke looked over at Diana. "Why do you think that? Have you had a vision lately?"

Diana shook her head. "No, but sometimes I wake up, and I can hear her talking. But she talks in a different language. I do not recognize it. It does not sound like Trahe, English, or even cat sounds. Just different somehow."

Brooke thought about this for a moment. "Well, perhaps. That would be a good thing if she is talking directly to the Creator. Maybe the Creator is guiding us in the right direction. Now go to sleep. You heard what Cleo said. We are going to have some long days."

The next few days were long. They rode hard and fast on a route that seemed well-hidden. It was on a day that they were feeling very exhausted that Archelaus demanded they slow down. Everyone was beat.

Aquila circled around them. "We are almost there."

246

The Trahe Chronicles

"Where?" asked Archelaus.

Aquila did not answer and kept flying ahead. She brought them to a very small ledge. It was barely big enough for all of them to fit. They were standing at the edge of a giant cliff that dropped into a canyon.

"Where is the bottom?" asked Brandon. No one could see it. It looked like the canyon went on forever. All they could see below them was a mist that looked like fog.

Directly across from them was the face of the large mountain. It was much too steep to climb. To the right was a very narrow path that none of them dared to walk on. The path looked like it rose from the bottom of the canyon and led all the way up the face of the mountain.

"Hey," said Brandon "is something actually walking up that path?" He pointed downward.

Aquila flew down and circled around the figures below. She flew back and informed them that it was Sir Bolivar, Skylar, Arcturus, and Methuselah down below.

Once Methuselah's group arrived at the ledge, the bear led everyone up the narrow path. The pegasi flew above the path instead of walking upon it; they were afraid they would lose their footing. The humans were amazed by how the rest of the animals stayed on the path. After what seemed like miles, they hit a dead end.

In front of them was a waterfall that cascaded down into the mist below. Much to their surprise, Methuselah kept walking and went through the waterfall. One by one, they followed. They were soaked, but they kept on going, pushing through the waterfall. Jereco enjoyed the sound of the rushing water. It reminded him of the water people.

It was only a few minutes before they emerged on the other side. They were standing in a dark and narrow tunnel which led into a damp cave. The humans mounted back onto the pegasi. They continued through the dark tunnels and caves for hours.

"Are we almost there?" whispered Diana. She was riding with Cleo on Midnight.

Cleo replied, "No. We will probably have to spend one night in the mountain before we get to the other side."

"Spend the night?" said Diana, with a frown. "I do not want to spend the night in here. I do not like this place. It is too dark." She looked around. Her eyes had not adjusted well to the darkness and she couldn't see much. "I bet there are bats, bugs, and other things here."

The path finally widened to a larger area. Brandon, who was riding Buster, caught up with Methuselah. "Can we take a break here?" Brandon asked. "I am hungry."

Methuselah shook his head. "Not here, but we are almost to the spot where we can camp for the night."

Buster spoke up this time. "We're going to camp in here for the night?"

247

Book One: The Chosen Ones

Methuselah nodded and continued ahead.

Buster kept up with him. "Where is here exactly?"

"We are in a mountain range of the Great Rock Mountains. This secret path will lead us out of this mountain range and into another which is called the Evadeam Mountains."

Buster whistled. "Wow. I am actually going to see Evadeam Mountain, the place that my ancestors have talked about—the place where many of our legendary stories took place."

"What is the big deal?" said Brandon.

Methuselah came to a halt. *"What's the big deal?"* he growled. "The Evadeam Mountain is the holiest place on this planet. It is where the great Creator created all seven tribes and all the creatures that belong to this world. It is the place where our ancestors were born." Methuselah looked Brandon in the eye. "And you are a descendant of the great Evadeam tribe—the tribe that was appointed by the Creator to live in the holy place while all others were placed in different parts of the world. Your ancestors were to be leaders and keep peace among all the creatures of Trahe." Methuselah turned and started walking again. "It is too bad that they could not uphold the peace. Instead, total chaos ran through this world."

Brandon did not know how to reply to Methuselah's last comment. He felt he should be insulted and defend his ancestors, but how does one argue with a giant grizzly bear?

It was not too long after their conversation that they rode down into a large cave. There was an opening at an angle above them where they could see the sky. Natural light shined through making it easier for the humans to see. Soon Methuselah stopped in an area that contained a waterfall that poured into a small lake. "This is where we will camp for the night." said Methuselah. "We will leave early in the morning and will be able to get out of the mountain before tomorrow evening." He walked over to the lake and started drinking out of it.

Archelaus jumped off Stal Lion. "This is perfect. We have water and a large area to set up camp."

Brooke looked over at him. "Perfect?" She gestured at the area around her. "This is nothing but perfect. We are in a cave in the middle of some mountain. It is dark, cold, and creepy."

Diana nodded in agreement. "Can we keep moving? I do not want to spend the night here."

Hachmoni was already taking his gear off Dale. "We need the rest. Tomorrow is a long ride. Besides, Brandon is hungry."

Brandon jumped off Buster. "Yes, I am starving. Let's eat."

Hachmoni threw a bag to Brandon. "First, we set up camp before we lose what little light we have. Then we need to feed our trusted friends."

Brandon opened the bag to find carrots, apples, and oats.

Buster peaked inside the bag. "Yummy."

The Trahe Chronicles

Brandon smiled. "Let me get this stuff off your back first."

They all pitched in and quickly made camp. They decided to tie all their tents together to make one large one. Hachmoni warned that the caverns could get really cold during the night. It would be better for them to stay close together. A few feet away, they were able to get a small campfire started for cooking and heat. They built it right below the opening in the sky. Methuselah warned them to keep the fire small so the smoke would not attract anyone outside the mountain. They huddled around the tiny fire and ate in a circle. The animals with their warm fur coats agreed to rest on the outside of the circle.

They were fortunate to have the moon and stars glowing bright in the sky. The moon shined light into the cavern. After their meals, most everyone fell asleep, except for the Evadeam kids. None of them liked sleeping in the cavern. The only other time that they had been in caves was when they had taken one of their family trips to the Mammoth Caves in Kentucky, and that was just a small hike with a guide and lights. This experience was totally different.

"Well, at least we have a grizzly bear for a guide," said Brandon. "There cannot be anything too creepy in this place that Methuselah could not handle."

"Yeah," replied Jereco, "but I prefer to be back on the island and out in the open sea air with the sounds of the water."

Buster sighed. "I miss home, but how could I pass up an adventure of a lifetime? I mean, we get to go to the holiest place on this planet. How cool is that? Besides, we will find your parents and be back home before we know it."

Their parents—where are they? Maybe they made it back home, thought Brooke.

Home, what was home to them now? Was it Willow for Brandon? Was it the Island of the Pegasi for Jereco? The kids lay there silently, each in their own deep thoughts. Their minds wandered as they remembered their home back on Earth in a small town in Michigan. One by one, the thoughts turned into dreams.

Brandon felt something cold on his face. He kept brushing it away, but it was being persistent. "Get up Brandon," said a voice.

Get up? Brandon thought. *No way.* They had just gone to bed. He rolled over and covered his head with his blanket. Brandon felt his blanket being yanked off him and then something with large teeth bit into his shirt. He was then dragged over to the lake and thrown in. Brandon woke from the shock of cold water sweeping over his body. He sputtered, "What the—" He tried to get his footing on the slippery rocks. After falling a few times back into the water, he finally pulled himself up and out. He dragged himself to the edge and found himself facing a laughing grizzly bear. Brandon gave Methuselah a dirty look.

Book One: The Chosen Ones

Methuselah kept chuckling and shook his head. "Come on. Get yourself together. You are going to miss breakfast."

"Breakfast?" said Brandon. "It can't be breakfast. It is still dark out." He pointed toward the small opening. Sure enough, it was still dark.

Jereco walked over and splashed water on his face. He, too, looked like he had just woken up. "Apparently, if we start out before day break," he said, "we have a better chance of getting out of this mountain before the sun goes down tonight."

Brandon mumbled something under his breath and went to dig up some dry clothes.

After breakfast, they packed and moved on. Methuselah was right. They spent the whole day traveling inside the mountain. It was a rougher ride than the day before. The terrain was more rugged, and at some points in the cave, the path was extremely narrow, or there was no path at all. The Pegasi tried to fly, but too often the caves were too small.

They were exhausted. There was no good area to stop to eat, so they ate while traveling.

"I am starting to think we are never going to get out of here," said Brandon.

"Don't say that!" scolded Diana. She hated the thought of them staying another night in this mountain.

Then, all of a sudden, everyone stopped. They faced a tall flat wall of rock. Methuselah sniffed along the rock, walking back and forth.

"Oh, great!" said Brandon. "We hit a dead end." He turned in his saddle and looked around. "Yep, we are at a dead end. Methuselah took a wrong turn. Now we will be here for another night."

Diana moaned, and Cleo jumped off. Cleo went up to Methuselah, and they talked. Cleo then came back to the rest of the group. "We need help with all the strength we can get."

Hachmoni, Silver Kat, Skylar, and Sir Bolivar went over to the wall. The rest of them just sat there looking at Cleo like she was nuts.

"Help with what?" asked Brandon.

"Help move the rock, of course," said Cleo.

"Move the rock!" He looked at the rock. "Are you kidding me? I hate to tell you guys this, but that is not a rock. It is a whole mountain wall! It is not going anywhere. You are wasting your time."

Jereco hopped off Clyde. "Unless—it is not a rock or a wall. Maybe it is a door." Jereco, who was always very smart at figuring out puzzles, went over to the wall of rock. "Wait a minute," he told everyone. He ran his fingers over it for a long time.

Brandon, who still did not get off Buster, impatiently waited. "Jereco, there is nothing there. This is a flat mountain. A wall of rock. There is no way we are going to move it. We just need to turn around and find the right path out of here."

250

The Trahe Chronicles

"Got it!" yelled Jereco. He had found a crack in the rock. He took his knife out of the sheath. He jammed his knife into the crack and continued to follow it. When he was done there was a partial outline of what could be a large door. "I cannot reach the part above my head, but I think this is the door. How do we open it?"

"Do you think with all of our strength that we could push it open?" asked Methuselah. Jereco shook his head. "I do not think it is that simple. I need some more light."

Archelaus lit a torch for him.

Jereco started to study the surrounding walls.

"What are you looking for?" Archelaus asked.

"I think there is a lever. If our ancestors wanted their city to be hidden from the rest of the world and also wanted the Chosen Ones to find it someday, then they would probably build this door in a way that it could be opened by us."

Archelaus lit up more torches. "Then come on, everyone. Let us search for this lever." They started to look, but minutes turned into hours.

Brandon finally sat down. "Okay, it was a great idea, Jereco, but I think you are wrong. I do not think there is a magical lever."

Jereco was tired of Brandon's complaining. He glared at him. "So I am wrong? And Methuselah is wrong? And you think you are right? Do you have any of your fancy trees around to tell you that you are right?" Jereco did not wait for a reply. "No, you do not. Because we are in the middle of the mountain. There are no trees here to help you, Brandon."

Brandon jumped up. "Yeah, and there are no mermaids to help you here either."

"Well," said Jereco, "at least I am trying to help. All you do is complain and tell everyone else that they are wrong."

"If Methuselah is right, then why are we still stuck in this mountain?" asked Brandon as he pointed at the mountain walls. "And if you are right, where is the magical lever? I do not see one, do you?" The torch he had in his hand almost hit Jereco in the face.

"Hey, watch it!" yelled Jereco. He knocked Brandon's hand away. The torch fell to the ground, and the flames went out.

"Great, now look what you have done!" Brandon turned and grabbed for Jereco's torch. "Give me yours since you blew mine out."

Jereco kept his torch out of Brandon's reach and pushed Brandon backward with his free hand. Brandon tripped over a rock and fell into the mountain wall.

"Ouch!" He grabbed his back. "That hurt!" He flung himself toward Jereco. Jereco sidestepped out of the way and pushed Brandon again. This time, Brandon fell on the rock he had just tripped over. Brandon struggled to get up, and he fell on the rock again. Finally, he regained his balance and stood up. "Now I am really mad!"

251

Book One: The Chosen Ones

But before Brandon could pounce, Jereco had moved away. So had the others. They were staring in the direction of the flat wall rock. The wall had opened up! "How did that happen?" asked Brandon.

Jereco looked at him and then pointed his torch toward the rock that Brandon had just fallen on. "You did it." He smiled. "You found the lever."

Brandon walked over to the rock. It wasn't actually an ordinary rock; indeed, it was a narrow lever made out of rock. When he fell on it, it triggered the door to open. "I did?" said Brandon. "Hey, I did! *I* found the lever!"

Brooke walked over. "Do not get too smug about it. You found the lever by accident."

Brandon crossed his arms. "So? I still found it, didn't I?"

Brooke rolled her eyes and walked back to Midnight.

Archelaus walked over to the boys. "I think you both deserve credit for discovering the door and a way to open it. Now make up and shake hands."

The boys had forgotten that they had even been fighting. They shrugged and gave each other a high five.

"Come on, you guys," yelled Diana, who was sitting atop Midnight. "Let's get out of here."

As they walked back to the party, Brandon whispered, "Good job, Jereco. You are the one who really figured out how to get us out of here."

Jereco shrugged. "Well, at least your hot temper was good for something today."

The boys smiled at each other and mounted their pegasi friends.

Methuselah led the way out of the Great Rock Mountain.

Grandpa took a deep breath once he was outside. "Ah, smell that fresh air."

Everyone did the same and agreed that it was nice to be out in the open air again and not inside the mountain.

"Check out the view!" Brandon said.

Most of the party had expected they would step out into the bottom of a valley. Instead, they were on a plateau high on the mountain. The view was incredible. The sun was just starting to set in the west. Rays of sunlight reflected off the surrounding mountains. It was a crisp, cool, and sunny autumn day.

"Welcome to the Evadeam Mountain Range." announced Methuselah.

"So now where do we go?" asked Jereco.

Methuselah pointed straight ahead. "To that mountain across the valley."

They looked across and then down. The only way down to the valley was by flight or climbing down over treacherous, rocky cliffs. At the edge of the plateau, they looked down into a small basin that had a small running stream and some trees.

Methuselah pointed down to the basin. "That will be a good place to camp for the night. The sun will set soon." He swung around and went back

The Trahe Chronicles

to the opening that they had just come out of. "But first, we need to seal this door back up."

Afterward, they headed down into the basin. The pegasi and humans traveled by flight while the others walked cautiously down the cliffs.

It was a great evening. After they set up camp, a meal was prepared, and they admired the sunset as they ate. They chose a spot near the stream. The mountain wall was behind them. Even though time was of the essence, they decided they would spend the next day at this spot. Everyone would have a chance to rest, bathe, and make plans on how to get across the valley to reach Evadeam Mountain.

The next day was a fine day. Everyone took turns washing up. Spirits were lifted due to the good rest and fresh air. As the men and animals made their travel plans, Brooke and Diana took the time to relax and brush out their hair. None of them had had haircuts since they had arrived on Trahe. The girls' hair was getting long, and they had been wearing their hair in braids or ponytails to keep the hair out of their faces.

Brooke was brushing Diana's hair as Diana played with the doll that Michael had bought for her back in Bethemek. Brooke paused for a minute when she noticed Diana had stopped chatting with her doll. "Are you okay, Diana?" she asked, bending forward to see Diana's face. Diana looked like she was in a trance.

"Diana?" repeated Brooke.

Diana snapped out of it and looked back at Brooke. She nodded. "I'm fine."

"Just daydreaming?" Brooke asked.

Diana looked at the rock they had been sitting next to. "I think it is alive," she whispered.

Brooke looked confused. "You think what is alive?"

Diana leaned over toward Brooke and continued to whisper. "The rock." She pointed at it.

Brooke, who was getting used to unusual things on this planet, cautiously looked at the rock. She admitted it looked a little bit unusual. But the rock did not look alive to her. She reached out and touched the brown rock. It was awfully smooth and warm. She knocked on it a little. "No, I think it is just a rock."

"What is just a rock?" said a voice behind the girls.

They both jumped.

"Don't do that!" said Brooke.

"Do what?" asked Archelaus.

"Sneak up on us," she whispered.

"I wasn't sneaking up on you, and why are you whispering?"

"Because the rock might hear you," whispered Diana.

"The rock?" Archelaus whispered back.

Diana nodded toward the rock. "Uh huh."

253

Book One: The Chosen Ones

Brooke got up and shrugged. "Diana thinks this rock is alive."

"Hmm—" Archelaus scratched his chin. "Well, let us see if it is." He touched the large rock. "Pretty smooth and oddly warm." He knocked on it. "Sounds like a rock." He stepped back. "I have concluded that this is a smooth and oddly warm rock. But it's still a rock. Sorry, Diana."

Diana did not look convinced, so Archelaus decided to change the subject. "Brandon found a nut tree on the other side of the basin. Apparently, the tree told Brandon we could help ourselves to its nuts. The nuts are good food we can store for the winter months ahead. Want to help us gather some?" He handed Diana a burlap bag.

Diana, who did not always feel like she was very helpful, jumped at the chance. "Yeah. Brooke, are you going to help too?"

"I think I have time to help before dinner." Brooke smiled at Archelaus. "Are you going to help too?"

"I certainly am," replied Archelaus.

They spent the rest of the afternoon, gathering nuts. They also collected any other supplies they came across.

At dinner, the group discussed their travel plans. They decided that Pinto would carry the extra supplies. Silver Kat, who had been riding Pinto, would run with Methuselah, Skylar, and Sir Bolivar until they reached their next meeting point at Lake Evadeam. The evening ended early, and everyone rested for the journey the next day.

The early morning brought clouds in the sky. Hachmoni and Silver Kat got everyone up and moving. "A storm is coming," explained Hachmoni. "If we start now, we might get ahead of it and make good time before we have to seek shelter again." They quickly ate breakfast together and packed.

Brooke was almost ready when she realized Diana was missing. "Great," said Brooke. "I swear, I cannot take my eye off her for one minute. Where did that child go?"

Archelaus laughed. "Spoken like a true mom."

Brooke was clearly frustrated. "Yeah, but I am not her mom. In fact, I wish her mom was here right now. Maybe then she would listen when I tell her not to wander off."

Grandpa walked over. "Are you girls ready yet?"

Brooke's head snapped up. "Do I look ready? I can't do everything! I cannot pack my stuff, Diana's stuff, and keep an eye on that child at the same time!"

Grandpa eyed Brooke, warily.

Archelaus leaned over and whispered, "Diana's gone missing again."

Grandpa sighed and shook his head. "Brooke, you finish packing, we will go find Diana." Grandpa put his hand on Archelaus's shoulder. "Come on. There aren't too many places Diana could go in this small basin."

They started hollering her name and came across her by the stream. She was walking around, crying.

The Trahe Chronicles

Archelaus ran over to her. "What is wrong? Are you hurt?"

Diana shook her head.

Grandpa kneeled down. "Diana, if you are not hurt, then what is wrong?"

Now Diana was crying so hard that she could barely speak.

Cleo, who had been walking along the edge of the stream, came up to them. Cleo bowed down. "It seems that our Vision Keeper has lost her doll."

Shock came across Archelaus face. "Doll?" he asked.

Cleo nodded. "Yes, doll. It is of upmost importance that we find her doll."

Archelaus shook his head. "Are you kidding me? She is crying because of a doll?!" Archelaus's reaction made Diana even more upset. She cried harder.

Cleo spoke. "I believe you have forgotten the importance of a little girl's doll. Especially, since it is the only one she has at the moment."

"It is the one I gave her," said Michael's voice from behind them. "I am packed and ready, so I can help find the missing doll." He bent down and scooped Diana up in his arms and handed her his handkerchief. "Wipe and blow. We will help find your doll."

As Diana wiped her tears away and blew her nose, Michael asked questions about where she had the doll last.

Michael started stepping backward. "So let's retrace our steps. Did you have your doll at breakfast?"

Diana shook her head.

"Did you have your doll last night when you slept?"

Diana nodded because she always had her doll with her in bed every night, ever since they left Bethemek. Then Diana paused. "No, I forgot. I didn't have her last night. Cleo slept with me instead, so I must have forgotten to take my doll to bed with me."

Michael stopped walking. "That is good that you remembered that. So do you remember where you had her yesterday?" Diana's little face scrunched up as she tried to remember.

"Did you have her when we were gathering the nuts?" asked Archelaus.

Diana shook her head and then her face lit up. "I remember now! I had her by the rock."

"The rock?" Michael looked around the basin, which was full of rocks. "Which rock?" "The rock that is alive," she whispered.

Michael looked confused and then looked over at Archelaus.

Archelaus nodded his head and signaled for them to follow him. He led them to a big, round, and smooth rock. "This is the rock Diana thinks is alive." explained Archelaus.

Diana, who was already upset, yelled at Archelaus. "It *is* alive!"

Archelaus was starting to lose patience from looking for a silly doll and arguing with Diana about a rock being alive. "Diana, the rock is not alive. Rocks cannot be alive. See?" He knocked on the rock really hard.

"Don't do that! You might hurt it!" she yelled back.

255

Book One: The Chosen Ones

"Okay, Diana, that is enough," scolded Grandpa. "Stop yelling at Archelaus."

Diana gave Grandpa a sour look.

Grandpa wagged a finger at Diana. "Now look here, granddaughter of mine—"

"Enough!" said Michael. "I think Diana is still upset because we have not found her doll. So let's look for her doll, and then we can leave."

Archelaus and Grandpa agreed and started to look around.

Diana jumped out of Michael's arms. "There she is." The doll was on the ground half-hidden behind the rock. As Diana picked it up, she noticed something on the rock. "You hurt it!" she shouted.

All three men looked at her.

She clutched her doll in one hand and pointed at the rock with the other. "See? You knocked so hard that you hurt it!"

"What is all the shouting about?" asked Brandon, who had walked up behind them. Brandon and Jereco were following Skylar.

"We recruited Skylar to find Diana." explained Jereco.

"Now why didn't I think of that?" said Archelaus after listening to Jereco.

"Because you are just a dumb old man!" said Diana.

Archelaus was taken by surprise. He was beginning to wonder what happened to the sweet little girl he was protecting.

Jereco kneeled down by Diana to make sure she was all right while Grandpa scolded her for calling Archelaus a dumb old man.

Meanwhile, Michael filled Brandon in about the rock argument that started the commotion.

Brandon walked up to the rock while Skylar and Cleo started sniffing around it. "You have to admit," said Brandon, "it is a cool-looking rock," He ran his hand over it. "Weird. It is warm."

Archelaus leaned over. "Just don't knock on it."

"Why?" asked Brandon.

"Apparently, you might hurt it," he explained.

"It's a rock." Brandon kept rubbing it.

Archelaus just shrugged and glanced over at Diana.

Brandon sat next to Diana, who was still on the ground, rubbing a spot on the rock.

"Diana, this is just a rock. It's not alive." He gestured at everyone else. "But we are all alive and need to leave now. It's time to stop fooling around or playing pretend. We need to go."

The trees branches and leaves started to blow in the wind. Brandon looked up. "The trees are saying a storm is coming. We need to go now."

Diana looked up at Brandon, with her big blue eyes. "If your trees can be alive, why can't my rock be alive?"

Brandon took a deep breath. "Okay. Your rock can be alive, but we still have to leave. We can't take it with us. It is way too big. So why don't you say

256

The Trahe Chronicles

goodbye to it?"

Diana looked at Jereco, who nodded and gestured for her to say goodbye to it.

The three adult men decided to just back away from what they thought was a ridiculous idea—saying goodbye to a rock. But they'd do anything to get moving.

Diana rubbed the rock. "I am sorry Archelaus hurt you. I am sure he didn't mean it."

Archelaus was glad to hear she was no longer calling him a dumb man.

Diana leaned closer and whispered, "I know you are alive." She kissed it and got up. "I am ready now."

They were starting to walk away when Skylar and Cleo both jumped on top of the rock. Skylar let out a load roar. Startled, they turned back toward the rock. Skylar and Cleo both jumped off the rock, but then they turned to face the rock and slowly backed up.

Diana's eyes got big and pointed toward the rock. "See? I told you it got hurt. Its scar is getting bigger."

The scar was a small line in the rock that was now becoming longer. *Crack, crack, crack!* The crack was getting bigger and bigger. Other cracks on the rock appeared.

Diana squeezed her doll. "Oh no," she cried. "It is dying!"

Meanwhile, the rest of their group joined them. Silver Kat moved in front of Diana and pulled out his knife. The others followed suit as Grandpa pulled Diana behind him.

"It is not dying," said Jereco as he also pulled out his knife. "I think it is becoming alive!"

Archelaus looked back at Brooke, who had just arrived. "Get Diana back to camp," Archelaus said. "You girls get in the air!" he ordered.

Brooke nodded and grabbed Diana, but they froze when the large rock began to move. Something they had never seen before was trying to come out of the rock. They now realized the rock was actually an overgrown egg. A dark, scaly, and ugly creature tried to make its way out.

"What is it?" asked Archelaus.

"It's a lizard!" answered Jereco.

Sure enough, it looked like a big lizard. It cried out and then flicked its tongue. They all stepped back. Then the lizard cried again. Skylar and Cleo started talking to it in the Trahe language.

Diana broke free of Brooke's grip and ran toward the lizard. Brooke ran after her "Diana, get back here!"

Diana ignored her "Didn't you hear? She is crying because she can't find her mommy!" Diana stopped next to Cleo and Skylar.

The lizard stopped crying when it saw Diana.

Cleo looked over at Diana. "She recognizes your voice."

The lizard's head came down toward Diana and sniffed her.

Book One: The Chosen Ones

Archelaus, Michael, Brooke, Jereco and Brandon slowly walked toward the lizard and Diana. They quietly withdrew their weapons, but the lizard heard. She looked at them and let out a roar. A small puff of smoke came out of its nostrils.

Brandon stopped. "Whoa!"

Diana lifted up her hands. "Stop! Stop!" she yelled at the lizard.

The lizard looked down at her.

"It is okay," Diana said. "They are my friends."

"Why don't we back up and give the baby some room," said Skylar.

Everyone backed up, including Diana.

They watched the lizard break completely free of the egg. They had to back up more as the lizard stretched out.

As it did so, something caught Silver Kat's eye. "Everyone, back up more." He gestured toward the top of the lizard's back. The lizard had a pair of wings jutting out of its back.

"It's a dragon!" said Brandon. "Wow!"

Sure enough, standing before them was a baby dragon.

The Trahe Chronicles

Diana's Dragon

"Now what?" whispered Brooke. "Do we make a run for it?" Brooke was ready to flee even though the dragon was only the size of a pony.

"No!" growled Skylar.

The dragon's head turned toward Skylar.

Skylar continued. "Hachmoni, do you, by chance, speak dragon language?"

Hachmoni, who seemed very calm, replied, "No, however, I do believe Cleo may."

Everyone turned his attention to Cleo, who was standing behind Diana's legs.

"Cleo, are you hiding?" asked Brandon.

Cleo, who never hid from anything, was clearly afraid. The hair on her back was standing on end, and she looked ready to run at a moment's notice.

"A newborn dragon is going to be hungry," replied Cleo, without taking her eyes off the dragon. "It may look at me as its first meal."

Diana was confused. "But you are Cleo. Doesn't it know who you are?" Before Cleo could reply, something dawned on Diana. "Or is this a bad dragon?" She took a step back.

Cleo shook her head. "Nothing is born bad. Newborn babies are from the good spirit world. They learn to be bad or good. In this case, this type of dragon is naturally a carnivore."

"A what?" Diana asked.

"An animal that eats meat," replied Cleo.

"Can we save the lessons for later?" asked Brandon. "If this dragon woke up hungry, what are we going to do about it? I don't feel like being a dragon's meal today."

"I don't think she is going to eat you. I think she wants to be friends." replied Diana.

Brandon gave Diana a look that strongly suggested he didn't believe that.

"Actually, Diana may have a point," said Cleo. "Diana had talked to the egg and protected it when we thought it was just a rock. Diana, pick me up, and maybe I can talk to the dragon while you hold me. Just be careful not to look like you are presenting me as her meal."

"How do you know it is a girl dragon?" asked Brandon.

Diana shrugged. "Instinct. Plus, I remember a dream I had once about a dragon. She was a girl. I think the dream was about this dragon." Diana scooped up Cleo and started petting her like she was a dear friend of hers. Diana slowly moved closer to the dragon while the rest of them continue to keep their weapons out in case something went wrong.

Cleo started speaking to the dragon in a language that none of them understood. Cleo was hissing a lot, and they assumed that hissing was part of the dragon language. The dragon seemed to listen at first, but it hardly

Book One: The Chosen Ones

responded. Then all of a sudden, it started to make a crying noise and moved toward them. Everyone naturally stepped back, which made the dragon even more upset.

"It is no use," said Cleo. "It is like talking to a big baby. It is just hungry and confused. It needs the comfort of a mom."

"Aw," said Diana as she walked toward the dragon. She put her hand on its nose. "There, there. It will be okay."

"*Is she nuts?*" whispered Brandon.

Jereco was already in motion. He moved in front of his sister, just in case the dragon tried to do something. The dragon looked at Jereco as a threat, but Diana stepped between the two of them.

"It is okay," she told the dragon. "He is my brother."

The dragon did not understand Diana, but realized that Diana was trying to protect Jereco.

Skylar, who had disappeared earlier, returned with some large, dead rodents in her mouth. She dropped them at the dragon's feet. But the dragon didn't eat the meat and looked at Diana.

"It is waiting for you to eat them first, I think," said Jereco.

Diana made a face. "I am not eating those."

"You don't have to," Cleo said. "Give some of the meat to Skylar and me, and we will eat it. Then offer some to the dragon. She might think you are feeding your kids, and maybe she will follow our actions."

Skylar tore apart some of the rodents for Diana. Diana proceeded to feed the meat to Skylar and Cleo. Afterward, she turned to the dragon and held out the largest rodent to her. The dragon caught on and snatched the meat from Diana's fingertips. In one big bite, the dragon gulped down the whole piece.

Diana clasped her hands together. "Good job." She petted the dragon on the head.

The dragon looked pleased and then looked at Skylar and Cleo for more rodent meat.

Skylar tore some more meat apart, gave some to Diana, who turned around and gave the meat to the dragon.

"I think we will need more food," suggested Jereco.

"I am already on it." Methuselah walked up behind him and dropped a small deer at Diana's feet.

Diana turned away from the dragon. "I can't feed her this poor little deer."

"Yes, you can," said Jereco. "Come on. I will help you carry it toward her. If we lay it down at her feet, maybe she will start eating it."

Brooke and Brandon also stepped forward. The four kids lifted the deer and put it in front of the dragon. Diana gestured at Skylar and the dragon to come eat. Remarkably, it worked. The tiger and the dragon ate, sharing the kill.

260

The Trahe Chronicles

Jereco put his hand on Diana's shoulder. "It is the circle of life."

"Speaking of the circle of life," said Grandpa, "where do you think the dragon came from?"

"I have been thinking about that," replied Hachmoni. "If you look above where her egg had been resting, you can see that it might have come from a nest somewhere up in those cliffs. The dragons of the Evadeam Mountains are legend. The dragons moved into the area after the Evadeam tribe disappeared. The dragons were supposed to protect the ancient grounds until the return of the Evadeam people."

Methuselah moved toward the egg. "We need to return this newborn to its mother." He started sniffing around the baby dragon. The dragon eyed Methuselah warily as she ate her meal.

"Methuselah is right," said Silver Kat. "We must delay our trip to Evadeam Mountain and try to return this baby dragon to its home."

Diana spoke up. "She needs a name. We can't just keep calling her a baby dragon." Methuselah walked up to the dragon, who was still eyeing him.

"I believe she does have a name," replied Methuselah. He looked over at Cleo.

Cleo sat there for a minute, and she glowed a little. This caught the dragon's attention, and it stopped eating. Still glowing, Cleo walked up to the dragon and spoke to her in the dragon's own tongue. This time, the dragon seemed to understand Cleo and spoke back. Cleo turned to the others. "Her name in the Trahe language is Uriel."

"The fire of God," acknowledged Silver Kat. "That is fitting."

"In our native language back on Earth," said Grandpa, "it also means the same thing."

Brooke stepped forward and looked closely at the dragon. "Correct me if I am wrong, but wasn't Uriel also one of the angels of God?"

They all turned to look at the dragon.

Diana walked up to Uriel and petted her scaly head and neck. "See, you are a good dragon after all."

Sir Bolivar, who had been staying as far away from the dragon as possible, finally came up to the group. "If we are going to go hunt for other dragons, we should leave soon before the storm clouds blow in."

Hachmoni looked up at the sky and nodded in agreement. "Yes, we have already wasted the morning away. Methuselah, do you think you have a general idea where Uriel's family might be?"

Methuselah nodded. "We can start by investigating those cliffs."

Once again, the group was off. Based upon the position of the cliffs, they would have to head slightly off-course. They went up the mountain they had just left and then went north. They had to travel slowly; the new baby dragon was learning how to walk, and its wings were not ready for flight yet. As they walked on, the baby dragon acted much like a human toddler. It was distracted constantly by its surroundings. Diana was trying to get her to

Book One: The Chosen Ones

follow and keep up with the group.

"This is going to take forever," complained Brandon.

"Well, look at it this way," said Jereco, "At least we have a dragon on our side now. Besides, I thought you thought the dragon was cool."

Brandon looked over at Jereco. "It would be cooler if it could fly, breathe fire, and stop acting like a big baby."

Hachmoni laughed at Brandon's comments. "Do you not want to help your sister babysit a baby dragon?"

Brandon shook his head. "No thank you."

Buster and the other pegasi had been very quiet since they discovered the dragon.

"So what do you think of our newfound friend?" Brandon asked Buster.

Buster replied very quietly. "On our island, there were stories about dragons, but I have never seen one until today. Dragons eat pegasi and unicorns."

Overhearing their whispered conversation, Luke Thunder stepped up next to Buster. "Nonsense!" said Luke Thunder. "Those stories were made up out of fear of the unknown. In ancient times, dragons were our allies. They fought side by side with us against the evil serpents."

Midnight also came up by his son. "It is true. Over time the stories were distorted and exaggerated. The evil serpents were confused with the dragons. Son, there is a difference between an evil serpent and a dragon. Cleo was correct by saying that all living things are born good. Evil is a learned behavior. Unfortunately, the serpents have passed their evil ways on to future generations while the dragons continue to stand behind the good and honest—qualities of the Evadeam way."

"So the big snake that we encountered when we got here was one of those evil serpents?" asked Brandon.

Midnight nodded. "Perhaps."

"And this baby dragon is a good dragon?" continued Brandon.

"I believe so," replied Midnight.

"Well, let's hope so," said Brandon. "I would hate to be fighting a big snake and a dragon."

They finally came upon a clearing by a large running stream. It was decided they would camp there for the night and continue the next morning. The evening brought rain. They huddled under their tents while taking turns watching the sleeping dragon, who had found shelter under the trees.

The next day, the rain storm was gone, and Uriel picked up the pace. She seemed to know that they were heading somewhere important, so they were able to cover more ground. At dusk, they came to a huge lake. The lake looked very dark and deep. On one side the lake poured into the river while the opposite side of the lake was filled by a waterfall.

Methuselah looked across the lake. "Up there near the waterfall are some cave dwellings. There might be dragon lairs."

262

The Trahe Chronicles

"If there are any dragons, they will be hunting at night," added Hachmoni. "We will never make it to those cave dwellings before nightfall. We will take cover in the woods tonight and approach the caves in the morning."

It was a long and restless evening. Everyone was a little on edge. They camped close together and had only a small fire for cooking. They did not want to attract any dragons. As the night got darker, Brandon thought everything seemed scarier.

"Do you hear that?" asked Brandon. They were sitting around in a circle, trying to keep each other warm in front of the small fire.

"Here what?" asked Brooke. "I don't hear anything."

"That is what I mean," whispered Brandon, "I don't hear anything. I don't hear any night creatures. Not even the trees are talking." That gave him the creeps. He always had comfort in the trees. But there was an eerie silence.

Everyone quieted and listened. They agreed with Brandon and heard nothing. "It makes my fur stand on end," concurred Sir Bolivar.

Uriel noticed the tension in the air and tried to speak to Diana. Diana didn't understand the dragon's language, but she placed her little arm around Uriel's neck. "It is okay," she said. She patted Uriel's neck. "Everything will be okay. We will find your mommy. We will be safe."

"Did you have a dream showing we would be safe?" asked Brandon, hoping that she had. Diana shook her head.

That's discouraging, thought Brandon.

"But I didn't have a dream showing we would be unsafe either," said Diana.

Diana and Uriel probably slept the best out of everyone. They slept together with Cleo curled up at Diana's feet. Cleo kept her eyes open and was on high alert.

It was just past midnight when Cleo's ears heard something. Her ears twitched back and forth. *There. There it is.* The sound was so faint that human ears would not have picked it up. Cleo's head popped up from her curled position. Her fur stood on end. A low growl came from deep in her throat. It was Cleo's growl that woke up Uriel and Diana.

"Cleo?" asked Diana.

Cleo was in a ready-to-pounce position. She didn't answer Diana but looked back at Uriel. She said something to Uriel in the dragon language. Uriel seemed to understand. She got up and pulled Diana under the protection of one of her wings. "Where are the others?" asked Diana, who was now becoming fully awake.

As if reading Diana's mind, Skylar was now beside them. "I've alerted the others. We must protect Diana and Uriel."

Brooke came up behind them. "What is it? I don't see or hear anything."

Someone screamed from behind them.

Skylar's and Cleo's heads turned sharply. "Stay here with Uriel and Diana!" Skylar told Brooke.

263

Book One: The Chosen Ones

Brooke got her knife out and nodded her head. She backed up under Uriel's wing and grabbed Diana's hand. Cleo also stood guard in front of them.

"Brooke, what was that?" said Diana in a shaky voice. "I can't see anything?"

Brooke didn't reply. She just held onto Diana tighter. She could not see anything either. It was so dark outside. She was counting on their animal friends to be their eyes for them. Brooke looked up toward the sky. "We could really use some moonlight right now."

Diana tugged on Brooke's hand. "Let's wish for some moonlight."

Brooke nodded in agreement and squeezed Diana's hand. She didn't dare close her eyes to pray, so she prayed out loud as her eyes tried to adjust to the darkness to see what her fellow friends could see. She whispered loud enough for Diana to hear. "Dear God, dear Creator of Trahe, please protect us tonight. Please bring us some light, so we may see our enemies." As she continued, she also said a prayer that her dad had taught her. "May the light of the Creator encircle us. May the power of the Creator protect us. May the love of the Creator enfold around us. May you be here with us."

Another scream pierced the air. The scream was followed by voices.

Brooke eyes were starting to adjust to the darkness. She turned and noticed the red embers from their small fire. "We need light. We need fire. Come on." She dragged Diana with her to the fire pit. Brooke and Diana concentrated on making the flames bigger while Cleo and Uriel stood guard. The red embers started to spread, and slowly a fire developed. The girls put more wood on the fire, but the flames were not building up fast enough. "I need the matches," mumbled Brooke. "Where are the matches?"

She was starting to panic because there was obviously some fighting going on. Sounds came from the lake. She wished she could see well. She tried to find the matches, but had no luck. She did not want to wander too far away from Diana and Uriel. She bent down to the fire and tried to stir up more flames. "It is no use." Brooke said frustrately as she heard more yelling echo from the waters.

It had all happened so fast, thought Jereco.

Archelaus and Jereco had just finished their guard duty. They switched shifts with Brandon and Michael. Jereco felt like he had only been asleep for a few minutes when he heard his brother screaming. He grabbed his sword and was on his feet when he saw Brandon being dragged to the lake. It was so dark, it was hard to see. Archelaus heard the cry also and was right beside him. Before they got to the lake, they saw Michael with a sword run into the water.

"What is it?" called Archelaus.

"A snake!" called back Michael as he swung his sword at the slimy creature. "And he has Brandon!"

264

The Trahe Chronicles

Jereco looked around the surface of the water. He only saw parts of the snake's body, but he didn't see Brandon. "Where?" he yelled. "Where is Brandon?"

"Under the water," replied Michael as he swung his sword down into the snake.

Jereco didn't hesitate. He dove into the water. Once under the water, he couldn't see anything. It was too dark. *Come on. What good is being a Water Guardian if I can't see under water?* he thought.

Discouraged, he swam back to the top and wiped the water from his eyes. Archelaus and Michael were both swinging at the huge snake. The snake was slashing back with his fangs.

Then, suddenly he saw Brandon resurface. Brandon had a knife in his hand and was stabbing the snake. Brandon was almost free when he was pulled back under.

Jereco dove into the water and swam toward Brandon. He couldn't let the snake drown his brother. He felt something swim past him, but could not see it. He had a hard time seeing under water. He reached down and grabbed his knife sheath that was strapped around his calf. As he pulled out the knife, a thought entered his brain. He remembered the green mark that was wrapped around the same ankle. He was the Water Guardian.

In his mind, he calmed himself. He pushed his thoughts outward. "I am the Water Guardian, and I am seeking anyone, anything that can help my brother and me. Please, I pray for your help, your guidance, and light to bring Brandon to safety." Almost instantly, a light shined from above and down into the murky waters. He later discovered that was moonlight.

The light fell upon a figure fighting something that was wrapped around him. *Brandon!* Jereco quickly swam toward him. The snake still had a grip on Brandon. Jereco bore his knife into the snake's skin. That must have surprised the snake. It loosened its grip around Brandon. Jereco quickly took advantage of the moment and tugged on his brother. Brandon was almost out of the snake's grip, but the snake realized it was losing its victim and quickly coiled around Brandon again.

Oh no, you don't, thought Jereco. He dug his knife deeper into the snake. At the same time, Archelaus and Michael had driven their swords into the upper body of the snake that was still in a shallow end of the waters. This was enough to distract the snake. The lower part of his body released Brandon. Jereco quickly grabbed his brother and swam to the surface.

Jereco dragged Brandon onto the shore. Hachmoni and Silver Kat were there to meet them. Brandon was unconscious. Jereco, who was exhausted, mustered up the strength to start CPR on his brother. "Come on, Brandon! Don't die on me now. Don't let this snake win!" Silver Kat joined in, helping Jereco.

Brandon began to cough up water. He was coming around. Jereco rolled him onto his side, so he wouldn't choke on the water that was coming out of

Book One: The Chosen Ones

his lungs. Brandon was finally breathing.

"Did you get him?" Brandon asked in a weak voice. "The snake?"

"Yeah, I got him," Jereco replied as he patted Brandon's back.

"Are you sure?" Brandon asked as he motioned to the lake. Jereco looked over his shoulder to see that the snake's upper body rearing out of the water. It hissed at Archelaus and Michael.

"Darn!" exclaimed Jereco. He looked back at Brandon.

"I am okay. Go get him," encouraged Brandon.

Jereco looked over Brandon's shoulders at Silver Kat, who instructed him to go. "I will give him some herbal remedies," Silver Kat said. "He will be fine."

Jereco nodded and went off to help Michael and Archelaus.

Hachmoni saw Madeave men and another snake approaching from the river. "Looks like we've got more trouble." He kneeled down by Brandon and Silver Kat. "Take care of Brandon," he ordered, and then he was off to meet the newcomers.

Silver Kat gave Brandon some natural herbs. "How do you feel?" he asked.

"I am okay," coughed Brandon.

"You should be feeling better in no time." Silver Kat put the herbs back in his pouch. "Go to Buster and take flight. I need to help Hachmoni." He took off.

Brandon nodded in reply and watched Silver Kat run and yell, firing arrows at the enemy at the same time.

Now that is a warrior, thought Brandon. Brandon heard water splashing. He turned his attention turned toward his brother. He was not about to run away on Buster. Despite that he almost drowned and his asthma was kicking in, he found the strength to get up. The trees started to blow. He took a deep breath and went to help Jereco.

Meanwhile, Brooke continued to hear the outcries from the lake and the river as she frantically tried to increase the flames of the fire. Suddenly, Uriel came forward and tried to sweep Diana under her wing again. Brooke and Diana fell to the ground.

"Uriel!" yelled Brooke.

"Don't yell at Uriel," Diana said. "It is not her fault. She was told to protect me." "Protect you! Protect you?" yelled Brooke. "I am supposed to protect you. Why don't you have her do something useful like start this fire," She pointed at the fire pit.

"I don't think she can breathe fire," mumbled Diana.

"Then what good is she?!" Brooke continued to yell.

Uriel didn't like Brooke's tone of voice. Uriel stepped toward Brooke and roared. Brooke stood up to full height with her knife in one hand. "Don't you roar at me! I am not your enemy. If you want to protect us, then help us.

266

The Trahe Chronicles

Start a fire." She pointed toward the fire pit. Uriel looked at the fire pit and opened its mouth. It coughed out a very small puff of smoke but not enough to start a fire. However, it was enough to catch Diana and Brooke's attention.

"Good job!" Diana said as she petted Uriel's neck. As Uriel turn to look at Diana, the clouds from above slowly broke away. A full moon shined light on their camp. The light appeared just in time for Brooke to see a huge snake coming up behind Uriel.

"Uriel! Look out!" Brooke went into action and threw her dagger at the snake's head. The knife hit the snake between the eyes, sending it into a screaming, hissing fit.

Uriel turned around and roared. Uriel immediately attacked the snake. Her small wings brought her up in the air enough to get over the top of the snake. She landed on it with her claws and then bore her teeth into the snake's head. The snake put up a short-lived fight.

Brooke made sure the snake was dead before she fetched her knife from the snake's head.

Uriel roared as it stood over the snake. When she was done, she looked over at Brooke and gave her a nod of acknowledgement. Brooke may have saved Uriel's life, and the dragon obviously understood this.

"Brooke!" shouted Diana.

Brooke turned to see Diana pointing toward the river. With the moonlight now shining down upon them, they could finally see. There was a larger snake partially in the river and partially into the lake. The snake was having a stand off with Brandon, Jereco, and Archelaus.

"How many snakes are there?" Brooke whispered to herself.

Cleo came up beside Brooke. "Stay with Diana and Uriel!"

Brooke nodded and grabbed for Diana's hand. Uriel, who was much more alert and in a fighting mood, brought its wing over them, protecting Brooke and Diana. Brooke watched Cleo head toward the river connection. Suddenly, Cleo stopped, looked down the river, and started meowing and growling. Brooke turned her head and saw shadows coming from the woods. The shadows were not those of a snake or a four-legged creature. Brooke could make out two-legged creatures coming from the woods. "Men!" she yelled. "They are men!"

Both Methuselah and Skylar came running from the direction of the river. "Ma-leave!" growled Methuselah. The men realized that they had been discovered. They raised their weapons at the bear and tiger. Brooke could see that the men had swords, knifes, and clubs. When Skylar crossed Cleo's path, she roared something to Cleo. Cleo nodded and ran fast toward Brooke and Diana.

"We need to get you two up in the air," Cleo said. "To the pegasi!"

Brooke turned to run holding Diana's hand.

Diana yanked free and stopped. "What about Uriel?"

"Well, she better learn to fly." Brooke reached for Diana's hand

Book One: The Chosen Ones

again."Now come on. Listen to Cleo!"

As Brooke pulled Diana toward the pegasi, Diana yelled at Uriel. "Come on. You have to fly. You have to fly!" Diana continued to urge Uriel along as they mounted Midnight. "Midnight," ordered Diana, "show Uriel how to fly!"

Midnight shook his mane. "She is too young. Her wings are not fully developed. She cannot fly."

Diana started to cry as Brooke threw Cleo up on Midnight. Brooke got on and held on to Diana for dear life. She knew they had to get away from the Madeave quickly.

Listening to Diana cry about Uriel brought tears to Brooke's eyes. "I'm sorry," Brooke said to Diana. "I'm sorry." With tears streaming down both girls' faces, Midnight got ready to jump in the air. Brooke looked over at Uriel. "I am sorry!"

Diana's hand shot out. "Uriel!" she wailed.

Uriel roared a small cry after the girls. The dragon did not understand what was happening.

"Cleo!" Diana shouted as she pointed at some Madeave men coming from behind Uriel. Cleo didn't see the men use their weapons against Uriel's back. Uriel's scales were not developed enough to protect her from their jabs. Uriel cried out as the Madeave attacked her. She spun around and roared. She used her claws and tail, trying to ward them off.

"Cleo, do something!" yelled Diana.

Brooke had already jumped off Midnight. "Midnight—get Diana out of here!" she yelled.

As Midnight flew into the sky, Brooke rushed over to Uriel. Within moments, Brooke was sparring with a Madeave. This particular Madeave man was small and had been taken off guard by Brooke's arrival. Brooke quickly defeated him using her knife. Another Madeave man, who was much bigger than the first man, came up with a larger sword in hand. Uriel came up on one side of the man and swung at him with his front claws. It was enough to make the man face Uriel. Brooke grabbed her chance and attacked him from behind. And that is how the two of them fought—side by side as one Madeave man after another came up to them.

Diana watched the fight below as she clung to Cleo and Midnight.

Grandpa who was fighting Madeave by the riverbed saw Midnight take flight. After defeating the Madeave, they flew to Diana. "Where is Brooke?" he yelled.

Diana pointed down below.

Grandpa's face became fierce. "That is my granddaughter they are messing with! Luke Thunder—"

"No need old man," Luke Thunder interrupted. "I am already on it." He flew toward Brooke.

Brooke and Uriel were now fighting back to back, surrounded by

The Trahe Chronicles

Madeave men. This was the first time Brooke had been this close to them. They actually looked just like humans or similar to the Evadeam tribe. Their hair color and skin tone varied, but most of them had brown or black hair that was long and straggly. Their bodies were muscular and on the larger side. As Brooke got near them, she could smell earth and sweat.

Grunts came from the sweaty men. They spoke a language Brooke didn't understand. *Concentrate*, Brooke kept telling herself. She was not used to fighting in general or fighting this hard and long. Brooke was relying on natural instinct and training. They had not practiced much since they left Willow.

Just as Brooke was starting to feel worn out, Luke Thunder tried to come down on the man Brooke was fighting. Luke Thunder missed, striking the ground with his hooves. The man was surprised at first but quickly recovered. He turned and thrust his sword into Luke Thunder.

"No!" Brooke shouted.

With the sword stuck in his belly, Luke Thunder reared. He came down on the Madeave man with one crushing blow from his hooves.

Diana felt Midnight jerk as Luke Thunder fell to his side. Everything felt like it was happening in slow motion. She watched as Grandpa slid off Luke Thunder, with no time to check on his beloved, old friend, before another Madeave man was attacking Grandpa.

How many men are there? Diana thought. She counted. Six were lying on the ground. Four more were fighting Grandpa, Brooke and Uriel. There were shadows coming from the woods. She looked toward the lake and checked on her brothers.

The moonlight shined upon them. Archelaus, Jereco and Brandon were still fighting a snake that was halfway in the water. Downstream she saw Skylar, Methuselah, Sir Bolivar, Michael, and Hachmoni fighting more Madeave men and snakes.

"We are outnumbered," she whispered. "Cleo, do something!"

Cleo's green eyes shined in the dark. She glanced below. Calmly, she spoke, "You are the Vision Keeper. You are a Chosen One. What would you do?"

Diana's mouth dropped, and before she replied, Cleo continued. "What can you do?"

Diana stared into Cleo's eyes—they started to glow. Thoughts came to Diana's mind. *Glow. Light. Circle of light.* Earlier, when Brooke and Diana had prayed, embers of the fire shined upon them, followed by the moonlight, which they badly needed. "Pray," she whispered. Cleo nodded, and Diana closed her eyes. As she petted Cleo, she started to pray. "Creator of Trahe, *please* help us. We haven't even made it to Evadeam Mountain yet. Please bring your light to us, to Cleo, to Uriel. Please encircle and protect us from harm. We need you. We need a miracle." As Diana continued to pray, she felt a great calm wash over her. She also heard Cleo start to purr. Diana repeated

269

Book One: The Chosen Ones

the prayer and didn't give up as the battle below continued.

Diana heard a loud roar. The sound scared Diana and her eyes snapped open. She hung on tight to Midnight and Cleo as she looked around to see where the sound had originated.

A loud crashing sound came from behind.

"Hang on!" yelled Midnight. He turned, sensing that something very large was coming up behind them.

Diana saw a huge dragon flying toward them. It roared again and spat fire.

Midnight dove just in time. Diana could feel the heat above her. The dragon flew past them and down toward the ground.

"It's a dragon!" Diana yelled. It was much larger than Uriel and was headed for the Madeave men. Everyone was caught off guard by the fire-breathing dragon. Even Uriel stood still as it saw a creature of her own kind heading toward her. The dragon roared again. Fire came out of its mouth and scorched the men.

Diana turned her head toward the lake to see another dragon flying across the water. "Yes!" she cheered. *Dragons had come to save the day.* She looked up at the sky and said a silent thank you to the Creator—to God. Then Diana turned her head toward the water, looking desperately for her brothers.

Jereco, Brandon and Archelaus were fighting the same snake that had dragged Brandon into the water. "Come on, guys," yelled Brandon. "Let's bring this snake down!" As Brandon arrived to help, another snake had come from downstream. The snake lashed out at Michael. Michael turned and fought back, luring the snake toward Hachmoni and Silver Kat.

Soon after that, a miracle happened. They heard a large roar. The noise distracted all of them, including the snakes. The snake Brandon was fighting had turned its head to see a large dragon coming its way.

"Now!" yelled Archelaus. All three men drove their weapons into the snake, finally bringing it down. It disappeared into the murky waters.

Archelaus put his hand on Brandon's back. "A snake can't keep you down for long." Brandon smiled and then looked over at Jereco, who was standing behind them. "Thanks, bro. For saving me, that is."

Jereco smiled. "Any time. We better go check on the rest of our family." They started out of the water when the moonlight shined onto their camp.

For the first time, Archelaus noticed another dragon was fighting near the campfire. He squinted and saw Brooke, who was combating side by side with Uriel, and her grandfather. "Come on!" he said as he broke into a run.

Brandon also saw the scene where Brooke was fighting a large group of what he assumed was the Madeave. However, he stopped in his tracks when he heard a scream from behind him. Brandon turned in time to see Jereco, who was still in the water, being dragged down by another snake. *More snakes must have come from downriver,* thought Brandon. "No!" yelled Brandon. "Archelaus! It's Jereco!"

270

The Trahe Chronicles

Brandon ran toward the spot where he saw Jereco last, but there was no sign of him. He was careful not to slash his sword into the water for fear he might hit his brother.

Brandon put his sword away and was about to dive into the water when Archelaus stopped him. "You don't have the strength," he ordered. "Go get help!" He dove in.

Brandon turned around to find help. Help. *Who could help?* Everyone was fighting something or someone. The dragons! *Can dragons go underwater?* He ran toward Silver Kat and Hachmoni, who were closest to him. As Brandon ran toward them, he saw the battle unfold in front of them. The dragons pretty much had wiped out the enemy. Those that had escaped were being followed into the woods by Skylar, Sir Bolivar, and Methuselah.

"I would like one of them alive!" called Hachmoni.

"Alive? Why?" asked Michael.

"I would like to question one of them. It concerns me that Madeave men are this close to Evadeam Mountain."

Michael nodded.

The experience in the river and all the running had taken a toll on Brandon. Once he reached Hachmoni, he fell down to his knees.

Hachmoni bent down to hear Brandon.

Gasping for breath, Brandon pointed toward the river. "Jer ... Jereco ... snake ... got him."

"Where is Archelaus?" asked Michael.

Brandon, who held his chest, took deep breaths to calm down—spoke more clearly. "He's in the water...to save Jereco."

Michael and Hachmoni broke out into a run and headed up the riverbed. Brandon slowly got up and was about to turn to follow them when a large male dragon's head came down to peer at him. Brandon looked up at him and pointed downstream. "Can you help Jereco?"

The dragon didn't understand him. Then something happened. The trees started to sway and become noisy. They started to talk in their tree language, which Brandon understood. They kept repeating, "Help the Water Guardian." The dragon raised its head, cocked it to the side, and listened. Then the dragon roared, lifted off into the air, and flew after Hachmoni and Michael.

Brandon whispered a thought to the trees. *Thank you.*

You're welcome, they replied.

"If anyone can help, Uriel's father can," said Buster as he walked up to Brandon.

"That is Uriel's father?" asked Brandon.

Buster nodded toward the campfire. "And that is Uriel's mother."

Brandon looked over and saw another dragon next to Uriel. He noticed that Brooke and Diana were safe. He turned back toward the lake and river. "Come on. We have to help find my brother."

271

Book One: The Chosen Ones

"Hop on," replied Buster. As Brandon pulled himself onto Buster's back, Buster explained that once the attack had started, the pegasi flew to the caverns in search of Uriel's family. They thought the dragons would be their best defense. It was Luke Thunder's idea, and he was supposed to lead them to where he thought the dragon's lair would be. But he turned back once the fighting broke out. It was up to the rest of the pegasi to find the lair and get help. Luckily, Aquila had met up with them in the air and showed them the way.

Brandon glanced back at the outline form of Aquila standing by the fire. He seemed to be standing and looking at something on the ground. Brandon was curious, but he had to concentrate on finding his brother. He turned his head back to the waters looking for any sign of movement.

Diana watched her brother climb on Buster and head back to the lake. Why were they heading back that way? Wasn't the battle over? She squinted, but it was still dark, and she could only make out shadows by the river. The moon was starting to hide behind the clouds again.

Midnight landed next to the fire. The Madeave had been defeated. Diana noted that someone must have removed the bodies because she no longer saw them lying around. She eyed the large dragon suspiciously. Was she licking her lips? Diana shuddered at the thought. Uriel walked over to Midnight and Diana as soon as they landed. Uriel was very happy to see Diana again. Cleo made introductions. Uriel's mother bowed down to Diana. Diana looked at Cleo, confused.

"She is honored to meet a Chosen One," Cleo explained. "She has fought many years to keep the Evadeam Mountain safe for your return. She is also grateful for the rescue and safe return of her baby."

Diana smiled, but her happy thoughts were soon interrupted by a low moan from Midnight. Brooke came running up to Diana and gestured for her to come down from Midnight's back.

"What is it?" asked Diana once her feet met the ground.

With tears in her eyes, Brooke held Diana tightly. "It's Luke Thunder. He took a sword for me and saved my life."

Diana turned remembering Luke Thunder falling to the ground. He still laid there with Grandpa and Silver Kat bent over him. Midnight touched his muzzle to Luke Thunder's head. Midnight and Luke Thunder were neighing to each other.

"Is he badly hurt?" asked Diana.

Brooke squeezed her shoulder. "Yes" was all she could choke out.

Diana looked up at Brooke. "Is he dying?"

Tears continued to run down Brooke's face. She nodded.

"No!" Diana broke free from Brooke's grasp and ran to Luke Thunder's side.

Brooke's hand flew up to her mouth as she tried to control the sobbing.

The Trahe Chronicles

She needed a Kleenex. She needed to blow her nose and dry the tears. But she couldn't stop crying. She was exhausted. She just wanted to drop to the ground and keep crying. She heard Diana cry out when she saw Luke Thunder, who was lying in his own pool of blood.

Grandpa kneeled down, grabbed Diana, and cried with her. That was all it took to break Brooke. She felt all her energy drain out as she sank to her feet. She brought her knees up to her chin and wrapped her arms around her legs. She bowed her head down and cried more. The eerie silence was back. All she could hear was the very slow breathing of Luke Thunder and the crying of those friends surrounding him. Then it stopped. Brooke held her breath and listened, but there was no more breath from Luke Thunder.

The silence was broken by the cries of the pegasi. Hooves pounded the ground, and all the pegasi, except for Midnight, took flight. They circled above Luke Thunder as a tribute.

Buster, who was over by the river, saw the circling of his family and friends. He pricked his ears forward and backward. He neighed and pawed at the air with his hooves. Brandon unaware of the death continued to search for Jereco.

Brooke's tears had finally run dry. She wiped her face the best she could. She started to get up to console Grandpa, who had just lost one of his best friends. Then she saw figures slowly walking up from the waters edge. She watched the shadows approach.

As the shadows continued toward camp, Brooke noticed Silver Kat and Hachmoni were holding onto Brandon. He looked upset and exhausted.

Archelaus trailed behind them. He looked up and met Brooke's eyes.

Something is wrong, Brooke thought. She saw it in Archelaus's eyes, and she felt it in her heart. She jumped up. Something was definitely wrong.

Archelaus looked straight ahead. He saw the light slowly go out of Brooke's eyes. He could see it register on her face. Brooke stared at Archelaus as he got closer. Her eyes were asking him, *Who?*

Archelaus did not know what to tell her. He did not know how to tell Brooke that he could not save her cousin—that Jereco was lost to the snake and the raging river?

Book One: The Chosen Ones

PART SIX

The Lost Evadeam Tribe

The Trahe Chronicles

"In all worlds there is darkness and there is light.
It is the light which shines and prevails.
It is our will that chooses between the darkness and the light.
Look deep.
Deeper into the heart of the mountain.
Deeper into the heart...your heart.
The silence of the winter snow brings forth silence in our thoughts.
All wonder why.
Some try to remember.
Some try to forget.
As the snow falls, it buries and claims our strength.
Our will rises to the top.
Hands break free through the snow.
We reach for help.
We grasp for life, for meaning, for answers.
As we tire, we let go.
Let go and let the Creator take us.
Surrender and reach out to the light.
The small beacon of light breaks through the snow.
The light grows and melts, grows and melts,
grows and melts the coldness away,
We feel the light.
We feel the warmth.
We break free!
Surrender!
Surrender our hearts.
Love and peace shall prevail!"
- Hachmoni

Book One: The Chosen Ones

Evadeam City

No one was able to sleep well that evening. The night Jereco disappeared into the cold mountain lake; Silver Kat had given Diana and Brooke herbal tea to help them relax. Diana finally slept and woke to find Brandon staring at her.

"What?" she asked.

"Did you have a dream?" he asked.

She thought about it for a moment. "No."

"Are you sure?"

She thought again. "No, I don't think so. Why? Did I have a seizure?"

Brandon shook his head. "I was just hoping you might have had a vision about Jereco."

"No. Have they found him yet?" she asked.

Brandon shook his head. "No." He jabbed his knife into the ground. "I wish they would have let me go with them!"

Diana remembered the fight Brandon had had with everyone. Archelaus and Silver Kat had to drag him from the lake when they lost Jereco to the snake. Brandon only agreed to leave with a promise that they would go hunt for him.

Meanwhile, Hachmoni insisted that they could not delay getting to Evadeam Mountain. However, the pegasi informed everyone that they were not going anywhere until they had a decent burial for Luke Thunder since they could not fly him back to their island. They would go after a proper mourning period had ended.

That evening, while everyone debated and argued about what to do, Brandon quickly packed his gear, including additional weapons. He ran past the lake and downstream to find his brother. No one realized he was missing until Diana spoke up.

In her small voice, Diana reminded them of the Evadeam family pact. They were not to be split up, so they were going nowhere until Jereco was found. Now they had to find Brandon too.

While searching for Jereco down river, Brandon found their other friends. Skylar, Sir Bolivar, and Methuselah were chasing the remaining Madeave when Jereco had been taken by the snake. They stopped chasing the Madeave to help Brandon search for Jereco. The male dragon that was assisting in the search landed next to them.

It had been hours and they were debating about continuing the search. "He is still alive!" exclaimed Brandon. "I know it. We need to find him."

Methuselah shook his head in doubt. "I am afraid he wouldn't survive the river's swift current."

Brandon was furious. "Are you kidding me?! He is the Water Guardian!" He stomped away and back toward the water's edge.

276

The Trahe Chronicles

"The Water Guardian?" asked the dragon.

Skylar quickly explained that the dragon was in the presence of the Chosen Ones.

The dragon flew ahead of Brandon and landed in front of his path. "I will find your brother, the Water Guardian. It is my duty and honor. I owe it to thee for the rescue of my daughter." The dragon bowed down.

"Great! I can use your help," replied Brandon. "Now let's go!"

Skylar growled something to the dragon.

The dragon stepped in front of Brandon. "You must stay and go back to your sister."

Brandon looked up at the dragon. "What? Are you kidding me? You are wasting time! Now let's go!"

This time, the dragon puffed out a few flames from his mouth. "Forest Friend, heed my warning! It is not your place to go further with this pursuit." The dragon paused. "Do you not hear the trees?"

Brandon shook his head angrily. "I do not hear anything from these trees! They seem to be speechless at the moment!"

The dragon growled. "Or perhaps you are refusing to listen! Sometimes you must do what you do not want to do. Sometimes you must do what is best even if you don't understand why!"

Brandon looked up into the dragon's eyes. "I must find my brother. He could be dying!" The dragon's face became sympathetic. "I thought once that my child was dying. I thought it was my place to find her, but it wasn't. I couldn't. Something inside me died. The child's mother felt the same way."

He waved a wing toward the trees, and then above to the stars. "With all things, we must remember to believe. Believe and follow the Creator." The dragon spoke sternly at Brandon. "The Vision Keeper found my daughter, and now I must find the Water Guardian."

The dragon let out a low growl. Soon, water animals emerged from all around. There were beavers, otters, and even some fish coming close to shore. "I have plenty of help and we can move quicker without the two-legged land creatures."

Skylar walked up to Brandon. "Besides, your good friend Buster needs you now."

Brandon was reminded that Luke Thunder, Buster's grandpa, had just died in battle. The dragon took his front claw and gently placed it on Brandon's shoulder. "I vow to find your brother, the Water Guardian, and I shall not return until I do. You have my word."

Brandon looked up at the dragon. "I don't know you; your word means nothing to me." The dragon was horrified by Brandon's comment.

Sir Bolivar shook his head. "Forgive him, but he is not of our world."

"Hmm ..." The dragon thought of something. "Come, Brandon. I will tell you a secret—

how to kill a dragon. If I do not keep my word, you may kill me."

Book One: The Chosen Ones

"What?" said Brandon.

Sir Bolivar jumped forward. "What? You cannot do that!" he told the dragon.

The dragon just lifted an eyebrow.

Sir Bolivar quickly turned to Brandon. "Brandon, this is serious stuff. No one, I mean, no one, knows how to kill a dragon."

Brandon shrugged. "Then, how come there are so few of them? How do they die?"

Methuselah was the one to speak. "Once upon a time, there were many dragons. In ancient times, ancestors of the Madeave—an evil tribe—fought the dragons. One of those tribe members accidently discovered how to quickly kill a dragon. But afterward, a terrible dread and sadness came over him. You see, he killed a mother dragon, and an unhatched egg was left in the nest. When the mother dragon died, the egg hatched, and the baby dragon cried for its mother. This tribe member was about to kill the baby dragon until he looked into its eyes. Do not ever look into the eyes of the dragon unless you want to see its soul. The soul of that baby dragon spoke to this tribe member. It spoke right to his heart, so the legend says.

The tribe member felt terrible for what he did. He could not even remember why he killed a dragon in the first place. He could not remember what the dragon had even done to him personally. From that day on, he vowed to protect that baby dragon and the secret. He knew the only way to keep the baby dragon safe was to turn it over to the Evadeam tribe. The Evadeam tribe was known to be honest and trustworthy. And from that day on, only trustworthy Evadeam tribe members were allowed to know the secret."

The dragon continued the story. "As time passed, the Evadeam tribe was broken up. Members were killed. Many disappeared. The secret became a true mystery. "

Brandon saw the extremely serious looks on their faces. Time was ticking away, and Jereco's life was in danger. He looked up at the dragon, and he noticed the tree branches above him.

Brandon closed his eyes and silently prayed. "Willow, can you hear me? Please tell me what to do. I need your spirit to guide me." He stood there in silence, waiting for an answer. He listened and listened. He pleaded in his mind to Willow. He pleaded to the Creator. He desperately needed guidance.

He heard water splash. He turned and peered into the darkness. The moon shined upon the water. What was that? A sign? Perhaps. He turned toward the dragon and meekly replied, "Okay."

Brandon was pulled aside and was told the most secret thing about a dragon.

As Brandon watched the death ceremony for Luke Thunder, his thoughts wandered. He wondered where Jereco was and if his brother was alive. He

The Trahe Chronicles

wondered if he should have not been told the dragon's best kept secret. He didn't feel privileged; he felt burdened. The knowledge weighed on his shoulders. No one, especially man, should have had this information. He looked around the valley and realized that if the wrong creatures discovered this place, then the remaining dragons could perish. He briefly wondered if Earth had dragons at one time. If so, how did they perish? He suddenly had an overwhelming urgency to leave the area to keep the dragons safe.

Brandon did not have to wait long. It was decided they would leave the very next morning. Diana was teary-eyed as they said their goodbyes to the dragons. She wanted Uriel to go with them, but Hachmoni explained that it was much too dangerous for Uriel. Besides, Uriel was reunited with her family, and she needed to stay home. The creatures of the valley reassured everyone that they would send word about Jereco to them as soon as they heard anything.

The group, now a little smaller, started out once again for Evadeam Mountain. It was a very rugged mountain terrain. They spent most of their time flying while Methuselah, Skylar, and Sir Bolivar moved on the ground ahead of them.

As they were in the air, Diana noticed how beautiful the scenery was. *Jereco would have enjoyed this flight*, she thought. The aerial view reminded her of a movie that they saw back on Earth. It was a nature movie about the Rocky Mountains. The movie had played at an Imax theatre, and she remembered feeling like she was flying through the mountains, just like she felt now.

Diana noticed the dense forest below had a large river that cut through the mountains. Now and then, they would come across a small lake or body of water and camp for the evening. Diana was losing track of the days. One morning, Diana woke up, colder than normal. She was really missing Jereco and did not want to get out of bed. She snuggled deeper into her blankets to get warm. As she did so, she heard noises and voices outside. *Snow? Did someone use the word snow?* Curiosity got her up. She quickly dressed in warmer clothes. As she stepped outside, she felt blinded by a light. As her eyes adjusted to the morning sun, she noticed that the blinding light was coming from sunlight reflecting off the white snow. The ground was covered with snow!

Diana ran back into the tent. "Brooke! Brooke, wake up. It snowed last night. We have snow!"

Brooke, who had also dug deeper into her covers for warmth, mumbled something about it being too cold and too early to get up.

Diana was wide awake and excited. They had not seen snow since they left their home on Earth. She dug into her pack of clothes and found the coat, gloves, and hat that Michael had bought for her in Bethemek. She quickly searched for Brandon. To her dismay, he was still sleeping, but Archelaus gave her permission to wake Brandon. Diana almost hated to wake up her brother because she knew that he hadn't slept well since Jereco had

Book One: The Chosen Ones

disappeared. She very carefully and quietly tried to wake up Brandon. She did not want to startle him, knowing he now slept with his weapons.

Snow. The word *snow* was winding its way into Brandon's mind. *Snow. Snow!* Brandon woke with a start and found Diana leaning over him. She was talking about snow, how pretty it was, how she missed it, and did he want to go play in it?

"Snow? Did you say snow?" he asked Diana.

Diana nodded eagerly. "Yes, it snowed last night. And I think there is enough to have a snowball fight or make a snowman."

Brandon quickly got up and peeked outside. He saw the ground was covered with the white, fluffy stuff. To Diana's dismay, Brandon cursed the snow as he went to grab his winter gear out of his pack.

"Brandon?" Diana wondered why he wasn't happy. He had always loved the snow back home. He used to love to ski, snowboard, and even make snowmen with her.

Brandon looked back at his sister.

For the first time, Diana realized how much older Brandon was beginning to look.

"It's too early for snow!" said Brandon. "Has anyone checked the pegasi?"

Diana shrugged her shoulders to indicate that she didn't know.

As Brandon continued to put on his winter gear, he explained that the pegasi did not have their winter coats yet. They had slept outside last night under a makeshift tent, and they must have been freezing.

These thoughts had never occurred to Diana. She suddenly felt very guilty for wanting to play in the snow. She followed Brandon's quick pace to see their friends. They found Michael, Archelaus, and Hachmoni already warming up the pegasi. Michael was dressing the pegasi with winter blankets and leggings. Brandon immediately went to his friend Buster. Brandon and Buster had become even closer since the lost of their loved ones.

"Hey, Buster. How are you?" asked Brandon as he walked up behind him.

"Good morning." Buster lifted his head and had a mouth full of snow. "This is so cool, Brandon! I have never seen snow before." Brandon and Buster had been learning each other's language, including slang words like *cool.* Buster buried his head back in the snow, and when his head popped back up, he was eating it.

Diana started laughing. "You look like Santa Claus?"

"Santa who?" Buster asked as he dove down for another mouthful of snow.

Even Brandon smiled. Santa Claus. He hadn't thought of Santa Claus in forever. So as Diana and Brandon helped Buster get into his winter gear, they explained who Santa Claus was.

"Brandon," Diana said, "do you think Santa Claus travels all the way to Trahe?"

The Trabe Chronicles

Brandon shook his head. "I doubt it."

Diana looked disappointed.

"Well, think about it Diana. He can barely get around Earth in one night. How in the world is he going to fly across the universe into another world? I doubt he has a spaceship." Diana gave it some thought. "Well, maybe Cleo would let him borrow the spaceship to come here."

Brandon looked at Diana. "Even if Cleo would let him borrow it, the spaceship is buried in the jungle, remember?"

Diana was thinking hard for another solution when Archelaus walked up behind them. He had overhead their conversation. He remembered Brooke explaining Christmas and some of the festivities that came with it, like the visit from Santa Claus. He wondered if Diana realized that they had been in his world for almost a year now, and that she had missed Christmas back on Earth. He could tell by the look on Brandon's face that Brandon desperately wanted the subject changed.

"Brandon," said Archelaus, "if you are almost done here, would you help me pack a load of dead wood? There is plenty here at this location, and I am not sure if our next stop will have much around."

Brandon nodded. "And if this weather is any indication, we are going to need it."

Archelaus turned to Diana. "Can you go wake up Brooke? We need to start breakfast soon." As Diana nodded, they heard the pegasi neigh.

Buster popped his head back out of the snow and stepped forward. "Look in the air."

They looked up and saw a tiny figure in the sky, soaring toward them. Brandon held his breath, hoping it was the dragon with news of Jereco, but as the figure came closer he saw, that it was much too small.

"It is Aquila," observed Archelaus.

They quickly moved to meet him. Aquila landed in the center of camp. Everyone was happy to see him and started to talk at once. They asked Aquila about Methuselah and Skylar. It wasn't until Brandon asked about Jereco that Aquila spread his wings and quieted everyone else down. Aquila used his eagle eyes to take a quick look around, and then he turned to Hachmoni.

"How about we explain over breakfast?" Hachmoni suggested.

"Fast," Aquila replied. "Must move fast. Winter storm moving here fast."

That caught everyone's attention. Aquila spoke quickly in eagle language to Hachmoni. Hachmoni listen intently while everyone quietly watched. Finally, with a nod, Aquila flew back into the air.

"Where is he going?" asked Brandon. "Does he know anything about Jereco?"

Hachmoni held up his hand. "Aquila is going to the river for his breakfast and will be back. And no, he does not know anything new about Jereco. However, he has other good news. They made it to Evadeam City."

281

Book One: The Chosen Ones

This news stunned everyone. It seemed like they have been traveling forever and now they were almost there.

"They found Evadeam City?" asked Archelaus.

Hachmoni nodded. "It seems Methuselah's, Skylar's, and Aquila's memories served them well. They found it right over that mountain ridge." He pointed west. "That is the good news."

Brandon cocked his head. "And the bad news?"

"A winter storm is blowing in from the west. If we do not move fast, we will be heading right into it before we hit the ancient city."

"Then we better get going," said Archelaus. He turned to Diana to tell her to get Brooke, but she was already running toward her tent.

Diana knew it would be hard to wake up Brooke this morning since Brooke did not do well in cold weather. She tried using some magic words. "Archelaus needs you ...." She yanked off Brooke's covers. As Brooke slowly got up and dressed, Diana filled her in with the news she had just learned.

Brooke paused when Diana told her about finding Evadeam City. "Are there people at the city?" Brooke asked.

"I don't know," replied Diana, "but Aquila said that there is a winter storm coming from the west."

"Didn't you say that is where we are heading?" said Brooke as she finished getting dressed.

"Uh huh, so we have to hurry," said Diana as she went back out of the tent.

Winter storm. Brooke was not looking forward to that. It was one thing to be caught in a winter storm in a warm house or car back on Earth, but to be caught in one outdoors on horseback was not going to be fun.

Brooke and Diana made a quick hot breakfast for everyone. Afterward, they hurriedly packed, and soon they were up in the air, following Aquila. It was a very hard day for the pegasi. They flew fast and hard, but being bundled in their winter gear slowed them down. They decided that they would not make it over the mountain ridge before nightfall, so they decided to set up camp for the night. They kept close together in a circle. The fire and the pegasi were right in the middle of camp while everyone's tents circled them to help break the wind or snow that might occur overnight. Within the tents, they slept close together to keep each other warm. It did snow that night. They were lucky a snow blizzard had not hit yet. They started off bright and early again the next day.

It was a rough flight over the ridge, but they made it over safely. Brooke looked down to see yet another beautiful untouched landscape. The valley was green with tall pine trees. There was also a mix of hard and soft wood trees. A river weaved through the valley. She noticed that the valley was surrounded by rugged mountain terrain. She doubted anyone could enter easily without flying. She could see why the Evadeam used this as their home for thousands of years. As she enjoyed the sight, her stomach started to

282

The Trahe Chronicles

growl. She looked up and noticed where the sun was located. Had they really been traveling all day without stopping? Shouldn't they stop for lunch? Someone else must have been thinking the same thing because they started to descend. They headed toward a large lake. It was surrounded mostly by forest, except for one side where a mountain bordered the lake's edge. A tall, raging waterfall flowed from the mountain's cliffs into the lake.

They landed in a small clearing at the lake's edge. After the group took a break, they settled down to eat a late lunch. There was a debate about whether to camp for the night or keep going. Aquila said that they could arrive at the city at dusk. Michael did not like the idea of going into a strange city just before nightfall and wanted to leave early in the morning. He also pointed out that they had not hit really bad weather yet. Hachmoni disagreed and wanted to continue. He said it would better to be stuck in a storm at the ancient city than here at the lake.

As the discussion continued, Brandon ate his meal quietly near Buster. All of a sudden, a chill ran up Brandon's back. Instantly, he put his lunch down and grabbed his sword.

"You felt it too," asked Buster.

Brandon looked at Buster, realizing he wasn't the only one who had felt a chill. Brandon got up and put his hand onto the nearest tree trunk. He was trying to catch a vibe from the tree. "Come on," he whispered. "Talk to me."

It was Buster who answered with a stomp of his hooves. He pointed his head in the direction of the waterfall.

Brandon narrowed his eyes and swore he saw something within the waterfall. "What is it?" he asked Buster.

'It is Luke Thunder," said Buster. "Get on."

Brandon didn't hesitate. He knew enough to follow Buster's instinct. However, he figured that what they saw could not have been Luke Thunder. Luke Thunder was dead. *Maybe it's a dragon*, he thought.

They quickly flew toward the waterfall. Once they arrived at the falls, they realized that there was no access behind the waterfall where Buster insisted he had seen Luke Thunder.

"Now what?" Brandon yelled to Buster.

Buster was frustrated. He was sure he had seen Luke Thunder's spirit, but how were they supposed to get into the waterfall? Buster and Brandon flew up and down looking for an entrance. Not only could they not find a way into the powerful waterfalls, they no longer saw the large creature behind it. In fact, Brandon was wondering if they had seen anything at all. "Brandon!" Buster yelled. "Look down there in the lake, just outside the falls."

Brandon looked down. "What? I don't see anything."

Buster, who had great eyesight, flew down closer for his friend's benefit. "Look there on that large rock."

Brandon squinted and looked down, but he saw only water beating against the rocks.

Book One: The Chosen Ones

"When the water recedes, look on that big rock on the south side," said Buster.

Brandon waited and looked. *There*. He saw it. Brandon's heart started pounding. It was a human on the rock. Water spray and lake grass covered the person. He couldn't tell if it was a he or she—dead or alive. "Can you get us down closer?" yelled Brandon. The rushing of the water and the flapping of Buster's wings drowned out Brandon's voice. As he yelled, he pointed down toward the rock. Buster nodded and flew in closer.

Acting on total instinct, Brandon took his rope lasso and tied it to his saddle. He tied the other end around himself. Due to the wind and the water from the falls, Buster could not fly right down to the rock, so Brandon decided to lower himself down. He worked quickly but carefully. He did not want to lose himself and Buster in the waterfall.

Brandon finally reached the rock and jumped on top of it. His heart was racing as he reached for the person who was lying face down across the rock. Brandon determined this person was a man. Brandon's heart started to race as he placed his fingers on the man's neck, looking for a pulse. As he did so, he wiped water from his own eyes. Brandon held his breathe as he carefully turned the person over.

Tears formed in Brandon's eyes as he looked at the bloody and bruised face. "Jereco?" he whispered.

Brandon wiped his eyes again. It was Jereco. Brandon desperately tried to find a pulse.

Splash!

Water poured over Brandon and Jereco. The rope around Brandon jerked upward as Buster tried to avoid getting wet. As the water cleared, Brandon thought he saw a large fin go through the waterfall.

Jereco began to cough in Brandon's arms. Then Brandon heard a moan come from Jereco's lips. "He is alive!" Brandon yelled. Brandon locked his arms and legs around Jereco's body. He yanked on the rope and yelled up to Buster. "Can you carry us both to the shore?"

Buster didn't need to answer. He was already lifting them both off the rock. It took all of Brandon's strength to keep the rope steady while hanging onto Jereco. As Buster slowly flew over the lake, Brandon could see Midnight flying toward them.

Midnight had noticed right away that Buster and Brandon had taken off for the waterfalls. The rest of the group did not think much about it. Midnight insisted that Archelaus hop on. Archelaus did not hesitate. The others were not sure what was going on, but they automatically knew to protect Diana and Brooke while Midnight and Archelaus were gone.

Archelaus helped lower Jereco onto Midnight, and then Brandon was able to hop back onto Buster. They flew safely back to camp, and there were cheers of joy when everyone realized Jereco was alive. However, Jereco was unconscious again, so Silver Kat gave medical attention to Jereco immediately. Silver Kat pulled something out of his saddle bag and placed it under Jereco's nose. Jereco started to moan and speak incoherently.

Silver Kat nodded. "Good." He called over Archelaus and Michael. "I will need some plants from the forest." He verbally made a list. "Take Midnight with you. He will be able to recognize the plants."

While they were gone, Brooke and Diana gathered water and clothes to clean up Jereco. They talked to him, hoping he would awaken. But all he did was mumble words like *water people*, *cave*, and *mad*.

"What is he saying?" Diana whispered as she handed Brooke a wet cloth. Diana turned to Silver Kat. "Is he going to be all right?"

Silver Kat never got a chance to reply as Archelaus, Michael, and Midnight had just returned with his ingredients. Silver Kat went to work right away as everyone watched intently.

As the day and night progressed, it seemed Jereco was not getting any better. Silver Kat pulled Hachmoni, Archelaus, and Michael aside. "We need to move Jereco to better shelter. Snow is coming."

Michael nodded in agreement. "I can feel it in the air and in my bones. I am concerned about what happened to Jereco. He keeps saying the word *mad*. What if Jereco means Madeave?"

"If there are Madeave near here," replied Archelaus, "then none of us will be safe out in the open like this. We need to get to Evadeam City."

Hachmoni rubbed his chin. "Since when has the Madeave tribe been back in Evadeam Mountain?"

Brooke, who had walked up behind the men, asked, "Is it safe to move Jereco?"

Hachmoni shook his head. "We have no choice. The storm is fast approaching, and until Jereco wakes up to tell us what has happened, we have to assume the Madeave are somewhere nearby. Let's get some sleep tonight and start first thing in the morning."

"I will take the first watch," volunteered Michael.

"Me too," piped up Brandon, who had walked up behind Brooke. "Besides I don't think I can sleep right now."

The night continued with members of the group switching guard duty as they looked after Jereco and kept an eye out for possible Madeave.

The night brought in snow, but they woke to a bright and sunny day. The light was sparkling across the white snow that covered most of the ground. Diana quickly got ready for the day and ran over to Jereco's tent. Inside, Brandon and Silver Kat were bent over Jereco. "How is he going to fly in this condition?" said Brandon.

Diana thought Brandon looked terrible. "Have you been up all night with Jereco?" she asked.

Brandon simply nodded and kept his attention on Silver Kat. He waited for an answer to his question. Diana looked at Jereco and also wondered how

Book One: The Chosen Ones

he was going to fly in his condition. He was still asleep. Diana noticed that Silver Kat had not answered Brandon yet.

Archelaus popped his head into the tent. "Aquila is back," he announced.

Silver Kat put his hand on Brandon's shoulder. "Come. Let's see what Aquila has to say." Sensing Brandon's hesitation, he continued, "Aquila will know how close we are to Evadeam City. Plus, he scouted the land for Madeave this morning."

"Go ahead, Brandon," Diana encouraged. "I will stay with Jereco."

Brandon looked at Jereco one more time before getting up and following Archelaus outside. Silver Kat started to follow and then hesitated for a moment. He looked back at Diana "Jereco could use a good prayer this morning." He smiled with encouragement before leaving the tent.

Diana looked at Jereco. Silver Kat was right. All of them seemed to be slacking with the prayers lately. Their lives had changed so much that their routine prayers were being forgotten.

Diana kneeled down beside Jereco. She folded her hands and closed her eyes in the fashion that she had been taught. She spoke softly to the Creator. She believed God was the same as the Creator on Trahe. "Dear Creator," she began, "I know I have not been good in praying to you lately. I am sorry. But I hope you will hear me today. My brother Jereco is injured and not waking up yet. Please, Creator, help him."

Brooke walked up to the tent as she heard Diana praying. She smiled as she listened to Diana's prayer. Diana was right. They hadn't been praying to the Creator like they should —only when they desperately needed help. Maybe that was why Jereco was lying there, and why they had not arrived at Evadeam City yet.

Brooke kneeled down next to Diana.

Diana looked up with surprise.

"Two praying is always better than one," Brooke explained.

They both prayed for the healing of Jereco, that they would find Evadeam City before the winter snowstorm hit, and for their new friends on this planet. They prayed for the safe return of their parents. Diana ended with a prayer for their family and friends back on Earth.

A few moments later, Jereco began to mumble. "Water ... people ... writing ... cave ... Madeave ..."

Brooke opened her eyes and saw Jereco's hazel-brown eyes staring at her. She could not believe it. Jereco had been mumbling in his sleep on and off so much that she did not expect for him to be awake this time.

Brooke turned to Diana. "Go get Silver Kat."

Diana looked at Jereco. "I will be right back." She ran off as fast as she could.

Brooke smiled at Jereco. "Good to have you back, Cousin."

She silently prayed a thank you to God, the Creator.

Silver Kat checked Jereco. The natural medicines were working; he would

286

The Trahe Chronicles

be fine after more rest. Some of them were crowded outside of Jereco's tent, debating whether or not they should wait another day before traveling to Evadeam City. This would give Jereco another day of rest, but that would also mean the winter storm would be getting closer.

"Leave," Jereco whispered.

"What?" Diana asked as she leaned closer to him.

"Need to leave," he said in a hoarse voice.

No one heard him, except Diana. Diana yelled to the others standing outside, "Hey, Jereco is saying something."

Cleo ran in and jumped onto Jereco's sleeping bag and walked right up to his face.

Jereco looked at Cleo and said in a very hoarse and tired voice, "We need to leave. Get to Evadeam City. Close. It is close by."

Cleo agreed, "The land has changed a little bit since I have been here last. But by my calculations, Evadeam City should be nearby."

Hachmoni walked into the tent. "That is what Aquila also confirmed."

"Yes, but Aquila was not specific," said Michael. "Is close by an hour, a day, or a week?"

Jereco lifted himself up on his elbows and said loudly, "Waterfall. The city is high up. On the other side of the waterfall." Then he sank into bed again.

"That is what Aquila meant when he chirped the words *falling water*." concluded Hachmoni.

With Jereco's encouragement, they packed right away and headed toward the waterfall where Brandon and Buster had found Jereco. Aquila led the way over the falls. Once they reached the top of the falls, they saw a raging river running between high walls of massive mountain rocks.

They flew above the river, following it. The river split off multiple times. It was easy to see how someone could lose their way. They flew fast, knowing it was critical to get Jereco back on the ground so he could fully recover. It was late afternoon when they arrived at another huge lake.

They landed in a clearing near the edge of a lake. Calm water stretched before them. On the opposite side of the lake was a waterfall. Behind them was a massive mountain wall. The lake offered a place to quench their thirst. Methuselah was already there. He had a large fish in his mouth as he walked up. He dropped the fish. "Welcome to Evadeam City."

Brooke looked around. "Where? I don't see a city. All I see is a lake, some overgrown brush, and rocks." A slight breeze whipped Brooke's hair into her eyes.

"It's here," Brandon said. "I can feel it. The trees are talking to me. It's here. We've finally made it!"

Brooke and Diana looked around confused.

Hachmoni slowly walked toward the massive mountain wall and put his hand on it. A flat mountain of rock was so tall that the top of it disappeared into the clouds. "Here," patting the wall. "Here is our beloved city. Evadeam

Book One: The Chosen Ones

City is built within Evadeam Mountain."

"Are we at the top of the mountain?" asked Diana.

"No," Hachmoni pointed his walking stick upwards "the peak of the mountain is over fourteen thousand feet above sea level. Our ancestors and we could not live much further up without getting altitude sickness. The city is about five thousand feet above sea level."

"I still don't see the city—only mountain rock," exclaimed Brooke.

"Caves," said Jereco in a hoarse voice. "In the caves."

"Oh great!" said Brooke. "More caves. I would rather it be a tree, like Willow."

Brandon nodded in agreement, but Archelaus looked pleased. "This is fantastic," Archelaus said. "The city entrance must be hidden behind all that brush. If the Madeave were in the area, they would have a hard time finding this place." He turned to Brooke. "Plus, this is our history. We are talking hundreds of years—maybe *thousands* of years old. This is where our Evadeam ancestors once lived."

Brooke had a memory of the brief history lessons Grandpa had given them before they left Earth. The very old books had talked about the Evadeam tribe, Princess Skylar, and her great white tiger friend. As these thoughts flooded her mind, she saw Skylar, the white tiger of today, climbing out of the rocks from the city her ancestors once called home.

"Let's refill all of our water jugs before heading into the city," instructed Hachmoni. "With any luck, we can find shelter in the city before the night falls."

After they got the water they needed, they followed Skylar and Methuselah into the mountain rock called Evadeam City.

Archelaus was right. Overgrown brush hid the entrance within the creases of the mountain wall. The entrance looked so natural that they would have easily missed it if they hadn't known the entrance was there.

Once inside the mountain city, the group entered a network of passageways. Someone could easily have gotten lost inside this rock city. Unlit torches, which at one time were used as lights, were anchored along the cave walls. The passageways were large enough for all of them to get through. Skylar and Methuselah seemed to be leading them upward. They walked into a huge room. The top of the room was open to the sky, which let in the natural light.

"This was once a grand city," explained Hachmoni. "It is written in the chronicles that this particular cave is two hundred and eighty two feet tall." As they looked around, they realized this must have been a massive courtyard.

"How large is the city?" asked Jereco.

"The books record that the city is forty square miles. The mountain walls that surround this courtyard have an assortment of approximately three hundred caves." continued Hachmoni. "Not to mention what may be below

288

The Trabe Chronicles

us."

"The caves must have been their homes," suggested Archelaus.

"They were," replied Methuselah.

"And there?" Diana asked as she pointed to a large hill in the center of the courtyard. It was now covered with snow. "What was that?"

Buster and Brandon made their way over. Brandon kicked off the snow to find stone steps that lead to a huge platform. "It is some kind of stage," Brandon announced.

"Oh, maybe they used to have plays on it," exclaimed Diana.

They watched as Archelaus followed Brandon to the platform. At that moment, the sun peeped through the hole above and light cascaded down on them.

Brooke looked up at Archelaus. "Or maybe that is where the ancient leaders gave their speeches to the people."

Archelaus looked down into Brooke's eyes, and she knew he was thinking the same thing. Brooke's heart went out to Archelaus. Being in Evadeam City brought back memories of Archelaus' family. He must really miss them. She suddenly felt homesick herself.

Skylar jumped onto the raised area. "There is no time to hypothesize about the past. Let's set up camp before the sun sets." As she headed down the steps, she reminded them that their eyes were not as good in the dark as hers. "I suggest making a fire before the caverns become dark."

Led by Skylar, they continued down a different passageway that headed in the direction of the lake. And as they climbed up, they started to feel a chill in the air. Skylar finally turned into another passageway that opened up into another huge room that was a size of a house.

Skylar turned toward Archelaus. "Since you are the descendant of the leaders of the Evadeam people, this will be your den."

"This is big enough for all of us," Archelaus stated as he glanced at Brooke. "I think we need to stay together."

The room had other rooms leading off of it. In the middle of the room was a grand circular fireplace built out of stone. On the far side of the room, they could see light filtering in. They walked over to the light to find a huge balcony. The balcony had boulders stacked up along its outer edges to make a railing. It was a good thing a railing was there; the drop-off was huge. The stone balcony overlooked the lake and waterfalls, and it was high enough to see down the river.

Brandon looked around them and noticed there were more balconies throughout the mountain city. However, the one they were standing on was the largest. "This is the perfect view," observed Brandon. "From here, you can see if any enemies are approaching."

"I have to admit that this is much nicer than I thought it would be," said Brooke. She also pointed to the vines hanging over the sides. "This would explain why we couldn't see the caves from down below."

Book One: The Chosen Ones

"The vines not only act as coverage," commented Michael, "but they also break the wind during a storm."

"What storm?" asked Brandon. "Everyone keeps talking about a storm, but all I have seen is a little snow."

Michael pulled Brandon forward and turned him toward the western sky. "I imagine that the worst of the storm is from the north, which is blocked by the city walls."

Brandon saw the storm clouds rolling in, and his shoulders slumped.

"You arrived just in time," said a voice from behind them.

"Sir Bolivar!" they exclaimed. Everyone was excited to see him.

"Anyone else hungry?" he asked.

Hachmoni insisted that they make camp first. They decided that it would be safest for all of them to stay in this large room until all the caverns were thoroughly checked out. Brooke noticed some homemade hooks from the ceilings, so she hung up a tent between the cave opening and the fireplace. This would help block the storm winds. Their tents were set up side by side on the other side of the fireplace.

The pegasi and the other animals would bed down between the tents and the cave entrance along the inner city walls. Brooke set up the kitchen on the east side of the fireplace. There was a room located off the east side that they decided to store their supplies in.

As Brooke, Archelaus, Hachmoni, and Diana set up camp, the others searched the rooms to make sure there were no other creatures inhabiting the cavern rooms. After Methuselah assured them that he had already checked out the den, Michael and Brandon were able to light all the torches that lined the walls. The room now had a nice glow from the torches' flames. The sun had set by the time they were done.

As they finally sat down for dinner, Methuselah and Skylar talked about their search of the city caverns. They had enlisted other animals to help search the area. Bears, wolves, mountain goats, mountain lions, and even small animals such as squirrels helped out. So far the city was deserted, except for creatures of the mountain that had taken refuge in the caves.

Sir Bolivar explained that communication with friendly creatures had enabled them to find the ancient city. They sent Aquila out to tell the rest of the group about the location of the city.

"Where is Aquila?" asked Diana.

"He is doing a search of the area by air before the storm hits," explained Hachmoni.

"So now what?" asked Brandon. "Now that we have found Evadeam City, what are we supposed to do next?"

Everyone turned to Hachmoni for an answer.

"All will reveal itself in time," he answered.

Brandon let out a frustrated sigh.

Cleo moved into the half circle of friends, toward the fire. "It is time for

The Trabe Chronicles

the Evadeam people to reclaim their city," she said.

"But why us?" Brandon asked. "Why did we have to come from Earth to help you?"

Cleo walked up to Brandon and looked into his eyes. "Because you are the Chosen Ones."

Before Brandon could ask another question Jereco's hoarse voice interrupted him. "Brandon, haven't you learned by now not to ask why? Follow your heart. Follow the Creator. We belong here. At least I feel that way. I can feel it even more when I am with the water people. Don't you when you talk to the trees?"

Brandon thought for a minute. "Yeah, I guess so."

Diana spoke quietly. "What about our parents? We still haven't found them. I thought they would be here."

No one answered at first. Brooke, Jereco, and Brandon were thinking the same thing though.

"We will find them, little one," replied Sir Bolivar. He looked over at Jereco. "At least we found Jereco. But you don't look so good."

"Yeah, I am kind of tired," Jereco replied.

"What happened to you, Water Guardian?" continued Sir Bolivar.

Hachmoni looked over at Jereco. "Are you up to telling us now?"

Jereco nodded and took a drink. He closed his eyes and tried to remember everything that had happened to him since he last saw his friends and family.

Book One: The Chosen Ones

The River People

Jereco put his hand to his temple as he collected his thoughts. He remembered thinking he was dead. He felt alive, but knew he should have been dead by then. He recalled being in a dark and murky place. It had all happened so fast. One minute he was walking behind Brandon and Archelaus, and then the next minute he was being dragged underwater. Another snake had come out of nowhere. The snake wrapped himself around Jereco and dragged him quickly back into the lake. The snake had moved fast, so fast that Jereco had barely enough time to realize what was happening.

As the snake raced down the lake into the river's mouth, it dawned on Jereco that the snake was occasionally pushing Jereco up and out of the water. It was as if the snake wanted Jereco to live and was giving him time to breathe. *He must be taking me somewhere*, thought Jereco. It was during one of those moments that Jereco was brought up to the surface that he saw them.

Something else was now swimming as fast as the snake, if not faster. There were several of them. *Fish maybe,* he thought. The snake must have realized he had company, and he didn't like it. The snake dragged Jereco back under the water. The snake began to swim faster.

Jereco had a feeling he needed to break loose, but on the other hand, he wasn't sure what was following the snake. Maybe they were crocodiles, eels, or something more dangerous. These creatures were obviously not friends of the snake. They started to attack the snake. The new predators gained on the snake and its prey. Suddenly, things got crazy. The snake was thrashing and swimming at the same time. At one point, Jereco felt his body slam into something—perhaps a rock.

Jereco thought he would have to break free before he drowned or got smashed to pieces. He struggled, but the snake wrapped tighter around Jereco. Jereco worried he wouldn't be able to breathe. He was going to drown.

Crack!

The sound jerked Jereco to his senses. He wasn't moving anymore. The snake wasn't moving either. Jereco opened his eyes. He was still underwater and could see these creatures attacking the snake. The creatures had something that was making a cracking sound. A light! There was a light. *An electric eel? I have to get out of here*, Jereco thought. Jereco pushed with all his might against the snake's body in attempt to free him. He couldn't do it. The snake must still be alive and still had a grip on him. One of the eels seemed to have noticed Jereco and swam toward him. *Great*, Jereco thought. *Now I will be an eel's lunch.* Jereco started to panic, trying to break free.

Crack!

There was that cracking sound again.

A bright light flashed near Jereco. Jereco turned to see the eel attacking the snake's body as if the eel was trying to free Jereco.

The Trahe Chronicles

Crack! There was the sound and light again, but this time Jereco swore that he did not see an electric eel but some sort of three-prong sword attacking the snake.

Mermaids! The thought hit Jereco like a lightning bolt. One more crack and a blast of light released Jereco. The moment Jereco felt the snake let go, he swam to the surface. Jereco broke through the water's surface, coughing and sputtering. He was exhausted and could barely stay above the water's surface. He felt something grab his arm. He started to panic, but whatever grabbed him didn't give him much time. It quickly pulled him to the riverbank.

The riverbank was steep here, so Jereco grabbed for a fallen tree trunk lying across the river. He didn't even try to pull himself out of the water. He just hung on and breathed. His arms wrapped around a thick branch, and he laid his head on the tree trunk. He was alive. That was all that mattered. He was alive and breathing. That was a good sign. He hung onto the tree trunk and rested there for about fifteen minutes until he felt water splash on his face.

He had to get out of the river. He lifted his head to look around. The riverbank was steep, but he was pretty sure he could climb it. It was still dark outside, but the moonlight provided some light. He was just about to let go of the tree trunk when he saw movement in the water. He thought it might be another snake. He quickly pulled the rest of his body out of the water and lay on the tree trunk. Once he was on the trunk, he looked at the water. The currents were still rough, so maybe the movement he saw in the river had just been his imagination.

Splash!

A huge wave of water washed over him. He hung onto the tree trunk, determined not to be pulled back into the raging river. When the water cleared, Jereco wiped his eyes. Staring back at him was a girl, or at least the shadows of the nighttime made her look like a girl. A water girl! But how was that possible? The water people lived in salt water.

Wait a minute. Jereco remembered his encounter with Chislon at Willow. Hadn't she come to him in fresh water? He looked more closely at the face staring back at him. This wasn't Chislon. He was slightly disappointed. As if feeling his disappointment, the water girl said something to him. She spoke in a language he didn't understand, but the expression on her face and the splash of her tail confirmed that she understood his thoughts.

"I am sorry," he said in the Trahe language. "Thank you for saving my life."

She seemed to be thinking over what he said. She was much smaller than Chislon. Maybe she was smaller because she was a freshwater person living in a smaller area of water. Then Jereco remembered that there were others. He looked out at the water and thought he could see shadows swimming under the water, just at the surface.

Jereco looked back at the water girl. "I am Jereco, the Water Guardian.

293

Book One: The Chosen Ones

Who are you?"

She squeaked something out that Jereco didn't understand.

"Don't you speak the Trahe language?" he asked.

She squeaked something else.

"Obviously not," Jereco mumbled. He pointed at the riverbank. "I need to go up there. I need to go back to my friends."

The girl looked at the riverbank and shook her head.

"But I need to go up there," said Jereco. "I can't swim in this water anymore. It is cold, and I am tired." He pointed in the direction he had come. "I need to go back."

The girl looked in the direction he was pointing and shook her head again.

Jereco gave up and started to get off the tree trunk to head toward the bank. He was almost off the tree trunk when he felt himself being pulled back down. Jereco looked down at his right leg. His green mark was glowing and matched the hand that was holding his leg. The water girl was dragging him back into the water.

Jereco was tired, cold, hungry, and cranky. He kicked his foot free. "No, I need to get back." He started to climb up again. He heard a screeching and squeaking noise coming from the water. He looked back, and there were more water people. They seemed anxious and were saying something to the water girl. She seemed to be explaining to them what Jereco was doing. A water person shook his head and quickly swam up to Jereco. He jumped up and pulled on both of Jereco's legs. Jereco was pulled into the water. The water person caught him before Jereco went under. Jereco noticed that this water person looked like a grown male—a small water man, but definitely older and much stronger than the water girl.

"Now look here. I am the Water Guardian and you can't just—"

The water man put his hand over Jereco's mouth. He screeched something, and then the water girl swam up to Jereco. She motioned Jereco to be quiet by putting a finger to her lips. She pointed up toward the bank. Jereco was confused for a moment, and then he heard it. *Crash!* Someone was up on the land. Jereco nodded his head to show he understood. The water man released him, and they swam up to the bank but stayed in the water. Jereco was listening really hard now. If it was one of his friends or family members looking for him, then he could shout for help. But if it wasn't, he was best to stay with the water people.

It sounded like a group of people were running fast. Jereco wished they would say something, so he would know who they were.

As if reading his mind, the water man screeched a sound. It worked. Whoever was running on land stopped. They paused and then yelled out something Jereco didn't understand. They definitely were not his people. Jereco peered up, but all he could see were shadows looking over the edge. A cloud in the sky had moved causing the moonlight to cast a light on those on the land. Jereco's eyes got big as he saw what looked like Madeave men.

294

The Trahe Chronicles

Afraid that he might say something, the water man put his hand over Jereco's mouth again. This slight movement caught the eye of one of the men above. He yelled something and pointed down into the water. The next thing Jereco knew, they were being bombarded with spears. The water people acted quickly. The water man motioned Jereco to take a breath. Jereco knew exactly what was coming next. The water people dragged him under the water, and they were off.

The water people swam as fast as the snake had, but much smoother. They pulled Jereco along and were much more delicate with him. Jereco was brought up to the surface to breathe. But as soon as he took a breath, he was pulled back under to swim again. Jereco knew they were going the wrong way. They had to go back toward his camp, but he never got a chance to tell his rescuers. They swam with Jereco between their bodies and always took him to the surface to breathe. Jereco lost track of time and knew his body needed to get out of the water soon.

Jereco was brought back up to the surface again, and this time they were near what looked like the side of a mountain. "Good," Jereco thought. They were near land again. The water girl motioned Jereco to take a deep breath. "Again?!" he asked in frustration. "I need to go back! Why do we keep swimming?"

But it was no use. She just motioned Jereco to get ready to swim again. He was exhausted and wanted to get out of the water, but his instincts told him to trust these water people. He thought about Chislon and did a silent prayer. He nodded his head to show he was ready for another plunge into the river. He thought he saw the water girl smile, and then they were off and under the water again. This time they swam downward and deeper into the river. It confused Jereco, but he went with the flow. They swam for a long time. The waters were getting darker and Jereco couldn't see where they were going.

Crack!

The same water man who had pulled Jereco under water had struck his fork against something. The fork lit up with a green glow and served as a lantern. Jereco could see that they were swimming into an underwater cavern. As soon as they entered the cavern, they pulled Jereco up for another breath. This time, Jereco sputtered and coughed. He was extremely tired and cold. The water people held him up in the water as Jereco regained some warmth from their body heat. The water girl motioned for him to take another breath. Jereco gave her a look that said, *I can't do it anymore.*

She smiled and held up one finger, gesturing as if to say, *Just one more time.*

Jereco closed his eyes. "God give me strength." Then he nodded to continue.

They swam deeper and farther into the underwater cavern. Just about the time Jereco was ready to give up, they brought him to the surface again. Jereco gasped for breath. "I'm ... I'm done. I'm done." He was done. Totally

Book One: The Chosen Ones

exhausted, he felt his body collapse into the arms of the water people. He felt himself being dragged through the water, and then he was placed on what felt like solid rock.

He is not sure how long he had lain there, but while he did, he felt the water people taking care of him. They placed something over him to keep him warm. He once opened his eyes to see the water girl smiling over him and then wiping his face with something. A while later, he felt someone holding him upright to feed him freshwater. Jereco remembered thinking how cool and sweet the water had tasted. He dozed off and on for a while. Finally, after feeling warmer and rested, he opened his eyes again.

Where am I? he thought. Slowly, the evening's events returned to his thoughts. He rubbed his eyes and face, trying to wake himself up. The first things he saw were stars. It looked like little stars way out in the distance. He heard the soft splashing of water. *Cavern ... cave.* Hadn't they swum into a cave?

He slowly turned his head, taking in his surroundings. He was in a cave. It was quite large. Most of it was submerged in water. What he thought was stars were actually some sort of glittering rock or mineral embedded into the walls of the cavern. There was a soft glow of light, which he realized was coming from the water people various forks, staffs, and swords. The water people seemed to be napping or relaxing in various places around the cavern. He propped himself up a little and noticed what was covering him and keeping him warm. It looked like a blanket of sea grass with some piles of lumpy fur placed at his feet and along his sides. He touched the fur out of curiosity. *Where can you get fur in an underwater cavern?*

"Pardon me!" a voice boomed.

Jereco jumped, snatching his hand back. The fur had a voice. As Jereco's eyes adjusted, he realized that the lumpy furs surrounding him looked like beavers. Jereco, who was becoming more used to Trahe's surprises, regained his composure quite quickly. "No, pardon me!" he said to the beaver. "I didn't know. I am sorry, and thank you for keeping me warm."

"Oh, you're welcome," said the beaver. "It is quite an honor to keep the Water Guardian warm. Are you warm now?"

"Yes, I believe so," Jereco replied.

"We are very glad to be of service." The beaver let out a low whistle. The other beavers snapped to attention, and so did the water people. "The Water Guardian is warm and alive," he announced. Then the beaver turned to Jereco. "May our warmth heal you. May the lights of the Creator guide you. May the wind always be at your back." Then his face got closer to Jereco. "And may the Water Guardian always protect the good and prevail over the evil." The beaver chattered something in beaver talk, and the beavers dove into the water and swam off.

"I didn't even get their names," Jereco muttered.

Splash!

296

The Trahe Chronicles

Jereco was sprayed by some water. It was the water girl who had just popped out of the water. She was holding some sort of grassy basket. She opened it and then motioned Jereco to eat what was inside. It looked like a variety of raw fish. Jereco made a face. "No thank you."

The water girl pouted.

Oh shoot, Jereco thought. *I hurt her feelings.* It was at that moment that his stomach chose to growl. He held his hand to his stomach. He was hungry, and he needed to eat something. So he gave the water girl a small smile and thanked her just before he held his breath and ate the fish. Luckily, the water girl had a wooden bowl of water for him too. He drank all the water right after he ate the fish. At least the water tasted good.

He felt a little better now. Having rested and eaten, his mind started to think more clearly. He needed to get back to his family and friends, but first he needed to find out why he had been taken to this place. The Creator must have had a purpose for this event. He slowly looked around. It looked like this might be a home for the water people. Jereco started to stand up, but he bumped his head on the ceiling. The water girl giggled. She motioned for him to follow her. As she swam through the cavern, he walked along the edge the best he could. At times, he had to get down and crawl on his hands and knees. He came to a place that he had to squirm through on his stomach.

The water girl, looking annoyed, gestured for him to come down in the water.

"No way—I am finally dry and warm." Jereco continued on until he ran into a dead end. There was a small crack that he could peer though, but there no way was he able to squeeze his body through it. Through the crack, he could see the most wonderful scene. It was like another world. It was a huge cavern that had a large lake with a waterfall coming down the opposite wall. And there were water people everywhere. "So this is their home," Jereco said.

He felt a tug on his right ankle. The water girl was gesturing for him to get in the water again. He looked back through the crack and motioned to her, asking if that is where they were going. She nodded.

"Okay then. Here I go," said Jereco as he jumped into the water. It was just a short swim underneath the rock to get to the large cavern on the other side.

It was a magnificent sight. Waterfalls were everywhere. Water people were laughing, eating, and playing. In the middle of the lake was a large flat plateau of green precious stone where there were several older water people. The water girl gestured to Jereco to swim to the plateau. When he reached a large boulder, she screeched something that made everyone stop and look. She motioned Jereco to get out of the water and climb onto the green, glistening plateau. As he did, the water people moved to the side, making a path for him that led to an older male water person.

"Welcome, Water Guardian," said an older water man.

Jereco's mouth dropped. The water man spoke Trahe.

Book One: The Chosen Ones

"You seem surprised."

Before Jereco could answer, the water man said, "I can see why. I see why my cousin Chislon admired you. You are a very humble Evadeam. You do not know what makes you a Water Guardian, and why it is so." The water man paused for Jereco to speak.

"Well, to be honest," said Jereco, "I was surprised that you could speak Trahe." He gestured to the water girl who had led him over. "She doesn't."

The older water man laughed. "Unfortunately, the younger generation does not care to learn the ancient language. However, times are changing. And with your presence, I do hope it sparks interest for the young ones to learn the ancient tongue."

"Chislon is your cousin?" Jereco asked.

"I beg your pardon; I have not introduced myself yet. I am Zephaniah. I am the chosen king of the river water people. Chislon is my cousin, and the great Abijam is my uncle."

"It is nice to meet you," said Jereco. "I did not know that water people lived in freshwater."

"We are the Creator's secret, and for our own safety, we must stay well-hidden from the land people. That is why you have been brought here during the darker hours. The time we rest deep within the mountain is during your daylight hours." Zephaniah bowed his head slightly. "But someday our time will end altogether as foretold by the prophets. Unless..." He looked up into Jereco's eyes. "...our world is kept safe."

All was silent for a moment. Zephaniah was the first to look away as he gazed out to his people. Jereco looked around and noticed all eyes were upon him. Was this his purpose? To somehow make it safe for these people? And from whom? The Madeave? A vision suddenly popped in his head. It was not of this world. It was of a world where he once belonged—a world where freshwater was becoming more scarce. Where freshwater was overrun by humans, boats, homes, and pollution. Did that world once have people like these? People who had perished at the hands of the land people?

"Come!" said Zephaniah.

Zephaniah's voice snapped Jereco out of his thoughts. He shook his head to clear his mind, and he was brought back to this world, where water people still existed. Maybe he could do something to help them.

Zephaniah moved to the end of the flat rock and pointed toward the large waterfall at one end of the cavern. "There you will find what you are seeking." He looked into Jereco's eyes again. "Remember it well. Bury it deep within your mind." He turned back toward the waterfall. "And do not forget these people you leave behind."

A look of confusion came across Jereco's face. "Leave behind? Am I leaving?"

Zephaniah nodded.

"Leaving already?" said Jereco. "I just got here." Once Jereco had entered

The Trahe Chronicles

this cavern, he immediately had wanted to stay. He had missed the water people of the sea and his longing had not subsided.

Zephaniah smiled. "You must. You have a mission. Have you forgotten the friends and family are looking for you?"

Jereco slapped his head with his hand. "They must be worried about me. They probably think the snake killed me." He imagined how upset Brooke and Diana must have been. Brandon was still probably looking for him and may have been getting himself killed in the process. He looked back at the cavern and the river water people. Though he longed to stay, he knew he had to go. He did not know how long his friends and family would look for him before continuing onto Evadeam City. So he shook hands with Zephaniah and said his goodbyes to everyone.

The water girl led him to the waterfall. It was just a brief swim. They continued under the waterfall. The churning of the water was hard to swim through. Jereco was glad for the water girl's help. They finally made it through the falls, and on the other side was another small cave. This one was tall enough for him to stand in, but narrow.

Crack!

The water girl had a staff that she lit against the floor.

"I have to get me one of those," Jereco said.

As if reading his mind, she handed the staff to him. He took it, confused. She pointed to the walls. As he turned and held the light up to it, he noticed something unusual about the wall. It was all coming together now. On the walls of this caves were pictures and markings. These were similar writings that had been on the walls he had found on the Island of the Pegasi.

Pieces to a puzzle, he thought. *Pieces scattered in underwater places.* As the Water Guardian, he had been brought to all these places.

He looked at the water girl, who smiled knowingly. "I still don't know your name," Jereco said.

She screeched something that he couldn't understand or speak. "How about I just call you River Girl?" he replied. "So River Girl, I don't suppose you have a pencil and paper on you?"She just looked confused.

"No, I suppose not," he muttered. "So this is what Zephaniah meant when he said, 'Remember it well.'"

It was a good thing that Jereco did have a great memory. He briefly thought back to his days on Earth. His memory helped him get great school grades. "It is not just about being smart," his grandma used to say. "It is also about studying hard and remembering." He loved his grandma. He wondered how Grandpa was doing now. Grandpa probably was worried about him. *Well, I can't go back until I have all of this memorized,* Jereco thought. As he looked at the wall, he realized there was a lot to remember. He shut his eyes. "Please, Grandma, may your spirit help me to remember now." He opened his eyes and began reading and memorizing the written words.

Jereco rubbed his eyes. He was developing a slight headache.

Book One: The Chosen Ones

"So what happened next?" asked Brandon.

Jereco opened his eyes to see his friends and family looking at him. He glanced around the mountain cavern that he now lay in.

"So what happened after you memorized the carved walls?" repeated Brandon.

Brooke noticed Jereco's hesitation. "Maybe we need to hear the rest of the story tomorrow."

"No. It is okay," said Jereco. "I was just missing the water people." He decided to give them the short version of the story, since he was beginning to feel unwell again. "Zephaniah received news that you had moved on. So after I was done reading the cavern wall markings, the river people took up me the river in hopes of finding your trail. As soon as daylight started to appear, the river people returned home and left me with some beaver friends. The animals of the forest were to bring me back to you." Jereco sadly shook his head. "But it did not turn out that way.

"We were attacked by the Madeave and snakes," continued Jereco. "I thought for sure I was going to die this time. We had too many to fight off. I was making a run for it and was diving back into the river when …" Jereco's voice trailed off. He looked up at Hachmoni. "I thought I would be safer in the water. I thought I could make it back to the river people."

"What happened next, Water Guardian?" said Hachmoni.

Jereco shrugged. "I was swooped into the air, I guess. Something grabbed me just before I hit the river water. Claws—no, talons—talons grabbed me. I can still feel them as they dug into my skin." He wiggled his shoulders and back.

"What was it?" asked Sir Bolivar.

Jereco shrugged. "I am not sure. I couldn't swing around to see it. But I heard it. It roared. And I remember hearing the swoosh of large wings. Larger than pegasus wings. I thought this was it. This was finally my time. I mean, I have already escaped death so many times here on this planet. But I didn't want to die, so I struggled. However, the more I tried to break free, the more the creature hung on tighter."

Jereco put one hand up to his mouth and another to his stomach as memories came flooding back to him. "We flew forever. It was horrible. It was like riding the worst roller coaster ever. It was nothing like riding on a pegasus."

Jereco paused and looked up. "That is why I don't remember much after that. I was overwhelmed by the idea that I was going to die, without seeing any of you again, and the nauseous feeling I had from being on the worst air flight ever."

Jereco looked down at his ankle with the green mark and muttered, "I lost it. I mean I literally got sick. I vomited. I heaved some more, broke out in a sweat, and remembered thinking that I was going to pass out." He looked over at Brandon with tears in his eyes. "That is the last thing I remember."

The Trahe Chronicles

Diana stood up and gave her brother a hug. "It is okay, Jereco. You are alive and you are here with us. Besides, I know what happened to you."

Jereco smiled slightly. "You do?"

"Sure. Isn't it obvious?"

No one responded as Diana looked around at everyone. "The dragon! Uriel's dad. He fulfilled his promise to Brandon."

Brandon's head snapped up. "Oh my gosh! You are right." He stood up. "It had to be. It had to be the dragon. He found you, saved you, and brought you to us."

"But how did he know how to find Jereco and then us?" asked Grandpa.

It was Buster, who replied, "Your friend. He found us through the guidance of your friend. Through the spirit of my grandfather Luke Thunder." Buster and Brandon quickly explained the shadow figure that they saw at the waterfall. The figure who called them to Jereco. Midnight also agreed with the theory as he had felt and seen Luke Thunder's presence too.

"Thank the Creator, and bless Luke Thunder," said Silver Kat.

Grandpa nodded in agreement. "Because of them, we are now all back together, and we have arrived at Evadeam City."

"Well, not everyone," said Brooke. "We still have not found our parents."

"We will. But first we need a good night's sleep," replied Grandpa. "Besides, Jereco needs more rest."

Michael got up and stretched. "I think we all need to go to bed."

Everyone reluctantly agreed, except for Cleo and Skylar, who volunteered to be on night watch.

The next morning, they were eager to start their new search. However, they did not search for the Evadeam parents the next day or the day after, for that evening, the winter storm hit, and it continued for several more weeks.

The stormy days and nights gave time for Jereco to rest and regain his strength. It also gave him time to think about and remember the river people.

Book One: The Chosen Ones

A Day of Peace

When Jereco felt better, he told Hachmoni about the writings he had found in the river cavern walls.

"Do you remember what the writings on the walls had said?" Hachmoni asked.

"I think so," replied Jereco as he touched his bandaged temple.

"Good," said Hachmoni. "Then if you want something to do, how about writing it down for me?"

Jereco was more than eager to feel useful. Hachmoni pulled some parchment paper and writing instruments from one of his bags. That became Jereco's new job. By memory, he transferred the words from the cavern walls.

Brooke smiled as she watched Jereco write down the markings he had found from the cavern walls. Jereco was sitting comfortably by the fire, and he decided he would also write down everything he remembered since they had landed on Trahe. Brooke wondered if Jereco's documentation would someday go down in Trahe's history books.

Brooke's eyes were drawn to the flicker of the fire. Brooke was surprised how warm the mountain home felt, considering it was not like a home back on Earth. Besides the fires, they also kept warm by bundling up in their woolen clothes and blankets that Michael had brought from Bethemek.

Winter was beginning to claim Evadeam Mountain and because of the impending snowstorms, the girls decided to spend their days cleaning and trying to make the mountain home as cozy as possible. Now and then, they would squeal with delight when they found pieces of furniture that were not yet crumbled to pieces. Michael was extremely handy at fixing up the broken wood furniture. They soon had a dining table and chairs.

"I wonder," said Brooke, "if we go through all the rooms and other homes, maybe we will find more furniture."

Michael and Archelaus were more than happy to try to please the girls by finding more furniture, so they volunteered themselves and Brandon to help, to Brandon's dismay.

"It will give us a chance to help Skylar and Methuselah to explore the caverns too," Archelaus told Brandon. "Plus, it gives us something to do while the storms blow outside."

Jereco also wanted to go, but Hachmoni thought it would be best that he stay and rest. Besides, Hachmoni wanted Jereco to continue writing his findings onto paper.

"Hey!" Jereco hollered to the three guys as they were leaving. "If you find any writings on the walls, let me know."

Michael, Archelaus, and Brandon came back with more pieces of furniture.

"There was nothing on the walls, except for very old tapestries," reported

302

Archelaus.

Brooke and Diana were excited with the men's findings, and they were able to put a small sitting area together. They were also able to put beds together for everyone. The beds would bring their bodies off the cold stone floor and would keep them warmer during the night.

"It feels more like a home now," complimented Hachmoni one evening during dinner. They had been living in Evadeam City for weeks. The winter had blanketed Evadeam Mountain with white snow. The Evadeam ancestors and their friends continued spending their wintry days exploring Evadeam City. They were sitting down for a hot dinner meal, sharing the day's findings, when Diana interrupted the conversation.

"All we need now is a Christmas tree," said Diana.

Her comment surprised everyone.

"Christmas tree?" asked Sir Bolivar.

"Do you think we missed Christmas?" asked Diana.

The rest of her family knew they had missed the celebration day, but they were not sure if Diana realized how long they had been gone. When the silence continued, Diana piped up. "I am not a baby! I know we missed it last year." She crossed her arms. "I want to know if we missed it this year."

Archelaus looked at the tent that blocked the cave's entrance. "Didn't you say it snows during the Christmas season on Earth?" he asked.

Diana nodded.

"Then I do not think you missed it," Archelaus said. "I think we truly did get to Evadeam City just in time."

Diana smiled with hope.

"In fact," continued Archelaus, "I think Jereco and Hachmoni can spend the day tomorrow to see exactly what day Christmas day will be this year."

Diana looked at Jereco. "Can you?"

Jereco didn't think he could since he did not have a calendar, a calculator, or a computer; but he refrained from saying that. "Yeah, I am sure Hachmoni and I can figure it out."Hachmoni smiled. "Well, of course, we can. It is the holiest night of them all. Here on Trahe, we also celebrate a holy time. I believe the Creator designs similar incidents throughout the planets of man." He looked over at Archelaus and Michael. "One of your Evadeam ancestors was thought to be the savior of mankind—the Savior of Trahe." Hachmoni looked over at Grandpa. "But our savior was a woman—Princess Skylar."

Michael spoke. "But some do not believe she was the actual savior. There are those who believe that the savior has yet to arrive." Michael turned toward the kids. "They believe the arrival of our savior is the arrival of the Chosen Ones. And here you are."

"Well, I do not feel like a savior," said Brandon, "and I do not think we brought one with us either."

Archelaus turned toward Hachmoni. "So can you figure out the date that we can celebrate this Christmas day?"

Book One: The Chosen Ones

"Yes. In fact, I already know the date."

Diana was so excited, "When?"

Hachmoni rubbed his chin. "It will be exactly thirty days from tomorrow."

Diana jumped up. "Yay! Jereco, Brandon, we are going to have a Christmas this year!"

Everyone, except Brooke, smiled at her.

Brooke was thinking. If it was really thirty days from tomorrow, then it would be Thanksgiving back home. She looked up and saw Grandpa looking at her. She knew he was thinking the same thing. They'd been here for almost a year. They were missing the holidays back home. Would they ever return to celebrate future holiday time with their families?

Holding back tears, Brooke started cleaning up after dinner. She heard Archelaus start to follow her, but Grandpa held him back and said something to him in a quiet voice. Brooke went to bed shortly after that and dreamed about past family holidays.

Brooke slept in the next morning, saying she was not feeling well. It was early afternoon when Archelaus popped his head into Brooke and Diana's tent bedroom. "Hey, are you sleeping?"

Brooke turned over and mumbled, "Not anymore."

Archelaus stepped in to the tent, uninvited. "I heard you are not feeling well."

Brooke just nodded without opening her eyes.

"Well, that is too bad," said Archelaus, "Now I will have to cook this myself."

"You have to be kidding me," Brooke said as she finally looked at him with frustration. "I am sick, and all you care about is if I can cook for you."

She jumped when she saw a huge bird hanging over her. She gasped. "What the—?"

"It is a turkey," Archelaus said proudly.

"I can see that," Brooke replied.

"And I hear that you celebrate something called Thanksgiving on Earth with a turkey."

Brooke's eyebrows gathered together as Archelaus continued. "Skylar and Cleo dug up some wild vegetables in what used to be a garden, I think. Methuselah caught a whole bunch of fish." He frowned. "But I do not have any bread to make something called stuffing."

Brooke had to smile at that. Obviously, Grandpa told him what was really bothering her last night. Everyone was pitching in to try and bring her spirits up. She could either lie there and feel sorry for herself or get up and share a nice dinner with the family she had here on Trahe.

"Okay, you win," said Brooke.

Archelaus grinned. "So does the winner get a kiss?"

Brooke laughed and pushed him away. "No, I have not brushed my teeth

The Trahe Chronicles

this morning." Archelaus laughed. "You mean, this afternoon."

As Archelaus bent down toward Brooke, Diana came running into the tent. "Hey, Brooke you have to see what Michael just brought."

Diana apparently did not notice the awkward moment.

Brooke was flustered. "What?"

"Come see what Michael brought," said Diana. Then she noticed Archelaus standing there. "Why are you holding a dead bird in our tent?"

Archelaus recovered well. "I was trying to motivate Brooke to get up and cook it for us. I think she is feeling better and might be able to manage it. Do you think you can help her?" Diana nodded. "But first, come and see." She ran out of the tent.

Out of curiosity, Archelaus left the tent as well.

Brooke got dressed for the day. When she came out, standing in the far southwest corner of their new home was a pine tree.

Diana was jumping up and down with glee. "Look, Brooke, our very own Christmas tree."

Brooke's eyebrow shot up. She looked at Brandon.

"I already talked to the trees," Brandon reassured everyone, "and this was a pine tree that had been uprooted during the storm. They said it was okay for us to take it."

Archelaus helped Michael get the tree in a handmade stand. When they were all done, everyone stood back.

"Now we just need decorations," said Diana. "But where are we going to get some?"

"Well," said Grandpa, "we will do what I used to do when I was a kid. We made decorations out of anything we could find in nature. Berries, pinecones, bird feathers left on the ground, and whatever else we can find."

"That is a great idea, Grandpa," said Brooke.

He smiled at her, glad to see that her mood had improved.

Brooke, with help from everyone, made their first Thanksgiving dinner on the planet Trahe. They sat around sharing memories of their best Thanksgiving dinners until the late hours of the night. Brooke went to bed in a much better mood than the one she had been in when she woke up that morning.

The following weeks went by fast. During stormy days, they continued to explore Evadeam City, looking for any writings on the walls or evidence of their parents or signs of any other living Evadeam people. Silver Kat also reminded everyone that they needed to stay fit and to be prepared for any unexpected surprises, so they also spent every day exercising and sparring.

Finally, they had a break in the weather, so they ventured out to find Christmas tree decorations and food. Soon Christmas Eve on Trahe was upon them. Diana was so excited that she could barely sleep. But she did, and her dreams were filled with a new vision.

Book One: The Chosen Ones

Diana was flying, flying fast. She was flying through Evadeam City. She was flying toward someone crying. She came into a room with many pools. The pools were steaming. The crying was stronger here. She flew slowly over the pools until she came to one where a little girl was sitting at the edge of the pool. The girl was crying as she looked into the pool. Then she looked up at Diana. She looked like Diana. *Is this me?* Diana thought. The crying stopped, but the girl turned her tear-stained face away and pointed to a cave wall in the darkest part of the room. Diana knew she should go there, but she was too scared.

All of a sudden, something pounced on Diana.

Diana woke up in bed. "Oh, Cleo it is just you."

Purring, the cat had lain on Diana's chest.

"I was just dreaming," Diana murmured. She felt much safer with Cleo sleeping on her. Diana closed her eyes and snuggled into the covers. She felt a draft come through the tent. *It must be another storm*, she thought. There was another draft, stronger than the first. She felt Cleo jump off her. Diana opened her eyes to see Cleo leaving the tent. When the door flap shut, Diana jumped as she saw the same girl in her dream floating above her. Diana sank into the covers.

"Do not be afraid," the ghostly figure said. "I need you. We need you. Come. Come to the pools. The Water Guardian will understand."

Then another shadow appeared beside the spirit. It was Nicolas. "Diana. It is me. Listen. Go to the pools."

"Nicolas?" Diana whispered.

Then the two spirits were gone.

Diana woke up with a start. She looked around and saw Cleo peering over her. "Are you okay?" Cleo asked.

Diana nodded. She must have had a dream in a dream. "Am I still dreaming?" she asked Cleo.

"No," Cleo replied.

"Are you sure?" said Diana.

In response, Cleo licked her face, pawed at her, and started kneading her belly.

"Okay, okay," Diana said. Feeling better, she lay there and tried to not think of the dream. Instead, she tried to think about the next day—Christmas Day. But it was hard not to think about Nicolas, and Diana wondered if he had found his way to Evadeam City.

While Diana had been dreaming, Brooke had stepped outside for some fresh air. It was a crisp, cool, and clear night. The white snow was gently falling over the mountain and down to the valley below. Brooke looked at the sky and could still make out the bright stars. She took a deep breath of fresh air and closed her eyes. It felt holy. This night felt holy and special. She opened her eyes again. *Or maybe I just want it to feel holy*, she thought.

306

The Trahe Chronicles

One year. They had been away from planet Earth for a year already. At this very moment, she really, really missed her home. She missed her dad, her friends, and even her school. She closed her eyes again, and a tear trickled down her cheek as she tried to remember what her dad looked like. It almost felt like her life on Earth was a dream. This very moment—this very time and place on Trahe—felt more real. It seemed like they had always belonged here, yet she had a deep feeling of missing her home in Michigan. "Michigan," she whispered.

"Cannot sleep?" a voice quietly asked.

She jumped. "Don't do that! You scared me."

Archelaus innocently shrugged. "What? Hasn't Silver Kat's training taught you to hear even the slightest footstep in the soft, fallen snow?"

Brooke said nothing as she looked away brushing her tears. She felt his hand touch her shoulder, and they just stood there in silence.

A shooting star flew across the sky.

"It is a sign," said Archelaus.

Brooke just nodded. They stood there, watching the sky, until they agreed it was time to go inside.

"Brooke, Brooke, get up," came an anxious voice.

Brooke moaned, turned over, and pulled the blankets over her head.

"Come on," said a gleeful voice. "It is Christmas morning."

Brooke peeked out of the blankets and saw Diana hovering over her. Brooke looked around. "It is not even light outside yet." She proceeded to go back under the covers. "I just got to bed."

"But Santa came. Come on. Come see what he brought us."

As Diana ran outside their bedroom into the other room of the cave, Brooke thought, *Santa?* Curiosity got the best of Brooke, and she slowly made it to the living room area of their current home. She noticed that everyone else was also slowly coming to the living room. Diana had apparently made her morning wake-up rounds.

Brooke was looking at some packages under their Christmas tree when Archelaus thrust a cup of coffee into her hands. "Good morning," he said with a big smile.

Brooke looked at him suspiciously. "You are too cheery this morning."

His smile grew wider. "I have good reason to be happy. It looks like the Earth's Santa Claus made it to Trahe." He gestured toward the tree.

Brooke's right eyebrow shot up, and the thought that she was about to voice was interrupted by Diana insisting that everyone get ready to open up gifts. For the past month, everyone had been busy making Christmas gifts. They had decided during their Thanksgiving feast to draw names. They had agreed to make or find a Christmas gift. Living in an abandoned ancient mountain city with no stores nearby forced everyone to be creative with gift giving.Diana was the first to unwrap her handmade gift. It was a new outfit

Book One: The Chosen Ones

for her doll. The outfit was made out of scraps of worn clothing. Diana was delighted and raced right away to get her doll. This gave everyone a break to fill up with morning refreshments.

Brandon was next to eagerly open up a gift. It was a walking stick. Hachmoni demonstrated how the walking stick could also be used as a weapon. After the demonstration, Brandon noticed the engravings on the stick, which were of a willow tree and the words *from Willow* scratched into the bark. With misty eyes, Brandon rubbed his hand over the words and said a quiet thank you.

The unwrapping continued. Jereco received a necklace made out of a leather strap and a small green stone. Engraved on the stone was the symbol that matched the one on his right ankle from the water people.

Brooke received handmade handkerchiefs, which Diana proclaimed Brooke needed with all the crying she had done lately.

Hachmoni also received a new walking stick that had the words *The Wise Man* engraved on it. Hachmoni laughed and looked at Brandon. "Two wise men think alike."

Brandon just grinned ear to ear.

Silver Kat was very grateful for a new leather pouch that could carry his natural herbal medicine ingredients.

Sir Bolivar was puzzled at first by his gifts until it was explained to him that they were paw coverings to keep his paws warm in the upcoming wintry months. The girls helped him put them on.

Skylar's gift was not in the room as it was a huge piece of raw meat made from a kill earlier that morning. Skylar licked her chops and then excused herself to go to another room.

Then, there was Michael. He had tears in his eyes after he un-wrapped his gift. When he did not say anything, Jereco spoke quietly. "I saw the picture that you keep folded in your pocket, so I drew the picture on a new piece of paper. It is a Christmas tree ornament. You can hang it on the tree, and during the other seasons, you can hang it wherever your heart desires."

Michael did not look up as he whispered, "Thank you." He hung the ornament on the tree and stared at it in silence for a while. The ornament was a sketch of his deceased wife and baby boy. No one dared say anything. He slowly walked out of the room, and as he did so, the ornament slightly swayed.

"It was a touching gift," Brooke quietly told Jereco. Everyone else agreed, but Jereco wondered if he had made a mistake.

Archelaus tactfully changed the subject. "What is it that you Earthlings say?" He clasped his hands. "Oh yes, save the best for last." He earnestly un-wrapped his gift to find parchment paper inside. As he unrolled the parchment, his eyebrows came together in thought. "A map?"

Hachmoni nodded and spread out the map. "This is where your brother was last known to be." Hachmoni pointed to another part of the map. "And

308

The Trahe Chronicles

this is where I had brought your sister. It will soon be time for you to find your siblings, Archelaus."

Archelaus stood up and gave Hachmoni a hug. "Thank you." He knew that this knowledge could put his siblings in more danger.

Meanwhile, Michael had come back and was thanking Jereco once again for the gift. He assured him that he would treasure it which made Jereco feel a little better.

Diana watched the adults as they continued to be mushy. Finally, she reminded them about the gifts still under the tree from Santa Claus.

"Santa Claus?" asked Brandon.

Archelaus gladly volunteered to hand out the rest of the gifts. Everyone received new winter clothes. The men received new weapons, sharpening stones, and weapon cases. Diana also received a new doll.

As everyone was looking at his gifts, Archelaus pulled Brooke aside. He handed her a small box. Brooke opened it carefully and found a gold necklace with a small golden heart-shaped pendant on it. She touched it. "It's beautiful. Thank you." She asked if he would put it on.

Diana walked up to Brooke and noticed her necklace. "Did you get that from Santa?" she asked. Before Brooke had a chance to answer, a loud roar came from outside the cavern entrance. There was a pause, and then weapons were drawn. Everyone ran toward the entrance, only to be greeted by Methuselah.

Methuselah left them days ago when they had a break in the weather. He had now returned, followed by two small black bears.

"Arcturus's cubs!" Silver Kat exclaimed.

Hachmoni nodded in agreement. "And they look almost frozen."

They noticed that the bears had icicles hanging from their bodies.

Methuselah growled. "Another storm is coming."

Skylar walked up to the bears. "Follow me." Then she looked at the others. "Everyone follow me." No one questioned Skylar. The men grabbed their weapons and torches. Skylar led them through corridors that they had not yet explored.

"How did we miss these?" asked Jereco.

Brooke shrugged. "I don't know, but I wish I would have changed first."

Jereco nodded in agreement as most of them were still in their sleeping garments. Their sleeping garments were warm, but their shoes were soft. The corridors were a little rugged and cool. The corridors had not been used in a while and were filled with cobwebs.

Just about the time Brooke was thinking about asking Skylar where they were going, they came into a large, steamy cavern. She blinked her eyes to see, and as if on cue, Hachmoni lit torches that lined the walls. Slowly, the scenery came alive in front of their eyes.

Brooke gasped as she saw pools and streams of steamy water. The bears were greeted by their mother Arcturus. After their joyous reunion, Arcturus

Book One: The Chosen Ones

instructed her cubs to climb into the pools to thaw their bodies. It did not take long for them to warm up since they already had thick fur and skin.

As if reading Brooke's mind, Archelaus said, "It's a bathing room. I have not seen one of these in years. At least, not one that is this large and grand."

Skylar and Silver Kat walked up to the girls. "Merry Christmas." Silver Kat turned to Archelaus. "As you would put it, we saved the best for last."

Grandpa cheered, "More of our friends have been found. We now have luxuries of a hot bath. Splendid! I get first dibs."

That led into an argument between the girls about who would get to take a bath first, since there was no privacy, and they would have to take turns. Skylar and Cleo volunteered to watch over the girls as they took their baths.

A whistle was blown, and everyone stopped talking. They turned their heads toward Jereco. Jereco had a torch and was walking along the round wall that encircled the bathing room.

Once Jereco had everyone's attention, he shined his torch toward the wall. "I think we just found the last inscriptions we have been seeking."

"Whoa!" Brandon exclaimed as he looked at the wall.

Everyone turned and looked at the walls, which were filled with writings and pictures.

They all knew what this meant. They may have finally found the writings that would lead them to the end of their quest.

"Merry Christmas," whispered Brooke.

310

The Trahe Chronicles

The Gray Protector

Christmas day was coming to an end. Brandon tried to salvage what was left of the holiday. He wanted to make Christmas on the planet Trahe as close to the times he had celebrated back on their farm. They missed their parents and talked about Christmas past. They wondered where their parents might be—if they were alive. The subject turned to discussing the writings on the cavern walls. Jereco, Hachmoni and Silver Kat had translated a lot of Evadeam history, but they had found nothing that would help find the Evadeam children's parents.

Almost a month passed, and as far as Brandon was concerned, nothing more had been accomplished, except a lot of discussions. Winter had blown in snowy storms, and the group was confined to the walls of Evadeam City. It was decided no action would be taken until the storms passed. They would wait until spring when the passageways outside of Evadeam Mountain would be open.

The bears took this opportunity to hibernate deep within the mountain caverns. "We will return when winter thaws," said Methuselah as he said goodbyes. He growled something low to Hachmoni and Skylar before heading off.

"Don't you hibernate?" Brandon asked Skylar.

She shook her head and said something about standing guard over the Evadeam family.

Brandon thought that she couldn't be comfortable in this cold mountain. He could not imagine this was anything like her natural habitat. Then again, her coat was white and blended well with the snow. Skylar reassured him that her tiger breed was native to cold climates.

Brandon was soon tired of being inside the city. He ventured outside the mountain walls as much as possible when the storms dissipated. One winter sunny morning, Brandon talked Silver Kat into letting him go into the woods. Brandon wanted to find some fallen logs that he could use to make snow toboggans. Silver Kat agreed it was time for the children to have some winter fun.

The forest had turned into a winter wonderland. The forest floor was covered with deep snow, which, on occasion, was broken up by the tracks of forest creatures. Tree branches were covered in white snow and glistening icicles.

Brandon and Silver Kat took a break on a fallen log. They ate a snack packed by Diana. They were enjoying the silence and were quietly admiring the wintry forest when they both heard a twig snap. They jumped up with weapons in hand. Silver Kat pointed to a faraway tree. Brandon almost missed seeing it. Standing very still next to a huge pine tree was a very big deer. Brandon counted at least twelve points on the buck's antlers. With only the slight noise of their breaths in the air, the men stood still as they watched

Book One: The Chosen Ones

the buck.

Whoosh!

The sound broke the silence. Brandon recognized the sound. A flying arrow. The arrow struck a pine tree.

Silver Kat motioned him to crouch low to the ground as the huge buck broke into a run. Brandon's and Silver Kat's gaze roamed the area, looking for the owner of the arrow. Suddenly, there he was. A man covered in buckskins and fur was quickly, but silently running after the buck. He hardly paused when he ran past the tree and pulled out his arrow that had missed the buck.

Brandon instantly knew that this man was an experienced hunter. There could be more of his kind. Brandon scanned the forest quickly. He looked over at Silver Kat who motioned to him that there was only the one man and that they should follow him. Brandon was not sure if this was a wise decision, yet he wondered who this other being living in Evadeam Mountain was.

They quickly and quietly followed the man, who was obviously tracking the buck. Brandon was just thinking that there was no way they would catch up with the buck on foot. But they came across it at the river. Brandon shook his head, thinking how stupid this deer was. It should have been far away by now. At that moment, the buck's head popped up out of the river and seemed to look straight at Brandon. The buck walked slowly and steadily toward a large oak tree. He rubbed his antlers against the tree trunk.

"What is he doing?" whispered Brandon. Didn't he know this would be the perfect opportunity to be shot?

Again, the buck stopped and seemed to look right at Brandon.

I wonder, Brandon thought. He whispered, "Do you speak the Trahe language?" The buck seemed to answer by nodding his head. Brandon looked over at Silver Kat, who had a look of surprise on his face. Not many of the deer family spoke Trahe. The Creator had provided deer as a source of meat for other creatures.

Brandon's head snapped around when he heard the familiar whooshing sound again. The buck was no longer standing next to the oak tree, but an arrow now stuck out of the tree.

The chase began again. When the stranger was out of hearing range, Brandon whispered to Silver Kat, "I don't get it. This buck is faster than any of us. Why isn't he just running away? It is almost like he is enjoying the chase or playing a game."

"Or leading us somewhere," Silver Kat pointed out.

He pointed up the river and Brandon realized what Silver Kat was thinking. They were almost back at the entrance of Evadeam City.

Why would a Trahe-speaking deer lead this stranger to their hidden city? Brandon decided not to find out. They had to stop the stranger before he discovered their winter hideaway. Silver Kat must have been thinking the same thing, because he decided to shoot an arrow at the stranger. The arrow

312

landed on a small white birch tree just in front of the man. The man whipped around with surprise. Silver Kat quickly hid among the trees and made his way toward the stranger from behind. The man was already armed with a large knife in hand.

Brandon was debating what his move should be when he felt a chill go up his back. "Darn!" he whispered. He had concentrated so much on this man in front of him that he forgot to keep his eyes out for anyone else. He slowly reached for his knife when he heard a low growl. Brandon rolled over just in time to see a white wolf jumping onto him.

One of the wolf's front paws landed on his hand that was holding the knife while the other paw landed right on Brandon's chest. Brandon used his free arm and went for the wolf's throat, pushing the wolf's head as far back as possible. Brandon felt lucky that the full weight of the wolf hadn't landed on his chest; his ribs would have been broken. Brandon was trying to speak, but he could barely breathe, let alone ask this wolf if he spoke Trahe.

Thump!

A pile of snow had fallen from a tree branch above and landed right on the wolf's head. The wolf growled and impatiently shook it off.

Thump!

This time a tree branch had fallen on his head. The wolf whimpered, and Brandon took the opportunity to throw the wolf off of him. Brandon quickly jumped to his feet with knife in hand. The wolf also reacted quickly and was about to attack Brandon when a larger tree branch fell right between them. Brandon knew that this was no coincidence. The trees were helping him.

Brandon thanked the trees in the Trahe language, which caught the wolf's attention. In a low growl, the wolf asked, "You speak Trahe?"

Brandon said that he did and asked why the wolf was attacking him.

The wolf didn't answer. He let out a few barks, which were answered by other barks that echoed in the woods.

"There are more of you?" asked Brandon.

Again, the wolf did not answer Brandon. He continued to bark at the other wolves in his own language. Brandon was now wondering what had happened to Silver Kat, but he did not dare turn his back to the wolf to find out.

Brandon decided to take another approach. In the language of Trahe, he said, "I am the Forest Friend. I mean you no harm."

The trees above rustled and dropped more snow on the wolf.

The wolf growled with irritation. "The forest speaks of you. I will not harm you." His eyes looked into Brandon's eyes.

Brandon swore he saw hunger in those eyes and thought it was wise to leave before the wolf changed his mind. Brandon nodded and backed up slowly. As he did so, a gray wolf came out from behind the trees. Then a black wolf revealed herself. And then another and another. Soon, Brandon was surrounded by a pack of wolves. *Where is Silver Kat?* thought Brandon.

Book One: The Chosen Ones

Silver Kat was nearby and had approached the man. The man was wearing fur, which made Silver Kat's skin crawl. Silver Kat asked the man who he was and why he dared to hunt a speaking Trahe animal. The man answered by lunging at Silver Kat with his knife. Silver Kat quickly stepped out of the way and tried talking to the man again. This time he looked into the man's eyes, trying to read his thoughts. Once again the man did not answer. He tried to fight instead.

Silver Kat decided to honor the man's request. Silver Kat was much quicker and smoother. He decided to wear down his opponent before delivering the final blow. He then heard the sound of barking wolves. He noticed the slight smile on the man's face. *So this man knows these wolves.* Silver Kat decided it was time to put the man down before a pack of wolves showed up. Silver Kat quickly disarmed the man and had him on the ground before the man realized what had happened.

"Who are you?" asked Silver Kat as his weight kept the man down on the snow-covered ground. "One who travels with a pack of wolves? You dare hunt Trahe-speaking animals on Evadeam Mountain?"

Silver Kat noticed a flicker of surprise come across the man's face. The pounding of hooves on the ground made both of them look up. Standing nearby was the huge buck that the man had been hunting. The buck bowed his head low, turned, and walked back into the forest, never to be seen again.

Silver Kat looked down at the man. "The buck is the shadow of the forest. He brought you to us. It must be the Creator's desire." Silver Kat slowly got up, put his knife in his sheath, and offered his hand to the stranger.

The man looked warily at Silver Kat, debating whether he should trust him or take this opportunity to attack Silver Kat. As if reading his mind, Silver Kat pointed out that the man would lose in another fight, and he would also lose his chance to find what he was seeking. The man decided to take the offer and let Silver Kat pull him up. As he stood, a pack of wolves escorting yet another man came their way.

Silver Kat and the leader of the wolf pack, a white wolf, acknowledged each other with a nod of heads. The white wolf turned to the man dressed in fur. "The forest has revealed what you seek."

Brandon stepped forward. "I am the Forest Friend. The Creator has guided you here to our home." Brandon gestured at his surroundings. "To Evadeam Mountain."

The stranger looked around as if he had just noticed his true surroundings for the first time.

Back at Evadeam City, Brooke and Diana had just finished preparing a lunch.

"So what is this called again?" asked Jereco as he spooned a dish from a large black pot.

The Trahe Chronicles

"A yummy surprise!" said a proud Diana, who had helped make it.

"So leftover stew?" mumbled Jereco.

Brooke elbowed Jereco in the ribs and gave him a dirty look.

"What?" he innocently asked.

"I think the meal tastes fantastic, Diana," Michael declared in between bites. "Don't you, Archelaus?"

Archelaus nodded and started to comment but choked instead when Michael hit him on the back.

"Ladies, the yummy surprise stew is indeed tasty," commented Hachmoni. He was just about to take his next bite when he heard Skylar roar near the cavern entrance. He dropped his spoon and jumped up. Skylar and Cleo also jumped up and flew over the table.

Diana watched as her yummy surprise meal spilled on the table and floor. Everyone was up in arms and approaching the front cavern entrance, except Brooke and Diana. Brooke grabbed Diana and put her behind her. Brooke was armed with a knife and in attack mode.

"What is going on?" Diana whispered.

"I do not know," Brooke responded as she pushed Diana farther back inside the cavern. Instinct took over, and the girls quickly and quietly gathered other weapons.

"The other entrance," Diana whispered as she pointed toward the entrance that led into the interior of Evadeam City.

Brooke knew that Diana had a special gift—an instinct stronger than hers. Brook squinted as she looked toward the entrance. There. She saw it—a shadow. She scolded herself. The lazy winter months had brought her guard down. They would have the best luck if they went back toward the outside cavern entrance, where the others had gone. Brooke motioned Diana to follow her. As soon as they stepped toward the other entrance, the shadow grew larger and lunged toward them, growling.

The shadowed figure landed in front of them, cutting off their path to the front entrance. Diana peered from behind Brooke. Diana was now making eye contact with the largest wolf she had ever seen. His fur had a mixture of dark gray and white. He continued to growl and bared his large canine teeth.

Brooke waved her knife at the wolf. "Do you speak the Trahe language?"

The wolf growled back. "Who is it that dares to threaten a member of the gray wolf pack?"

"The Protector of the Evadeam people," Brooke replied as she held her ground.

The wolf paused for a moment.

"Liar!" he growled as he stepped toward Brooke.

"I am so tired of being called a liar," Brooke declared. She lunged at the wolf with her knife. But something pushed Brooke to the side and into Diana. The two girls fell to the ground.

"Sir Bolivar!" Diana exclaimed.

315

Book One: The Chosen Ones

Brooke looked up to see Sir Bolivar, their overgrown mongoose friend, fighting with the wolf.

Sir Bolivar tossed the wolf toward the cavern wall. The wolf quickly shook the attack off and was heading back toward Sir Bolivar when they both heard a large bark.

"Enough!" Hachmoni said.

Everyone turned to see Hachmoni and Archelaus standing next to a large white wolf and a smaller black wolf. Slowly, more of the gray wolf pack came in.

"You need to keep your pack in line," Sir Bolivar said to the white wolf. "Teach them to respect the Protector of the Chosen Ones!"

The gray wolf responded, "Liar! She is not the Protector of the Evadeam tribe. He is!" He nodded toward a man who was now standing behind the large white wolf, arm in arm with Archelaus.

Sir Bolivar, Brooke, and Diana studied the young, dark-haired man. Brooke thought he resembled Archelaus in many ways. Before she had a chance to ask who he was, Sir Bolivar barked out, "Adamah!"

"Adamah," Brooke whispered. Archelaus nodded in acknowledgement. It was Archelaus's missing younger brother. She could not believe it.

Archelaus stepped forward. "Adamah, I would like you to meet Brooke, the other Protector of the Evadeam tribe. And this is Diana, the Vision Keeper."

Adamah walked forward, bowed and took their hands. "It is my honor. I have been looking a long time for you." He helped both girls get up off the floor.

Adamah looked at the gray wolf. "It looks like you may have met your match Gray Protector."

Brooke looked over at the large gray wolf and could see why he was named the Gray Protector. He must be the wolf who protected the pack. The white wolf was the leader. Gray Protector looked at Brooke with disdain. Brooke knew that she would have to watch her back when it came to this wolf.

Adamah made the rest of the introductions, including Silver Fang, the white wolf leader. "How did you come across Evadeam Mountain?" asked Jereco.

Adamah explained that he travelled with a small group of people that broke off from their village. Their village was attacked many years ago. Hachmoni had led their group to a safe haven at another faraway mountain, but their safe haven was recently discovered by Madeave tribe members. The Madeave had attacked their new village. "Those of us who survived have been traveling ever since," explained Adamah. "We do not stay in one place long. One evening, the gray wolf pack came across our tribe. They said the Creator had asked the pack to lead the Evadeam people to a new safe place. We have been following them ever since."

316

"So why did we find you alone with the pack?" asked Brandon. "Where is the rest of your tribe?"

Adamah did not answer.

Archelaus looked at his younger brother. "Why are you the one hunting with the pack? Why are you not back with the tribe protecting them? You are royal Evadeam blood."

Adamah looked up at his older brother. "There is no single leader anymore, Archelaus. We all pick the duty that is right for us. Mine was selected by Silver Fang. Silver Fang sought me out as the hunter for the tribe."

Archelaus was about to say something when Adamah held up his hand. "We found it was best to send only a few out to hunt food. The pack and I can move faster and get better results. The women and children have to be protected by the rest of the men."

Archelaus was about to say something again, but he was interrupted by Diana. "You have children traveling with you?" she said.

Adamah looked over and smiled at Diana. "Yes, little one. We have children and women." He looked around their cavern home. "They would be very happy to call a place like this home."

Diana clasped her hands and squealed with delight. "Then bring them here right away."

Michael, who was just as shocked as everyone else by finding Adamah, said, "Diana is right. The buck obviously led you here to Evadeam City. The Evadeam tribe should be brought back home."

Everyone nodded in agreement, and soon talk was under way about how to go about retrieving Adamah's small band of people. Grandpa thought it was risky to venture too far away from Evadeam City during the middle of the winter months. But Adamah had no intention of staying within the safe haven of Evadeam Mountain until spring. He, after all, was on a hunt for food that was needed by his people. Plus, the tribe would keep moving if he did not get back to them soon. "They are constantly trying to avoid being found by the Madeave," Adamah explained. He did not want to risk losing track of them.

So it was decided that Silver Kat, Archelaus, Michael, Hachmoni and Adamah would fly back to the tribe on the pegasi. The gray wolf pack would follow below on foot. They were fast runners in the snow.

Grandpa, the Evadeam children, Sir Bolivar, and Skylar would stay behind at Evadeam City. Midnight also told Buster that he should stay behind. When Buster started to protest, Hachmoni and Midnight took Buster, Jereco, and Brandon aside. "If something happens and an emergency arises at the cavern," said Midnight, "we will need you to be available to fly to us to let us know."

Hachmoni added, "Jereco and Brandon, you two, along with your Grandpa, will be the men in charge now. Stand guard. Keep a night watch at

317

Book One: The Chosen Ones

all times. If anything unusual arises, send word through Buster immediately."

After Hachmoni and Midnight left to prepare for travel, Jereco confessed he was suspicious about Adamah's sudden appearance at Evadeam Mountain. It was all going too smoothly. "If it was really this simple," said Jereco, "then why are we even here, right?"

Brandon thought about it. "Buster and I will go see if the trees can tell me anything."

Brandon did not hear anything unusual. In fact, the trees seemed quiet—maybe too quiet.

"Or peaceful," Buster suggested. He shook his mane. "Brrr. It is cold out here though, I am going back inside." As Buster walked back into Evadeam City, he admitted that he did not mind staying behind. The thought of flying through the mountains in the middle of winter was not appealing. As Buster looked up at the other pegasi who were discussing their upcoming trip, he realized he might miss the pegasi though. It had been hard to accept the death of his grandfather Luke Thunder, and being around his dad and the other pegasi helped with the loss.

Later that evening, everyone ate dinner and relaxed for the night. Jereco decided to step outside. He was quietly looking over the balcony and staring down into the Evadeam Lake when he heard footsteps come from behind. Jereco turned to see Hachmoni approaching.

Hachmoni smiled. "Your ears have improved."

Jereco just nodded.

Hachmoni studied Jereco's facial expression. "What is it that bothers you, Water Guardian?"

Jereco knew he could not hide anything from Hachmoni. He looked at the nighttime landscape. "It is too easy," he simply replied. When Hachmoni did not respond, he continued. "Something doesn't feel right. It's too easy for Adamah and the gray wolf pack to have come here. If everything were that simple in the first place, then why do we have to be here? Why the writings on the cavern walls?" Jereco looked up at Hachmoni's face.

Hachmoni did not respond right away, but Jereco could tell by his facial expression that he was thinking the same thing.

Hachmoni simply nodded and said, "You have a good point. We all need to be on high alert. This also means we need to get plenty of sleep."

Jereco shook his head. "I can't sleep. I will take the first watch."

Much to his surprise, Hachmoni did not argue and let Jereco be the first night guard. That somehow made Jereco uneasy. If Hachmoni wanted more guards posted, then he definitely knew something was wrong.

The time for them to adjust to the idea of the group's departure was brief. The party got ready to leave early the following morning before daybreak. Brooke and Diana were particularly sad to see them go. They said their goodbyes with tears in their eyes. Archelaus took Brooke's hand and led her

The Trahe Chronicles

down to the bathing pools for a private goodbye.

"We shall not be long," Archelaus tried to reassure Brooke. He caressed her face with his hand. "I will miss you. Be safe and send word immediately if you need us."

Brooke just nodded. She was too choked up for words. "Brooke," she heard Archelaus whisper as his head came down to kiss her.

It was an innocent and nice kiss. She flung her arms around Archelaus's neck and cried, "Please be careful and come back soon."

He held her and reassured her for a long time. Their embrace was finally broken by a subtle cough from Cleo.

"It is time," said Cleo.

As they walked back, Brooke held Cleo close. She petted Cleo like she would any household cat, forgetting for a moment that Cleo was more than just a cat. Cleo did not seem to mind, knowing that Brooke needed some comfort at the moment.

Many hours later after the sun had set; Skylar patrolled the interior walls of Evadeam City. Large, thick white paws softly and quietly hit the mountain rock floor. These paws could kill a man in an instant. Ironically, these paws protected man on this planet called Trahe. She had been told distant tiger breeds ate men for lunch. They were not allies.

The enormous white tiger paused for a moment as she felt a chill run through the passageway. Spirits—she could feel them. She needed to return to her man tribe. She picked up her pace and thought of the Vision Keeper, the Chosen One who could see ghosts.

Skylar found the Evadeam family huddled around the fire in their cave. "What is wrong?"

Brandon was surprised by Skylar's question, "Nothing—why?"

"Nothing?" asked Grandpa.

Brandon looked down and poked at the fire.

"Where is the Vision Keeper?" asked Skylar.

Jereco noticed Skylar had used the chosen name and not Diana. "She is in bed. She had a rough night. She was missing home."

When Skylar gave Jereco a confused look, he explained, "Home, as in planet Earth. So our sympathetic brother here, the one you call the Forest Friend, decided to inform her that we are never going back to Earth. Evadeam Mountain is our home now."

Skylar turned to Brandon. "And how did the Vision Keeper accept the news?"

Brandon proceeded to push the stick deeper into the fire. "Not very well. I got yelled at a lot."

Skylar nodded and started to turn when Grandpa asked, "Is something wrong? You asked us what was wrong as if you were expecting something."

Skylar answered with a question, "Is Cleo with the Vision Keeper?"

319

Book One: The Chosen Ones

Grandpa's eyebrow shot up. "Yes. Why?"

"Then they will be fine." She turned back to the fire and lay down. "I will stand guard tonight. There is a chill in the air—the chill of a spirit."

"A good spirit? Or a bad one?" asked Brandon.

"We shall see," the white tiger responded.

"Great. I better go warn Buster. He hates ghosts."

Jereco watched Brandon walk away and decided to check in on Diana. He would be able to tell by looking at her if she was being visited by a bad spirit. He peered behind the curtain and saw the two of them sleeping soundly. Diana and Cleo. No signs of ghosts. Bad or good. He smiled as he remembered that it was not too long ago that his biggest concern was running to her bedroom to calm her down after an epileptic seizure. Now he was running to her side to fend off spirits or worse. He sighed and let the tent curtain fall.

He said a little prayer to the Creator. "May the Creator's light surround us. May the Creator's power protect us. May the Creator's love enfold around us. May the Creator watch over us. May we find our parents, and may we someday return to planet Earth."

Jereco started to turn when he heard Diana's voice. "He is here," she said. "Who?"

"The ghost of Nicolas. He says that the Evadeam tribe is no longer lost. The past has brought the future. Now all will be one." Diana's eyes slowly closed, and she fell back to sleep.

Cleo looked up at Jereco. "Watch over her while I go speak to Skylar and find Brooke."

Jereco simply nodded and then sat down on the bed to watch over his baby sister, the Vision Keeper.

Brooke was standing on the balcony. She crossed her arms and tugged on her winter coat as she remembered watching her friends fly away into the rising sun this morning. She was happy for Archelaus. Happy that he had found a family member. Happy that some of his people were coming home to Evadeam City. But at the same, she felt sad that she had not yet found her father. As she continued to stare out into the mountain darkness, she wondered if her dad had watched a morning sun. A setting sun? A sun at all?

"Dad, where are you?" she whispered in the wintry wind.

The Trahe Chronicles

The Beginning

On the planet Trahe, miles away from Evadeam Mountain was a woman. A woman named Maria. She was deep in thought as she felt the man with the cowboy hat watching her. She could feel his eyes upon her. She let her long, curly, light brown hair fall forward to cover her hazel eyes. Her eyes might show the terrible feelings she had against that man. Feelings of hate—pure hate for the man who killed her brother. She paused for a moment, prayed to the Creator for strength, and continued her duties.

She went through the motions of clearing the dishes off the table that belonged to another man who called himself Master. Master, indeed! Some day she would be free again. Free from this new life as a slave.

She slightly shook her head to clear her thoughts and concentrate. She listened to the news that the cowboy man was relaying to the master. As she listened, she tried very hard to contain her excitement. The mention of her hometown had made her flush.

Maria almost dropped a dish as the master yelled at the cowboy for his ignorance. "Fool! You had the Chosen Ones in your grasp and let them get away!"

"But I did not know who they were, and they had help," argued the cowboy. "There were many of them, including a ghost tiger."

Maria had to give the cowboy credit for standing up to the master. The master turned and asked for detailed descriptions of every creature that traveled with the Chosen Ones. He ordered the cowboy to find and capture the Chosen Ones. "And I would take extra precautions with the smaller cat," he advised.

The cowboy was excused from the dining room as Maria finished her job. She was off to deliver the dishes to the kitchen area. She made her normal stop at the workshop that was adjacent to the master's living quarters.

In the workshop, she calmly cleared more dishes. She was happy to see Larry working there. He would be glad to hear about the recent developments she had overheard.

Larry watched Maria as she cleaned the workshop. She was a slave like himself. She worked in the master's quarters, so she was able to gather information there. Any information could help with their escape. *Someday, they will escape,* he thought. He turned his attention to the spaceship in front of him.

It seemed like just yesterday that their ship had landed on this planet. They crash-landed right into enemy hands. They were captured and forced to repair their own spaceship for the alien master they called Tartak.

Tartak, the Prince of Darkness. Larry had heard of Tartak through Cleo. Luckily, Tartak did not know Larry and his family. Tartak was smart though. He knew that Larry was not of this world, and surprisingly, Tartak was good to Larry and his brother. Tartak needed them, and that was good. As long as

321

Book One: The Chosen Ones

they were essential to Tartak's plan, they would stay alive. Luckily, Larry had the skills to fulfill Tartak's requests and execute his own tasks at the same time. Maria was assisting with that mission.

As Maria cleared the dishes at Larry's workstation, she whispered what she had just learned. Larry was grateful that this barren prison was not equipped with monitors. The only things that monitored the slaves were Tartak's guards who were too lenient as far as Larry was concerned. He did a silent prayer, thankful for the guards' lack of experience.

"Wait," whispered Larry. "What did you just say, Maria?" His thoughts had wandered, and he must have misunderstood her. She repeated the information that she overheard from Tartak and the cowboy's conversation. The Chosen Ones have landed. Larry looked up at her with surprise and concern. He started to sweat. He closed his eyes and took a deep breath. He had to get under control. He felt Maria's hand squeeze his for a moment. A reassuring gesture—one that lasted only a moment. She continued to pick up the dishes by his side.

Before she left, he quickly spoke in a low tone. "Tartak will be very happy that his ship will be ready soon." He paused. "*We* will be ready soon." Larry turned his head back to his work desk. His eyebrows came together in deep thought.

Maria had just told him that one of Tartak's men had run into a band of Evadeam members south of here. Larry was guessing by the descriptions that one of them was Cleo, the Guide. Another was likely his father. He was not surprised that Cleo and his dad had come to Trahe on a rescue operation. However, Larry was concerned by one of the other people reported in the traveling party. A young lady described as having dark flowing hair and a strong fist. An Earth woman deemed as the Protector.

Larry cringed. He prayed and hoped that this young lady, this Protector, was not who he thought she was. "Oh Creator, please let my intuition be wrong. Please do not let her be my daughter, my Brooke."

It was late in the evening when Maria was locked into her room. She sighed. Her room was a cell. It was better than most of the slave quarters, but she yearned to be free again. Free to go home. Free to find her people. She listened. All was quiet. It usually was during this time of the evening. *It is time,* she thought.

She reached over to the candleholder that sat upon the small table next to her bed. She moved the candleholder. A piece of wood in the table slid open and revealed a small secret compartment that she had made. It held only four things. One was a thing called a pen. It was given to her by Larry. He showed her how to use it to make writings on paper. The second object was paper. She had used it to draw maps of this mountain city that had imprisoned her. The third was a picture of her beloved brother Nicolas. She ran her hand over the picture and kissed it. "This is for you," she whispered.

322

The Trahe Chronicles

Maria picked the fourth object—a knife—and closed the compartment. Afraid of unexpected intruders, she placed the candle over the tabletop compartment door to conceal the compartment. She lit the candle and watched the flames flicker. Soon shadows danced across the fur rug that hung on the wall behind her bed.

To keep her room warm, furs had been hung on all the rock walls. Since the one behind her bed was not easily accessible, she thought it would be a good hiding place. She slowly pulled back the fur and temporality taped it to the wall so it was out of the way. She used an item that was called duct tape, another object Larry had given to her.

Maria decided that Larry was a very good ally. She smiled at this thought and then looked at her masterpiece. The uncovered rock wall now revealed a written story. The story was about what happened to herself, her brother, the rest of her family, and friends. It was also a story about the evil Tartak, her new friend Larry and the life that she now lived as a slave in this place—this prison.

Maria took the knife and started to carve into the rock wall. She remembered Larry asking her why she spent her evenings carving into a rock. Maria looked at him thoughtfully. "This is the way our people leave our legacy. This is how legends are created. By truth—true tales of our people. If I never leave this mountain and die here, I want the chronicles of the Evadeam people to continue, to be heard and retold."

The soft candlelight shimmered on the pale-skinned woman as she wrote her story. She had just finished carving the tiger called Skylar. The cowboy had seen the tiger. The rumors she had heard were true.

The Evadeam tiger had returned and now lived with the Chosen Ones. She only wished that they had arrived sooner—soon enough to save them from the evil that had entered her world and killed her brother Nicolas.

As this thought formed in her head, a chill instantaneously ran up her back and neck. For a moment, there was a ghostly shadow in the reflected light that danced on the cavern wall. Maria paused and ran her hand over the wall carving of a boy. "Nicolas?"

Book One: The Chosen Ones

Continue the Adventure with the Chosen Ones in
Book Two of *The Trahe Chronicles*

It had been days since Archelaus left Evadeam City to find Adamah's small tribe. In their cavern home, Brooke sighed as she cleared the breakfast dishes. Suddenly, she heard an unfamiliar sound. She held her breath. *There.* A slight noise came from the cave entrance that led into the internal mountain city.

Cleo must of heard it too because she jumped in front of Brooke and Diana. Cleo's ears and tail twitched. She let out a low growl.

Brooke grabbed Diana and told her to go to the hiding spot they had made for Diana just for emergencies. Diana shook her head no. In a stronger and firmer voice, Brooke ordered Diana one more time to hide.

The sound of barking came from the inner mountain entrance. It was a warning from Sir Bolivar. That was enough to make Diana finally run to her hiding spot. Brooke was beginning to wonder where Sir Bolivar was specifically. He had been on guard duty while Skylar and the guys were out hunting for food.

Diana barely had enough time to hide before the cave entrance was filled with Madeave men. The last thing Diana saw before retreating was her cat jumping into the face of a Madeave man. The man screamed as Cleo clawed at him. The glowing light came off Cleo's body, stunning the rest of the men, which gave Brooke a moment to grab her knife and a nearby sword.

Brooke moved quickly into action. She fought fiercely against the men, but they were backing her toward the outside cavern entrance.

A loud roar echoed through their cavern home. Skylar came running in behind the Madeave. Her jaws and claws tore into a couple of men quickly, bringing them down.

Brooke noticed a glimpse of fear in the eyes of the man she was fighting. "Now you are in trouble," she yelled in the Trahe language. Brooke's voice caught him off guard, and she was able to cut into him with her knife and slash him with her sword. As the man fell, she looked behind him to see Skylar, Sir Bolivar, Jereco, and Grandpa fighting more men.

"Thank the Creator," whispered Brooke.

Thump!

A large thud came from behind her, and she turned to see Buster and Brandon had just landed in the cavern. They'd come in from the exterior cave entrance that could only be accessed from the air. As Brandon shot arrows at the Madeave men, he yelled to Brooke, "Where is Diana?"

"She is in the safe haven."

He yelled back. "I will get her, and then you two will go get help."

"But we can take them."

Brandon shook his head. "There are more!"

Brooke's heart sank. *More?* How did they find Evadeam City? Before she

324

The Trahe Chronicles

had time to think about it, another Madeave man came after her. Buster stepped in front of Brooke and pounded the man with his hooves. As if that was not enough, Buster ran his unicorn horn into the man. "That is for the death of my grandfather!"

Brooke stood there for a moment as she realized what they had become. They were warriors. A year ago, she was a teenage girl from Nashville, Michigan, USA, Earth.

The deadliest thing she did then was kill a bug. Now she was a young woman fighting for her life and killing another being—a Madeave.

"Brooke!" yelled Brandon.

Brooke snapped to attention.

Brandon thrust Diana forward. "Ride Buster and get help," he ordered and then he turned to fight.

Brooke threw Diana on Buster's back and got on the pegasi herself. Buster wanted to stay and fight, but he knew that they were outnumbered. He also knew it was important to get the Vision Keeper and the Protector to safety.

As Buster turned to take flight, he yelled to Brandon, "I will be back, my friend!"

Brandon never heard him as he fought. Their Evadeam City Mountain home was being destroyed. Brandon watched as their Christmas tree toppled over. His heart sank. He was going to die before ever seeing his parents again. "If there is a Creator, we could use some help now."

Jereco came up behind Brandon. "Do not say *if*. Say, 'Creator, we need your help now!'" And the boys fought back to back while waiting for help.

Help finally came in the form of four bears and other creatures that had made Evadeam City their home. They were led by the fierce Methuselah. When he entered, he stood tall and roared. A huge grizzly bear standing full height can be very intimating. But one particular Madeave was not intimated. He simply growled back and threw a spear right into Methuselah. Methuselah paused for a moment and then looked down at the embedded spear. Methuselah broke off the end of the spear with his teeth, dropped to all four paws, walked over to the Madeave, and spit the spear at the man's feet. "It is your day to die evil two-legged creature."

Brandon had to give the man credit. He stood his ground and fought fiercely against the grizzly bear. The man lost.

Soon all the Madeave lost. They either died at the hands of the Chosen Ones and their allies, or they ran away. Brandon figured that the ones who had run away would soon be hunted down by their furry friends. The Madeave attack did, after all, wake his friends up from their winter slumber.

Brandon turned toward one of Arcturus's cubs. "Thank you, Silver Paw."

The cub with a silver paw had saved Brandon's life more than once during the battle. Silver Paw nodded and then paused. He lifted his nose in the air, cried out, and ran toward a fallen black bear on the cavern floor.

325

Book One: The Chosen Ones

Brandon ran after him. The bear was Silver Paw's twin cub. Brandon tried to find any sign of life. "Grandpa!" he yelled in desperation.

Grandpa quickly came over, followed by Arcturus, the cubs' mother. Arcturus wept as Grandpa shook his head. "May you be at peace with the Creator," whispered Grandpa.

As Grandpa stood and walked away to give Arcturus and Silver Paw some privacy, Brandon noticed that Grandpa was grabbing his leg. Grandpa was limping.

Brandon ran up to him. "You are hurt!"

"I will be fine." Grandpa waved Brandon away. "I can attend to myself. There are others that will need your help."

Brandon looked around. Not only was their cavern home in shambles, but many of their allies were also lying around, licking their wounds. That is when Brandon noticed Methuselah lying in a corner. Jereco was already bent over the large grizzly bear.

When Brandon arrived, he saw tears flowing down Jereco's face. Methuselah was bleeding profusely from a spot where a spear had struck him.

In a raspy voice, the bear said, "Silver Paw."

Brandon let Methuselah know that Silver Paw was okay.

"Get him," Methuselah ordered.

When Silver Paw came to Methuselah's side, the others stepped back. But Brandon could still hear what Methuselah was telling Silver Paw. "My son, it is now your turn to fulfill the prophecy. It is your turn to protect the Evadeam tribe."

Brandon's eyes widened with surprise. Was Silver Paw really Methuselah's son? Was he half grizzly, half black bear? Brandon remembered the written word. The prophecy about Silver Paw was coming true.

Skylar came up behind them. "The gray wolf pack has returned."

The pack of wolves piled into the cavern with the announcement that their friends would soon arrive with the Evadeam tribe. Skylar told the pack leader that some Madeave men had escaped and needed to be found. The leader nodded and barked orders. They set off on a hunt.

As they waited for the arrival of their friends, they tended to the wounded the best they could. Finally, Brandon heard the familiar sound of hooves landing at the cavern entrance. Brandon looked up as the rest of their party entered the cavern.

Archelaus hopped off Midnight and simply asked, "Brooke?"

Brandon stopped and stared at Archelaus. "Isn't she with you?"

Archelaus shook his head.

Brandon quickly explained that he had sent Brooke and Diana off on Buster to get them. "Isn't that why you are here? Didn't they find you?"

Hachmoni, who was now next to Archelaus, replied, "No, the bird messengers came and told us about the attack in Evadeam City. Adamah sent the gray wolf pack ahead of us and we followed on the pegasi. The rest of

326

The Trahe Chronicles

Adamah's tribe is coming on foot. We never came across Buster and the girls."

Brandon, now worried, turned toward Grandpa. "Then what happened to them?"

As soon as Brooke left the mountain city of Evadeam, they were met by a flock of birds who pointed them in the direction of their friends. Brooke thought it was odd that the birds continued in the opposite direction. Soon, another huge flock of birds crossed their path. This flock was squawking and flying as if they were panicked.

Buster turned his head. "They are saying danger, danger."

Then Brooke heard it—a sound of an aircraft. It was a sound that she had not heard in a long time. She felt Buster shift underneath her. She put her hand on his neck. "Don't panic, my friend."

"What is that sound?"

Before she had a chance to answer, the spaceship appeared. It was flying toward them and perhaps to Evadeam City. Brooke noticed that the spaceship was damaged. Maybe that was why it was flying so slowly.

"We need to bring it down," Brooke said out loud.

"What is it?" asked Buster.

"A spaceship. It's a machine that could do some serious damage to Evadeam City."

"And how are we supposed to bring that creature down?"

"It is not a creature. It is a machine run by the creatures inside it."

Diana squeezed Brooke. "What if our parents are driving it?"

Brooke thought about this. It had not occurred to Brooke that this could be their parents' aircraft. Diana could be right.

Brooke made an executive decision. "Buster, let's hide and go find help."

Brooke did not have to tell Buster twice. He flew away from the metal creature. But Diana protested. "Brooke! What if my mom and dad are in there? What if your dad is in there?"

"But what if they are not?" said Brooke. "We do not know who is driving that spaceship. So until we do, we are staying away from it. The best thing for us to do is to get help. Cleo can deal with the spaceship."

"Brooke!" yelled Buster. "I think the creature has seen us."

Sure enough, the spaceship had shifted directions and was coming their way.

"Fly! Fly away from it!" Brooke yelled. "Hang on, Diana!"

And they were off. Buster flew the fastest he had ever flown. He was not sure which direction to go though. He did not want to lead the metal creature back toward Evadeam City, but he also did not want to lead it toward Adamah's people who were mostly traveling by foot. So Buster flew in all directions to try to shake the spaceship from his trail. When they flew above the tree line, Buster saw that the metal creature was much larger than himself,

327

Book One: The Chosen Ones

so Buster decided to fly toward the ground. It would be tough for Buster with his wingspan, but once they were on the ground, he could just gallop across the snow-covered mountain floor. Buster flew toward a dense area in the mountain forest where perhaps the metal creature could not fit.

However, Buster was not prepared for the metal creature to follow him, breaking down tree branches as it did. "Why is the breaking of the trees not breaking its own wings?"

"It will eventually. It is too big." Brooke pointed toward a rocky terrain surrounded by large evergreen trees. "Keep flying toward the ground."

The spaceship continued to follow them, and as anticipated, it crashed. Flames shot out from the back of the metal machine.

Buster landed on the ground. They took cover behind some trees and looked at the spaceship. Brooke wondered if Diana might be right. What if her dad was flying the ship? "The metal creature makes fire?" said Buster.

The spaceship door opened. Buster started to take off, but Brooke stopped him.

"Hold on. I want to see who was flying the ship."

That was a mistake. Four men came rushing out the door. One man had a fire extinguisher and rushed to the flames. Another man come out, shooting arrows in their direction.

"Buster, fly!" Brooke yelled.

Two other men held something some sort of machine she didn't recognize. By the time she realized what it was, it was too late. As Buster took flight, a large net shot up at them. The net had come out of the machine that the two men had been holding. The net landed over the girls and the back end of Buster. Brooke and Diana got tangled up in the net, but Buster's front half was still free, including one wing. Brooke acted fast. She grabbed her knife and started to cut at the rope. The net was dragging them down, but Buster was strong. He tried with all his might to break free.

Brooke kept cutting at the net hanging on Buster's wing while Diana tried to untangle herself. Trashing around only made the situation worse. Then Brooke heard one of the men speak Trahe. "Get the girls! The master wants them alive. Kill the beast! I want that horn!"

"Diana, hang on to me!" Brooke stood up and lifted the net off Buster. "Buster get help!" Buster took the cue and flew out of the net. The girls, who were still entangled in the net, toppled backward. Brooke landed hard on the ground. Diana had fallen on top of her, crying.

Brooke mustered all her strength to get Diana out of harm's way. But Diana was so tangled up, she couldn't get her free. Before she had a chance to protect herself with her knife, the two men were there.

The men removed the net and grabbed the girls. As they did so, Brooke turned to see Buster fly away as arrows were being shot at him. *Good, he got away safely*, she thought. Brooke turned to face their attackers. Surprise registered on her face.

The Trahe Chronicles

"Surprised to see me again, sweetheart?" the man sneered.

Brooke was staring into the face of the man that they had left to die with Skylar at Great Rock Canyon. She almost did not recognize him. He had a large cowboy hat that covered most of his dark brown hair and eyes. He also had grown a beard and mustache.

"Skylar should have killed you!" spat Brooke. "She should have eaten you!"

"Your white tiger friend was feeling generous that day. Should I thank the Creator for that?" He laughed. "Come on. My boss will be very pleased to meet you."

He turned toward the other men. "Get this ship back in the air. We have two packages to deliver."

As Brooke and Diana were dragged to the ship, Brooke tried to think of a way to escape. She noticed that the two other men looked like Madeave men, but the fourth was something different. The fourth man looked at Brooke briefly before turning into the ship.

Diana grabbed Brooke's hand. "He is an alien."

Brooke thought Diana was right. That man did not have the look of an Earthling or a creature of Trahe. As if reading her thoughts, her captor remarked, "I would not think of trying to escape. They say aliens, as you call them, have special powers. You can die now, or live and meet the master."

For Diana's safety, Brooke decided it would be safer to go along with her captors and wait for their rescue. She looked at her cousin, the Vision Keeper, for reassurance. Diana nodded and whispered, "Nicolas is with us."

Nicolas—Diana's ghost friend. Brooke's heart sank. Having an invisible spirit with them was not very reassuring. As they were pushed into the spaceship, she glanced back. There was no sign of rescuers. Brooke thought she heard a cry of a bird, a sound made from a great bald eagle. The spaceship door slid shut.

Book One: The Chosen Ones

GLOSSARY

Abijam: Father of the sea. Leader of the water people.

Adam Evadeam: Earth son of Larry Evadeam. Deceased brother of Brooke Evadeam.

Adamah: The blood brother of Archelaus.

Adeline Evadeam: The deceased grandmother of the Chosen Ones. The seven children of Adeline include Brandon Scott, Coby, Larry, Gregory, Peter, Tricia, and Rhonda.

Annette: A friend of Diana Evadeam.

Agnes Evadeam: The wife of Ronald Evadeam. The mother of Brandon, Jereco, and Diana.

Aquila: The great eagle.

Archelaus: The leader of the Evadeam tribe. The prince of his people.

Arcturus: The great black bear. Mother of Silver Paw.

Areli: The blood sister of Archelaus. The light of the Creator.

Bathsheba Bethharan: The wife of Sir Bolivar. A mongoose.

Bethemek: The home of Michael Evadeam. Bethemek is located in a remote valley in the Great Rock Mountain.

Brandon Evadeam: The youngest son of Ronald Evadeam. A Chosen One who speaks to the trees. The Forest Friend.

Brandon Scott Evadeam: A son of Ovid Evadeam.

Bright Eyes: The ancient white tiger. Protector of Princess Skylar. The mother of white tiger Skylar.

Brooke Evadeam: The daughter of Larry Evadeam. A Chosen One who is known as the guardian of Diana Evadeam while on planet Trahe. The Protector.

Buster: The son of Midnight, the pegasus, and Prisca, the unicorn. A brown

330

The Trahe Chronicles

and white flying pegasus with a horn. The Great Horned Wing One.

Cheyenne: The leader of a dog pack.

Chislon: The daughter of Abijam. The hope of the water people.

Cleopatra: Also known as Cleo. The Guide. A messenger for the Creator.

Clyde: A pegasus that looks like a Clydesdale horse on Earth. Twin brother of Dale. Travels with and protects the Chosen Ones.

Creator: The Creator of all things on the planet Trahe. It is believed that the Creator and God are the same being. The creator of the universe.

Coby Evadeam: A son of Ovid Evadeam.

Color River: A great river that leads to and winds through Evadeam Mountain.

Dale: A pegasus that looks like a Clydesdale horse on Earth. Twin brother of Clyde. Travels with and protects the Chosen Ones.

Diana Lorraine Evadeam: Daughter of Ronald Evadeam. A Chosen One who has sign dreams. The Vision Keeper.

Evadeam Tribe: The Creator's first tribe of Trahe. Habitants of the Evadeam City located in Evadeam Mountain. Ancestors of the Evadeam family on Earth.

Evadeam City: Ancient city of the Evadeam Tribe. The city is located in Evadeam Mountain. The city is forty square miles and five thousand two hundred eighty feet above sea level. It has approximately three hundred caves.

Evadeam Mountain: Home of the ancient city of the Evadeam Tribe. The location where the Evadeam were first placed into the world of Trahe by the Creator. The mountain is over fourteen thousand feet above sea level.

Edamave Tribe: The Creator's second tribe of Trahe. Habitants of the Great River.

Evemada Tribe: The Creator's third tribe of Trahe. Habitants of the southern mountain region.

Book One: The Chosen Ones

Ghost Tribe: Silver Kat's tribe.

Great Blue Sea: The sea surrounding the Island of the Pegasi.

Gregory Evadeam: A son of Ovid Evadeam.

Gray Protector: A gray wolf of the gray wolf pack. The protector of Adamah.

Hachmoni: A wise elder of the Evadeam Council. A protector of the Chosen Ones.

Heart: A planet located in the seventh solar system away from the planet Earth.

Ibhar: Princess Skylar's husband. Father of all fathers of the Chosen Ones.

Jereco Evadeam: The oldest son of Ronald Evadeam. A Chosen One who speaks to the water creatures. The Water Guardian.

Kedar: The Trahe cowboy who is Tartak's right hand man.

Koa: The tropical bird from the Island of the Pegasi. Ally of the Evadeam people and the Chosen Ones.

Larry Evadeam: The father of Brooke Evadeam. Son of Ovid Evadeam.

Larry, the monkey: A monkey from the Island of the Pegasi. Friend of Larry Evadeam.

Lightning Thunder: A male pegasus. Father of Luke Thunder, the pegasus.

Luke Thunder: A black male pegasus. Father of Midnight, the Pegasus.

Madeave Tribe: The Creator's fourth tribe of Trahe. Habitants of the southern jungle region. Enemies of the Evadeam Tribe during the tribal wars.

Madevea Tribe: The Creator's fifth tribe of Trahe. Habitants of the swamp region.

Mangus Village: The home of Sir Bolivar, the Mongoose. The village of many creatures, managed by the council.

The Trahe Chronicles

Maria Edamave: The sister of Nicolas, the ghost of the Great Rock Canyon.

Melkart Sasquatch: A bigfoot creature of Trahe.

Methuselah: The great ancient grizzly bear. Keeper and protector of Arcturus's cubs.

Michael: A cousin of Archelaus. A leader of the people of Bethemek.

Midnight: A blue and black male Pegasus horse. Leader of the pegasi. The partner of Prisca, the unicorn. Father of Buster. Son of Luke Thunder.

Muhans Tribe: The Creator's seventh tribe of Trahe. Habitants of the desert caverns.

Nahash: The mighty Evadeam dragon. Father of Uriel.

Nashville: The Chosen Ones' hometown located in Michigan on planet Earth.

Nicolas Edamave: The ghost of the Great Rock Canyon. The brother of Maria.

Nicolas Christmas Evadeam: An orphaned baby boy.

Osprey: A bird ally of the Mongoose Tribe. A guide for the Chosen Ones.

Ovid Evadeam: The grandfather of the Chosen Ones. The Returner. The seven children of Ovid include Brandon Scott, Coby, Larry, Gregory, Peter, Tricia, and Rhonda.

Pinto Dreams: A pegasus that looks like a Pinto horse on Earth. Travels with and protects the Chosen Ones.

Princess Skylar: Daughter of Chief Evadeam. Wife of Ibhar. Mother of all mothers of the Chosen Ones.

Prisca: A white female unicorn. The partner of Midnight, the pegasus. Mother of Buster.

Rhonda Evadeam: The daughter of Ovid Evadeam.

River Girl: The river water girl who befriends Jereco.

Book One: The Chosen Ones

Ronald Evadeam: The father of Brandon, Jereco, and Diana. Son of Ovid Evadeam.

Ryan: A boy enslaved by Tartak.

Seven Tribes of Trahe: The Creator's first seven tribes of Trahe consisting of two-legged creatures. The tribes are the Evadeam, the Edamave, the Evemada, the Madevea, the Madeave, the Suhman and the Muhans.

Sheba: The mother of Cheyenne. Protector of Willow, the great willow tree.

Sir Bolivar Bethharan: A leader of the Mongoose tribe.

Silver Fang: A white wolf and leader of the gray wolf Pack.

Silver Kat: An ally and friend of the Evadeam Tribe. Friend and keeper of the white tiger Skylar.

Silver Paw: A great black bear cub. The son of Arcturus.

Skylar: The white tiger who is the daughter of Bright Eyes. Named after Princess Skylar.

Stal Lion: A Pegasus that looks like a thoroughbred horse on Earth. Travels with and protect the Chosen Ones.

Suhman Tribe: The Creator's sixth tribe of Trahe. Habitants of the flat desert lands.

Tartak: Alien from the planet Heart. The Prince of Darkness.

The Ark: The spaceship the Evadeam family flew to the planet Trahe.

The Island of the Pegasi: The island home of the pegasi and unicorns. The island is located in the southern hemisphere of planet Trahe.

Trahe (pronounced *Trah*): A planet located in the third solar system away from Earth. Trahe is the third planet from its sun, similar to Earth's position in its own solar system.

Tricia Evadeam: The daughter of Ovid Evadeam.

Uriel: The baby dragon found by Diana.

The Trahe Chronicles

Water people: The creatures who live in the waters on the planet Trahe.

Willow: A living willow tree that acts as a secret stronghold for the Mangus Village creatures and surrounding tribes. Befriends the Chosen Ones and protects them.

Zacchaeus: The leader of the woodsmen of Bethemek.

Zephaniah: The chosen leader of the river water people. Cousin of Chislon and nephew of the great Abijam.

Zippor: Falcon friend of Michael and Zacchaeus.

Book One: The Chosen Ones

A NOTE FROM THE AUTHOR

I am a proud survivor of Epilepsy. Epilepsy is a chronic neurological condition characterized by the recurrence of seizures. As a child I had medicated treatment and was cured by the age of twelve.

My imagination soared as an adolescent. The creativity continued into my adulthood. I have always had stories floating through my head. After years of writing, I am fulfilling my childhood dream of publishing one of these stories.

I grew up and live in the wonderful state of Michigan. I love Michigan with its fabulous seasons and magnificent terrain. Many places that I have enjoyed in my home state, has helped me create the magical world of Trahe.

Trahe is a world with adventure and discovery. Trahe has many places similar to Earth. In honor of these locations, they are mentioned in the book out of fondness and good memories.

I hope you enjoyed my imaginary world.

D. L Price

Made in the USA
Lexington, KY
29 October 2019